PRAISE FOR RICHARD MATHESON

"The author who influenced me the most
as a writer was Richard Matheson."
—Stephen King

"Ever since he started writing for sci-fi magazines
and for *The Twilight Zone*, Richard Matheson has
been giving readers a grand tour in the gardens of
menace. . . . Matheson's a writer who just has the
special knack, the deft skill to imagine terrifying
scenarios on any scale, large and small,
and give them chilling possibility."
—*Los Angeles Times*

"His stories not only entertain but touch
the mind and heart."
—Dean Koontz

"One of the great names in American terror fiction."
—*The Philadelphia Inquirer*

"Richard Matheson is worth our time,
attention, and great affection."
—Ray Bradbury

**ALSO BY RICHARD MATHESON
FROM TOM DOHERTY ASSOCIATES**

THE BEARDLESS WARRIORS

BUTTON, BUTTON (THE BOX)

DUEL

EARTHBOUND

HELL HOUSE

HUNTED PAST REASON

I AM LEGEND

THE INCREDIBLE SHRINKING MAN

JOURNAL OF THE GUN YEARS

THE GUN FIGHT

THE MEMOIRS OF WILD BILL HICKOK

NIGHTMARE AT 20,000 FEET

NOIR

NOW YOU SEE IT . . .

THE PATH: A NEW LOOK AT REALITY

7 STEPS TO MIDNIGHT

SOMEWHERE IN TIME

A STIR OF ECHOES

WHAT DREAMS MAY COME

DUEL

TERROR STORIES BY
RICHARD MATHESON

TOR

A TOM DOHERTY ASSOCIATES BOOK
NEW YORK

This is a work of fiction. All of the characters, organizations, and events portrayed in this collection are either products of the author's imagination or are used fictitiously.

DUEL: TERROR STORIES BY RICHARD MATHESON

Copyright © 2003 by Richard Matheson

An Appreciation copyright © 1988 by Ray Bradbury. Reprinted by permission of the author.

All rights reserved.

A Tor Book
Published by Tom Doherty Associates
175 Fifth Avenue
New York, NY 10010

www.tor-forge.com

Tor® is a registered trademark of Macmillan Publishing Group, LLC.

ISBN 978-0-7653-9993-9

Our books may be purchased in bulk for promotional, educational, or business use. Please contact your local bookseller or the Macmillan Corporate and Premium Sales Department at 1-800-221-7945, extension 5442, or by e-mail at MacmillanSpecialMarkets@macmillan.com.

First Edition: January 2003
First Mass Market Edition: December 2017

Printed in the United States of America

0 9 8 7 6 5 4 3 2 1

To Ray Bradbury,
a mentor, guide, and inspiration to me
for more than fifty years.

CONTENTS

AN APPRECIATION BY RAY BRADBURY   ix

DUEL   1

THIRD FROM THE SUN   36

WHEN THE WAKER SLEEPS   47

BORN OF MAN AND WOMAN   67

RETURN   72

BROTHER TO THE MACHINE   102

F —   111

LOVER WHEN YOU'RE NEAR ME   135

SHIPSHAPE HOME   168

SRL AD   194

DEATH SHIP   207

THE LAST DAY   236

LITTLE GIRL LOST   259

TRESPASS   276

BEING   329

THE TEST   376

ONE FOR THE BOOKS   402

STEEL   427

BIBLIOGRAPHY: ORIGINAL PUBLICATIONS   463

AN APPRECIATION

SOME THIRTY-ODD YEARS AGO, LETTERS BEGAN to fall into my mailbox from a young man across the country who very much desired to become a writer. I don't recall how many letters there were or in what manner I responded to them. I remember thanking the young writer for his compliments on my books and telling him, I think, to write every day of his life from that time on. At least I hope I told him this. For the end result, over the years has been:

Richard Matheson

I look back on Richard Matheson's accomplishments with great fondness. For he has done what he set out to do: become a very fine writer indeed. And if he is not known quite as well as, say, Arthur C. Clarke or Isaac Asimov, still his readers are a good legion and the quality of their attention makes up for any faint lack of numbers. And, anyway, the numbers are *growing!*

Perhaps the most immediate thing one would note about Richard is that no one label fits him. Which is all to the good. Whether he is writing the weird, the horror, the science-fiction or the fantasy tale, all are more than each label implies. He is, in sum, a mainstream writer. Take my word for it and forget all the malarkey that the New York snob critics publish about all of us.

I would go on at greater length but Matheson doesn't

need me to explain him to you. He, himself, is the best explainer.

Richard Matheson is worth our time, attention and great affection.

RAY BRADBURY

DUEL

DUEL

He was heading west, en route to San Francisco. It was Thursday and unseasonably hot for April. He had his suitcoat off, his tie removed and shirt collar opened, his sleeve cuffs folded back. There was sunlight on his left arm and on part of his lap. He could feel the heat of it through his dark trousers as he drove along the two-lane highway. For the past twenty minutes, he had not seen another vehicle going in either direction.

Then he saw the truck ahead, moving up a curving grade between two high green hills. He heard the grinding strain of its motor and saw a double shadow on the road. The truck was pulling a trailer.

He paid no attention to the details of the truck. As he drew behind it on the grade, he edged his car toward the opposite lane. The road ahead had blind curves and he didn't try to pass until the truck had crossed the ridge. He waited until it started around a left curve on the downgrade, then, seeing that the way was clear, pressed down on the accelerator pedal and steered his car into the eastbound lane. He waited until he could see the truck front in his rearview mirror before he turned back into the proper lane.

Mann looked across the countryside ahead. There were ranges of mountains as far as he could see and, all around him, rolling green hills. He whistled softly as the car sped down the winding grade, its tires making crisp sounds on the pavement.

At the bottom of the hill, he crossed a concrete bridge and, glancing to the right, saw a dry stream bed strewn with rocks and gravel. As the car moved off the bridge, he saw a trailer park set back from the highway to his right. How can anyone live out here? he thought. His shifting gaze caught sight of a pet cemetery ahead and he smiled. Maybe those people in the trailers wanted to be close to the graves of their dogs and cats.

The highway ahead was straight now. Mann drifted into a reverie, the sunlight on his arm and lap. He wondered what Ruth was doing. The kids, of course, were in school and would be for hours yet. Maybe Ruth was shopping; Thursday was the day she usually went. Mann visualized her in the supermarket, putting various items into the basket cart. He wished he were with her instead of starting on another sales trip. Hours of driving yet before he'd reach San Francisco. Three days of hotel sleeping and restaurant eating, hoped-for contacts and likely disappointments. He sighed; then, reaching out impulsively, he switched on the radio. He revolved the turning knob until he found a station playing soft, innocuous music. He hummed along with it, eyes almost out of focus on the road ahead.

He started as the truck roared past him on the left, causing his car to shudder slightly. He watched the truck and trailer cut in abruptly for the westbound lane and frowned as he had to brake to maintain a safe distance behind it. What's with you? he thought.

He eyed the truck with cursory disapproval. It was a huge gasoline tanker pulling a tank trailer, each of them having six pairs of wheels. He could see that it was not a new rig but was dented and in need of renovation, its tanks painted a cheap-looking silvery color. Mann wondered if the driver had done the painting himself. His gaze shifted from the word FLAMMABLE printed across the back of the trailer tank, red letters on a white background, to the parallel reflector lines painted in red across the bottom of the tank to the massive rubber flaps swaying behind the rear tires, then back up again. The reflector lines looked as though they'd been clumsily applied with a stencil. The driver must be an independent trucker, he decided, and not too affluent a one, from the looks of his outfit. He glanced at the trailer's license plate. It was a California issue.

Mann checked his speedometer. He was holding steady at 55 miles an hour, as he invariably did when he drove without thinking on the open highway. The truck driver must have done a good 70 to pass him so quickly. That seemed a little odd. Weren't truck drivers supposed to be a cautious lot?

He grimaced at the smell of the truck's exhaust and looked at the vertical pipe to the left of the cab. It was spewing smoke, which clouded darkly back across the trailer. Christ, he thought. With all the furor about air pollution, why do they keep allowing that sort of thing on the highways?

He scowled at the constant fumes. They'd make him nauseated in a little while, he knew. He couldn't lag back here like this. Either he slowed down or he passed the truck again. He didn't have the time to slow down. He'd gotten a late start. Keeping it at 55 all the way, he'd just about make his afternoon appointment. No, he'd have to pass.

Depressing the gas pedal, he eased his car toward the opposite lane. No sign of anything ahead. Traffic on this route seemed almost nonexistent today. He pushed down harder on the accelerator and steered all the way into the eastbound lane.

As he passed the truck, he glanced at it. The cab was too high for him to see into. All he caught sight of was the back of the truck driver's left hand on the steering wheel. It was darkly tanned and square-looking, with large veins knotted on its surface.

When Mann could see the truck reflected in the rearview mirror, he pulled back over to the proper lane and looked ahead again.

He glanced at the rearview mirror in surprise as the truck driver gave him an extended horn blast. What was that? he wondered; a greeting or a curse? He grunted with amusement, glancing at the mirror as he drove. The front fenders of the truck were a dingy purple color, the paint faded and chipped; another amateurish job. All he could see was the lower portion of the truck; the rest was cut off by the top of his rear window.

To Mann's right, now, was a slope of shalelike earth with patches of scrub grass growing on it. His gaze jumped to the clapboard house on top of the slope. The television aerial on its roof was sagging at an angle of less than 40 degrees. Must give great reception, he thought.

He looked to the front again, glancing aside abruptly at a sign printed in jagged block letters on a piece of plywood: NIGHT CRAWLERS—BAIT. What the hell is a night crawler? he wondered. It sounded like some monster in a low-grade Hollywood thriller.

The unexpected roar of the truck motor made his gaze jump to the rearview mirror. Instantly, his startled look jumped to the side mirror. By God, the guy was passing him *again*. Mann turned his head to scowl at the leviathan form as it drifted by. He tried to see into the cab but couldn't because of its height. What's with him, anyway? he wondered. What the hell are we having here, a contest? See which vehicle can stay ahead the longest?

He thought of speeding up to stay ahead but changed his mind. When the truck and trailer started back into the westbound lane, he let up on the pedal, voicing a newly incredulous sound as he saw that if he hadn't slowed down, he would have been prematurely cut off again. Jesus Christ, he thought. What's *with* this guy?

His scowl deepened as the odor of the truck's exhaust reached his nostrils again. Irritably, he cranked up the window on his left. Damn it, was he going to have to breathe that crap all the way to San Francisco? He couldn't afford to slow down. He had to meet Forbes at a quarter after three and that was that.

He looked ahead. At least there was no traffic complicating matters. Mann pressed down on the accelerator pedal, drawing close behind the truck. When the highway curved enough to the left to give him a completely open view of the route ahead, he jarred down on the pedal, steering out into the opposite lane.

The truck edged over, blocking his way.

For several moments, all Mann could do was stare at it in blank confusion. Then, with a startled noise, he braked, returning to the proper lane. The truck moved back in front of him.

Mann could not allow himself to accept what apparently had taken place. It had to be a coincidence. The truck driver couldn't have blocked his way on purpose. He waited for more than a minute, then flicked down the turn-indicator lever to make his intentions perfectly clear and, depressing the accelerator pedal, steered again into the eastbound lane.

Immediately, the truck shifted, barring his way.

"*Jesus Christ!*" Mann was astounded. This was unbelievable. He'd never seen such a thing in twenty-six years of driving. He returned to the westbound lane, shaking his head as the truck swung back in front of him.

He eased up on the gas pedal, falling back to avoid the truck's exhaust. Now what? he wondered. He still had to make San Francisco on schedule. Why in God's name hadn't he gone a little out of his way in the beginning, so he could have traveled by freeway? This damned highway was two lane all the way.

Impulsively, he sped into the eastbound lane again. To his surprise, the truck driver did not pull over. Instead, the driver stuck his left arm out and waved him on. Mann started pushing down on the accelerator. Suddenly, he let up on the pedal with a gasp and jerked the steering wheel around, raking back behind the truck so quickly that his car began to fishtail. He was fighting to control its zigzag whipping when a blue convertible shot by him in the opposite lane. Mann caught a momentary vision of the man inside it glaring at him.

The car came under his control again. Mann was sucking breath in through his mouth. His heart was pounding almost painfully. My God! he thought. *He wanted me to hit that car head on.* The realization stunned him. True, he should have seen to it himself that the road ahead was clear; that was his failure. But to wave him on. . . . Mann felt appalled and sickened. Boy, oh, boy, oh, boy, he thought. This was really one for the books. That son of a bitch had meant for not only him to be killed but a totally uninvolved passerby as well. The idea seemed beyond his comprehension. On a California highway on a Thursday morning? *Why?*

Mann tried to calm himself and rationalize the incident. Maybe it's the heat, he thought. Maybe the truck driver had a tension headache or an upset stomach; maybe both. Maybe he'd had a fight with his wife. Maybe she'd failed to put out last night. Mann tried in vain to smile. There could be any number of reasons. Reaching out, he twisted off the radio. The cheerful music irritated him.

He drove behind the truck for several minutes, his face a mask of animosity. As the exhaust fumes started putting his stomach on edge, he suddenly forced down the heel of his right hand on the horn bar and held it there. Seeing that the route ahead was clear, he pushed in the accelerator pedal all the way and steered into the opposite lane.

The movement of his car was paralleled immediately by the truck. Mann stayed in place, right hand jammed down on the horn bar. Get out of the way, you son of a bitch! he thought. He felt the muscles of his jaw hardening until they ached. There was a twisting in his stomach.

"*Damn!*" He pulled back quickly to the proper lane, shuddering with fury. "You miserable son of a bitch," he muttered, glaring at the truck as it was shifted back in front of him. What the hell is wrong with you? I pass your goddamn rig a couple of times and you go flying off the deep end? Are you nuts or something? Mann nodded tensely. Yes, he thought; he is. No other explanation.

He wondered what Ruth would think of all this, how she'd react. Probably, she'd start to honk the horn and would keep on honking it, assuming that, eventually, it would attract the attention of a policeman. He looked around with a scowl. Just where in hell were the policemen out here, anyway? He made a scoffing noise. What policemen? Here in the boondocks? They probably had a sheriff on horseback, for Christ's sake.

He wondered suddenly if he could fool the truck driver by passing on the right. Edging his car toward the shoulder, he peered ahead. No chance. There wasn't room enough. The truck driver could shove him through that wire fence if he wanted to. Mann shivered. And he'd want to, sure as hell, he thought.

Driving where he was, he grew conscious of the debris lying beside the highway: beer cans, candy wrappers, ice-cream containers, newspaper sections browned and rotted by the weather, a FOR SALE sign torn in half. Keep America beautiful, he thought sardonically. He passed a boulder with the name WILL JASPER painted on it in white. Who the hell is Will Jasper? he wondered. What would he think of this situation?

Unexpectedly, the car began to bounce. For several anxious moments, Mann thought that one of his tires had gone flat. Then he noticed that the paving along this section of highway consisted of pitted slabs with gaps between them. He saw the truck and trailer jolting up and down and thought: I hope it shakes your brains loose. As the truck veered into a sharp left curve, he caught a fleeting glimpse of the driver's face in the cab's side mirror. There was not enough time to establish his appearance.

"Ah," he said. A long, steep hill was looming up ahead. The truck would have to climb it slowly. There would doubtless be an opportunity to pass somewhere on the grade. Mann pressed down on the accelerator pedal, drawing as close behind the truck as safety would allow.

Halfway up the slope, Mann saw a turnout for the eastbound lane with no oncoming traffic anywhere in sight. Flooring the accelerator pedal, he shot into the opposite lane. The slow-moving truck began to angle out in front of him. Face stiffening, Mann steered his speeding car across the highway edge and curved it sharply on the turnout. Clouds of dust went billowing up behind his car, making him lose sight of the truck. His tires buzzed and crackled on the dirt, then, suddenly, were humming on the pavement once again.

He glanced at the rearview mirror and a barking laugh erupted from his throat. He'd only meant to pass. The dust had been an unexpected bonus. Let the bastard get a sniff of something rotten smelling in his nose for a change! he thought. He honked the horn elatedly, a mocking rhythm of bleats. Screw you, Jack!

He swept across the summit of the hill. A striking vista lay ahead: sunlit hills and flatland, a corridor of dark trees, quadrangles of cleared-off acreage and bright-green vegetable patches; far off, in the distance, a mammoth water tower. Mann felt stirred by the panoramic sight. Lovely, he thought. Reaching out, he turned the radio back on and started humming cheerfully with the music.

Seven minutes later, he passed a billboard advertising CHUCK'S CAFE. No thanks, Chuck, he thought. He glanced at a gray house nestled in a hollow. Was that a cemetery in its front yard or a group of plaster statuary for sale?

Hearing the noise behind him, Mann looked at the rearview mirror and felt himself go cold with fear. The truck was hurtling down the hill, pursuing him.

His mouth fell open and he threw a glance at the speedometer. He was doing more than 60! On a curving downgrade, that was not at all a safe speed to be driving. Yet the truck must be exceeding that by a considerable margin, it was closing the distance between them so rapidly. Mann swallowed, leaning to the right as he steered his car around a sharp curve. Is the man *insane?* he thought.

His gaze jumped forward searchingly. He saw a turnoff half a mile ahead and decided that he'd use it. In the rearview mirror, the huge square radiator grille was all he could see now. He stamped down on the gas pedal and his tires screeched unnervingly as he wheeled around another curve, thinking that, surely, the truck would have to slow down here.

He groaned as it rounded the curve with ease, only the sway of its tanks revealing the outward pressure of the turn. Mann bit trembling lips together as he whipped his car around another curve. A straight descent now. He depressed the pedal farther, glanced at the speedometer. Almost 70 miles an hour! He wasn't used to driving this fast!

In agony, he saw the turnoff shoot by on his right. He couldn't have left the highway at this speed, anyway; he'd have overturned. Goddamn it, what was wrong with that son of a bitch? Mann honked his horn in frightened rage. Cranking down the window suddenly, he shoved his left arm out to wave the truck back. "*Back!*" he yelled. He honked the horn again. "Get back, you crazy bastard!"

The truck was almost on him now. He's going to kill me! Mann thought, horrified. He honked the horn repeatedly, then had to use both hands to grip the steering wheel as he swept around another curve. He flashed a look at the rearview mirror. He could see only the bottom portion of the truck's radiator grille. He was going to lose control! He felt the rear wheels start to drift and let up on the pedal quickly. The tire treads bit in, the car leaped on, regaining its momentum.

Mann saw the bottom of the grade ahead, and in

the distance there was a building with a sign that read
CHUCK'S CAFE. The truck was gaining ground
again. This is insane! he thought, enraged and terrified at once. The highway straightened out. He floored
the pedal: 74 now—75. Mann braced himself, trying
to ease the car as far to the right as possible.

Abruptly, he began to brake, then swerved to the
right, raking his car into the open area in front of the
cafe. He cried out as the car began to fishtail, then
careened into a skid. *Steer with it!* screamed a voice
in his mind. The rear of the car was lashing from side
to side, tires spewing dirt and raising clouds of dust.
Mann pressed harder on the brake pedal, turning further into the skid. The car began to straighten out
and he braked harder yet, conscious, on the sides of
his vision, of the truck and trailer roaring by on the
highway. He nearly sideswiped one of the cars parked
in front of the cafe, bounced and skidded by it, going
almost straight now. He jammed in the brake pedal as
hard as he could. The rear end broke to the right and
the car spun half around, sheering sideways to a
neck-wrenching halt thirty yards beyond the cafe.

Mann sat in pulsing silence, eyes closed. His heartbeats felt like club blows in his chest. He couldn't seem
to catch his breath. If he were ever going to have
a heart attack, it would be now. After a while, he
opened his eyes and pressed his right palm against his
chest. His heart was still throbbing laboredly. No wonder, he thought. It isn't every day I'm almost murdered
by a truck.

He raised the handle and pushed out the door,
then started forward, grunting in surprise as the

safety belt held him in place. Reaching down with shaking fingers, he depressed the release button and pulled the ends of the belt apart. He glanced at the cafe. What had its patrons thought of his breakneck appearance? he wondered.

He stumbled as he walked to the front door of the cafe. TRUCKERS WELCOME, read a sign in the window. It gave Mann a queasy feeling to see it. Shivering, he pulled open the door and went inside, avoiding the sight of its customers. He felt certain they were watching him, but he didn't have the strength to face their looks. Keeping his gaze fixed straight ahead, he moved to the rear of the cafe and opened the door marked GENTS.

Moving to the sink, he twisted the right-hand faucet and leaned over to cup cold water in his palms and splash it on his face. There was a fluttering of his stomach muscles he could not control.

Straightening up, he tugged down several towels from their dispenser and patted them against his face, grimacing at the smell of the paper. Dropping the soggy towels into a wastebasket beside the sink, he regarded himself in the wall mirror. Still with us, Mann, he thought. He nodded, swallowing. Drawing out his metal comb, he neatened his hair. You never know, he thought. You just never know. You drift along, year after year, presuming certain values to be fixed; like being able to drive on a public thoroughfare without somebody trying to murder you. You come to depend on that sort of thing. Then something occurs and all bets are off. One shocking incident and all the years of logic and acceptance are displaced and, suddenly, the jungle is in front of you again. *Man, part animal, part angel.* Where had he come across that phrase? He shivered.

It was entirely an animal in that truck out there.

His breath was almost back to normal now. Mann forced a smile at his reflection. All right, boy, he told himself. It's over now. It was a goddamned nightmare, but it's over. You are on your way to San Francisco. You'll get yourself a nice hotel room, order a bottle of expensive Scotch, soak your body in a hot bath and forget. Damn right, he thought. He turned and walked out of the washroom.

He jolted to a halt, his breath cut off. Standing rooted, heartbeat hammering at his chest, he gaped through the front window of the cafe.

The truck and trailer were parked outside.

Mann stared at them in unbelieving shock. It wasn't possible. He'd seen them roaring by at top speed. The driver had won; he'd *won!* He'd had the whole damn highway to himself! *Why had he turned back?*

Mann looked around with sudden dread. There were five men eating, three along the counter, two in booths. He cursed himself for having failed to look at faces when he'd entered. Now there was no way of knowing who it was. Mann felt his legs begin to shake.

Abruptly, he walked to the nearest booth and slid in clumsily behind the table. Now wait, he told himself; just wait. Surely, he could tell which one it was. Masking his face with the menu, he glanced across its top. Was it that one in the khaki work shirt? Mann tried to see the man's hands but couldn't. His gaze flicked nervously across the room. Not that one in the suit, of course. Three remaining. That one in the front booth, square-faced, black-haired? If only he could see the man's hands, it might help. One of the two others at the counter? Mann studied them uneasily. Why hadn't he looked at faces when he'd come in?

Now *wait*, he thought. Goddamn it, *wait!* All right, the truck driver was in here. That didn't automatically signify that he meant to continue the insane duel. Chuck's Cafe might be the only place to eat for miles around. It *was* lunchtime, wasn't it? The truck driver had probably intended to eat here all the time. He'd just been moving too fast to pull into the parking lot before. So he'd slowed down, turned around and driven back, that was all. Mann forced himself to read the menu. Right, he thought. No point in getting so rattled. Perhaps a beer would help relax him.

The woman behind the counter came over and Mann ordered a ham sandwich on rye toast and a bottle of Coors. As the woman turned away, he wondered, with a sudden twinge of self-reproach, why he hadn't simply left the cafe, jumped into his car and sped away. He would have known immediately, then, if the truck driver was still out to get him. As it was, he'd have to suffer through an entire meal to find out. He almost groaned at his stupidity.

Still, what if the truck driver *had* followed him out and started after him again? He'd have been right back where he'd started. Even if he'd managed to get a good lead, the truck driver would have overtaken him eventually. It just wasn't in him to drive at 80 and 90 miles an hour in order to stay ahead. True, he might have been intercepted by a California Highway Patrol car. What if he weren't, though?

Mann repressed the plaguing thoughts. He tried to calm himself. He looked deliberately at the four men. Either of two seemed a likely possibility as the driver of the truck: the square-faced one in the front booth and the chunky one in the jumpsuit sitting at the counter. Mann had an impulse to walk over to them and ask which one it was, tell the man he was sorry he'd irritated him, tell him anything to calm him, since, obviously, he wasn't rational, was a manic-depressive, probably. Maybe buy the man a beer and sit with him awhile to try to settle things.

He couldn't move. What if the truck driver were letting the whole thing drop? Mightn't his approach rile the man all over again? Mann felt drained by indecision. He nodded weakly as the waitress set the sandwich and the bottle in front of him. He took a swallow of the beer, which made him cough. Was the truck driver amused by the sound? Mann felt a stirring of resentment deep inside himself. What right did that bastard have to impose this torment on another human being? It was a free country, wasn't it? Damn it, he had every right to pass the son of a bitch on a highway if he wanted to!

"Oh, hell," he mumbled. He tried to feel amused. He was making entirely too much of this. Wasn't he? He glanced at the pay telephone on the front wall. What was to prevent him from calling the local police and telling them the situation? But, then, he'd have to stay here, lose time, make Forbes angry, probably lose the sale. And what if the truck driver stayed to face them? Naturally, he'd deny the whole thing. What if the police believed him and didn't do anything about it? After they'd gone, the truck driver would undoubtedly take it out on him again, only worse. *God!* Mann thought in agony.

The sandwich tasted flat, the beer unpleasantly sour. Mann stared at the table as he ate. For God's sake, why was he just *sitting* here like this? He was a grown man, wasn't he? Why didn't he settle this damn thing once and for all?

His left hand twitched so unexpectedly, he spilled beer on his trousers. The man in the jump suit had risen from the counter and was strolling toward the front of the cafe. Mann felt his heartbeat thumping as the man gave money to the waitress, took his change and a toothpick from the dispenser and went outside. Mann watched in anxious silence.

The man did not get into the cab of the tanker truck.

It had to be the one in the front booth, then. His face took form in Mann's remembrance: square, with dark eyes, dark hair; the man who'd tried to kill him.

Mann stood abruptly, letting impulse conquer fear. Eyes fixed ahead, he started toward the entrance. Anything was preferable to sitting in that booth. He stopped by the cash register, conscious of the hitching of his chest as he gulped in air. Was the man observing him? he wondered. He swallowed, pulling out the clip of dollar bills in his right-hand trouser pocket. He glanced toward the waitress. Come *on*, he thought. He looked at his check and, seeing the amount, reached shakily into his trouser pocket for change. He heard a coin fall onto the floor and roll away. Ignoring it, he dropped a dollar and a quarter onto the counter and thrust the clip of bills into his trouser pocket.

As he did, he heard the man in the front booth get

up. An icy shudder spasmed up his back. Turning quickly to the door, he shoved it open, seeing, on the edges of his vision, the square-faced man approach the cash register. Lurching from the cafe, he started toward his car with long strides. His mouth was dry again. The pounding of his heart was painful in his chest.

Suddenly, he started running. He heard the cafe door bang shut and fought away the urge to look across his shoulder. Was that a sound of other running footsteps now? Reaching his car, Mann yanked open the door and jarred in awkwardly behind the steering wheel. He reached into his trouser pocket for the keys and snatched them out, almost dropping them. His hand was shaking so badly he couldn't get the ignition key into its slot. He whined with mounting dread. Come on! he thought.

The key slid in, he twisted it convulsively. The motor started and he raced it momentarily before jerking the transmission shift to drive. Depressing the accelerator pedal quickly, he raked the car around and steered it toward the highway. From the corners of his eyes, he saw the truck and trailer being backed away from the cafe.

Reaction burst inside him. "No!" he raged and slammed his foot down on the brake pedal. This was idiotic! Why the hell should he run away? His car slid sideways to a rocking halt and, shouldering out the door, he lurched to his feet and started toward the truck with angry strides. *All right, Jack,* he thought. He glared at the man inside the truck. You want to punch my nose, okay, but no more goddamn tournament on the highway.

The truck began to pick up speed. Mann raised his right arm. "Hey!" he yelled. He knew the driver saw him. *"Hey!"* He started running as the truck kept moving, engine grinding loudly. It was on the highway now. He sprinted toward it with a sense of martyred outrage. The driver shifted gears, the truck moved faster. "Stop!" Mann shouted. "Damn it, *stop!*"

He thudded to a panting halt, staring at the truck as it receded down the highway, moved around a hill and disappeared. "You son of a bitch," he muttered. "You goddamn, miserable son of a bitch."

He trudged back slowly to his car, trying to believe that the truck driver had fled the hazard of a fistfight. It was possible, of course, but, somehow, he could not believe it.

He got into his car and was about to drive onto the highway when he changed his mind and switched the motor off. That crazy bastard might just be tooling along at 15 miles an hour, waiting for him to catch up. Nuts to that, he thought. So he blew his schedule; screw it. Forbes would have to wait, that was all. And if Forbes didn't care to wait, that was all right, too. He'd sit here for a while and let the nut get out of range, let him think he'd won the day. He grinned. You're the bloody Red Baron, Jack; you've shot me down. Now go to hell with my sincerest compliments. He shook his head. Beyond belief, he thought.

He really should have done this earlier, pulled over, waited. Then the truck driver would have had to let it pass. *Or picked on someone else*, the startling thought occurred to him. Jesus, maybe that was how the crazy bastard whiled away his work hours! Jesus Christ Almighty! was it possible?

He looked at the dashboard clock. It was just past 12:30. Wow, he thought. All that in less than an hour. He shifted on the seat and stretched his legs out. Leaning back against the door, he closed his eyes and mentally perused the things he had to do tomorrow and the following day. Today was shot to hell, as far as he could see.

When he opened his eyes, afraid of drifting into sleep and losing too much time, almost eleven minutes had passed. The nut must be an ample distance off by now, he thought; at least 11 miles and likely more, the way he drove. Good enough. He wasn't going to try to make San Francisco on schedule now, anyway. He'd take it real easy.

Mann adjusted his safety belt, switched on the motor, tapped the transmission pointer into drive position and pulled onto the highway, glancing back across his shoulder. Not a car in sight. Great day for driving. Everybody was staying at home. That nut must have a reputation around here. When Crazy Jack is on the highway, lock your car in the garage. Mann chuckled at the notion as his car began to turn the curve ahead.

Mindless reflex drove his right foot down against the brake pedal. Suddenly, his car had skidded to a halt and he was staring down the highway. The truck and trailer were parked on the shoulder less than 90 yards away.

Mann couldn't seem to function. He knew his car was blocking the westbound lane, knew that he should either make a U-turn or pull off the highway, but all he could do was gape at the truck.

He cried out, legs retracting, as a horn blast sounded behind him. Snapping up his head, he looked at the rearview mirror, gasping as he saw a yellow station wagon bearing down on him at high speed. Suddenly, it veered off toward the eastbound lane, disappearing from the mirror. Mann jerked around and saw it hurtling past his car, its rear end snapping back and forth, its back tires screeching. He saw the twisted features of the man inside, saw his lips move rapidly with cursing.

Then the station wagon had swerved back into the westbound lane and was speeding off. It gave Mann an odd sensation to see it pass the truck. The man in that station wagon could drive on, unthreatened. Only he'd been singled out. What happened was demented. Yet it was happening.

He drove his car onto the highway shoulder and braked. Putting the transmission into neutral, he leaned back, staring at the truck. His head was aching again. There was a pulsing at his temples like the ticking of a muffled clock.

What was he to do? He knew very well that if he left his car to walk to the truck, the driver would pull away and repark farther down the highway. He may as well face the fact that he was dealing with a madman. He felt the tremor in his stomach muscles starting up again. His heartbeat thudded slowly, striking at his chest wall. Now what?

With a sudden, angry impulse, Mann snapped the transmission into gear and stepped down hard on the accelerator pedal. The tires of the car spun sizzlingly before they gripped; the car shot out onto the highway. Instantly, the truck began to move. He even had the motor on! Mann thought in raging fear. He floored the pedal, then, abruptly, realized he couldn't make it, that the truck would block his way and he'd collide with its trailer. A vision flashed across his mind, a fiery explosion and a sheet of flame incinerating him. He started braking fast, trying to decelerate evenly, so he wouldn't lose control.

When he'd slowed down enough to feel that it was safe, he steered the car onto the shoulder and stopped it again, throwing the transmission into neutral.

Approximately eighty yards ahead, the truck pulled off the highway and stopped.

Mann tapped his fingers on the steering wheel. *Now* what? he thought. Turn around and head east until he reached a cutoff that would take him to San Francisco by another route? How did he know the truck driver wouldn't follow him even then? His cheeks twisted as he bit his lips together angrily. No! He wasn't going to turn around!

His expression hardened suddenly. Well, he wasn't going to *sit* here all day, that was certain. Reaching out, he tapped the gearshift into drive and steered his car onto the highway once again. He saw the massive truck and trailer start to move but made no effort to speed up. He tapped at the brakes, taking a position about 30 yards behind the trailer. He glanced at his speedometer. Forty miles an hour. The truck driver had his left arm out of the cab window and was waving him on. What did that mean? Had he changed his mind? Decided, finally, that this thing had gone too far? Mann couldn't let himself believe it.

He looked ahead. Despite the mountain ranges all around, the highway was flat as far as he could see. He tapped a fingernail against the horn bar, trying to make up his mind. Presumably, he could continue all the way to San Francisco at this speed, hanging back just far enough to avoid the worst of the exhaust fumes. It didn't seem likely that the truck driver would stop directly on the highway to block his way. And if the truck driver pulled onto the shoulder to let him pass, he could pull off the highway, too. It would be a draining afternoon but a safe one.

On the other hand, outracing the truck might be worth just one more try. This was obviously what that son of a bitch wanted. Yet, surely, a vehicle of such size couldn't be driven with the same daring as, potentially, his own. The laws of mechanics were against it, if nothing else. Whatever advantage the truck had in mass, it had to lose in stability, particularly that of its trailer. If Mann were to drive at, say, 80 miles an hour and there were a few steep grades—as he felt sure there were—the truck would have to fall behind.

The question was, of course, whether he had the nerve to maintain such a speed over a long distance. He'd never done it before. Still, the more he thought about it, the more it appealed to him; far more than the alternative did.

Abruptly, he decided. *Right*, he thought. He checked ahead, then pressed down hard on the accelerator pedal and pulled into the eastbound lane. As he neared the truck, he tensed, anticipating that the driver might block his way. But the truck did not shift from the westbound lane. Mann's car moved along its mammoth side. He glanced at the cab and saw the name KELLER printed on its door. For a shocking instant, he thought it read KILLER and started to slow down. Then, glancing at the name again, he saw what it really was and depressed the pedal sharply. When he saw the truck reflected in the rearview mirror, he steered his car into the westbound lane.

He shuddered, dread and satisfaction mixed together, as he saw that the truck driver was speeding up. It was strangely comforting to know the man's intentions definitely again. That plus the knowledge of his face and name seemed, somehow, to reduce his stature. Before, he had been faceless, nameless, an embodiment of unknown terror. Now, at least, he was an individual. All right, Keller, said his mind, let's see you beat me with that purple-silver relic now. He pressed down harder on the pedal. *Here we go*, he thought.

He looked at the speedometer, scowling as he saw that he was doing only 74 miles an hour. Deliberately, he pressed down on the pedal, alternating his gaze between the highway ahead and the speedometer until the needle turned past 80. He felt a flickering of satisfaction with himself. All right, Keller, you son of a bitch, top that, he thought.

After several moments, he glanced into the rearview mirror again. Was the truck getting closer? Stunned, he checked the speedometer. Damn it! He was down to 76! He forced in the accelerator pedal angrily. *He mustn't go less than 80!* Mann's chest shuddered with convulsive breath.

He glanced aside as he hurtled past a beige sedan parked on the shoulder underneath a tree. A young couple sat inside it, talking. Already they were far behind, their world removed from his. Had they even glanced aside when he'd passed? He doubted it.

He started as the shadow of an overhead bridge whipped across the hood and windshield. Inhaling raggedly, he glanced at the speedometer again. He was holding at 81. He checked the rearview mirror. Was it his imagination that the truck was gaining ground? He looked forward with anxious eyes. There had to be some kind of town ahead. To hell with time; he'd stop at the police station and tell them what had happened. They'd have to believe him. Why would he stop to tell them such a story if it weren't true? For all he knew, Keller had a police record in these parts. *Oh, sure, we're on to him,* he heard a faceless officer remark. *That crazy bastard's asked for it before and now he's going to get it.*

Mann shook himself and looked at the mirror. The truck *was* getting closer. Wincing, he glanced at the speedometer. Goddamn it, pay attention! raged his mind. He was down to 74 again! Whining with frustration, he depressed the pedal. Eighty!—80! he demanded of himself. There was a murderer behind him!

His car began to pass a field of flowers; lilacs, Mann saw, white and purple stretching out in endless rows. There was a small shack near the highway, the words FIELD FRESH FLOWERS painted on it. A brown cardboard square was propped against the shack, the word FUNERALS printed crudely on it. Mann saw himself, abruptly, lying in a casket, painted like some grotesque mannequin. The overpowering smell of flowers seemed to fill his nostrils. Ruth and the children sitting in the first row, heads bowed. All his relatives—

Suddenly, the pavement roughened and the car began to bounce and shudder, driving bolts of pain into his head. He felt the steering wheel resisting him and clamped his hands around it tightly, harsh vibrations running up his arms. He didn't dare look at the mirror now. He had to force himself to keep the speed unchanged. Keller wasn't going to slow down; he was sure of that. *What if he got a flat tire, though?* All control would vanish in an instant. He visualized the somersaulting of his car, its grinding, shrieking tumble, the explosion of its gas tank, his body crushed and burned and—

The broken span of pavement ended and his gaze jumped quickly to the rearview mirror. The truck was no closer, but it hadn't lost ground, either. Mann's eyes shifted. Up ahead were hills and mountains. He tried to reassure himself that upgrades were on his side, that he could climb them at the same speed he was going now. Yet all he could imagine were the downgrades, the immense truck close behind him, slamming violently into his car and knocking it across some cliff edge. He had a horrifying vision of dozens of broken, rusted cars lying unseen in the canyons ahead, corpses in every one of them, all flung to shattering deaths by Keller.

Mann's car went rocketing into a corridor of trees. On each side of the highway was a eucalyptus windbreak, each trunk three feet from the next. It was like speeding through a high-walled canyon. Mann gasped, twitching, as a large twig bearing dusty leaves dropped down across the windshield, then slid out of sight. Dear God! he thought. He was getting near the edge himself. If he should lose his nerve at this speed, it was over. Jesus! That would be ideal for Keller! he realized suddenly. He visualized the square-faced driver laughing as he passed the burning wreckage, knowing that he'd killed his prey without so much as touching him.

Mann started as his car shot out into the open. The route ahead was not straight now but winding up into the foothills. Mann willed himself to press down on the pedal even more. Eighty-three now, almost 84.

To his left was a broad terrain of green hills blending into mountains. He saw a black car on a dirt road, moving toward the highway. *Was its side painted white?* Mann's heartbeat lurched. Impulsively, he jammed the heel of his right hand down against the horn bar and held it there. The blast of the horn was shrill and racking to his ears. His heart began to pound. Was it a police car? *Was it?*

He let the horn bar up abruptly. *No,* it *wasn't.* Damn! his mind raged. Keller must have been amused by his pathetic efforts. Doubtless, he was chuckling to himself right now. He heard the truck driver's voice in his mind, coarse and sly. *You think you gonna get a cop to save you, boy? Shee-it. You gonna die.* Mann's heart contorted with savage hatred. *You son of a bitch!* he thought. Jerking his right hand into a fist, he drove it down against the seat. Goddamn you, Keller! I'm going to kill you, if it's the last thing I do!

The hills were closer now. There would be slopes directly, long steep grades. Mann felt a burst of hope within himself. He was sure to gain a lot of distance on the truck. No matter how he tried, that bastard Keller couldn't manage 80 miles an hour on a hill. But *I* can! cried his mind with fierce elation. He worked up saliva in his mouth and swallowed it. The back of his shirt was drenched. He could feel sweat trickling down his sides. A bath and a drink, first order of the day on reaching San Francisco. A long, hot bath, a long, cold drink. Cutty Sark. He'd splurge, by Christ. He rated it.

The car swept up a shallow rise. Not steep enough, goddamn it! The truck's momentum would prevent its losing speed. Mann felt mindless hatred for the landscape. Already, he had topped the rise and tilted over to a shallow downgrade. He looked at the rearview mirror. *Square*, he thought, everything about the truck was square: the radiator grille, the fender shapes, the bumper ends, the outline of the cab, even the shape of Keller's hands and face. He visualized the truck as some great entity pursuing him, insentient, brutish, chasing him with instinct only.

Mann cried out, horror-stricken, as he saw the ROAD REPAIRS sign up ahead. His frantic gaze leaped down the highway. Both lanes blocked, a huge black arrow pointing toward the alternate route! He groaned in anguish, seeing it was dirt. His foot jumped automatically to the brake pedal and started pumping it. He threw a dazed look at the rearview mirror. The truck was moving as fast as ever! It *couldn't*, though! Mann's expression froze in terror as he started turning to the right.

He stiffened as the front wheels hit the dirt road. For an instant, he was certain that the back part of the car was going to spin; he felt it breaking to the left. "No, don't!" he cried. Abruptly, he was jarring down the dirt road, elbows braced against his sides, trying to keep from losing control. His tires battered at the ruts, almost tearing the wheel from his grip. The windows rattled noisily. His neck snapped back and forth with painful jerks. His jolting body surged against the binding of the safety belt and slammed down violently on the seat. He felt the bouncing of the car drive up his spine. His clenching teeth slipped and he cried out hoarsely as his upper teeth gouged deep into his lip.

He gasped as the rear end of the car began surging to the right. He started to jerk the steering wheel to the left, then, hissing, wrenched it in the opposite direction, crying out as the right rear fender cracked into a fence pole, knocking it down. He started pumping at the brakes, struggling to regain control. The car rear yawed sharply to the left, tires shooting out a spray of dirt. Mann felt a scream tear upward in his throat. He twisted wildly at the steering wheel. The car began careening to the right. He hitched the wheel around until the car was on course again. His head was pounding like his heart now, with gigantic, throbbing spasms. He started coughing as he gagged on dripping blood.

The dirt road ended suddenly, the car regained momentum on the pavement and he dared to look at the rearview mirror. The truck was slowed down but was still behind him, rocking like a freighter on a storm-tossed sea, its huge tires scouring up a pall of dust. Mann shoved in the accelerator pedal and his car surged forward. A good, steep grade lay just ahead; he'd gain that distance now. He swallowed blood, grimacing at the taste, then fumbled in his trouser pocket and tugged out his handkerchief. He pressed it to his bleeding lip, eyes fixed on the slope ahead. Another fifty yards or so. He writhed his back. His undershirt was soaking wet, adhering to his skin. He glanced at the rearview mirror. The truck had just regained the highway. *Tough!* he thought with venom. Didn't get me, did you, Keller?

His car was on the first yards of the upgrade when steam began to issue from beneath its hood. Mann stiffened suddenly, eyes widening with shock. The steam increased, became a smoking mist. Mann's gaze jumped down. The red light hadn't flashed on yet but had to in a moment. How could this be happening? Just as he was set to get away! The slope ahead was long and gradual, with many curves. He knew he couldn't stop. Could he U-turn unexpectedly and go back down? the sudden thought occurred. He looked ahead. The highway was too narrow, bound by hills on both sides. There wasn't room enough to make an uninterrupted turn and there wasn't time enough to ease around. If he tried that, Keller would shift direction and hit him head on. "Oh, my God!" Mann murmured suddenly.

He was going to die.

He stared ahead with stricken eyes, his view increasingly obscured by steam. Abruptly, he recalled the afternoon he'd had the engine steam-cleaned at the local car wash. The man who'd done it had suggested he replace the water hoses, because steam-cleaning had a tendency to make them crack. He'd nodded, thinking that he'd do it when he had more time. *More time!* The phrase was like a dagger in his mind. He'd failed to change the hoses and, for that failure, he was now about to die.

He sobbed in terror as the dashboard light flashed on. He glanced at it involuntarily and read the word HOT, black on red. With a breathless gasp, he jerked the transmission into low. Why hadn't he done that right away! He looked ahead. The slope seemed endless. Already, he could hear a boiling throb inside the radiator. How much coolant was there left? Steam was clouding faster, hazing up the windshield. Reaching out, he twisted at a dashboard knob. The wipers started flicking back and forth in fan-shaped sweeps. There had to be enough coolant in the radiator to get him to the top. *Then* what? cried his mind. He couldn't drive without coolant, even downhill. He glanced at the rearview mirror. The truck was falling behind. Mann snarled with maddened fury. *If it weren't for that goddamned hose, he'd be escaping now!*

The sudden lurching of the car snatched him back to terror. If he braked now, he could jump out, run and scrabble up that slope. Later, he might not have the time. He couldn't make himself stop the car, though. As long as it kept on running, he felt bound to it, less vulnerable. God knows what would happen if he left it.

Mann started up the slope with haunted eyes, trying not to see the red light on the edges of his vision. Yard by yard, his car was slowing down. Make it, make it, pleaded his mind, even though he thought that it was futile. The car was running more and more unevenly. The thumping percolation of its radiator filled his ears. Any moment now, the motor would be choked off and the car would shudder to a stop, leaving him a sitting target. *No*, he thought. He tried to blank his mind.

He was almost to the top, but in the mirror he could see the truck drawing up on him. He jammed down on the pedal and the motor made a grinding noise. He groaned. It had to make the top! Please, God, help me! screamed his mind. The ridge was just ahead. Closer. Closer. Make it. "Make it." The car was shuddering and clanking, slowing down—oil, smoke and steam gushing from beneath the hood. The windshield wipers swept from side to side. Mann's head throbbed. Both his hands felt numb. His heartbeat pounded as he stared ahead. Make it, please, God, make it. Make it. *Make* it!

Over! Mann's lips opened in a cry of triumph as the car began descending. Hand shaking uncontrollably, he shoved the transmission into neutral and let the car go into a glide. The triumph strangled in his throat as he saw that there was nothing in sight but hills and more hills. Never mind! He was on a downgrade now, a long one. He passed a sign that read, TRUCKS USE LOW GEARS NEXT 12 MILES. Twelve miles! Something would come up. It had to.

The car began to pick up speed. Mann glanced at the speedometer. Forty-seven miles an hour. The red light still burned. He'd save the motor for a long time, too, though; let it cool for twelve miles, if the truck was far enough behind.

His speed increased. Fifty . . . 51. Mann watched the needle turning slowly toward the right. He glanced at the rearview mirror. The truck had not appeared yet. With a little luck, he might still get a good lead. Not as good as he might have if the motor hadn't overheated but enough to work with. There had to be some place along the way to stop. The needle edged past 55 and started toward the 60 mark.

Again, he looked at the rearview mirror, jolting as he saw that the truck had topped the ridge and was on its way down. He felt his lips begin to shake and

crimped them together. His gaze jumped fitfully between the steam-obscured highway and the mirror.
The truck was accelerating rapidly. Keller doubtless
had the gas pedal floored. It wouldn't be long before
the truck caught up to him. Mann's right hand
twitched unconsciously toward the gearshift. Noticing, he jerked it back, grimacing, glanced at the speedometer. The car's velocity had just passed 60. Not
enough! He had to use the motor now! He reached
out desperately.

His right hand froze in mid-air as the motor stalled;
then, shooting out the hand, he twisted the ignition
key. The motor made a grinding noise but wouldn't
start. Mann glanced up, saw that he was almost on the
shoulder, jerked the steering wheel around. Again, he
turned the key, but there was no response. He looked
up at the rearview mirror. The truck was gaining on
him swiftly. He glanced at the speedometer. The car's
speed was fixed at 62. Mann felt himself crushed in a
vise of panic. He stared ahead with haunted eyes.

Then he saw it, several hundred yards ahead: an
escape route for trucks with burned-out brakes. There
was no alternative now. Either he took the turnout or
his car would be rammed from behind. The truck was
frighteningly close. He heard the high-pitched wailing of its motor. Unconsciously, he started easing to
the right, then jerked the wheel back suddenly. He
mustn't give the move away! He had to wait until the
last possible moment. Otherwise, Keller would follow
him in.

Just before he reached the escape route, Mann
wrenched the steering wheel around. The car rear
started breaking to the left, tires shrieking on the

pavement. Mann steered with the skid, braking just enough to keep from losing all control. The rear tires grabbed and, at 60 miles an hour, the car shot up the dirt trail, tires slinging up a cloud of dust. Mann began to hit the brakes. The rear wheels sideslipped and the car slammed hard against the dirt bank to the right. Mann gasped as the car bounced off and started to fishtail with violent whipping motions, angling toward the trail edge. He drove his foot down on the brake pedal with all his might. The car rear skidded to the right and slammed against the bank again. Mann heard a grinding rend of metal and felt himself heaved downward suddenly, his neck snapped, as the car plowed to a violent halt.

As in a dream, Mann turned to see the truck and trailer swerving off the highway. Paralyzed, he watched the massive vehicle hurtle toward him, staring at it with a blank detachment, knowing he was going to die but so stupefied by the sight of the looming truck that he couldn't react. The gargantuan shape roared closer, blotting out the sky. Mann felt a strange sensation in his throat, unaware that he was screaming.

Suddenly, the truck began to tilt. Mann stared at it in choked-off silence as it started tipping over like some ponderous beast toppling in slow motion. Before it reached his car, it vanished from his rear window.

Hands palsied, Mann undid the safety belt and opened the door. Struggling from the car, he stumbled to the trail edge, staring downward. He was just in time to see the truck capsize like a foundering ship. The tanker followed, huge wheels spinning as it overturned.

The storage tank on the truck exploded first, the violence of its detonation causing Mann to stagger back and sit down clumsily on the dirt. A second explosion roared below, its shock wave buffeting across him hotly, making his ears hurt. His glazed eyes saw a fiery column shoot up toward the sky in front of him, then another.

Mann crawled slowly to the trail edge and peered down at the canyon. Enormous gouts of flame were towering upward, topped by thick, black, oily smoke. He couldn't see the truck or trailer, only flames. He gaped at them in shock, all feeling drained from him.

Then, unexpectedly, emotion came. Not dread, at first, and not regret; not the nausea that followed soon. It was a primeval tumult in his mind: the cry of some ancestral beast above the body of its vanquished foe.

THIRD FROM THE SUN

HIS EYES WERE OPEN FIVE SECONDS BEFORE THE
alarm was set to go off. There was no effort in wak-
ing. It was sudden. Coldly conscious, he reached out
his left hand in the dark and pushed in the stop. The
alarm glowed a second, then faded.

At his side, his wife put her hand on his arm.

"Did you sleep?" he asked.

"No, did you?"

"A little," he said. "Not much."

She was silent for a few seconds. He heard her
throat contract. She shivered. He knew what she was
going to say.

"We're still going?" she asked.

He twisted his shoulders on the bed and took a
deep breath.

"Yes," he said, and he felt her fingers tighten on his
arm.

"What time is it?" she asked.

"About five."

"We'd better get ready."

"Yes, we'd better."

They made no move.

"You're sure we can get on the ship without anyone noticing?" she asked.

"They think it's just another test flight. Nobody will be checking."

She didn't say anything. She moved a little closer to him. He felt how cold her skin was.

"I'm afraid," she said.

He took her hand and held it in a tight grip. "Don't be," he said. "We'll be safe."

"It's the children I'm worried about."

"We'll be safe," he repeated.

She lifted his hand to her lips and kissed it gently.

"All right," she said.

They both sat up in the darkness. He heard her stand. Her night garment rustled to the floor. She didn't pick it up. She stood still, shivering in the cold morning air.

"You're sure we don't need anything else with us?" she asked.

"No, nothing. I have all the supplies we need in the ship. Anyway . . ."

"What?"

"We can't carry anything past the guard," he said. "He has to think you and the kids are just coming to see me off."

She began dressing. He threw off the covering and got up. He went across the cold floor to the closet and dressed.

"I'll get the children up," she said.

He grunted, pulling clothes over his head. At the door she stopped. "Are you sure . . ." she began.

"What?"

"Won't the guard think it's funny that . . . that our neighbors are coming down to see you off, too?"

He sank down on the bed and fumbled for the clasps on his shoes.

"We'll have to take that chance," he said. "We need them with us."

She sighed. "It seems so cold. So calculating."

He straightened up and saw her silhouette in the doorway.

"What else can we do?" he asked intensely. "We can't interbreed our own children."

"No," she said. "It's just . . ."

"Just what?"

"Nothing, darling. I'm sorry."

She closed the door. Her footsteps disappeared down the hall. The door to the children's room opened. He heard their two voices. A cheerless smile raised his lips. You'd think it was a holiday, he thought.

He pulled on his shoes. At least the kids didn't know what was happening. They thought they were going to take him down to the field. They thought they'd come back and tell all their schoolmates about it. They didn't know they'd never come back.

He finished clasping his shoes and stood up. He shuffled over to the bureau and turned on the light. It was odd, such an undistinguished looking man planning this.

Cold. Calculating. Her words filled his mind again. Well, there was no other way. In a few years, probably less, the whole planet would go up with a blinding flash. This was the only way out. Escaping, starting all over again with a few people on a new planet.

He stared at the reflection.

"There's no other way," he said.

He glanced around the bedroom. Goodbye, this part of my life. Turning off the lamp was like turning off a light in his mind. He closed the door gently behind him and slid his fingers off the worn handle.

His son and daughter were going down the ramp. They were talking in mysterious whispers. He shook his head in slight amusement.

His wife waited for him. They went down together, holding hands.

"I'm not afraid, darling," she said. "It'll be all right."

"Sure," he said. "Sure it will."

They all went in to eat. He sat down with his children. His wife poured out juice for them. Then she went to get the food.

"Help your mother, doll," he told his daughter. She got up.

"Pretty soon, haah, pop?" his son said. "Pretty soon, haah?"

"Take it easy," he cautioned. "Remember what I told you. If you say a word of it to anybody I'll have to leave you behind."

A dish shattered on the floor. He darted a glance at his wife. She was staring at him, her lips trembling.

She averted her eyes and bent down. She fumbled at the pieces, picked up a few. Then she dropped them all, stood up and pushed them against the wall with her shoe.

"As if it mattered," she said nervously. "As if it mattered whether the place is clean or not."

The children were watching her in surprise.

"What is it?" asked the daughter.

"Nothing, darling, nothing," she said. "I'm just nervous. Go back to the table. Drink your juice. We have to eat quickly. The neighbors will be here soon."

"Pop, why are the neighbors coming with us?" asked his son.

"Because," he said vaguely, "they want to. Now forget it. Don't talk about it so much."

The room was quiet. His wife brought their food and set it down. Only her footsteps broke the silence. The children kept glancing at each other, at their father. He kept his eyes on the plate. The food tasted flat and thick in his mouth and he felt his heart thudding against the wall of his chest. Last day. This is the last day.

"You'd better eat," he told his wife.

She sat down to eat. As she lifted the eating utensil the door buzzer sounded. The utensil skidded out of her nerveless fingers and clattered on the floor. He reached out quickly and put his hand on hers.

"All right, darling," he said. "It's all right." He turned to the children. "Go answer the door," he told them.

"Both of us?" his daughter asked.

"Both of you."

"But . . ."

"Do as I say."

They slid off their chairs and left the room, glancing back at their parents.

When the sliding door shut off their view, he turned back to his wife. Her face was pale and tight; she had her lips pressed together.

"Darling, please," he said. "Please. You know I

wouldn't take you if I wasn't sure it was safe. You know how many times I've flown the ship before. And I know just where we're going. It's safe. Believe me it's safe."

She pressed his hand against her cheek. She closed her eyes and large tears ran out under her lids and down her cheeks.

"It's not that so m-much," she said. "It's just . . . leaving, never coming back. We've been here all our lives. It isn't like . . . like moving. We can't come back. Ever."

"Listen, darling," his voice was tense and hurried. "You know as well as I do. In a matter of years, maybe less, there's going to be another war, a terrible one. There won't be a thing left. We have to leave. For our children, for ourselves . . ."

He paused, testing the words in his mind.

"For the future of life itself," he finished weakly. He was sorry he said it. Early in the morning, over prosaic food, that kind of talk didn't sound right. Even if it was true.

"Just don't be afraid," he said. "We'll be all right."

She squeezed his hand.

"I know," she said quietly. "I know."

There were footsteps coming toward them. He pulled out a tissue and gave it to her. She hastily dabbed at her face.

The door slid open. The neighbors and their son and daughter came in. The children were excited. They had trouble keeping it down.

"Good morning," the neighbor said.

The neighbor's wife went to his wife and the two of

them went over to the window and talked in low voices. The children stood around, fidgeted and looked nervously at each other.

"You've eaten?" he asked his neighbor.

"Yes," his neighbor said. "Don't you think we'd better be going?"

"I suppose so," he said.

They left all the dishes on the table. His wife went upstairs and got garments for the family.

He and his wife stayed on the porch a moment while the rest went out to the ground car.

"Should we lock the door?" he asked.

She smiled helplessly and ran a hand through her hair. She shrugged. "Does it matter?" she said and turned away.

He locked the door and followed her down the walk. She turned as he came up to her.

"It's a nice house," she murmured.

"Don't think about it," he said.

They turned their backs on their home and got in the ground car.

"Did you lock it?" asked the neighbor.

"Yes."

The neighbor smiled wryly. "So did we," he said. "I tried not to, but then I had to go back."

They moved through the quiet streets. The edges of the sky were beginning to redden. The neighbor's wife and the four children were in back. His wife and the neighbor were in front with him.

"Going to be a nice day," said the neighbor.

"I suppose so," he said.

"Have you told your children?" the neighbor asked softly.

"Of course not."

"I haven't, I haven't," insisted his neighbor. "I was just asking."

"Oh."

They rode in silence a while.

"Do you ever get the feeling that we're . . . running out?" asked the neighbor.

He tightened. "No," he said. His lips pressed together. "No."

"I guess it's better not to talk about it," his neighbor said hastily.

"Much better," he said.

As they drove up to the guardhouse at the gate, he turned to the back.

"Remember," he said. "Not a word from any of you."

The guard was sleepy and didn't care. The guard recognized him right away as the chief test pilot for the new ship. That was enough. The family was coming down to watch him off, he told the guard. That was all right. The guard let them drive to the ship's platform.

The car stopped under the huge columns. They all got out and stared up.

Far above them, its nose pointed toward the sky, the great metal ship was beginning to reflect the early morning glow.

"Let's go," he said. "Quickly."

As they hurried toward the ship's elevator, he stopped for a moment to look back. The guardhouse looked deserted. He looked around at everything and tried to fix it all in his memory.

He bent over and picked up some dirt. He put it in his pocket.

"Goodbye," he whispered.

He ran to the elevator.

The doors shut in front of them. There was no sound in the rising cubicle but the hum of the motor and a few self-conscious coughs from the children. He looked at them. To be taken so young, he thought, without a chance to help.

He closed his eyes. His wife's arm rested on his arm. He looked at her. Their eyes met and she smiled at him.

"It's all right," she whispered.

The elevator shuddered to a stop. The doors slid open and they went out. It was getting lighter. He hurried them along the enclosed platform.

They all climbed through the narrow doorway in the ship's side. He hesitated before following them. He wanted to say something fitting the moment. It burned in him to say something fitting the moment.

He couldn't. He swung in and grunted as he pulled the door shut and turned the wheel tight.

"That's it," he said. "Come on, everybody."

Their footsteps echoed on the metal decks and ladders as they went up to the control room.

The children ran to the ports and looked out. They gasped when they saw how high they were. Their mothers stood behind them, looking down at the ground with frightened eyes.

He went up to them.

"So high," said his daughter.

He patted her head gently. "So high," he repeated.

Then he turned abruptly and went over to the instrument panel. He stood there hesitantly. He heard someone come up behind him.

"Shouldn't we tell the children?" asked his wife. "Shouldn't we let them know it's their last look?"

"Go ahead," he said. "Tell them."

He waited to hear her footsteps. There were none. He turned. She kissed him on the cheek. Then she went to tell the children.

He threw over the switch. Deep in the belly of the ship, a spark ignited the fuel. A concentrated rush of gas flooded from the vents. The bulkheads began to shake.

He heard his daughter crying. He tried not to listen. He extended a trembling hand toward the lever, then glanced back suddenly. They were all staring at him. He put his hand on the lever and threw it over.

The ship quivered a brief second and then they felt it rush along the smooth incline. It flashed up into the air, faster and faster. They all heard the wind rushing past.

He watched the children turn to the ports and look out again.

"Goodbye," they said. "Goodbye."

He sank down wearily at the control panel. Out of the corner of his eyes he saw his neighbor sit down next to him.

"You know just where we're going?" his neighbor asked.

"On that chart there."

His neighbor looked at the chart. His eyebrows raised.

"In another solar system," he said.

"That's right. It has an atmosphere like ours. We'll be safe there."

"The race will be safe," said his neighbor.

He nodded once and looked back at his and his neighbor's family. They were still looking out the ports.

"What?" he asked.

"I said," the neighbor repeated, "which one of these planets is it?"

He leaned over the chart, pointed.

"That small one over there," he said. "Near that moon."

"This one, third from the sun?"

"That's right," he said. "That one. Third from the sun."

WHEN THE WAKER SLEEPS

IF ONE FLEW OVER THE CITY AT THIS TIME OF
this day, which was like any other day in the year
3850, one would think all life had disappeared.

Sweeping over the rustless spires, one would search
in vain for the sight of human activity. One's gaze
would scan the great ribboned highways that swept
over and under each other like the weave of some tre-
mendous loom. But there would be no autocars to
see; nothing but the empty lanes and the colored traffic
lights clicking out their mindless progressions.

Dipping low and weaving in and out among the
glittering towers, one might see the moving walks,
the studied revolution of the giant street ventilators,
hot in the winter and cool in summer, the tiny doors
opening and closing, the park fountains shooting their
methodical columns of water into the air.

Farther along, one would flit across the great open
field on which the glossy spaceships stood lined before
their hangars. Farther yet, one would catch sight of

the river, the metal ships resting along shore, delicate froth streaming from their sterns caused by the never-ending operation of their vents.

Again, one would glide over the city proper, seeking some sign of life in the broad avenues, the network of streets, the painstaking pattern of dwellings in the living area, the metal fastness of the commercial section.

The search would be fruitless.

All movement below would be seen to be mechanical. And, knowing what city this was, one's eyes would stop the search for citizens and seek out those squat metal structures which stood a half mile apart. These circular buildings housed the never-resting machines, the humming geared servants of the city's people.

These were the machines that did all: cleared the air of impurities, moved the walks and opened the doors, sent their synchronized impulses into the traffic lights, operated the fountains and the spaceships, the river vessels and the ventilators.

These were the machines in whose flawless efficacy the people of the city placed their casual faith.

At the moment, these people were resting on their pneumatic couches in rooms. And the music that seeped from their wall speakers, the cool breezes that flowed from their wall ventilators, the very air they breathed— all these were of and from the machines, the unfailing, the trusted, the infallible machines.

Now there was a buzzing in ears. Now the city came alive.

There was a buzzing, buzzing.

From the black swirl of slumber, you heard it. You

wrinkled up your classic nose and twitched the twenty neural rods that led to the highways of your extremities.

The sound bore deeper, cut through swaths of snooze and poked an impatient finger in the throbbing matter of your brain. You twisted your head on the pillow and grimaced.

There was no cessation. With stupored hand, you reached out and picked up the receiver. One eye propped open by dint of will, you breathed a weary mutter into the mouthpiece.

"Captain Rackley!" The knifing voice put your teeth on edge.

"Yes," you said.

"You will report to your company headquarters immediately!"

That swept away sleep and annoyance as a petulant old man brushes chessmen from his board. Stomach muscles drew into play and you were sitting. Inside your noble chest, that throbbing meat ball, source of blood velocity, saw fit to swell and depress with marked emphasis. Your sweat glands engaged in proper activity, ready for action, danger, heroism.

"Is it . . . ?" you started.

"Report immediately!" the voice crackled, and there was a severe click in your ear.

You, Justin Rackley, dropped the receiver—plunko—in its cradle and leaped from bed in a shower of fluttering bedclothes.

You raced to your wardrobe door and flung it open. Plunging into the depths, you soon emerged with your skintight pants, the tunic for your forty-two chest. You donned said trousers and tunic, flopped upon a nearby seat and plunged your arches into black military boots.

And your face reflected oh-so-grim thoughts. Combing out your thick blond hair, you were sure you knew what the emergency was.

The Rustons! They were at it again!

Awake now, you wrinkled your nose with conscious aplomb. The Rustons made revolting food for thought with their twelve legs, sign of alien progenitors, and their exudation of foul reptilian slime.

As you scurried from your room, leaped across the balustrade and down the stairs, you wondered once again where these awful Rustons had originated, what odious interbreeding produced their monster race. You wondered where they lived, where proliferated their grisly stock, held their meetings of war, began the upward slither to those great Earth fissures from which they massed in attack.

With nothing approaching answers to these endless questions, you ran out of the dwelling and flew down the steps to your faithful autocar. Sliding in, pushing buttons, levers, pedals, what have you, you soon had it darting through the streets toward the broad highway that led to headquarters.

At this time of day, naturally, there were very few people about. In point of fact you saw none. It was only a few minutes later, when you turned sharply and zoomed up the ramp to the highway, that you saw the other autocars whizzing toward the tower five miles distant. You guessed, and were correct in guessing, that they were fellow officers, all similarly ripped from slumber by mobilization.

Buildings flew past as you pushed pedals deeper

into their cavities, your face always grim, alive to danger, grand warrior! True, you were not averse to the chance for activity after a month of idleness. But the circumstances *were* slightly distasteful. To think of the Rustons made a fellow shudder, eh?

What made them pour from their unknown pits? Why did they seek to destroy the machines, let the acid canker of their ooze eat through metal, make the teeth fall off the gears like petals off a dying flower? What was their purpose? Did they mean to ruin the city? Govern its inhabitants? Or slaughter them? Ugly questions, questions without answers.

Well, you thought as you drove into headquarters parking area, thank heaven the Rustons had only managed to get at a few of the outer machines, yours blessedly not included.

They, at least, had no more idea than you where the Great Machine was, that fabulous fountainhead of energy, driver of all machines.

You slid the seat of your military trousers across the seat of the autocar and jumped out into the wide lot. Your black boots clacked as you ran toward the entrance. Other officers were getting out of autocars, too, running across the area. None of them said anything; they all looked grim. Some of them nodded curtly at you as you all stood together in the rising elevator. Bad business, you thought.

With a tug at the groin, the door gave a hydraulic gasp and opened. You stepped out and padded silently down the hall to the high-ceilinged briefing room.

Already the room was almost filled. The young men, invariably handsome and muscular, stood in gregarious formations, discussing the Rustons in low voices. The gray soundproof walls sucked in their comments and returned dead air.

The men gave you a look and a nod when you entered, then returned to their talking. Justin Rackley, captain, that's you, sat down in a front seat.

Then you looked up. The door to Upper Echelons was jerked open. The General came striding through, a sheaf of papers in his square fist. *His* face was grim, too.

He stepped up on the rostrum and slapped the papers on the thick table which stood there. Then he plumped down on the edge of it and kicked his boot against one of its legs until all your fellow officers had broken up their groups and hurriedly taken seats. With silence creeping over all heads, he pursed his lips and banged a palm on the table surface.

"Gentlemen," he said with that voice which seemed to issue from an ancient tomb, "once more the city lies in grave danger."

He then paused and looked capable of handling all emergencies. You hoped that someday you might be General and look capable of handling all emergencies. No reason why not, you thought.

"I will not take up precious time," the General went on, taking up precious time. "You all know your positions, you all know your responsibilities. When this briefing is concluded, you will report to the arsenal and draw out your ray guns. Always remember that the Rustons must not be allowed to enter the machinery and live. Shoot to kill. The rays are *not* harmful, repeat, *not* harmful to the machinery."

He looked over you eager young men.

"You also know," he said, "the dangers of Ruston

poisoning. For this reason, that the slightest touch of their stingers can lead to abysmal agonies of death, you will be assigned, as you also know, a nurse trained in the combating of systemic poisons. Therefore, after leaving the arsenal, you will report to the Preventive Section."

He winked, a thoroughly out-of-place wink.

"And remember," he said, with a broad roll of import in his voice, "this is *war!* And *only* war!"

This, of course, brought on appreciative smiles, a smattering of leers and many unmilitary asides. Upon which the General snapped out of his brief role as chuckling confrere and returned to strict autocratic detachment.

"Once assigned a nurse, those of you whose machines are more than fifteen miles from the city will report to the spaceport, there to be assigned a spacecar. All of you will then proceed with utmost dispatch. Questions?"

No questions.

"I need hardly remind you," completed the General, "of the importance of this defense. As you are well aware, should Rustons penetrate our city, spread their ravaging to the core of our machine system, should they—heaven forfend!—locate the Great Machine, we may then expect nothing but the most merciless of butchery. The city would be undone, we would all be annihilated, Man would be overthrown."

The men looked at him with clenched fists, patriotism lurching through their brains like drunken satyrs, yours included, Justin Rackley.

"That is all," said the General, waving his hand. "Good shooting."

He jumped down from the platform and swept through the doorway, the door opening magically a split second before his imperious nose stood to shatter on its surface.

You stood up, muscles tingling. Onward! Save our fair city!

You stepped through the broken ranks. The elevator again, standing shoulder to shoulder with your comrades, a fluttering sense of hyperawareness coursing your healthy young body.

The arsenal room. Sound lost in the heavily padded interior. You, on line, grim-faced always, shuffling along, weapon bound. A counter; it was like an exchange market. You showed the man your identity card and he handed you a shiny ray gun and a shoulder case of extra ray pellets.

Then you passed through the door and scuffed down the rubberized steps to the Preventive Section. Corpuscles took a carnival ride through your veins.

You were fourth in line and she was fourth in line; that's how she was assigned to you.

You perused her contours, noting that her uniform, although similar to yours, somehow hung differently on her. This sidetracked martial contemplations for the nonce. *Zowie hoopla!*—your libido clapped its calloused hands.

"Captain Rackley," said the man, "this is Miss Lieutenant Forbes. She is your only guarantee against death should you be stung by a Ruston. See that she remains close by at all times."

This seemed hardly an onerous commission and you saluted the man. You then exchanged a flicker of lids with the young lady and intoned a gruff command relative to departure. This roused the two of you to walk to the elevator.

Riding down in silence, you cast glances at her. Long, forgotten threnodies twitched into life in your revitalized brain. You were much taken by the dark ringlets that hung over her forehead and massed on her shoulders like curled black fingers. Her eyes, you noted, were brown and soft as eyes in a dream. And why shouldn't they be?

Yet something lacked. Some retardation kept bringing you down from ethereal cogitation. Could it, you wondered, be duty? And, remembering what you were out to do, you suddenly feared again. The pink clouds marched away in military formation.

Miss Lieutenant Forbes remained silent until the spacecar which you were assigned was flitting across the sky beyond the outskirts of the city. Then, following your somewhat banal overtures regarding the weather, she smiled her pretty little smile and showed her pretty little dimples.

"I am but sixteen," she announced.

"Then this is your first time."

"Yes," she replied, gazing afar. "I am very frightened."

You nodded, you patted her knee with what you meant to be a parental manner, but which, posthaste, brought the crimson of modesty flaming into her cheeks.

"Just stay close to me," you said, trying hard for a double meaning. "I'll take care of you."

Primitive, but good enough for sixteen. She blushed more deeply.

The city towers flashed beneath. Far off, like a

minute button on the fringes of spiderweb, you saw your machine. You eased the wheel forward; the tiny ship dipped down and began a long glide toward Earth. You kept your eyes on the control board with strict attention, wondering about this strange sense of excitement running pell-mell through your body, not knowing whether it presaged combat fatigue of one sort or another.

This was war. The city first. Hola!

The ship floated down to and hovered over the machine as you threw on the air brakes. Slowly, it sank to the roof like a butterfly settling on a flower.

You threw off the switch, heart pounding, all forgotten but the present danger. Grabbing the ray gun, you jumped out and ran to the edge of the roof.

Your machine was beyond the perimeter of the city. There were fields about. Your keen eyes flashed over the ground.

There was no sign of the enemy.

You hurried back to the ship. She was still sitting inside, watching you. You turned the knob and the communicator system spilled out its endless drones of information. You stood impatiently until the announcer spoke your machine number and said the Rustons were within a mile of it.

You heard her drawn-in breath and noted the upward cast of frightened eyes in your direction. You turned off the set.

"Come, we'll go inside," you said, holding the ray gun in a delightfully shaking hand. It was fun to be frightened. A fine sense of living dangerously. Wasn't that why you were here?

You helped her out. Her hand was cold. You

squeezed it and gave her a half smile of confidence. Then, locking the door to the spacecar, to keep the foe out, you went down the stairs. As you entered the main room, your head was at once filled with the smooth hum of machinery.

Here, at this juncture of the adventure, you put down your ray gun and ammunition and explained the machinery to her. It is to be noted that you had no particular concern for the machinery as you spoke, being more aware of her proximity. Such charm, such youth, crying out for comfort.

You soon held her hand again. Then you had your arm around her lithesome waist and she was close. Something other than military defense planned itself in your mind.

Came the moment when she flicked up her drowsy lids and looked you smack-dab in the eye, as is the archaic literary passage. You found her violet eyes somewhat unbalancing. You drew her closer. The perfume of her rosy breath tied casual knots in your limbs. And yet there was still something holding you back.

Swish! Slap!

She stiffened and cried out.

The Rustons were at the walls!

You raced for the table upon which your ray gun rested. On the couch next to the table was your ammunition. You slung the case over your shoulder. She ran up to you and, sternly, you handed her the preventive case. You felt like the self-assured General when he was in a grim mood.

"Keep the needles loaded and handy," you said. "I may . . ."

The sentence died as another great slobbering Ruston slapped against the wall. The sound of its huge suckers slurped on the outside. They were searching for the machinery in the basement.

You checked the gun. It was ready.

"Stay here," you muttered. "I have to go down."

You didn't hear what she said. You dashed down the stairs and came bouncing out into the basement just as the first horror gushed over the edge of a window onto its metal floor like a stream of gravity-defying lava.

The row of blinking yellow eyes turned on you; your flesh crawled. The great brown-gold monstrosity began to scuttle across toward the machines with an oily squish. You almost froze in fear.

Then instinct came to the fore. You raised the gun quickly. A crackling, brilliantine-blue ray leaped from the muzzle, touched the scaly body and enveloped it. Screeching and the smell of frying oil filled the air. When the ray had dissipated, the dead Ruston lay black and smoking on the floor, its slime running across the welded seams.

You heard the sound of suckers behind. You whirled, blasted the second of the Rustons into greasy oblivion. Still another slid over the window edge and started toward you. Another burst from the gun and another scorched hulk lay twitching on the metal.

You swallowed a great lump of excitement in your throat, your head snapping around, your body leaping from side to side. In a second, two more of them were moving toward you. Two bursts of ray; one missed. The second monster was almost upon you before you

burst it into flaming chunks as it reared up to plunge
its black stingers in your chest.

You turned quickly, cried out in horror.

One Ruston was just slipping down the stairs, another swishing toward you, the long stingers aimed at
your heart. You pressed the button. A scream caught in
your throat.

You were out of pellets!

You leaped to the side and the Ruston fell forward.
You tore open the case and fumbled with the pellets.
One fell and shattered uselessly on the metal. Your
hands were ice, they shook terribly. The blood
pounded through your veins, your hair stood on end.
You felt scared and amused.

The Ruston lunged again as you slid the pellet into
the ray gun. You dodged again—not enough! The end
of one stinger slashed through your tunic, laid open
your arm. You felt the burning poison shoot into your
system.

You pressed the button and the monster disappeared
in a cloud of unguent smoke. The basement machinery
was secure against attack—the Rustons had bypassed it.

You leaped for the stairway. You had to save the
machines, save her, save yourself!

Your boots banged up the metal stairs. You lunged
into the great room of machines and swept a glance
around.

A gasp tore open your mouth. She was collapsed on
a couch, sprawled, inert. A Ruston line of slime ran
down the front of her swelling tunic.

You whirled and, as you did, the Ruston vanished
into the machinery, pushing its scaly body through

the gear spaces. The slime dropped from its body and watery jaws. The machine stopped, started again, the racked wheels groaning.

The city! You leaped to the machine's edge and shot a blast from the ray gun into it! The brilliantine-blue ray licked out, missed the Ruston. You fired again. The Ruston moved too fast, hid behind the wheels. You ran around the machine, kept on firing.

You glanced at her. How long did the poison take? They never said. Already in your flesh, however, the burning had begun. You felt as if you were going up in flames, as if great pieces of your body were about to fall off.

You had to get an injection for yourself and her.

Still the Ruston eluded you. You had to stop and put another pellet in the gun. The interior began to whirl around you; you were overpoweringly dizzy. You pressed the button again and again. The ray darted into the machine.

You reeled around with a sob and tore open your collar. You could hardly breathe. The smell of the singed suet, of the rays, filled your head. You stumbled around the machine, shot out another ray at the fast-moving Ruston.

Then, finally, when you were about to keel over, you got a good target. You pressed the button, the Ruston was enveloped in flame, fell in molten bits beneath the machine, was swallowed up by the waste exhaust.

You dropped the ray gun and staggered over to her.

The hypodermics were on the table.

You tore open her tunic and jabbed a needle into her soft white shoulder, shudderingly injected the antidote into her veins. You stuck another into your own shoulder, felt the sudden coolness run through your flesh and your bloodstream.

You sank down beside her, breathing heavily and closing your eyes. The violence of activity had exhausted you. You felt as though you would have to rest a month after this. And, of course, you would.

She groaned. You opened your eyes and looked at her. Your heavy breathing began again, but this time you knew where the excitement was coming from. You kept looking at her. A warm heat lapped at your limbs, caressed your heart. Her eyes were on you.

"I . . ." you said.

Then all holding back was ended, all doubt undone. The city, the Rustons, the machines—the danger was over and forgotten. She ran a caressing hand over your cheek.

"And when next you opened your eyes," finished the doctor, "you were back in this room."

Rackley laughed, his head quivering on the pillow, his hands twitching in glee.

"But my dear doctor," he laughed, "how fantastically clever of you to know everything. How *ever* do you do it, naughty man?"

The doctor looked down at the tall handsome man who lay on the bed, still shaking with breathless laughter.

"You forget," he said, "I inject you. Quite natural that I should know what happens then."

"Oh, quite! Quite!" cried Justin Rackley. "Oh, it was utterly, utterly fantastic. Imagine, me!" He ran strong fingers over the swelling biceps of his arm. "*Me,* a hero!"

He clapped his hands together and deep laughter rumbled in his chest, his white teeth flashed against the glowing tan of his face. The sheet slipped, revealing the broad suppleness of his chest, the tightly ridged stomach muscles.

"Oh, dear me," he sighed. "Dear me, what *would* this dull existence be without your blessed injections to case our endless boredom?"

The doctor looked coldly at him, his strong white fingers tightening into a bloodless fist. The thought plunged a cruel knife into his brain—this is the end of our race, the sorry peak of Man's evolution. This is the final corruption.

Rackley yawned and stretched his arms. "I must rest." He peered up at the doctor. "It was such a *fatiguing* dream."

He began to giggle, his great blond head lolling on the pillow. His hands striking at the sheet as though he would die of amusement.

"Do tell me," he gasped, "what on earth have you in those utterly delightful injections? I've asked you so often."

The doctor picked up his plastic bag. "Merely a combination of chemicals designed to exacerbate the adrenals on one hand and, on the other, to inhibit the higher brain centers. In short," he finished, "a potpourri of intensification and reduction."

"Oh, you always say that," said Justin Rackley. "But it *is* delightful. Utterly, charmingly delightful. You will be back in a month for my next dream and my dream playback?"

The doctor blew out a weary gust of breath. "Yes," he said, making no effort to veil his disgust. "I'll be back next month."

"Thank heavens," said Rackley. "I'm done with that awful Ruston dream for another five months. Ugh! It's so frightfully vile! I like the pleasanter dreams about mining and transporting ores from Mars and the Moon, and the adventures in food centers. They're so much nicer. But . . ." His lips twitched. "*Do* have more of those pretty young girls in them."

His strong, weary body twisted in delight.

"Oh, *do*," he murmured, his eyes shutting.

He sighed and turned slowly and exhaustedly onto his broad, muscular side.

The doctor walked through the deserted streets, his face tight with the old frustration. Why? Why? His mind kept repeating the word.

Why must we continue to sustain life in the cities? For what purpose? Why not let civilization in its last outpost die as it means to die? Why struggle to keep such men alive?

Hundreds, thousands of Justin Rackleys—well-kept animals, mechanically bred and fed and massaged into fair and handsome form. Mechanically restrained, too, from physically turning into the fat white slugs that, mentally, they already were and would bodily resemble if left untended. Or die.

Why not let them? Why visit them every month, fill their veins with hypnotic drugs and sit back and watch them, one by one, go bursting into their dream worlds to escape boredom? Must he endlessly send his suggestions into their loosened brainways, fly

them to planets and moons, crowd all forms of love
and grand adventure into their mock-heroic dreams?

The doctor slumped tiredly and went into another
dorm-building. More figures, strongly or beautifully
made, passive on couches. More dream injections.

He made them, watched the figures stand and stumble to the wardrobes. Explorers' outfits this time, pith
helmets and attractive shorts, snake boots and bared
limbs. He stood at the window, saw them clamber into
their autocars and drive away. He sat back and waited
for them to return, knowing every move they would
make, because he made them in his mind.

They would go out to the hydroponics tanks and
fight off an invasion of Energy Eaters. Bigger than the
Rustons and made of pure force, they threatened to
suck the sustenance from the plants in the growing
trays, the living, formless meat swelling immortally in
the nutrient solutions. The Energy Eaters would be
beaten off, of course. They always were.

Naturally. They were only dreams. Creatures of
fantastic illusion, conjured in eager dreaming minds
by chemical magic and dreary scientific incantation.

But what would all these Justin Rackleys say, these
handsome and hopeless ruins of torpid flesh, if they
found out how they were being fooled?

Found out that the Rustons were only mental fic-
tions for objectifying simple rust and wear and con-
verting them into fanciful monsters. Monsters which
alone could feebly arouse the dim instinct for self-
preservation which just barely existed in this lost
race. Energy Eaters—beetles and spores and exhausted growth solutions. Mine Borers—vaporous
beasties that had to be blasted out of the Lunar and

Martian metal deposits. And others, still others, all of them threats to that which runs and feeds and renews a city.

What would all these Justin Rackleys say to the discovery that each of them, in his "dreams," had done genuine manual work? That their ray guns were spray guns or grease guns or air hammers, their death rays no more than streams of lubrication for rusting machines or insecticides or liquid fertilizer?

What would they say if they found out how they were tricked into breeding with aphrodisiacs in the guise of anti-poison shots? How they, with no healthy interest in procreation, were drugged into furtherance of their spineless strain, a strain whose only function was to sustain the life-giving machines.

In a month he would return to Justin Rackley, *Captain* Justin Rackley. A month for rest, these people were so devoid of energy. It took a month to build up even enough strength to endure an injection of hypnotics, to oil a machine or tend a tray, and to bring forth one puny cell of life.

All for the machines, the city, for man . . .

The doctor spat on the immaculate floor of the room with the pneumatic couches.

The people were the machines, more than the machines themselves. A slave race, a detestable residue, hopeless, without hope.

Oh, how they would wail and swoon, he thought, getting grim pleasure in the notion, were they allowed to walk through the vast subterranean tunnel to the giant chamber where the Great Machine stood, that supposed source of all energy, and saw why they had to be tricked into working. The Great Machine had been designed to eliminate all human labor, tending the minor machines, the food plants, the mining.

But some wise one on the Control Council, centuries before, had had the wit to smash the Great Machine's mechanical brain. And now the Justin Rackleys would have to see, with their own unbelieving eyes, the rust, the rot, the giant twisted death of it.... But they wouldn't.

Their job was to dream of adventurous work, and work while dreaming.

For how long?

BORN OF MAN AND WOMAN

X—THIS DAY WHEN IT HAD LIGHT MOTHER called me retch. You retch she said. I saw in her eyes the anger. I wonder what it is a retch.

This day it had water falling from upstairs. It fell all around. I saw that. The ground of the back I watched from the little window. The ground it sucked up the water like thirsty lips. It drank too much and it got sick and runny brown. I didn't like it.

Mother is a pretty I know. In my bed place with cold walls around I have a paper things that was behind the furnace. It says on it SCREEN-STARS. I see in the pictures faces like of mother and father. Father says they are pretty. Once he said it.

And also mother he said. Mother so pretty and me decent enough. Look at you he said and didnt have the nice face. I touched his arm and said it *is* alright father. He shook and pulled away where I couldnt reach.

Today mother let me off the chain a little so I could

look out the little window. Thats how I saw the water falling from upstairs.

XX—This day it had goldness in the upstairs. As I know when I looked at it my eyes hurt. After I look at it the cellar is red.

I think this was church. They leave the upstairs. The big machine swallows them and rolls out past and is gone. In the back part is the little mother. She is much small than me. I am I can see out the little window all I like.

In this day when it got dark I had eat my food and some bugs. I hear laughs upstairs. I like to know why there are laughs for. I took the chain from the wall and wrapped it around me. I walked squish to the stairs. They creak when I walk on them. My legs slip on them because I dont walk on stairs. My feet stick to the wood.

I went up and opened a door. It was a white place. White as white jewels that come from upstairs some-time. I went in and stood quiet. I hear the laughing some more. I walk to the sound and look through to the people. More people than I thought was. I thought I should laugh with them.

Mother came out and pushed the door in. It hit me and hurt. I fell back on the smooth floor and the chain made noise. I cried. She made a hissing noise into her and put her hand on her mouth. Her eyes got big.

She looked at me. I heard father call. What fell he called. She said a iron board. Come help pick it up she said. He came and said now is *that* so heavy you need. He saw me and grew big. The anger came in his eyes. He hit me. I spilled some of the drip on the floor from one arm. It was not nice. It made ugly green on the floor.

Father told me to go to the cellar. I had to go. The light it hurt some now in my eyes. It is not so like that in the cellar.

Father tied my legs and arms up. He put me on my bed. Upstairs I heard laughing while I was quiet there looking on a black spider that was swinging down to me. I thought what father said. Oh god he said. And only eight.

XXX—This day father hit in the chain again before it had light. I have to try pull it out again. He said I was bad to come upstairs. He said never do that again or he would beat me hard. That hurts.

I hurt. I slept the day and rested my head against the cold wall. I thought of the white place upstairs.

XXXX—I got the chain from the wall out. Mother was upstairs. I heard little laughs very high. I looked out the window. I saw all little people like the little mother and little fathers too. They are pretty.

They were making nice noise and jumping around the ground. Their legs was moving hard. They are like mother and father. Mother says all right people look like they do.

One of the little fathers saw me. He pointed at the window. I let go and slid down the wall in the dark. I curled up as they would not see. I heard their talks by the window and foots running. Upstairs there was a door hitting. I heard the little mother call upstairs. I heard heavy steps and I rushed in my bed place. I hit the chain in the wall and lay down on my front.

I heard my mother come down. Have you been at the window she said. I heard the anger. *Stay* away from the window. You have pulled the chain out again.

She took the stick and hit me with it. I didnt cry. I cant do that. But the drip ran all over the bed. She saw it and twisted away and made a noise. Oh mygodmygod she said why have you *done* this to me? I heard the stick go bounce on the stone floor. She ran upstairs. I slept the day.

XXXXX—This day it had water again. When mother was upstairs I heard the little one come slow down the steps. I hidded myself in the coal bin for mother would have anger if the little mother saw me.

She had a little live thing with her. It walked on the arms and had pointy ears. She said things to it.

It was all right except the live thing smelled me. It ran up the coal and looked down at me. The hairs stood up. In the throat it made an angry noise. I hissed but it jumped on me.

I didnt want to hurt it. I got fear because it bit me harder than the rat does. I hurt and the little mother screamed. I grabbed the live thing tight. It made sounds I never heard. I pushed it all together. It was all lumpy and red on the black coal.

I hid there when mother called. I was afraid of the stick. She left. I crept over the coal with the thing. I hid it under my pillow and rested on it. I put the chain in the wall again.

X—This is another times. Father chained me tight. I hurt because he beat me. This time I hit the stick out of his hands and made noise. He went away and his face was white. He ran out of my bed place and locked the door.

I am not so glad. All day it is cold in here. The chain comes slow out of the wall. And I have a bad anger with mother and father. I will show them. I will do what I did that once.

I will screech and laugh loud. I will run on the walls. Last I will hang head down by all my legs and laugh and drip green all over until they are sorry they didnt be nice to me.

If they try to beat me again Ill hurt them. I will.

X—

RETURN

PROFESSOR ROBERT WADE WAS JUST SITTING down on the thick fragrant grass when he saw his wife Mary come rushing past the Social Sciences Building and onto the campus.

She had apparently run all the way from the house—a good half mile. And with a child in her. Wade clenched his teeth angrily on the stem of his pipe.

Someone had told her.

He could see how flushed and breathless she was as she hurried around the ellipse of walk facing the Liberal Arts Building. He pushed himself up.

Now she was starting down the wide path that paralleled the length of the enormous granite-faced Physical Sciences Center. Her bosom rose and fell rapidly. She raised her right hand and pushed back wisps of dark brown hair.

Wade called, "Mary! Over here!" and gestured with his pipe.

She slowed down, gasping in the cool September air. Her eyes searched over the wide sunlit campus until she saw him. Then she ran off the walk onto the grass. He could see the pitiful fright marring her features and his anger faded. Why did anyone have to tell her?

She threw herself against him. "You said you wouldn't go this time," she said, the words spilling out in gasps. "You said s-someone else would go this time."

"Shhh, darling" he soothed. "Get your breath."

He pulled a handkerchief from his coat pocket and gently patted her forehead.

"Robert, why?" she asked.

"Who told you?" he asked. "I told them not to."

She pulled back and stared at him. "Not tell me!" she said. "You'd go without telling me?"

"Is it surprising that I don't want you frightened?" he said. "Especially now, with the baby coming?"

"But Robert," she said, "you have to tell me about a thing like that."

"Come on," he said, "let's go over to that bench."

They started across the green, arms around each other.

"You said you wouldn't go," she reminded him.

"Darling, it's my job."

They reached the bench and sat down. He put his arm around her.

"I'll be home for supper," he said. "It's just an afternoon's work."

She looked terrified.

"To go five hundred years into the future!" she cried. "Is that just an afternoon's work?"

"Mary," he said, "you know John Randall has traveled five years and I've traveled a hundred. Why do you start worrying now?"

She closed her eyes. "I'm not just starting," she murmured. "I've been in agony ever since you men invented that—*that thing.*"

Her shoulders twitched and she began to cry again. He gave her his handkerchief with a helpless look on his face.

"Listen," he said, "do you think John would let me go if there was any danger? Do you think Doctor Phillips would?"

"But why you?" she asked. "Why not a student?"

"We have no right to send a student, Mary."

She looked out at the campus, plucking at the handkerchief.

"I knew it would be no use talking," she said.

He had no reply.

"Oh, I know it's your job," she said. "I have no right to complain. It's just that—" She turned to him. "Robert, don't lie to me. Will you be in danger? Is there any chance at all that you . . . won't come back?"

He smiled reassuringly. "My dear, there's no more risk than there was the other time. After all it's—" He stopped as she pressed herself against him.

"There'd be no life for me without you," she said. "You know that. I'd die."

"Shhh," he said. "No talk of dying. Remember there are two lives in you now. You've lost your right to private despair." He raised her chin with his hand. "Smile?" he said. "For me? There. That's better. You're much too pretty to cry."

She caressed his hand.

"Who told you?" he asked.

"I'm not snitching," she said with a smile. "Anyway, the one who told me assumed that I already knew."

"Well, now you know," he said. "I'll be back for supper. Simple as that." He started to knock the ashes out of his pipe. "Any errand you'd like me to perform in the twenty-fifth century?" he asked, a smile tugging at the corners of his lean mouth.

"Say hello to Buck Rogers," she said, as he pulled out his watch. Her face grew worried again, and she whispered, "How soon?"

"About forty minutes."

"Forty min—" She grasped his hand and pressed it against her cheek. "You'll come back to me?" she said, looking into his eyes.

"I'll be back," he said, patting her cheek fondly. Then he put on a face of mock severity.

"Unless," he said, "you have something for supper I don't like."

He was thinking about her as he strapped himself into a sitting position in the dim time-chamber.

The large, gleaming sphere rested on a base of thick conductors. The air crackled with the operation of giant dynamos.

Through the tall, single-paned windows, sunlight streamed across the rubberized floors like outflung bolts of gold cloth. Students and instructors hurried in and out among the shadows, checking and preparing Transposition T-3. On the wall a buzzer sounded ominously.

Everyone on the floor made their final adjustments,

then walked quickly to the large, glass-fronted control room and entered.

A short, middle-aged man in a white lab coat came out and strode over to the chamber. He peered into its gloomy interior.

"Bob?" he said. "You want to see me?"

"Yes," Wade said. "I just wanted to say the usual thing. On the vague possibility that I'm unable to return, I—"

"Usual thing!" snorted Professor Randall. "If you think there's any possibility of it at all, get out of that chamber. We're not that interested in the future." He squinted into the chamber. "You smiling?" he asked. "Can't see clearly."

"I'm smiling."

"Good. Nothing to worry about. Just keep strapped in, mind your P's and Q's and don't go flirting with any of those Buck Rogers women.

Wade chuckled. "That reminds me," he said. "Mary asked me to say hello to Buck Rogers. Anything you'd like me to do?"

"Just be back in an hour," growled Randall. He reached in and shook hands with Wade. "All strapped?"

"All strapped," Wade answered.

"Good. We'll bounce you out of here in, uh—" Randall looked up at the large red-dialed clock on the firebrick wall. "In eight minutes. Check?"

"Check," Wade said. "Say goodbye to Doctor Phillips for me."

"Will do. Take care, Bob."

"See you."

Wade watched his friend walk back across the floor

to the control room. Then, taking a deep breath, he pulled the thick circular door shut and turned the wheel, locking it. All sound was cut off.

"Twenty-four seventy-five, here I come," he muttered.

The air seemed heavy and thin. He knew it was only an illusion. He looked quickly at the control board clock. Six minutes. Or five? No matter. He was ready. He rubbed a hand over his brow. Sweat dripped from his palm.

"Hot," he said. His voice was hollow, unreal.

Four minutes.

He let go of the bracing handle with his left hand and, reaching into his back pants pocket, he drew out his wallet. As he opened it to look at Mary's picture, his fingers lost their grip, and the wallet thudded on the metal deck.

He tried to reach it. The straps held him back. He glanced nervously at the clock. Three and a half minutes. Or two and a half? He'd forgotten when John had started the count.

His watch registered a different time. He gritted his teeth. He couldn't leave the wallet there. It might get sucked into the whirring fan and be destroyed and destroy him as well.

Two minutes was time enough.

He fumbled at the waist and chest straps, pulled them open and picked up the wallet. As he started to rebuckle the straps, he squinted once more at the clock. One and a half minutes. Or—

Suddenly the sphere began to vibrate.

Wade felt his muscles contract. The slack waist band

snapped open and whipped against the bulkhead. A sudden pain filled his chest and stomach. The wallet fell again.

He grabbed wildly for the bracing handles, exerted all his strength to keep himself pressed to the seat.

He was hurled through the universe. Stars whistled past his ear. A fist of icy fear punched at his heart.

"Mary!" he cried through a tight, fear-bound throat.

Then his head snapped back against the metal. Something exploded in his brain, and he slumped forward. The rushing darkness blotted out consciousness.

It was cool. Pure, exhilarating air washed over the numbed layers of his brain. The touch of it was a pleasant balm to him.

Wade opened his eyes and gazed fixedly at the dull gray ceiling. He twisted his head to follow the drop of the walls. Slight twinges fluttered in his flesh. He winced and moved his head back to its original position.

"Professor Wade."

He started up at the voice, fell back in hissing pain.

"Please remain motionless, Professor Wade," the voice said.

Wade tried to speak but his vocal cords felt numb and heavy.

"Don't try to speak," said the voice. "I'll be in presently."

There was a click, then silence.

Slowly Wade turned his head to the side and looked at the room.

It was about twenty feet square with a fifteen-foot ceiling. The walls and ceiling were of a uniform dullish gray. The floor was black; some sort of tile. In the far wall was the almost invisible outline of a door.

Beside the couch on which he lay was an irregularly shaped three-legged structure. Wade took it for a chair.

There was nothing else. No other furniture, pictures, rugs, or even source of light. The ceiling seemed to be glowing. Yet, at every spot he concentrated his gaze, the glow faded into lusterless gray.

He lay there trying to recall what had happened. All he could remember was the pain, the flooding tide of blackness.

With considerable pain he rolled onto his right side and got a shaky hand into his rear trouser pocket.

Someone had picked his wallet up from the chamber deck and put it back in his pocket. Stiff-fingered, he drew it out, opened it, and looked at Mary smiling at him from the porch of their home.

The door opened with a gasp of compressed air and a robed man entered.

His age was indeterminate. He was bald, and his wrinkleless features presented an unnatural smoothness like that of an immobile mask.

"Professor Wade," he said.

Wade's tongue moved ineffectively. The man came over to the couch and drew a small plastic box from his robe pocket. Opening it, he took out a small hypodermic and drove it into Wade's arm.

Wade felt a soothing flow of warmth in his veins. It seemed to unknot ligaments and muscles, loosen his throat and activate his brain centers.

"That's better," he said. "Thank you."

"Quite all right," said the man, sitting down on the three-legged structure and sliding the case into his pocket. "I imagine you'd like to know where you are."

"Yes, I would."

"You've reached your goal, Professor—2475—exactly."

"Good. Very good," Wade said. He raised up on one elbow. The pain had disappeared. "My chamber," he said, "is it all right?"

"I dare say," said the man. "It's down in the machine laboratory."

Wade breathed easier. He slid the wallet into his pocket.

"Your wife was a lovely woman," said the man.

"Was?" Wade asked in alarm.

"You didn't think she was going to live five hundred years did you?" said the man.

Wade looked dazed. Then an awkward smile raised his lips.

"It's a little difficult to grasp," he said. "To me she's still alive."

He sat up and put his legs over the edge of the couch.

"I'm Clemolk," said the man. "I'm an historian. You're in the History Pavilion in the city Greenhill."

"United States?"

"Nationalist States," said the historian.

Wade was silent a moment. Then he looked up suddenly and asked, "Say, how long have I been unconscious?"

"You've been 'unconscious,' as you call it, for a little more than two hours."

Wade jumped up. "My God," he said anxiously, "I'll have to leave."

Clemolk looked at him blandly. "Nonsense," he said. "Please sit down."

"But—"

"Please. Let me tell you what you're here for."

Wade sat down, a puzzled look on his face. A vague uneasiness began to stir in him.

"Here for?" he muttered.

"Let me show you something," Clemolk said.

He drew a small control board from his robe and pushed one of its many buttons.

The walls seemed to fall away. Wade could see the exterior of the building. High up, across the huge entablature were the words: HISTORY IS LIVING. After a moment the wall was there again, solid and opaque.

"Well?" Wade asked.

"We build our history texts, you see, not on records but on direct testimony."

"I don't understand."

"We transcribe the testimony of people who lived in the times we wish to study."

"But how?"

"By the re-formation of disincarnate personalities."

Wade was dumbfounded. *"The dead?"* he asked hollowly.

"We call them the bodiless," replied Clemolk.

"In the natural order, Professor," the historian said, "Man's personality exists apart from and independent of his corporeal frame. We have taken this truism and used it to our advantage. Since the personality retains indefinitely—although in decreasing strength—the memory of its physical form and habiliments, it is only a matter of supplying the organic and inorganic materials to this memory."

"But that's incredible," Wade said. "At Fort—that's the college where I teach—we have psychical research projects. But nothing approaching this." Suddenly he paled. "Why am *I* here?"

"In your case," Clemolk said, "we were spared the difficulty of reforming a long bodiless personality from your time period. You reached our period in your chamber."

Wade clasped his shaking hands and blew out a heavy breath.

"This is all very interesting," he said, "but I can't stay long. Suppose you ask me what you want to know."

Clemolk drew out the control board and pushed a button. "Your voice will be transcribed now," he said.

He leaned back and clasped his colorless hands on his lap.

"Your governmental system," he said. "Suppose we start with that."

"Yes," Clemolk said, "it all balances nicely with what we already know."

"Now, may I see my chamber?" Wade asked.

Clemolk's eyes looked at him without flickering. His motionless face was getting on Wade's nerves.

"I think you can *see* it," Clemolk said, getting up.

Wade got up and followed the historian through

the doorway into a long similarly shaded and illuminated hall.

You can *see* it.

Wade's brow was twisted into worried lines. Why the emphasis on that word, as though to see the chamber was all he would be allowed to do?

Clemolk seemed unaware of Wade's uneasy thoughts.

"As a scientist," he was saying, "you should be interested in the aspects of re-formation. Every detail is clearly defined. The only difficulty our scientists have yet to cope with is the strength of memory and its effect on the re-formed body. The weaker the memory, you see, the sooner the body disintegrates."

Wade wasn't listening. He was thinking about his wife.

"You see," Clemolk went on, "although, as I said, these disincarnate personalities are re-formed in a vestigial pattern that includes every item to the last detail—including clothes and personal belongings— they last for shorter and shorter periods of time.

"The time allowances vary. A re-formed person, from your period, say, would last about three quarters of an hour."

The historian stopped and motioned Wade toward a door that had opened in the wall of the hallway.

"Here," he said, "we'll take the tube over to the laboratory."

They entered a narrow, dimly lit chamber. Clemolk directed Wade to a wall bench.

The door slid shut quickly and a hum rose in the air. Wade had the immediate sensation of being back in the time-chamber again. He felt the pain, the crushing weight of depression, the wordless terror billowing up in memory.

"Mary." His lips soundlessly formed her name.

The chamber was resting on a broad metal platform. Three men, similar to Clemolk in appearance were examining its exterior surface.

Wade stepped up on the platform and touched the smooth metal with his palms. It comforted him to feel it. It was a tangible link with the past—and his wife.

Then a look of concern crossed his face. Someone had locked the door. He frowned. Opening it from the outside was a difficult and imperfect method.

One of the students spoke. "Will you open it? We didn't want to cut it open."

A pang of fear coursed through Wade. If they had cut it open, he would have been stranded forever.

"I'll open it," he said. "I have to leave now anyway." He said it with forced belligerence, as though he dared them to say otherwise.

The silence that greeted his remark frightened him. He heard Clemolk whisper something.

Pressing his lips together, he began hesitantly to move his fingers over the combination dials.

In his mind, Wade planned quickly, desperately. He would open the door, jump in and pull it shut behind him before they could make a move.

Clumsily, as if they were receiving only vague direction from his brain, his fingers moved over the thick dials on the center of the door. His lips moved as he repeated to himself the numbers of the combination: 3.2—5.9—7.6—9.01. He paused, then tugged at the handle.

The door would not open.

Drops of perspiration beaded on his forehead and ran down his face. The combination had eluded him.

He struggled to concentrate and remember. He had to remember! Closing his eyes, he leaned against the chamber. Mary, he thought, please help me. Again he fumbled at the dials.

Not 7.6 he suddenly realized. It was 7.8.

His eyes flashed open. He turned the dial to 7.8. The lock was ready to open.

"You'd b-better step back," Wade said, turning to the four men. "There's liable to be an escape of . . . locked-in gasses." He hoped they wouldn't guess how desperately he was lying.

The students and Clemolk stepped back a little. They were still close, but he had to risk it.

Wade jerked open the door and in his plunge through the opening, slipped on the smooth platform surface and crashed down on one knee. Before he could rise, he felt himself grabbed on both sides.

Two students started to drag him off the platform.

"No!" he screamed. "I have to go back!"

He kicked and struggled, his fists flailed the air. Now the other two men held him back. Tears of rage flew from his eyes as he writhed furiously in their grip, shrieking, "Let me go!"

A sudden pain jabbed Wade's back. He tore away from one student and dragged the others around in a last surge of enraged power. A glimpse of Clemolk showed the historian holding another hypodermic.

Wade would have tried to lunge for him, but on the instant a complete lassitude watered his limbs. He slumped down on his knees, glassy-eyed, one numbing hand outflung in vain appeal.

"Mary," he muttered hoarsely.

Then he was on his back and Clemolk was standing over him. The historian seemed to waver and disappear before Wade's clouding eyes.

"I'm sorry," Clemolk was saying. "You can't go back—ever."

Wade lay on the couch again, staring at the ceiling and still turning over Clemolk's words in his mind.

"It's impossible that you return. You've been transposed in time. You now belong to this period."

Mary was waiting.

Supper would be on the stove. He could see her setting the table, her slender fingers putting down plates, cups, sparkling glasses, silverware. She'd be wearing a clean, fluffy apron over her dress.

Then the food was ready. She'd be sitting at the table waiting for him. Deep within himself Wade felt the unspoken terror in her mind.

He twisted his head on the couch in agony. Could it possibly be true? Was he really imprisoned five centuries from his rightful existence? It was insane. But he was *here*. The yielding couch was definitely under him, the gray walls around him. Everything was real.

He wanted to surge up and scream, to strike out blindly and break something. The fury burst in his system. He drove his fists into the couch and yelled without meaning or intelligence, a wild outraged cry. Then he rolled on his side, facing the door. The fierce anger abated. He compressed his mouth into a thin shaking line.

"Mary," he whispered in lonely terror.

The door opened and Mary came in.

Wade sat up stiffly, gaping, blinking, believing himself mad.

She was still there, dressed in white, her eyes warm with love for him.

He couldn't speak. He doubted that his muscles would sustain him, yet he rose up waveringly.

She came to him.

There was no terror in her look. She was smiling with a radiant happiness. Her comforting hand brushed over his cheek.

A sob broke on his lips at the touch of her hand. He reached out with shaking arms and grasped her, embraced her tightly, pressing his face into her silky hair.

"Oh, Mary," he mumbled.

"Shhh, my darling," she whispered. "It's all right now."

Happiness flooded his veins as he kissed her warm lips. The terror and lonely fright were gone. He ran trembling fingers over her face.

They sat down on the couch. He kept caressing her arms, her hands, her face, as though he couldn't believe it was true.

"How did you get here?" he asked, in a shaky voice.

"I'm here. Isn't that enough?"

"Mary."

He pressed his face against her soft body. She stroked his hair and he was comforted.

Then, as he sat there, eyes tightly shut, a terrible thought struck him.

"Mary," he said, almost afraid to ask.

"Yes, my darling."

"How did you get here?"

"Is it so—"

"How?" He sat up and stared into her eyes. "Did they send the time-chamber for you?" he asked.

He knew they hadn't, but he clutched at the possibility.

She smiled sadly. "No, my dear," she said.

He felt himself shudder. He almost drew back in revulsion.

"Then you're—" His eyes were wide with shock, his face drained of color.

She pressed against him and kissed his mouth.

"Darling," she begged, "does it matter so? It's me. See? It's really me. Oh my darling, we have so little time. Please love me. I've waited so long for this moment."

He pressed his cheek against hers, clutching her to him.

"Oh my God, Mary, Mary," he groaned. "What am I to do? How long will you stay?"

A person, from your period, say, would last about three quarters of an hour. The remembrance of Clemolk's words was like a whiplash on tender flesh.

"Forty min—" he started and couldn't finish.

"Don't think about it darling," she begged. "Please. We're together for now."

But, as they kissed, a thought made his flesh crawl.

I am kissing a dead woman—his mind would not repress the words—I am holding her in my arms.

They sat quietly together. Wade's body grew more tense with each passing second.

How soon? . . . Disintegrate . . . How could he bear it? Yet he could bear less to leave her.

"Tell me about our baby," he said, trying to drive away the fear. "Was it a boy or a girl?"

She was silent.

"Mary?"

"You don't know? No, of course you don't."

"Know what?"

"I can't tell you about our child."

"Why?"

"I died when it was born."

He tried to speak but the words shattered in his throat. Finally he could ask, "Because I didn't return?"

"Yes," she replied softly. "I had no right to. But I didn't want to live without you."

"And they refuse to let me go back," he said bitterly. Then he ran his fingers through her thick hair and kissed her. He looked into her face. "Listen," he said, "I'm going to return."

"You can't change what's done."

"If I come back," he said, "it *isn't* done. I can change it."

She looked at him strangely. "Is it possible—" she began, and her words died in a groan. "No, no, it can't be!"

"Yes!" he said, "It *is* poss—" He stopped abruptly, his heart lurching wildly. She had been speaking of something else.

Under his fingers her left arm was disappearing. The flesh seemed to be dissolving, leaving her arm rotted and shapeless.

He gasped in horror. Terrified, she looked down at her hands. They were falling apart, bits of flesh spiraling away like slender streamers of white smoke.

"No!" she cried. "Don't let it happen!"

"Mary!"

She tried to take his hands but she had none her-self. Quickly she bent over and kissed him. Her lips were cold and shaking.

"So soon," she sobbed. "Oh, go away! Don't watch me, Robert! Please don't watch me!" Then she started up, crying out, "Oh, my dear, I had hoped for—"

The rest was lost in a soft, guttural bubbling. Her throat was beginning to disintegrate.

Wade leaped up and tried to embrace her to hold back the horror, but his clutch only seemed to hasten the dissolution. The sound of her breaking down be-came a terrible hiss.

He staggered back with a shriek, holding his hands before him as though to ward off the awful sight.

Her body was breaking apart in chunks. The chunks split into fizzing particles which dissolved in the air. Her hands and arms were gone. The shoulders started to disappear. Her feet and legs burst apart and the swirls of gaseous flesh spun up into the air.

Wade crashed into the wall, his shaking hands over his face. He didn't want to look, but he couldn't help himself. Drawing his fingers down, he watched in a sort of palsied fascination.

Now her chest and shoulders were going. Her chin and lower face were flowing into an amorphous cloud of flesh that gyrated like wind-blown snow.

Last to go were her eyes. Alone, hanging on a veil of gray wall, they burned into his. In his mind came the last message from her living mind: "Goodbye, my darling. I shall always love you."

He was alone.

His mouth hung open, and his eyes were circles of dumb unbelief. For long minutes he stood there, shivering helplessly, looking hopefully—hopelessly—around the room. There was nothing, not the least sensory trace of her passing.

He tried to walk to the couch, but his legs were useless blocks of wood. And all at once the floor seemed to fly up into his face.

White pain gave way to a sluggish black current that claimed his mind.

Clemolk was sitting in the chair.

"I'm sorry you took it so badly," he said.

Wade said nothing, his gaze never leaving the historian's face. Heat rose in his body, his muscles twitched.

"We could probably re-form her again," Clemolk said carelessly, "but her body would last an even shorter period the second time. Besides we haven't the—"

"What do you want?"

"I thought we might talk some more about 1975 while there's—"

"You thought that, did you!" Wade threw himself into a sitting position, eyes bright with crazed fury. "You keep me prisoner, you torture me with the ghost of my wife. Now you want to talk!"

He jolted to his feet, fingers bent into arcs of taut flesh.

Clemolk stood up, too, and reached into his robe pocket. The very casualness of the move further enraged Wade. When the historian drew out the plastic case, Wade knocked it to the floor with a snarl.

"Stop this," Clemolk said mildly, his visage still unruffled.

"I'm going back," roared Wade. "I'm going back and you're not stopping me!"

"I'm not stopping you," said Clemolk, the first signs of peevishness sounding in his voice. "You're stopping yourself. I've told you. You should have considered what you were doing before entering your time-chamber. And, as for your Mary—"

The sound of her name pronounced with such dispassionate smugness broke the floodgates of Wade's fury. His hand shot out and fastened around Clemolk's thin ivory column of neck.

"Stop," Clemolk said, his voice cracking. "You can't go back. I tell you—"

His fish eyes were popping and blurred. A gurgle of delicate protest filled his throat as his frail hands fumbled at Wade's clutching fingers. A moment later the historian's eyes rolled back and his body went limp. Wade released his fingers and put Clemolk down on the couch.

He ran to the door, his mind filled with conflicting plans. The door wouldn't open. He pushed it, threw his weight against it, tried to dig his nails along its edge to pull it open. It was tightly shut. He stepped back, his face contorted with hopeless frenzy.

Of course!

He sprang to Clemolk's inert body, reached in the robe pocket, and drew out the small control board. It had no connections in the robe. Wade pushed a button. The great sign was above him: HISTORY IS LIVING. With an impatient gasp, Wade pushed another, still another. He heard his voice.

". . . The governmental system was based on the existence of three branches, two of which were supposedly subject to popular vote. . . ."

He pushed another button—and yet another.

The door seemed to draw a heavy breath and opened noiselessly. Wade ran to it and through. It closed behind him.

Now to find the machine lab. What if the students were there? He had to risk it.

He raced down the padded hallway, looking for the tube door. It was a nightmare of running. Back and forth he rushed frantically, muttering to himself. He stopped and forced himself back, pushing buttons as he went, ignoring sounds and sights around him—the fading walls, the speaking dead. He almost missed the tube door as he passed it. Its outline blended with the wall.

"Stop!"

He heard the weak cry behind him and glanced hurriedly over his shoulder. Clemolk, stumbling along the hall, waving him down. He must have recovered and got out while Wade was carrying on his desperate search.

Wade entered the tube quickly, and the door slid shut. He breathed a sigh of relief as he felt the chamber rush through its tunnel. Something made him turn around. He gasped at the sight of the uniformed man who sat on the bench facing him. In the man's hand was a dull black tube that pointed straight at Wade's chest.

"Sit down," said the man.

Defeated, Wade slumped down in a dejected heap. Mary. The name was a broken lament in his mind.

"Why do you re-forms get so excited?" the man asked. "Why do you? Answer me that?"

Wade looked up, a spark of hope igniting in him. The man thought—

"I—expected to go soon," Wade said hurriedly. "In a matter of minutes. I wanted to get down to the machine lab."

"Why there, for heaven's sake?"

"I heard there was a time-chamber there," Wade said anxiously. "I thought—"

"Thought you'd use it?"

"Yes, that's it. I want to go back to my own time. I'm lonely."

"Haven't you been told?" asked the man.

"Told what?"

The tube sighed to a halt. Wade started up. The man waved his weapon and Wade sank down again. Had they passed it? "As soon as your re-formed body returns to air," the man was saying, "your psychic force returns to the original moment of death—hrumph—separation from the body I mean."

Wade was distracted by nervous fear. "What?" he asked vaguely, looking around.

"Personal force, personal force," bumbled the man. "At the moment it leaves your re-formed body, it will return to the moment you originally—uh—died. In your case that would be—when?"

"I don't understand."

The man shrugged. "No matter, no matter. Take my word for it. You'll soon be back in your own time."

"What about the machine lab?" Wade asked again.

"Next stop," said the man.

"Can we go there, I mean?"

"Oh," grumbled the man, "I suppose I could drop in and take a look at it. Think they'd let me know. Never any cooperation with the military. Invariably—" His voice trailed off. "No," he resumed. "On second thought, I'm in a hurry."

Wade watched the man lower his weapon. He clenched his teeth and braced himself to lunge.

"Well," said the man, "on third thought . . ."

Closing his eyes, Wade slumped back and exhaled a long shuddering breath through his pale lips.

It was still intact, its gleaming metal reflecting the tiers of bright overhead lights—and the circular door was open.

There was only one student in the lab. He was sitting at a bench. He looked up as they entered.

"Can I help you, Commander?" he asked.

"No need. No need," said the officer in an annoyed voice. "The re-form and myself are here to see the time-chamber." He waved toward the platform. "That it?"

"Yes, that's it," said the student, looking at Wade. Wade averted his face. He couldn't tell whether the student was one of the four who had been there before. They all looked alike. The student went back to his work.

Wade and the Commander stepped up on the platform. The Commander peered into the interior of the sphere.

"Well," he mused, "who brought it here, I'd like to know."

"I don't know," Wade answered. "I've never seen one."

"And you thought you could use it!" The Commander laughed.

Wade glanced around nervously to make sure the student wasn't watching. Turning back, he scanned the sphere rapidly and saw that it wasn't fastened in any way. He started as a loud buzzer sounded and looking around quickly, saw the student push a button on the wall. He tightened in fear.

On a small teleview screen built into the wall, Clemolk's face had appeared. Wade couldn't hear the historian's voice but his face showed excitement at last.

Wade spun back, facing the chamber, and asked, "Think I could see what it's like inside?"

"No, no," said the commander. "You'll play tricks."

"I won't," he said, "I'll just—"

"Commander!" cried the student.

The Commander turned. Wade gave him a shove, and the corpulent officer staggered forward, his arms flailing the air for balance, and a look of astonished outrage on his face.

Wade dove into the time chamber, cracking his knees on the metal deck, and scrambled around.

The student rushed toward the sphere, pointing one of those dull black tubes ahead of him.

Wade grabbed the heavy door and with a grunt of effort pulled it shut. The heavy circle of metal grated into place, cutting off a flash of blue flame that was directed at him. Wade spun the wheel around feverishly until the door was securely fixed.

They would be cutting the chamber open any moment.

His eyes swept over the dials as his fingers worked on the strap buckles. He saw that the main dial was still set at five hundred years and reaching over, flipped it to reverse position.

Everything seemed ready. He had to take a chance that it was. There was no time to check. Already a deadly cutting flame might be directed at the metal globe.

The straps were fastened. Wade braced himself and threw the main switch. Nothing happened. A cry of mortal terror broke through his lips. His eyes darted around. His fingers shook over the control board as he tested the connections.

A plug was loose. Grabbing it with both hands to steady it, he slid it into its socket. At once the chamber began to vibrate. The high screech of its mechanism was music to him.

The universe poured by again, the black night washing over him like ocean waves. This time he didn't lose consciousness.

He was secure.

The chamber stopped vibrating. The silence was almost deafening. Wade sat breathlessly in the semidarkness, gasping in air. Then he grabbed the wheel and turned it quickly. He kicked open the door and jumped down into the apparatus lab of Fort College and looked around, hungry for the sight of familiar things.

The lab was empty. One wall light shone down bleakly in the silence, casting great shadows of machines, sending his own shadow leaping up the walls.

He touched benches, stools, gauges, machines, anything, just to convince himself that he was back.

"It's real." He said it over and over.

An overpowering weakness of relief fell over him like a mantle. He leaned against the chamber. Here and there he saw black marks on the metal, and pieces of it were hanging loose. He felt almost a love for it. Even partly destroyed it had gotten him back.

Suddenly he looked at the clock. Two in the morning. . . . Mary. . . . He had to get home. Quickly, quickly.

The door was locked. He fumbled for keys, got the door open and rushed down the hall. The building was deserted. He reached the front door, unlocked it, remembered to lock it behind him, although he was shaking with excitement.

He tried to walk, but he kept breaking into a run, and his mind raced ahead in anticipation. He was on the porch, through the doorway, rushing up to the bedroom. . . . Mary, Mary, he was calling. . . . He was bursting through the doorway. . . . She was standing by the window. She whirled, saw him, a look of glorious happiness crossed her face. She cried out in tearful joy. . . . They were holding each other, kissing; together, together.

"Mary," he murmured in a choked-up voice as, once more, he began running.

The tall black Social Sciences Building was behind him. Now the campus was behind him, and he was running happily down University Avenue.

The street lights seemed to waver before him. His chest heaved with shuddering breaths. A burning ache stabbed at his side. His mouth fell open. Exhausted, he was forced to slow down to a walk. He gasped in air, started to run again.

Only two more blocks.

Ahead, the dark outline of his home stood out against the sky. There was a light in the living room. She was awake. She hadn't given up!

His heart flew out to her. The desire for her warm arms was almost more than he could bear.

He felt tired. He slowed down, felt his limbs trembling violently. Excitement. His body ached. He felt numb.

He was on their walk. The front door was open. Through the screen door, he could see the stairs to the second floor. He paused, his eyes glittering with a sick hunger.

"Home," he muttered.

He staggered up the path, up the porch steps. Shooting pains wracked his body. His head felt as though it would explode.

He pulled open the screen door and lurched to the living room arch.

John Randall's wife was sleeping on the couch.

There was no time to talk. He wanted Mary. He turned and stumbled to the stairs. He started up.

He tripped, almost fell. He groped for the banister with his right hand. A scream gurgled up and died in his throat. *The hand was dissolving in air.* His mouth fell open as the horror struck him.

"No!" He tried to scream it but only a mocking wheeze escaped his lips.

He struggled up. The disintegration was going on

faster. His hands. His wrists. They were flying apart. He felt as though he had been thrown into a vat of burning acid.

His mind twisted over itself as he tried to understand. And all the while he kept dragging himself up the stairs, now on his ankles, now on his knees, the corroded remnants of his disappearing legs.

Then he knew all of it. Why the chamber door was locked. Why they wouldn't let him see his own corpse. Why his body had lasted so long. It was because he had reached 2475 alive and *then* had died. Now he had to return to that year. He could not be with her *even in death*.

"Mary!"

He tried to scream for her. She had to know. But no sound came. He felt pieces of his throat falling out. Somehow he had to reach her, let her know that he had come back.

He reached the top of the landing and through the open door of their room saw her lying on the bed, sleeping in exhausted sorrow.

He called. No sound. Tears of rage poured from his anguished eyes. Now he was at the door, trying to force himself into the room.

There'd be no life for me without you.

Her remembered words tortured him. His crying was like a gentle bubbling of lava.

Now he was almost gone. The last of him poured over the rug like a morning mist, the blackness of his eyes like dark shiny beads in a swirling fog.

"Mary, Mary—" he could only think it now "—how very much I love you."

She didn't awaken.

He willed himself closer and drank in the fleeting sight of her. A massive despair weighed on his mind. A faint groan fluttered over his wraith.

Then, the woman, smiling in her uneasy sleep, was alone in the room except for two haunted eyes which hung suspended for a moment and then were gone; like tiny worlds that flare up in birth and, in the same moment, die.

BROTHER TO THE MACHINE

HE STEPPED INTO THE SUNLIGHT AND WALKED among the people. His feet carried him away from the black tube depths. The distant roar of underground machinery left his brain to be replaced by myriad whispers of the city.

Now he was walking the main street. Men of flesh and men of steel passed him by, coming and going. His legs moved slowly and his footsteps were lost in a thousand footsteps.

He passed a building that had died in the last war. There were scurrying men and robots pulling off the rubble to build again. Over their heads hung the control ship and he saw men looking down to see that work was done properly.

He slipped in and out among the crowd. No fear of being seen. Only inside of him was there a difference. Eyes would never know it. Visio-poles set at every corner could not glean the change. In form and visage he was just like all the rest.

He looked at the sky. He was the only one. The others didn't know about the sky. It was only when you broke away that you could see. He saw a rocket ship flashing across the sun and control ships hovering in a sky rich with blue and fluffy clouds.

The dull-eyed people glanced at him suspiciously and hurried on. The blank-faced robots made no sign. They clanked on past, holding their envelopes and their packages in long metal arms.

He lowered his eyes and kept walking. A man cannot look at the sky, he thought. It is suspect to look at the sky.

"Would you help a buddy?"

He paused and his eyes flicked down to the card on the man's chest.

Ex-Space Pilot. Blind. Legalized Beggar.

Signed by the stamp of the Control Commissioner. He put his hand on the blind man's shoulder. The man did not speak but passed by and moved on, his cane clacking on the sidewalk until he had disappeared. It was not allowed to beg in this district. They would find him soon.

He turned from watching and strode on. The visiopoles had seen him pause and touch the blind man. It was not permitted to pause on business streets, to touch another.

He passed a metal news dispenser and, brushing by, pulled out a sheet. He continued on and held it up before his eyes.

Income Taxes Raised. Military Draft Raised. Prices Raised.

Those were the story heads. He turned it over. On the back was an editorial that told why Earth forces had been compelled to destroy all the Martians.

Something clicked in his mind and his fingers closed slowly in a tight fist.

He passed his people, men and robots both. What distinction now? he asked himself. The common classes did the same work as the robots. Together they walked or drove through the streets, carrying and delivering.

To be a man, he thought. No longer is it a blessing, a pride, a gift. To be brother to the machine, used and broken by invisible men who kept their eyes on poles and their fists bunched in ships that hung over all their heads, waiting to strike at opposition.

When it came to you one day that this was so, you saw there was no reason to go on with it.

He stopped in the shade and his eyes blinked. He looked in the shop window. There were tiny baby creatures in a cage.

Buy a Venus Baby For Your Child, said the card.

He looked into the eyes of the small tentacled things and saw there intelligence and pleading misery. And he passed on, ashamed of what one people can do to another people.

Something stirred within his body. He lurched a little and pressed his hand against his head. His shoulders twitched. When a man is sick, he thought, he cannot work. And when a man cannot work, he is not wanted.

He stepped into the street and a huge Control truck ground to a stop inches before him.

He walked away jerkily, leaped upon the sidewalk. Someone shouted and he ran. Now the photo-cells would follow him. He tried to lose himself in the moving crowds. People whirled by, an endless blur of faces and bodies.

They would be searching now. When a man stepped in front of a vehicle he was suspect. To wish death was not allowed. He had to escape before they caught him and took him to the Adjustment Center. He couldn't bear that.

People and robots rushed past him, messengers, delivery boys, the bottom level of an era. All going somewhere. In all these scurrying thousands, only he had no place to go, no bundle to deliver, no slavish duty to perform. He was adrift.

Street after street, block on block. He felt his body weaving. He was going to collapse soon, he felt. He was weak. He wanted to stop. But he couldn't stop. Not now. If he paused—sat down to rest—they would come for him and take him to the Adjustment Center. He didn't want to be adjusted. He didn't want to be made once more into a stupid shuffling machine. It was better to be in anguish and to understand.

He stumbled on. Bleating horns tore at his brain. Neon eyes blinked down at him as he walked.

He tried to walk straight, but his system was giving way. Were they following? He would have to be careful. He kept his face blank and he walked as steadily as he could.

His knee joint stiffened and, as he bent to rub it in his hands, a wave of darkness leaped from the ground and clawed at him. He staggered against a plate-glass window.

He shook his head and saw a man staring from inside. He pushed away. The man came out and stared at him in fear. The photo-cells picked him up and followed him. He had to hurry. He couldn't be brought back to start all over again. He'd rather be dead.

A sudden idea. Cold water. Only to drink?

I'm going to die, he thought. But I will know why I am dying and that will be different. I have left the laboratory where, daily, I was sated with calculations for bombs and gasses and bacterial sprays.

All through those long days and nights of plotting destruction, the truth was growing in my brain. Connections were weakening, indoctrinations faltering as effort fought with apathy.

And, finally, something gave, and all that was left was weariness and truth and a great desire to be at peace.

And now he had escaped and he would never go back. His brain had snapped forever and they would never adjust him again.

He came to the citizen's park, last outpost for the old, the crippled, the useless. Where they could hide away and rest and wait for death.

He entered through the wide gate and looked at the high walls which stretched beyond sight. The walls that hid the ugliness from outside eyes. It was safe here. They did not care if a man died inside the citizen's park.

This is my island, he thought. I have found a silent place. There are no probing photo-cells here and no ears listening. A person can be free here.

His legs felt suddenly weak and he leaned against a blackened dead tree and sank down into the moldy leaves lying deep on the ground.

An old man came by and stared at him suspiciously. The old man walked on. He could not stop to talk for minds were still the same even when the shackles had been burst.

Two old ladies passed him by. They looked at him and whispered to one another. He was not an old person. He was not allowed in the citizen's park. The Control Police might follow him. There was danger and they hurried on, casting frightened glances over their lean shoulders. When he came near they scurried over the hill.

He walked. Far off he heard a siren. The high, screeching siren of the Control Police cars. Were they after him? Did they know he was there? He hurried on, his body twitching as he loped up a sun-baked hill and down the other side. The lake, he thought, I am looking for the lake.

He saw a fountain and stepped down the slope and stood by it. There was an old man bent over it. It was the man who had passed him. The old man's lips enveloped the thin stream of water.

He stood there quietly, shaking. The old man did not know he was there. He drank and drank. The water dashed and sparkled in the sun. His hands reached out for the old man. The old man felt his touch and jerked away, water running across his gray-bearded chin. He backed away, staring open-mouthed. He turned quickly and hobbled away.

He saw the old man run. Then he bent over the fountain. The water gurgled in his mouth. It ran down and up into his mouth and poured out again, tastelessly.

He straightened up suddenly, a sick burning in his chest. The sun faded to his eye, the sky became black.

He stumbled about on the pavement, his mouth opening and closing. He tripped over the edge of the walk and fell to his knees on the dry ground.

He crawled in on the dead grass and fell on his back, his stomach grinding, water running over his chin.

He lay there with the sun shining on his face and he looked at it without blinking. Then he raised his hands and put them over his eyes.

An ant crawled across his wrist. He looked at it stupidly. Then he put the ant between two fingers and squashed it to a pulp.

He sat up. He couldn't stay where he was. Already they might be searching the park, their cold eyes scanning the hills, moving like a horrible tide through his last outpost where old people were allowed to think if they were able to.

He got up and staggered around clumsily and started for the path, stiff-legged, looking for a lake.

He turned a bend and walked in a weaving line. He heard whistles. He heard a distant shout. They *were* looking for him. Even here in the citizen's park where he thought he could escape. And find the lake in peace.

He passed an old shut-down merry-go-round. He saw the little wooden horses in gay poses, galloping high and motionless, caught fast in time. Green and orange with heavy tassels, all covered with thick dust.

He reached a sunken walk and started down it. There were gray stone walls on both sides. Sirens were all around in the air. They knew he was loose and they were coming to get him now. A man could not escape. It was not done.

He shuffled across the road and moved up the path. Turning, he saw, far off, men running. They wore black uniforms and they were waving at him. He hurried on, his feet thudding endlessly on the concrete walk.

He ran off the path and up a hill and tumbled in the grass. He crawled into scarlet-leaved bushes and watched through waves of dizziness as the men of the Control Police dashed by.

Then he got up and started off, limping, his eyes staring ahead.

At last, the shifting, dull glitter of the lake. He hurried on now, stumbling and tripping. Only a little way. He lurched across a field. The air was thick with the smell of rotting grass. He crashed through the bushes and there were shouts and someone fired a gun. He looked back stiffly to see the men running after him.

He plunged into the water, flopping on his chest with a great splash. He struggled forward, walking on the bottom until the water had flooded over his chest, his shoulders, his head. Still walking while it washed into his mouth and filled his throat and weighted his body, dragging him down.

His eyes were wide and staring as he slid gently forward onto his face on the bottom. His fingers closed in the silt and he made no move.

Later, the Control Police dragged him out and threw him in the black truck and drove off.

And, inside, the technician tore off the sheeting and shook his head at the sight of tangled coils and water-soaked machinery.

"They go bad," he muttered as he probed with pliers and picks. "They crack up and think they are men and go wandering. Too bad they don't work as good as people."

F—

GROUND CARS SHRIEKED TO A HALT. MUFFLED curses assailed windshields. Pedestrians jumped back, eyes widened, mouths spread into incredulous O's.

A great metal sphere had appeared out of thin air right in the middle of the intersection.

"What? What?" bumbled a traffic controller, leaving the fastness of his concrete island.

"Good heavens!" cried a secretary, gaping from her third story window. "What *can* this be?"

"Popped outta nowhere!" ejaculated an old man. "Outta nowhere, I'll be bound."

Gasps. Everyone leaned forward with pounding hearts.

The sphere's circular door was being pushed open.

Out jumped a man. He looked around interestedly. He stared at the people. The people stared at him.

"What's the meaning?" ranted the traffic controller, pulling out his report book. "Looking for trouble, eh?"

The man smiled. People close by heard him say, "My

name is Professor Robert Wade. I've come from the year 1954."

"Likely, likely," grumbled the officer. "First of all get this contraption out of here."

"But that's impossible," said the man. "Right now anyway."

The officer stuck out his lower lip.

"Impossible, eh?" he challenged and stepped over to the metal globe. He pushed it. It didn't budge. He kicked it. He howled, "Ow!"

"Please," said the stranger. "It won't do any good."

Angrily, the officer pushed aside the door. He peered into the interior.

He backed away, a gasp of horror torn from paled lips.

"What? What?" he cried in fabulous disbelief.

"What's the matter?" asked the professor.

The officer's face was grim and shocked. His teeth chattered. He was unnerved.

"If you'd . . ." began the man.

"Silence, filthy dog!" the officer roared. The professor stepped back in alarm, his face a twist of surprise.

The officer reached into the interior of the sphere and plucked out objects.

Pandemonium.

Women averted their faces with shrieks of revulsion. Strong men gasped and stared in frank paralysis. Little children glanced about furtively. Maidens swooned.

The officer hid the objects beneath his coat quickly. He held the lump of them with one trembling hand. Then he clapped violently on the professor's shoulder.

"Vermin!" he raved. "Pig!"

"Hang him, hang him!" chanted a group of out-raged ladies, beating time on the sidewalk with their canes.

"The shame of it," muttered a churchman, flushing a fast vermilion.

The professor was dragged down the street. He tugged and complained. The shouting of the crowd drowned him out. They struck at him with umbrel-las, canes, crutches and rolled-up magazines.

"Villain!" they accused, waving vindictive fingers. "Unblushing libertine!"

"*Disgusting!*"

But in alleys, in vein bars, in pool rooms, behind leering faces everywhere, squirmed wild fancies. Word got around. Chuckles, deeply and formidably obscene, quivered through the city streets.

They took the professor to jail.

Two men of the Control Police were stationed by the metal globe. They kept away all curious pass-ersby. They kept looking inside with glittering eyes.

"Right in *there!*" said one of the officers again and again, licking his lips excitedly. "Wow!"

High Commissioner Castlemould was looking at li-centious postcards when the televiewer buzzed.

His scrawny shoulders twitched violently, his false teeth clicked together in shock. Quickly, he scooped up the pile of cards and threw them in his desk drawer.

Casting one more inhaling glance at the illustra-tions, he slammed the drawer shut, forced a mask of official dignity over his bony face and threw the con-trol switch.

On the telecom screen appeared Captain Ranker of the Control Police, fat neck edges oozing over his tight collar.

"Commissioner," crooned the captain, his features dripping obeisance. "Sorry to disturb you during your hour of meditation."

"Well, well, what is it?" Castlemould asked sharply, beating an impatient palm on the glossy surface of the desk.

"We have a prisoner," said the captain. "Claims to be a time traveler from 1954."

The captain looked around guiltily.

"What are you looking for?" crackled the Commissioner.

Captain Ranker held up a mollifying hand. Then, reaching under the desk, he picked up the three objects and set them on his blotter where Castlemould could see.

Castlemould's eyes made an effort to pop from their sockets. His Adam's apple took a nose dive.

"Aaaah!" he croaked. "Where did you get those?"

"The prisoner had them with him," said Ranker uneasily.

The old Commissioner drank in the sight of the objects. Neither of the men spoke for gaping. Castlemould felt a sensuous dizziness creep over him. He snorted through pinched nostrils.

"Hold on!" he gasped, in a high cracking voice, "I'll be right down."

He threw off the switch, thought a second, threw it on again. Captain Ranker jerked his hand back from the desk.

"You better not touch those things," warned Castle-mould, eyes slitted. "Don't touch 'em. Understand?"

Captain Ranker swallowed his heart.

"Yes, sir," he mumbled, a deep blush splashing up his fleshy neck.

Castlemould sneered, threw off the switch again. Then he jumped up from his desk with a lusty cackle.

"Haah haah!" he cried. "Haah haah!"

He hobbled across the floor, rubbing his lean hands together. He scuffed the thick rug delightedly with his thin black shoes.

"Haah haah! Aha haah haah haah!"

He called for his private car.

Footsteps. The burly guard unlocked the door, slid it open.

"Get up, *you*," he snarled, lips a curleycue of contempt.

Professor Wade got up and, glaring at his jailer, walked past the doorway into the hall.

"Turn right," ordered the guard.

Wade turned right. They started down the hall.

"I should have stayed home," Wade muttered.

"Silence, lewd dog!"

"Oh, *shut up!*" said Wade. "You must all be crazy around here. You find a little . . ."

"Silence!" roared the guard, looking around hurriedly. He shuddered. "Don't even say that word in my clean jail."

Wade threw up imploring eyes.

"This is too much," he announced, "anyway you look at it."

He was ushered into a room which spread out behind the door reading: *Captain Ranker—Chief of Control Police.*

The chief got up hastily as Wade came in. On the desk were the three objects discreetly hidden by a white cloth.

A wizened old man in funereal garb looked at Wade, a shrewd deductive look on his face.

Two hands waved simultaneously at a chair.

"Sit down," said the chief.

"Sit down," said the Commissioner.

The chief apologized. The Commissioner sneered.

"Sit down," Castlemould repeated.

"Would you like me to sit down?" Wade asked.

Apoplectic scarlet spattered over Captain Ranker's already mottled features.

"Sit down!" he gargled. "When Commissioner Castlemould says to sit down, he means to sit down!"

Professor Wade sat down.

Both men circled him like calculating buzzards anticipating the first swoop. The professor looked at Chief Ranker.

"Maybe you'll tell me . . ."

"Silence!" snapped Ranker.

Wade slapped an irate hand on the chair arm. "I will not be silent! I'm sick and tired of this asinine prattle you people are talking. You look in my time chamber and find *these* idiotic things and . . ."

He jerked the cloth from its shielding drape. The two men jumped back and gasped as though Wade had torn the clothes from the backs of their grandmothers.

Wade got up, throwing the cloth on the desk.

"For God's sake, what's the matter!" he growled. "It's food. *Food.* A little food!"

* * *

The men wilted under the repeated impact of the word as though they stood in blasts of purgatorial wind.

"*Shut your filthy mouth*," said the captain in a choked, wheezy voice. "We refuse to listen to your obscenities."

"Obscenities!" cried Professor Wade, his eyes and mouth expanding in disbelief. "Am I hearing right?"

He held up one of the objects.

"This is a box of crackers!" he said incredulously. "Are you telling me that's obscene?"

Captain Ranker closed his eyes, all atremble. The old Commissioner regained his senses and, pursing his greyish lips, watched the professor with cunning little eyes.

Wade threw down the box. The old man blanched. Wade grabbed the other two objects.

"A can of processed meat!" he exclaimed furiously. "A flask of coffee. What in the hell is obscene about meat and coffee?"

Dead silence filled the room when the tirade had ended.

They all stared at one another. Ranker shivered bonelessly, his face suffused with hopeless fluster. The old man's gaze bounced back and forth between Wade's indignant face and the objects that were back on the desk. Cogitations strained his brain centers.

At length Castlemould nodded and coughed meaningfully.

"Captain," he said, "I want to be alone with this scoundrel. I'll get to the bottom of this outrage."

The captain looked at his superior and nodded his grotesque skull. He hurried from the room wordlessly. They heard him stumbling down the hall, breathing steam whistles.

"Now," said the Commissioner, dwindling into the immensity of Ranker's chair. "Just tell me what your name is." His voice cajoled. It was half joking.

He picked up the cloth between sedate thumb and forefinger and dropped it over the offending articles with the decorum of a minister throwing his robe over the naked shoulders of a strip teaser.

Wade sank down in the other chair with a sigh.

"I give up," he said, "I come from the year 1954 in my time chamber. I bring along a little . . . food . . . in case of a slight emergency. Then you all tell me that I'm an obscene dog. I'm afraid I don't understand a bit of it."

Castlemould folded his hands over his sunken chest and nodded slowly.

"Mmm-hmmm. Well, young man, I happen to believe you," he said. "It's possible. I'll admit that. Historians tell of such a period when, ahem . . . physical sustenance was taken orally."

"I'm glad someone believes," Wade said. "But I wish you'd tell me about this food situation."

The Commissioner flinched slightly at the word. Wade looked puzzled again.

"Is it possible," he said, "that the word . . . *food* . . . has become obscene?"

At the repeated sound of the word something seemed to click in Castlemould's brain. He reached over and drew back the cloth with glittering eyes. He seemed to drink in the sight of the flask, the box, the tin. His tongue flicked over dried lips. Wade stared. A feeling close to disgust rose in him.

The old man ran a shaking hand over the box of crackers as though it were a chorus girl's leg. His lungs grappled with the air.

"Food." He breathed the word in bated salacity.

Then, quickly, he drew the cloth back over the articles, apparently surfeited with the maddening sight. His bright old eyes flicked up into Professor Wade's. He drew in a tenuous breath.

"F— well," he said.

Wade leaned back in his chair, beginning to feel an embarrassed heat sluicing through his body. He shook his head and grimaced at the thought of it all.

"Fantastic," he muttered.

He lowered his head to avoid the old man's gaze. Then, looking up, he saw Castlemould peeking under the cloth again with all the tremor of an adolescent at his first burlesque show.

"Commissioner."

The ratty old man jerked in the chair, his lips drawing back with a startled hiss. He struggled for composition.

"Yes, yes," he said, gulping.

Wade stood up. He pulled off the cloth and stretched it out on the desk. Then he piled the objects in the center of it and drew up the corners. He suspended the bundle at his side.

"I don't wish to corrupt your society," he said. "Suppose I get the facts I want about your era and then leave and take my . . . take *this* with me."

Fear sprang into the lined features. "No!" Castlemould cried.

Wade looked suspicious. The Commissioner bit off his mental tongue.

"I mean," he glowed, "no point in going back so soon. After all . . ." He flourished his skinny arms in an unfamiliar gesture. "You *are* my guest. Come, we'll go to my house and have some . . ."

He cleared his throat violently. He got up and hurried around the desk. He patted Wade's shoulders, his lips wrenched into the smile of a hospitable jackal.

"You can get all the facts you need in my library," he said.

Wade didn't say anything. The old man looked around guiltily.

"But you . . . uh, better not leave the bundle here," he said. "Better take it with you."

He chuckled confidentially. Wade looked more suspicious. Castlemould stiffened the backs of his words. "Hate to say it," he said, "but you can't trust inferiors. Might cause terrible upset in the department. *That*, I mean."

He glanced with affected carelessness toward the bundle. His narrow throat suffered an honest contraction.

"Never know what might happen," he continued. "Some people are unprincipled, you know."

He said it as though the horrendous thought had just made its unwanted appearance in his pristine mind.

He started for the door to avoid argument. He turned, fingers clawed around the knob. "You wait here," he said, "I'll get your release."

"But . . ."

"Not at all, not at all," said Castlemould, springing out into the hallway.

Professor Wade shook his head. Then he reached into his coat pocket and drew out a bar of chocolate.

"Better keep this well hidden," he said to himself, "or it's the firing squad for me."

As they entered the hallway of his house, Castlemould said, "Here, let me take the package. We'll put it in my desk."

"I don't think so," Wade said, keeping back laughter at the Commissioner's eager face. "It might be too much of a . . . temptation."

"Who, for *me?*" cried Castlemould. "Haah, that's funny." He kept holding onto the professor's bundle, his lips molded into a pouting circle.

"Tell you what," he bargained furiously. "We'll go in my study and I'll guard your bundle while you take notes from my books. How's that, haah? Haah?"

Wade trailed the hobbling old man into the high-ceilinged study. It still didn't make sense to him. Food. He tested the sound of it in his mind. Just a harmless word. But, like anything else, it could have any meaning people assigned to it.

He noted how Castlemould's vein-popping hands caressed the bundle, noted the acquisitive, shifty-eyed look that swallowed up his dour old face. He wondered if he could leave the . . . He smiled to himself at the hesitation in his mind. It was getting to him too.

They crossed the wide rug. "Have the best collection in the city," bragged the Commissioner. "Complete." He winked a red-veined eyeball. "Unexpurgated," he promised.

Wade said, "That's nice."

He stood before the shelves and ran his eyes over the

titles surveying the parallel rows of books that walled the room.

"Do you have a . . ." he started, turning. The Commissioner had left his side and was seated at the desk. He had unwrapped the bundle and was looking at the can of meat with the leer of a miser counting his gold.

Wade called loudly, "Commissioner!"

The old man jumped wildly and dropped the can on the floor. Abruptly, he slid from sight and emerged from the desk surface a moment later, dripping with abashed chagrin, the can tightly gripped in both hands.

"Yes?" he inquired pleasantly.

Wade turned quickly, his shoulders shuddering with ill-repressed laughter.

"Have you . . . a history text?" His voice was shaky.

"Yes sir!" Castlemould burst out. "Best history text in the city!"

His black shoes squeaked over the floor. From a shelf overladen with dust, he tugged out a thick volume. "Reading it myself just the other day," he said proffering it to Professor Wade. Wade nodded as he blew off a cloud of dust.

"Here we are," Castlemould said. "Now you just sit right here." He patted the cracked leather back of an armchair. "I'll get you something to write on."

Wade watched him as he hustled back to the desk and jerked out the top drawer. May as well let the old fool have the food, he thought as Castlemould came back with a fat pad of artipaper. At first Wade was going to say he had a pad but then he changed his mind, thinking it would be nice to have a sample of the paper of the future.

"Now you just sit right here and take all the notes

you want," said Castlemould, "and don't you worry about your f— don't you worry." He soothed anciently.

"Where are *you* going?"

"Nowhere! Nowhere!" the Commissioner professed. "Staying right here. I'll guard the . . ." His Adam's apple dipped low as he surveyed the articles again and his voice petered out in depleting passion.

Wade eased down into the chair and opened the book. He glanced up once at the old man.

Castlemould was shaking the flask of coffee and listening to it gurgle. On his seamed face hung the look of a reflective idiot.

The destruction of Earth's f— bearing capacities was completed by the overall military use of bacterial sprays, the Professor read. *These minute germinal droplets permeated the earth to such a depth as to make plant growth impossible. They also destroyed the major portion of m— giving animals as well as ocean edibles, for whom no protective provision was made in the last desperate germ attack of the war.*

Also rendered unpalatable were the major water supplies of earth. Five years after the war, at the time of this writing, the heavy pollution still remains, undiminished by fresh rains. Moreover. . . .

Wade looked up from the history text, shaking his head grimly.

He looked over at the Commissioner. Castlemould was leaning back in his chair, juggling the box of crackers thoughtfully.

Wade went back to the book and hurriedly finished the selection. He glanced at his watch. He had to get back. He completed the notation and closed the book. Standing, he slid the volume back into its place and walked over to the desk.

"I'll be going now," he said.

Castlemould's lips trembled, drawing back from his china teeth.

"So soon?" he said, close to menace hovering in his words. His eyes searched the room, searching for something.

"Ah!" he said. Gently he put down the box of crackers and stood up.

"How about a vein-ball?" he asked. "Just a short one before you go."

"A what?"

"Vein-ball." Wade felt the Commissioner's hand touch his arm. He was led back to the armchair. "Come along," said Castlemould, weirdly jovial. Wade sat. No harm, he thought. I'll leave the food. That will mollify him.

The old man was wheeling a cumbersome wagon-like table from one corner of the room. On its dialed top rose numerous shiny tendrils, each dangling over the sides and ending in a stubby needle.

"Just our way of—" The Commissioner glanced around like a salesman of illicit postcards "—*drinking*," he finished softly.

Wade watched him pick up one of the tendrils. "Here, give me your hand," said the Commissioner.

"Will it hurt?"

"Not at all, not at all," said the old man. "Nothing to be afraid of."

He took hold of Wade's hand and jabbed the needle

into the palm. Wade gasped. The pain passed almost immediately.

"It might . . ." Wade started. Then he felt a soothing flow of muscle-easing liquors flowing into his veins.

"Isn't that good?" asked the Commissioner.

"This is how you drink?"

Castlemould stuck the needle into his own palm.

"Not everyone has such a deluxe set," he said proudly. "This veinwagon was presented to me by the governor of the state. For my services, y'know, in bringing the notorious Tom-Gang to justice."

Wade felt pleasantly lethargic. Just a moment more, he thought, then I'll go. "Tom-Gang?" he asked.

Castlemould perched on the edge of another chair.

"Short for, ahem, Tomato Gang. Group of notorious criminals trying to raise . . . tomatoes. Wholesale!"

"Horrors," said Wade.

"It was grave, grave."

"Grave. I think I've had enough."

"Better change this a little," Castlemould said, rising to fiddle with the dials.

"I've had enough," Wade said.

"How's that?" asked Castlemould.

Wade blinked and shook his head to clear away the fog. "That's enough for me," he said, "I'm dizzy."

"How's this?" Castlemould asked.

Wade felt the warmth rising. His veins seemed to run with fire. His head whirled. "No more!" he said, trying to rise.

"How's this?" Castlemould said, drawing the needle from his own hand.

"That's enough!" Wade cried. He reached down to

pull out the needle. His hands felt numb. He slumped back in the chair. "Turn it off," he said feebly.

"How's *this!*" cried Castlemould and Wade grunted as a hose of flames played through his body. The heat twisted and leaped through his system.

He tried to move. He couldn't. He was inert, in a liquored coma when Castlemould finally turned down the dials. He sagged in the chair, the shiny tentacles still drooping from his palm. His eyes were half closed. They were glassy and doped.

Sound. His thickened brain tried to place it. He blinked his eyes. It was like compressing his brain between hot stones. He opened his eyes. The room was a blurry haze. The shelves ran into each other, watery streams of book backs. He shook his head. He thought he felt his brains jiggling.

The mists began to slip away one by one like the veils of a dancer.

He saw Castlemould at the desk.

Eating.

He was bent over the desk, his face a blackish red as though he were performing some rabidly carnal rite. His eyes had glued themselves to the food spread out on the cloth. He was apart. The flask banged against his teeth. He held it in interlocked fingers, his body shivering as the cool fluid drained down his throat. His lips smacked ecstatically.

He sliced another piece of meat and stuck it between two crackers.

His trembling hand held the sandwich up to his wet mouth. He bit into their crisp layers and chewed loudly, his eyes glittering orbs of excitement.

Wade's face twisted in revulsion. He sat staring at the old man. Castlemould was looking at postcards while he ate. He gazed at them, jaws moving busily. His eyes shone. He looked at what he was eating, then looked at the cards again while he chewed.

Wade tried to move his arms. They were logs. He struggled and managed to slip one hand on the other. He drew out the needle, a sigh rasping in his throat. The Commissioner didn't hear. He was lost; absorbed in an orgy of digestion.

Experimentally, Wade shifted his legs. They felt like somebody else's legs. He knew that, if he stood, he'd pitch forward on his face.

He dug nails into his palms. At first there was no feeling. Then it came slowly, at last flaring up in his brain and clearing away more fog.

His eyes never left Castlemould. The old man shivered as he ate, caressing each morsel. Wade thought: he's committing an act of love with a box of crackers.

He fought to gain control. He had to get back.

Castlemould had polished off the cracker box. He was nibbling on the bits of crumb that remained. He picked them up with a moistened finger and popped them into his mouth. He made sure there were no remaining scraps of meat. He tilted up the flask and drained it. Practically empty, it was suspended over his gaping mouth. The remaining drops fell—*drip, drip*—into the white-toothed cavity and rolled over his tongue and into his throat.

He sighed and set down the flask. He looked at his pictures once more, his chest laboring. Then he pushed them aside with a drunken gesture and sank back in the chair. He stared in sleepy dullness at the desk, the empty box, the can and flask. He ran two weary fingers over his mouth.

After a few minutes his head slumped forward. His rattling snores echoed through the room.

The festival was over.

Wade struggled up. He stumbled across the floor. It tried to heave itself up in his face. He ran into the side of Castlemould's desk and held on dizzily. The old man still slept.

Wade edged around the desk, leaning against its surface. The room still spun.

He stood behind the old man's chair, looking down at the shambles of violent dining. He took a deep ragged breath and held onto the chair with eyes closed until the spasm of dizziness had passed. Then he opened his eyes and looked once more at the desk. He noticed the postcards. An incredulous look crossed his face.

They were pictures of food.

A head of cabbage, a roast turkey. In some of them, partially unclad women held desiccated lettuce leaves, lean tomatoes, dried up oranges; held them out in their hands in profane offering.

"God, I want to go back," he muttered.

He was halfway to the door when he realized that he had no idea where his chamber was. He stood weaving on the threadbare rug, listening to Castlemould's snores ring out.

Then he went back and squatted dizzily by the side of the desk. He kept his eyes on the open-mouthed Commissioner as he slid out the desk drawers.

In the bottom drawer he found what he wanted; a strange gun-like tube. He took hold of it.

"Get up," he said angrily, rapping the old man on the head.

"Aaahh!" cried Castlemould, starting up. His midriff collided with the desk edge. He fell back in the chair, the wind knocked out of him. "Get up," Wade said.

A confused Castlemould stared up. He tried to smile and a crumb fell from his lips.

"Now look here, young man!"

"*Shut up*. You're taking me back to my chamber."

"Now, wait a . . ."

"Now!"

"Don't fool with that thing," Castlemould warned. "It's dangerous."

"I hope it's very dangerous," Wade said. "Now get up and take me to your car."

Castlemould scurried to his feet. "Young man, this is . . ."

"Oh, be quiet, you senile goat. Take me to your car and hope I don't push this button."

"God, don't do that!"

The Commissioner suddenly stopped halfway to the door. He grimaced and bent over as his stomach began to protest against its violation.

"Oh! That food," he muttered wretchedly.

"I hope you have the belly ache of the century," said Wade, prodding him on. "You deserve it."

The old man clutched at his paunch. "*Ohhhh*." He groaned. "Don't shove."

They went into the hall. Castlemould spun against the closet door. He clawed at the wood. "I'm dying!" he announced.

Wade ordered, "Come on!"

Castlemould, heedless, pulled open the door and plunged into the closet depths. There, in the stuffy blackness, he was very sick.

Wade turned away in disgust.

At last the old man stumbled forth, face white and drawn. He shut the door and leaned back against it. "Oh," he said weakly.

"You deserved that," Wade said. "Richly."

"Don't talk," begged the old man. "I may die yet."

"Let's go," Wade said.

They were in the car. A recovered Commissioner was at the wheel. Wade sat across the wide front seat from him holding the weapon level at Castlemould's chest.

"I apologize for . . ." started the Commissioner.

"Drive."

"Well, I don't like to feel inhospitable."

"Shut up."

The old man's face tightened. "Young man," he said tentatively, "how would you like to make some money?"

Wade knew what was coming. "How?" he asked anyway.

"Very simple."

"Bring you food," Wade finished.

Castlemould's face twitched. "Well," he whined, "what's so bad about that?"

"You have gall to ask me that," Wade said.

"Now look, young man. *Son*."

"Oh, God, *shut* up," Wade said, twisting his shoulders in disgust. "Think of your hall closet and shut up."

"Now son," insisted the Commissioner, "that was only because I'm not used to it. But now I . . ." His face became suddenly clever and evil. "I have a taste for it."

"Then lose your taste," Wade said, never taking his eyes off the old man.

The Commissioner looked desperate. His scrawny fingers tightened on the wheel. His left foot drummed resolutely on the floorboards. "You won't change your mind?" he said, threateningly.

"You're lucky I don't shoot you."

Castlemould said no more. He watched the road with slitted calculating eyes.

The car hissed up beside the chamber and stopped. "Tell the officers you want to examine the chamber," Wade told him.

"If I don't?"

"Then whatever comes out of this tube, you'll get right in the stomach."

Castlemould forced a brisk smile to his lips and the officers came up.

"What's the meaning—ohhh *Commissioner!*" the officer said, shifting noticeably from truculence to reverence. "What can we do for you?" He doffed his cap with a face-halving smile.

"Want to look over that . . . thing," said Castlemould. "Want to check something."

"Yes *sir,* sir," said the officer.

"I'm putting the tube in my pocket," Wade said quietly.

The Commissioner said nothing as he opened the door. The two of them approached the chamber. Then Castlemould said loudly, "I'll go in first. Might be dangerous."

The officers murmured appreciatively of his courage.

Wade's mouth tightened. He contented himself by thinking how hard he was going to boot the old man right out into the street.

The Commissioner's bones crackled energetically as he reached up for the two door rungs. He pulled himself up with a teeth-clenching grunt. Wade gave him a shove and enjoyed the sound of the old Commissioner flying against the steel bulkhead.

He reached up his free hand. But he couldn't get in with just one hand. He had to reach up both. He grabbed the rungs and swung in quickly.

The moment Wade entered Castlemould plunged his hand into Wade's pocket and jerked out the weapon.

"Aaah-haah!" His high pitched voice echoed shrilly inside the small shell.

Wade pressed against the bulkhead. He could see a little in the dimness. "What do you think you're going to do now?" he asked.

The porcelain teeth flashed. "You're taking me back," Castlemould said. "I'm going with you."

"There's only room for one person in here."

"Then it'll be *me.*"

"You can't operate it."

"You tell me," Castlemould ordered.

"Or what?"

"Or I'll burn you up."

Wade tensed himself. "And if I tell you?" he asked.

"You stay here till I come back."

"I don't believe you."

"You have to, young man," cackled the Commissioner. "Now tell me how it works."

Wade reached for his pocket. "Watch it!" warned Castlemould.

"Do you want me to get out the instruction sheet or not?"

"Go on. But watch it. Instruction sheet, hah?"

"You wouldn't understand a word of it." Wade reached into his pocket.

"What's that you got?" Castlemould asked. "That's not paper."

"A bar of chocolate," Wade breathed the words. "A thick, sweet, creamy, rich bar of chocolate."

"Gimme it!"

"Here. *Take* it."

The Commissioner lunged. He fell off balance, the weapon pointed at the floor. As he pitched forward, Wade grabbed the old man by the collar and the seat of the pants. He hurled Commissioner Castlemould out through the doorway and the old man went sprawling into the street.

Shouts. The officers were horrified. Wade tossed out the chocolate bar.

"Obscene dog!" he roared, choking with laughter as the bar bounced off Castlemould's ridged skull.

Then he jerked the door shut and turned the wheel until he was sealed. He flipped switches and strapped himself down, chuckling at the thought of the Commissioner trying to explain the bar of chocolate so he could keep it.

Next, the intersection was empty on that spot except for a few wisps of acrid smoke. There was only one sound in the dead stillness.

The contemplative wail of a hungry old man.

The chamber shuddered to a halt. The door opened and Wade jumped out. He was surrounded by men and students who came flooding from the control room.

"Hey!" said his friend. "You made it!"

"Of course," Wade said, feeling the pleasure of understatement.

"This calls for a celebration," said his friend. "I'm taking you out tonight and buying you the biggest steak you ever saw—hey, what's the matter?"

Professor Wade was blushing.

LOVER WHEN YOU'RE NEAR ME

THE SILVERY WELDED SHIP CAME RUSHING BACK-wards through the veils of broken cloud, tobog-ganing down the atmosphere of Station Four. Fires of deceleration jetted red from the reactor ports, roaring their hurricane thrust against the clutch of gravity.

Air thickened; the glittering rocket speck slid eas-ier, settling itself downward like a parachuting mis-sile. Sunlight splashed its metal sides with light and the blue ocean waters billowed wide to swallow it. The ship dipped in a wide arc and backed down to-ward the reddish-green clad land.

Inside its tiny cabin, the two men lay strapped and waiting for the shock of contact. Their eyes were closed, their hands tight and blood-drained. Muscle blocks struggled against the drag.

The earth swept up and blocked its way; the ship settled hard on its rear braces, trembling. Then, in an instant, it stood motionless and silent, successfully navigated through a thousand billion miles of vacu-umed night.

A quarter mile away were the warehouse, the village and the house.

Critical. That was the official record. It was supposed to be secret but David Lindell knew it; all the Wentner men had known it. Station Four The Birds and the Three-Moon Psycho Ward. That was scuttlebutt and to be taken with a fistful of salt. Lindell knew that too.

But it all meant something; the laughter, the ribbing, the silence from upstairs. They put a man on other stations for two years at a clip. Here on Four it was only for six months. That meant something. It adds up, they used to say in the briefing room on Earth. *Wentner's Interstellar Trading Company* doesn't break its heart for nothing. And Lindell believed it.

"But like I always say," he said, "it's no use worrying myself."

He said it to Martin, the ship's pilot as the two of them trudged across the wide meadow toward the distant compound carrying Lindell's luggage.

"You have the right idea," said Martin. "Don't worry yourself."

"That's what I always say," said Lindell.

After a while they passed the silent gargantuan warehouse. The sliding doors were half open and, inside, Lindell could see the concrete floor empty and sunlight filtering through the skylight. Martin told him the cargo ship had emptied it out a few weeks before. Lindell grunted and shifted his luggage.

"Where are the workers?" he asked.

Martin gestured his helmeted head toward the workers' village about three hundred yards away.

There was no sound from the low-slung white dwellings methodically arranged to form three sides of a rectangle. The windows blinked fiercely in the sunlight.

"Guess they're sacked out," Martin judged. "They sleep a lot when work is done. You'll see them tomorrow when shipments start coming in again."

"Got their families with them?" Lindell asked.

"Nope."

"Thought it was company policy."

"Not here. The Gnees don't have much family life. Too few men and they're all pretty dumb."

"Great," Lindell said. "Dandy." He shrugged. "Well, it's no use worrying myself about it."

While they were on the stairs to the hallway of the house, he asked Martin where Corrigan was.

"He went home with the cargo ship," Martin said. "They do that once in a while. There's nothing here to do anyway after the goods are picked up."

"Oh," said Lindell. "What's this door?" He kicked it open and looked in at the combination living room–library.

"All the comforts of," he said.

"More," said Martin, looking over Lindell's shoulder. "Over there you have a movie projector and a tape recorder."

"Swell," Lindell said. "I can talk to myself legal." Then he grimaced. "Let's dump these bags. My arms are falling off."

They shuffled down the hall and Lindell glanced into the small kitchen as they passed. It was porcelain paneled and well kept.

"Can this Gnee woman cook?" he asked.

"From what I hear," said Martin, "you'll be packing it in like a king."

"Glad to hear it. Say, incidentally, you got any idea why they call this joint the Three-Moon Psycho Ward?"

"Who calls it?"

"The boys back on Earth."

"The boys are all wet. You'll like it here."

"But why is it only a six month stint?"

"Here's your bedroom," Martin said.

As they entered, she was making the bed, her back turned to the door. They thumped down the bags and she turned.

Lindell's hands twitched. Oh well, he rallied, I've seen worse in my day.

She wore a heavy robe fastened at the neck and falling to the floor like a truncated cone of cloth. All he could see was her head.

It was a squat, coarsely-grained head, pink and hairless. Like the mottled belly of an expecting bitch, he decided. For ears there were cavities on the sides of her flat, chinless face. Her nose was a stub, single nostriled. Her lips were thick and monkey-like, outlining a small circle of mouth. Hello Beautiful, Lindell decided not to say.

She came across the room quietly and he blinked at her eyes. Then she placed a moist, spongy hand in his.

"Hi," he said.

"She can't hear," Martin said. "Telepathic."

"That's right, I forgot." *Hello,* he thought, and *Hello*

came back the answering welcome. *It is good to have you.*

"Thanks," he said. She seemed a decent kid, he thought to himself; weird but homey. A question touched his brain like a timid hand.

"Yeah, sure," he said. Yes, he added in his mind.

"What's that?" Martin asked.

"She asked if she should unpack, I think." Lindell slumped down on the bed. "Ahhh," he said. "This I like." He pushed exploring fingers into the mattress.

"Say, how do you know it's a she?" he asked when he and Martin were walking back down the hall while the Gnee woman unpacked.

"The robe. The males don't wear robes."

"That's all?"

Martin grinned. "A few other things of absolutely no interest to you."

They moved into the living room and Lindell tried out the easy chair for size. He leaned back and stroked the arms with satisfied fingers.

"Critical or no," he said, "this station has 'em all beat for comfort."

He sat there, momentarily reflecting on her eyes. They were huge eyes, covering a full third of her face; like big glass saucers with dark cup rings for pupils. And they were moist; bowls of liquid. He shrugged and let it go. So what, he thought, it's nothing.

"Hah? What?" he asked, hearing Martin's voice.

"I said——be careful." Martin was holding up a shiny gas pistol. "This is loaded," he warned.

"Who needs it?"

"You won't. Just standard equipment." Martin put

it back in the desk drawer and shoved the drawer back in. "And you know where all your books are," he said. "The warehouse office is set up like all the other station offices." Lindell nodded.

Martin glanced at his watch. "Well, I have to be going."

"Let's see," he continued as he and Lindell started for the door. "Anything else to tell you? You know the rule about not harming the people, of course?"

"Who's gonna harm—whoops!"

They'd almost knocked her over as they exited from the room. She jumped back one more bouncy step and stared at them, eyes wide and frightened.

"Take it easy, kiddo," Lindell soothed. "What's up?"

Eat? The thought cringed before him like a beggar at the back door of his mind. He pursed his lips and nodded. "You took the words right out of my head."

He looked at her and concentrated. *I'll be back as soon as I walk the co-pilot back to his ship. Make something good.*

She nodded violently and rushed toward the kitchen.

"Where's she off to like a bat?" Martin asked as they turned for the stairs and Lindell told him.

"That's what I call service deluxe," he said, chuckling, as they descended. "This telepathy is okay. At the other stations it was either learn half the language to get a ham sandwich or try and teach 'em English so I wouldn't starve. Either way I really had to sweat for my supper until things got settled."

He looked pleased. "This is hot," he said.

Their heavy boots crushed down the tall crisp blue grass as they approached the upright ship. Martin held out his hand. "Take it easy, Lindell. See you in six."

"Right enough. Give old man Wentner a kick in the pants for me."

"Will do."

He watched the pilot dwindle in size ascending the metal ladder to the hatchway. A midget Martin pulled himself into the ship and clanged the metal port shut behind himself. Lindell waved back at the tiny figure at the port and then turned and ran away to escape the blast.

He stood on a hill underneath the heavy scarlet foliage of a tree. Inside the ship's belly he heard a liquid cough, a rush of exploding gasses. He watched the ship hang for a moment on its flaming exhaust and then flash up into the green-blue sky, leaving scorched plant life in its wake. In a moment it was gone.

He walked in lazy strides back toward the house, gazing appreciatively at the profusion of livid plants and flowers in the meadow around him, bulbous insects hanging over them.

He took off his jacket and let it hang from one hand as he walked. The sun felt good on his lean back.

"Boys," he said to the fragrant air. "You're all wet."

The great blazing sun was almost gone, spraying the sky with the blood of its cyclic dying. Soon the three moons would rise; guaranteed to drive insane a man looking for a shadow to call his own.

Lindell sat at the living room window gazing out over the countryside. You couldn't beat it, he thought; for air or climate or all the things that grew in Earth's paling technicolor. Nature had outdone herself in this tucked away corner of the galaxy. He sighed and stretched, wondering about supper.

Drink?

He started, chopping a yawn in half, and drew his fingers together so fast that the knuckle bones crackled.

He saw her standing at his side, proffering a tray with a glass on it. He reached for it, feeling his heart placate itself after the initial jolt.

"I'd knock or something," he suggested. The big eyes were elliptical now. They stared at him without comprehension.

"Well, let it go," he said, after a sip of the warm tangy liquid. He smacked his lips and took another sip, a long one.

"Damn good," he said. "Thanks, Lover."

He blinked at himself. That brings a guy up short, he decided. *Lover?* Of all the unlikely names in the universe—He glanced at her with a chuckle bubbling up in his throat.

She hadn't moved. Her face was screwed up into what he assumed was a smile. But her mouth wasn't designed for smiling.

"Hey, when are we eating?" he asked, feeling an edge uncomfortable under the unmoving gaze of her watery eye globes.

She turned and hurried to the door. There she turned.

All ready already, he got the message.

He grinned, downed the drink, got up and followed her eager shuffle down the dim hallway.

* * *

He pushed away the plate with a sigh and leaned back in the chair.

"That's what I call good," he said.

Like a hidden spring, he felt her pleasure well up in his mind. *Lover thanks you.* She certainly picked up the name fast, he thought. She looked at him, eyes wide. Was she trying to smile again, he wondered? To him the expression looked like all her others; the facial poses of an idiot. He thought she was smiling though because of the thoughts that accompanied the expression.

Then he found his eyes watering in empathy and he turned his head, blinking. A trifle nervously, he dumped a teaspoon of sugar in his coffee and stirred. He could feel her eyes on him. A twinge of displeasure marred his thoughts and she turned away abruptly. That's better, he thought, and felt all right again.

"Hey, tell me Lover," he started to say. Well, might as well get used to it, he figured. *You have a husband?* Her returned thoughts were confused.

A mate? he reworded.

Oh, yes.

In the workers' village?

They have no mates, she answered and he thought he sensed a note of hauteur in her reply.

He shrugged and took a sip of coffee. "Well," he said to himself, "one satisfied worker would drive the rest of 'em crazy anyway. They'd be biting their nails if they had nails. And on that note, good night."

In bed he sat writing in his much-used diary. Between its beat-up covers were inscribed the sparse comments he had made on half a dozen different planets. This was his seventh selection. *My lucky number*, he paragraphed in blue ink.

Again no sound. *To sleep?* His pen skidded and spit out three fat blots. He looked up and saw her with the tray again.

"Yeah," he said. *Yeah. Thanks, Lover. But, look, will you just let me know when you . . .*

He stopped, seeing it was hopeless.

"This will make me sleep?" he asked. *Oh, yes*, was the reply.

He took a sip, looking down at the ink-blotted page. Just started it anyway, he thought, no loss of priceless literature. He ripped out the page and crumpled it in one hand.

"This is good stuff," he said, nodding his head toward the glass. He held up the paper. *Throw it away, haah? Throw away?* she asked.

"That's right," he said. "Now clear out. What in 'ell are you doing in a gent's boudoir anyway?"

She scuttled across the floor and he grinned as she closed the door quietly behind herself.

Finishing the drink, he set the glass down on the bedside table and turned off the lamp. He settled back on the soft pillow with a sigh. Some critter, he thought in drowsy satisfaction.

Good night.

He opened his heavy-lidded eyes and looked around. There was no one in the room. He sank back.

Good night.

He raised up on one elbow, squinting into the darkness.

Good night. "Oh," he said. "Good night yourself."

The thoughts abated. He fell back again and made his mouth a tooth-edged cave with yawning.

"How 'bout that?" he muttered, thickly, turning on his side. "Absolutely no mirrors. See? Nothin' up my sleeves. Howboutha—"

He had a dream. The dream covered him with sweat.

After breakfast, he left the house with her farewells tugging at his brain and headed across for the warehouse. Already, he saw, the Gnee men were formed in a moving line, carrying bundles on their heads. They marched into the warehouse, deposited their burden on the concrete and had it checked off by a Gnee foreman who stood in the center of the floor holding a clipboard thick with tissue-thin vouchers.

As Lindell approached, the men all bowed and looked more subservient as they continued on their rounds. He noticed that their heads were flatter than Lover's, a little more darkly tinted with smaller eyes. Their bodies were broad and thick-muscled. They *do* look stupid, he thought.

As he came up to the man who was doing the checking and sent out an unanswered thought, he saw that they weren't telepathic either; or didn't want to be.

"How doody," said the man in a squeaky voice. "I check. You check?"

"That's okay," Lindell said, pushing back the clipboard. "Just bring it into the office when the first batch is all in."

"What, haah?" said the man. Jeez, are you a case, Lindell thought.

"Bring *this*," he said, tapping the clipped sheaf of paper. "Bring to office." He pointed again. "Bring to me—*me*. When goods all in."

The man's splotchy face lit up with a look of vibrant stupidity and he nodded sharply. Lindell patted his shoulder. Good boy, rasped his mind, I bet you're dynamite in a crisis. He headed for the office, gritting his teeth.

Inside, he shut the plastiglass door behind him and looked around the office. It was the same as he remembered from other stations. Except for the cot in one corner. Don't tell me I have to sleep out here nights?—he thought with a groan.

He moved closer. On the flat soil-cased pillow was the imprint of a head. He picked up a light brown hair. And what the hell is this? he wondered.

Under the cot he found a buckleless belt. On the wall by the cot there were violent scratches as though a man in fever had tried to get out of the office the hard way. He stared at them.

"This joint is haunted," he concluded with a vague shake of his head. Then he turned away with a shrug. No use worrying myself, he thought. I got six months to go and nothing's going to get *me* down.

He sat down quickly before the desk and dragged the heavy station log before himself. With a shrug he flipped open the heavy cover and started reading from the beginning.

The first entries were twenty years dry. They were signed *Jefferson Winters*, or, a little later, a hasty *Jeff*. At the end of six months and fifty-two closely packed pages, Lindell found page 53 covered with a floridly penned message—*Station Four, goodbye forever! Jeff* didn't seem to have had any difficulties adjusting to the life there.

Lindell shifted back in the creaking chair and pulled the heavy book on his lap with a sigh of boredom.

It was after the first replacement's second month that the entries started to get ragged. There were blurred words, hurried scrawling, mistakes deleted and re-done. Some of the errors apparently had been corrected much later by still another replacement.

It was that way through the next four hundred or so sleep-inducing pages; a sorry chain of flaws and eventual corrections. Lindell flipped through them wearily, without the slightest interest in their content.

Then he reached entries signed *Bill Corrigan* and, with a blinking yawn, he straightened himself up, propped the book on the desk and paid closer attention.

They were the same as in every case before, excluding the first one; efficient beginnings declining markedly to increased wildness, the penmanship erring more extravagantly with each month until, at last, it became almost illegible. He found a few blatantly miscalculated additions which he corrected in his careful hand.

Corrigan's writing, he noted, broke off in the middle of a word one afternoon. And, for the last month and a half of Corrigan's stay, there were nothing but blank pages. He thumbed through them carelessly, shaking his head slowly. Have to admit it, he thought, I don't get it.

Sitting in the living room through twilight, and later at supper, he began to get the sensation that Lover's

thoughts were, somehow, alive; like microscopic insects crawling in and out among the fissures of his
brain. Sometimes they barely moved; other times they
leaped excitedly. Once, when he became a little irritated with her staring, the thoughts were like invisible suppliants pawing clumsily at his mind.

What was worse, he realized later while reading in
bed, the sensation occurred even when she wasn't in
the same room with him. It was disconcerting enough
to feel an endless stream of thoughts flowing into him
while she was close; this remote control business was
just a little too much for his taste.

Hey, how about it? he tried to reason her away good
naturedly. But all he got back was the picture of her
looking at him wide-eyed and uncomprehending.

"Aah, nuts," he muttered and tossed his book on
the bedside table. Maybe that's it, he thought, settling down for the night. This telepathy gimmick,
maybe that was what got the other men. Well, not
me, he vowed. I just won't worry myself about it. And
he turned out the lamp, said good night to the air and
went to sleep.

"Sleep," he muttered, unaware, only half conscious.
It wasn't sleep; not deep enough by half. A cloudy
haze submerged his mind and filled it with the same
detailed scene. It telescoped and sank away in a burst.
It magnified, welling up and swallowing him and
everything.

Lover. Lover. Echo of a shriek in a long black corridor.
The robe fluttering close by. He saw her pale features.
No, he said, stay away. Far—close—beyond—upon. He
cried out. No. *No*. NO!

He jolted up in the darkness with a choking grunt,

eyes full open. He stared groggily around the empty bedroom, his thoughts roiling.

He reached out in the darkness and flicked on the lamp. Hurriedly he stuck a cigarette between his lips and lay slumped against the headboard blowing out clouds of curling smoke. He raised his hand and saw that it shook. He muttered words without sense.

Then his nostrils twitched and his lips drew back in revulsion. What the hell died? he thought. There was a heavy saccharine odor in the air, getting worse every second. He tossed off the covers.

At the foot of the bed he found them; a thick pile of livid purple flowers arranged there.

He looked at them a moment and then bent over to pick them up and throw them away. He drew back gasping as a thorn punctured his right thumb.

He pressed out fat blood drops and sucked the wound, his brain assailed by the thickening smell.

It's very nice of you, he sent her the message, *but no more flowers.*

She looked at him. She doesn't get it, he knew.

"Do you understand?" he asked.

Floods of affection gurgled over the layers of his brain like syrup. He stirred his coffee restlessly and the transfer eased as though she were determined not to offend him. The kitchen was silent except for the clink of his silver on the breakfast dishes and the slight whispering rustle of her robe.

He gulped down coffee and stood to leave. *I'll eat lunch around . . .*

I know. Her thought cut into his, mildly commanding. He grinned a little to himself as he headed down the hall. Her telepathied message had come with an almost mother-like chiding.

Then, crossing the grounds, he recalled the dream again and the departing grin emptied his features of amusement.

All morning he wondered irritably what made the Gnee men so stupid. If they dropped a bundle it was a project to pick it up again. They're like brainless cows, he thought, watching them through the office windows as they plodded through their tasks, eyes dull and unblinking, their thick shoulders sloping inward.

He knew definitely now that they weren't telepathic. He'd tried several times to give them orders with his mind alone and there was no receipt of message. They only reacted to loudly repeated words of two, or preferably less, syllables. And they reacted moronically at that.

In the middle of the morning he looked up from the backlog of paper work that Corrigan had left and realized, with some shock, that her thoughts were reaching him all the way from the house.

And yet they weren't thoughts he could translate into words. They were sensations, amorphously present. He got the feeling that she was checking, sending out exploratory beams now and again to see if all were well with him.

The first few times it did no worse than amuse him. He chuckled softly and went back to his work.

But then the proddings assumed an annoyingly regular time pattern and he began to squirm in his chair. He found himself becoming rigidly erect and anticipating seconds before they came.

By late morning he was repulsing them consciously; tossing his pen on the desk and ordering her angrily to leave him alone when he worked. Her thoughts would break off penitently. And soon come back again, like creeping things that stole upon him, insinuating and beyond insult.

His nerves began to fray a little. He left the office and prowled the warehouse floor, tearing open bundles and checking goods with impatient fingers. The thoughts followed him around faithfully. "How doody," said the Gnee foreman every time Lindell passed, making him angrier yet.

Once he straightened up suddenly over a bundle and said loudly, "*Go away!*"

The foreman jumped a foot in the air, his pencil and clipboard went flying and he hid behind a pillar and looked fearfully at Lindell. Lindell pretended not to notice.

Later, back in the office, he sat thinking, the open log book before him.

No wonder the Gnee men didn't telepathize, he thought. They knew what was good for them.

Then he looked out the window at the plodding line of workers.

What if they weren't just *avoiding* telepathy? What if they were incapable of it; had once held the ability and, because of it, had been broken to their present state of hopeless stolidity.

He thought of what Martin had said about the women outnumbering the men. And a phrase entered his mind—*matriarchy by mind*. The phrase offended him but he was suddenly afraid it might be true. It would explain why the other men had cracked. For, if the women were in control, it might well be that, in their inherent lust for dominance, they made no distinction between their own men and the men from Earth. A man is a man is a man. He twisted angrily at the idea of possibly being considered on a level with the dolts who lived in the village.

He stood up abruptly. I'm not hungry, he thought, not at all. But I'm going back to the house and order her to make me lunch and let her know I'm not hungry either. I'll make her used to being dominated herself and then she'll get no chance to pick at me. No bug-eyed Gnee woman, by God, is going to get *me* down.

Then he blinked and turned away quickly when he realized that he was staring at the wild pattern of scratches on the far office wall. And the belt without a buckle that still curled limply underneath the cot.

The dream again. It tore at his brain tissues with claws of razor. Sweat covering him. He tossed on the bed with a groan and was suddenly awake, staring into the darkness.

He thought he saw something at the foot of the bed. He closed his eyes and shook his head and looked again. The room was empty. He felt mind-drenching thoughts recede like some alien tide.

His fists contracted angrily. She's been at me while I slept, he thought, Goddamn her hide, she's been at me.

He pushed aside the covers and crawled to the foot of the bed nervously.

He couldn't see them. But the cloying fumes undulated up from the floor like erected serpents slithering into his nostrils. Gagging, he slumped down on the mattress, his stomach wrenched. Why? his brain mumbled over and over.

My God, *why?*

Angrily, he threw the flowers away in her sight and the thoughts pleaded and showered over him like raindrops.

"I said *no*, didn't I?" he yelled at her.

Then he sat down at the table and controlled himself as well as he could. I've a long way to go, he told his will, ease off, ease off.

Now he was sure he knew why it was only six months. That would be more than enough. But I won't crack. He commanded himself. It's a cinch she isn't going to crack so conserve yourself. *She's too stupid to crack,* he thought deliberately, hoping she'd pick it up.

She apparently did for her shoulders slumped dejectedly all of a sudden. And during breakfast, she circled him like a timorous wraith, keeping her face averted and her thoughts aloof. He found himself almost sorry for her then. It probably wasn't her fault, he thought, it was just an inborn trait among Gnee women to dominate men.

Then he realized that her thoughts were at him again, tender and gratefully maudlin. He tried to neutralize himself and ignore them as they sought to break through his apathy like honeyed picks.

All day he worked hard and made payments in

spices and grain to the Gnee foreman to be forwarded to the workers. He wondered if the payments would go eventually to the women. Wherever they were.

"I'm taping my voice," he dictated later that night. "I want to hear myself talking so I can forget her. There's no one else to talk to so I'll have to talk to myself. A sad case. Well, here goes.

"Here I am on Station Four, folks, having a wonderful time and wish you were here instead of me. Oh, it's not *that* bad, don't get me wrong. But I guess I know what knocked out Corrigan and the poor bastards before him. It was Lover and her cannibal mind eating them up. But I'll tell you this; it's not going to eat *me* up. That much you can put bets on. Lover isn't going to . . .

"No, I didn't call you! Come on, get out of my life, will ya? Go to a movie or something. Yeah, yeah, I know. Well, go to bed then. Just leave me alone." *Alone*.

"There. That's for her. She'll have to go some to get me clawing at the walls."

But he carefully locked the door to his room when he went to bed. And he groaned in his sleep because of the same nightmare and his limbs thrashed and all peace and rest were crowded out.

He twisted into wakefulness in mid-morning and stumbled up to check the door. He fumbled at the lock with heavy fingers. Finally his thickened brain divined the fact that the door was still locked and he went back to bed in a weaving line and fell on it into a stupored sleep.

When he woke up in the morning there were flowers at the foot of his bed, luxuriantly purple and foul-smelling and the door was locked.

He couldn't ask her about it because he left the kitchen in revulsion when she called him *dear*.

No more flowers! I'll promise! cried her pursuing thoughts. He locked himself in the living room and sat at the desk, feeling sick. Get hold of yourself!—he ordered his system, clasping his hands tightly and holding his teeth firmly clenched.

Eat?

She was outside the door; he knew it. He closed his eyes. *Go away, leave me alone,* he told her.

I'm sorry, dear, she said.

"Stop calling me 'dear'!" he shouted, slamming his fist on the desk surface. As he twisted in the chair, his belt buckle caught on the drawer handle and it jerked out. He found himself staring down at the shiny gas pistol. Almost unconsciously he reached down and touched its slick barrel.

He shoved in the drawer with a convulsive movement. None of that! he swore.

He looked around suddenly, feeling alone and free. He got up and hurried to the window. Down below, he saw her hurrying across the grounds with a basket on her arm. She's going for vegetables, he thought. But what made her leave so suddenly?

Of course. The pistol. She must have gotten his thoughts of violent intent.

He sighed and calmed down a little, feeling as if his brain had been drained of thick, noxious fluids.

I've still got cards in my hand, he soothed himself.

While she was out he decided to look in her room and see if he could find the shifting panel that enabled her to enter his room with the flowers. He hurried down the hall and pushed open the door to her barely furnished little chamber.

His brain was immediately attacked by the odor of a reeking pile of the purple flowers in one corner. He held a hand over his mouth and nose as he looked down in distaste at the living and dead blossoms.

What did they represent?—he wondered. An offering of thoughtfulness? His throat contracted. Or was it more than thoughtfulness? He grimaced at the thought and remembered that first evening when he'd dubbed her Lover. What had possessed him to choose that name from the infinity of possible names? He hoped he didn't know.

On the couch he found a small pile of odds and ends. There was a button, a pair of broken shoe laces, the piece of crumpled paper he had told her to throw away. And a belt buckle with the initials W. C. stamped on it.

There were no secret panels.

He sat in the kitchen staring into an untouched cup of coffee. No way she could get in his room. W. C.—William Corrigan. He had to fight it, keep fighting it.

Time passed. And suddenly, he realized that she was back in the house again. There was no sound; it was like the return of a ghost. But he knew it. A cloud of feeling preceded her, came plunging through the rooms like an excited puppy, searching. Thoughts swirled. *You are well? You are not angry? Lover is back*—all hastily and eagerly clutching at him.

She swept into the room so quickly that his hands twitched and he upset the cup. The hot liquid splashed over his shirt and trousers as he jumped back, knocking over the chair.

She put down the basket and got a towel as she patted the stains dry. She'd never been so close to him. She'd never actually touched him before except for that first handshake.

There was an aroma about her. It made his chest heave painfully. And all the time, her thoughts caressed his mind as her hands seemed to be caressing his body.

There. There . . . I am here with you.

David dear.

Almost in horror, he stared at her spongy pink skin, her huge eyes, her tiny wound of a mouth.

And, in the office that morning, he made three straight mistakes in the log book and tore out a whole page and hurled it across the room with a choking cry of rage.

Avoid her. No point in remonstration. He tried to raze his mental ground so that her thoughts could not find domicile there. If he relaxed his mind enough, her thoughts flowed through and out. Perhaps taking part of his will as they left but he'd have to risk that.

And if he worked hard and crowded his head with stodgy banks of figures, it kept her at a distance and his hands did not tremble so badly.

Maybe I should sleep in the office, he thought. Then he found Corrigan's note.

It was on a white slip of paper stuck away in the

log book, hidden white on white. He only found it because he was going through the pages one at a time, reciting the dates in a loud voice to keep his mind filled.

God help me, read the note, black and jagged-lettered, *Lover comes through the walls!*

Lindell stared. *I saw it myself*, attested the words, *I'm going out of my mind. Always that damn animal mind tugging and tearing at me. And now I can't even shut away her body. I slept out here but she came anyway. And I . . .*

Lindell read it again and it was a wind fanning the fires of terror. *Through the walls*. The words agonized him. Was it possible?

And it was Corrigan then who had named her Lover. From the very start, the relationship had been on her terms. Lindell had had nothing to say about it.

"Lover," he muttered and her thoughts enveloped him suddenly like a carrion's wings swooping down from the sky. He flung up his arms and cried out—"Leave me alone!"

And, as her phantom mind slipped off, he had the sense that it was with less timidity, with the patience such as a man knowing his own great strength can afford to display.

He sank back on the chair, exhausted, suddenly, depleted with fighting it. He crumpled the note in his right hand, thinking of the scratches on the wall behind him.

And he saw in his mind: Corrigan tossing on the cot, burning with fever, rearing up with a shriek of horror to see her standing before him. But then. *Then?* The scene was dark.

He rubbed a shaking hand over his face. Don't crack, he said to himself. But it was more a frightened entreaty than a command. Wasting fogs of premonition flooded over him in chilling waves. *She comes through the walls.*

That night again, he poured the potion she made down his bathroom sink. He locked the door and, in the lightless room, he squatted in one corner, peering and waiting, lungs bellowing in spasmodic bursts.

The thermostat lowered the heat. The floorboards got icy and his teeth started chattering. I'm not going to bed, he vowed angrily. He didn't know why it was that suddenly the bed frightened him. I don't know, he forced the words through his brain because he felt vaguely that he *did* know and he didn't want to admit it, even for a second.

But after hours of futile waiting, he had to straighten up with a snapping of joints and stumble back to bed. There, he crawled under the blankets and lay trembling, trying to stay awake. She'll come while I'm asleep, he thought, I mustn't sleep.

When he woke up in the morning there were the flowers on the floor for him. And that was another day before a mass of days that sank crushed into the lump of months.

You can get used to horror, he thought. When it has lost immediacy and is no longer pungent and has become a steady diet. When it has degraded to a chain of mind-numbing events. When shocks are like scalpels picking and jabbing at delicate ganglia until they have lost all feeling.

Yet, though it was no longer terror, it was worse. For

his nerves were raw and bleeding a hemophilia of rage. He fought his battles to the dregs of seconds, gaunt willed, shouting her off, firing lances of hate from his jaded mind; tortured by her surrenders that were her victories. She always came back. Like an enraging cat, rubbing endless sycophantic sides against him, filling him with thoughts of—*yes, admit it!*—he screamed to himself through midnight struggles . . .

Thoughts of *love.*

And there was the undercurrent, the promise of new shock that would topple his already shaking edifice. It needed only that—an added push, another stab of the blade, one more drop of the shattering hammer.

The shapeless threat hung over him. He waited for it, poised for it a hundred times an hour, especially at night. Wait. Waiting. And, sometimes, when he thought he knew what he was waiting for, the shock of admission made him shudder and made him want to claw at walls and break things and run until the blackness swallowed him.

If he could only forget her, he thought. Yes, if you could forget her for a while, just a little while, it would be all right.

He mumbled that to himself as he set up the movie projector in the living room.

She begged from the kitchen—*Can I see?*

"No!"

Now all his replies, worded or thought, were like the snapping retorts of a jangled old man. If only the six months would end. That was the problem. The months weren't moving fast enough. And time was like her—not to be reasoned with or intimidated.

There were many reels on the wall shelf. But his hand reached out without hesitation and picked out one. He didn't notice it; his mind was calloused to suggestion.

He adjusted the reel on the spindle and turned out the lights. He sat down with a tired groan as the flickering milky cone of light shot out from the lens, throwing pictures on the screen.

A lean, dark-bearded man was posing, arms crossed, white teeth showing in an artificial smile. He came closer to the camera. The sun flashed, blurring the film a second. Black screen. Title: *Picture of me*.

The man, high cheek-boned, bright-eyed, stood laughing soundlessly out from the screen. He pointed to the side and the camera swung around. Lindell sat up sharply.

It was the station.

Apparently it was autumn. For, as the camera swung past the house, the village, jerking a moment as though changing hands, he saw the trees surrounded by heaps of dead leaves. He sat there shivering, waiting for something, he didn't know what.

The screen blacked. Another title roughly etched in white. *Jeff In the Office*.

The man peered at the camera, an idiotic smile on his face, white skin accentuated by the immaculate black outline of his beard.

Fadeout—in. The man doing a jig around the empty warehouse floor, hands poised delicately in the air, his dark hair bouncing wildly on his skull.

Another title flashing on the screen. Lindell stiffened in his seat, his breath cut off abruptly.

Title: *Lover*.

There was her face horribly repellent in black and white. She was standing by his bedroom window, her face a mask of delight. He could tell now it was delight. Once he would have said she looked like a maniac, her mouth twisted like a living scar, her grotesque eyes staring.

She spun and her robe swirled out. He saw her puffy ankles and his stomach grew rock taut.

She approached the camera; he saw filmy eyelids slide down over her eyes. His hands began to tremble violently. It was his dream. It made him sick. It was his dream to the detail. Then it had never been a dream—not from his own mind.

A sob tore at his throat. She was undoing the robe. *Here it is!* he screamed in his panic-stricken mind. He whimpered and reached out shakily to turn off the projector.

No.

It was a cold command in the darkness. *Watch me,* she ordered. He sat bound in a vise of terror, staring in sick fascination as the robe slid from her neck, pulled down over her round shoulders. She twisted sensuously. The robe sank into a heavy, swirling heap on the floor.

He screamed.

He flung out an arm and it swept into the burning projector. It crashed down on the floor. The room was night. He struggled up and lurched across the room. *Nice? Nice?* The word dug at him mercilessly as he fumbled for the door. He found it, rushed into the hall. Her door opened and she stood in the half light, the robe hanging from one smooth shoulder.

He jolted to a halt. "Get out of here!" he yelled.

No.

He made a convulsive move for her, hands out like rigid claws. The sight of her pink, dewy flesh spun him away. *Yes?* her mind suggested. It seemed as if he heard it spoken in a slyly rising voice . . .

"Listen!" he cried, reaching out for the door to his room. "Listen, you have to go, do you understand? Go to your mate!"

He twisted back in utter horror.

I am with him now—her message had said.

The thought paralyzed him. He stared, open-mouthed, heart pounding in slow, gigantic beats as the robe slipped over her shoulders and started down her arms.

He whirled with a cry and slammed the door behind him. His fingers shook on the lock. Her thoughts were a wailing in his mind. He whimpered in fright and sickness and knew it was no good because he couldn't lock her out.

There were monkeys chattering in his brain. They lay on their backs in a circle and kicked at the inside of his skull. They grabbed juicy blobs of grey in their dirty paws and they squeezed.

He rolled on his side with a groan. I'll go crazy, he thought. Like Corrigan, like all of them but the first one; that slimy one who started it all; who added a new and hideous warp to the corrugation of her dominating Gnee mind; who had named her Lover because he meant it.

Suddenly he sat up with a gasp of terror, staring at the foot of the bed. *She comes through the walls!*— howled his brain. Nothing there, his eyes saw. His fingers clutched at the sheets. He felt sweat dripping off his brow and rolling down the embankment of his nose.

He lay down. Up again! He whimpered like a frightened child. A cloud of blackness was falling over him. Her. Her. He groaned. "No." In the blackness. No use.

He whined. Sleep. Sleep. The word throbbed, swelled and depressed in his brain. This is the time. He knew it, knew it, knew. . . .

The blade falling, sanity decapitated and twitching bloody in the basket.

No! He tried to push himself up but he couldn't. Sleep. A black tide of night hovering, tracking.

Sleep.

He fell back on the pillow, pushed up weakly on one elbow.

"No." His lungs were crusted. "No."

He struggled. It was too much. He screamed a thick, bubbling scream. She threw his will aside, snapped and futile. She was using all her strength now and he was enervated, beaten. He thudded back on the pillow, glassy-eyed and limp. He moaned weakly and his eyes shut—opened—shut—opened—shut. . . .

The dream again. Insane. Not a dream.

When he woke up there were no flowers. The courtship was ended. He gaped blankly and unbelievingly at the imprint of a body beside him on the bed.

It was still warm and moist.

He laughed out loud. He wrote curse words in his diary. He wrote them in tall black letters, holding the pencil like a knife. He wrote them in the log book too. He tore up vouchers if they weren't the right color.

His entries were crooked lines of figures like wavy-numbered tendrils. Sometimes he didn't care about that. Mostly he didn't notice.

He prowled the filled warehouse behind locked doors, red-eyed and muttering. He clambered up on the bundles and stared out through the skylight at the empty sky. He was lighter by fifteen pounds, unwashed. His face was black with wiry growth. He was going to have an immaculate beard. She wanted it. She didn't want him to wash or shave or be healthy. She called him Jeff.

You can't fight that, he told himself. You can't win because you lose. If you advance you are retreating because, when you are too tired to fight, she comes back and takes your city and your soul.

That's why he whispered to the warehouse so no one would hear, "There is a thing to do."

That's why, late at night, he sneaked to the living room and put the gas pistol in his pocket. Never harm the Gnees. Well, that was wrong. It was kill or be killed. That's why I'm taking the pistol to bed with me. That's why I'm stroking it as I stare up at the ceiling. Yes, this is it. This is my rock to rest on through the daynights.

And he turned over plans as an animal snuffles over flat stones to find bugs for supper.

Days. Days. Days. He whispered, "Kill her."

He nodded and smiled to himself and patted the cool metal. You're my friend, he said, you're my only friend. She has to die, we all know that.

He made lots of plans and they were all the same one. He killed her a million times in his mind—in secret chambers of his mind that he had discovered and opened; where he could crouch clever and undisturbed while he made his plans.

Animals. He walked and looked at the workers' village. Animals. I'm not going to end up like you. I'm not going to I'm not going to I'm not going to I'm . . .

He lurched up from his office desk, eyes wide, slaver running over his lips. He held the pistol tight in his palsied hand.

He flung open the office door and staggered over the concrete, through the lanes between roof-high stacks. His mouth was a line. He held the pistol pointing.

He flung up the catch and dragged back one heavy door. He plunged into the pouring sunlight and broke into a run. Wisps of terror licked out from the house. He reveled in them. He ran faster. He fell down because his legs were weak. The pistol went flying. He crawled to it and brushed off the dust. Now we'll see, he promised the monkeys in his head, *now*.

He stood up dizzily. He started to hobble for the house.

He heard a rushing in the air, a flicker of light dashed over his cheeks and eyes. He looked up and blinked and saw the cargo ship.

Six months.

He dropped the pistol and slumped down beside it and plucked at blue grass stupidly. He stared at the ship dumbly as it came down and stopped and the hatches opened and men climbed out.

"Why," he said, "that's cutting it too thin for me."

And his voice was quite normal except that he broke

into giggling and sobbing and had a fist fight with the air.

"You'll be all right," they told him on the way back to Earth. And they shot more sedative to his shrieking nerves to make him forget.

But he never did.

SHIPSHAPE HOME

"THAT JANITOR GIVES ME THE CREEPS," RUTH SAID
when she came in that afternoon.

I looked up from the typewriter as she put the bags
on the table and faced me. I was killing a second draft
on a story.

"He gives you the creeps," I said.

"Yes, he does," she said. "That way he has of slink-
ing around. He's like Peter Lorre or somebody."

"Peter Lorre," I said. I was still plotting.

"*Babe*," she implored. "I'm serious. The man is a
creep."

I snapped out of the creative fog with a blink.

"Hon, what can the poor guy do about his face?" I
said. "Heredity. Give him a break."

She plopped down in a chair by the table and started
to take out groceries, stacking cans on the table.

"Listen," she said.

I could smell it coming. That dead serious tone of
hers which she isn't even aware of anymore. But

which comes every time she's about to make one of her "revelations" to me.

"Listen," she repeated. Dramatic emphasis.

"Yes, dear," I said. I leaned one elbow on the type-writer cover and gazed at her patiently.

"You get that look off your face," she said. "You always look at me as if I were an idiot child or something."

I smiled. Wanly.

"You'll be sorry," she said. "Some night when that man creeps in with an axe and dismembers us."

"He's just a poor man earning a living," I said. "He mops the halls, he stokes the furnaces, he . . ."

"We have oil heat," she said.

"If we had a furnace, the man would stoke it," I said. "Let us have charity. He labors like ourselves. I write stories. He mops floors. Who can say which is the greater act?"

She looked dejected.

"Okay," she said with a surrendering gesture. "Okay, if you don't want to face facts."

"Which are?" I prodded. I decided it was best to let it out of her before it burned a hole in her mind.

Her eyes narrowed. "You listen to me," she said. "That man has some design in being here. He's no janitor. I wouldn't be surprised if . . ."

"If this apartment house were just a front for a gambling establishment. A hideout for public enemies one through fifteen. An abortion mill. A counterfeiter's lair. A murderer's rendezvous."

She was already in the kitchen thumping cans and boxes into the cupboard.

"Okay," she said. "*Okay.*" In that patient if-you-get-murdered-then-don't-come-to-me-for-sympathy voice. "Don't say I didn't try. If I'm married to a wall, I can't help it."

I came in and slid my arms around her waist. I kissed her neck.

"Stop that," she said. "You can't disconcert me. The janitor is . . ."

She turned. "You're serious," I said.

Her face darkened. "Honey, I *am*," she said. "The man looks at me in a funny way."

"How?"

"Oh," she searched. "In . . . in . . . *anticipation.*"

I chuckled. "Can't blame the man."

"Be serious now."

"Remember the time you thought the milkman was a knife killer for the Mafia?" I said.

"I don't care."

"You read too many fantasy pulps," I said.

"You'll be sorry."

I kissed her neck again. "Let's eat," I said.

She groaned. "Why do I tell you anything?"

"Because you love me," I said.

She closed her eyes. "I give up," she said quietly, with the patience of a saint under fire.

I kissed her. "Come on, hon, we have enough troubles."

She shrugged. "Oh, all right."

"Good," I said. "When are Phil and Marge coming?"

"Six," she said. "I got pork."

"Roast?"

"Mmmm."

"I'll buy that."

"You already did."

"In that case, back to the typewriter."

While I squeezed out another page I heard her muttering to herself in the kitchen. I didn't catch it all. All that came through was a grimly prophetic, "Murdered in our beds or something."

"No, it's flukey," Ruth analyzed as we all sat having dinner that night.

I grinned at Phil and he grinned back.

"I think so too," Marge agreed. "Whoever heard of charging only sixty-five a month for a five-room apartment furnished? Stove, refrigerator, washer—it's fantastic."

"Girls," I said. "Let's not quibble. Let's take advantage."

"*Oh!*" Ruth tossed her pretty blonde head. "If a man said—Here's a million dollars for you, old man—you'd probably take it."

"I most definitely would take it," I said. "I would then run like hell."

"You're naïve," she said. "You think people are . . . are . . ."

"Steady," I said.

"You think everybody is Santa Claus!"

"It *is* a little funny," Phil said. "Think about it, Rick."

I thought about it. A five-room apartment, brand new, furnished in the best manner, dishes . . . I pursed my lips. A guy can get lost in his typewriter. Maybe it was true. I nodded anyway. I could see their point.

Of course I wouldn't say so. And spoil Ruth's and my little game of war? Never.

"I think they charge too much," I said.

"Oh . . . Lord!" Ruth was taking it straight, as she usually did. "Too much! Five rooms yet! Furniture, dishes, linens, a . . . a television set! What do you want—a swimming pool!"

"A small one?" I said meekly.

She looked at Marge and Phil.

"Let us discuss this thing quietly," she said. "Let us pretend that the fourth voice we hear is nothing but the wind in the eaves."

"I am the wind in the eaves," I said.

"Listen," Ruth re-spun her forbodings, "what if the place is a fluke? I mean what if they just want people here for a cover-up. That would explain the rent. You remember the rush on the place when they started renting?"

I remembered as well as Phil and Marge. The only reason we'd got our apartment was because we happened to be walking past the place when the janitor first put out the renting sign. We went right in. I remember our amazement, our delight, at the rental. We thought it was Christmas.

We were the first tenants. The next day was like the Alamo under attack. It's a little hard to get an apartment these days.

"I say there's something funny about it," Ruth finished. "And did you ever notice that janitor?"

"He's a creep," I contributed blandly.

"He *is*," Marge laughed. "My God, he's something out of a B-picture. Those eyes. He looks like Peter Lorre."

"See!" Ruth was triumphant.

"Kids," I said, raising a hand of weary conciliation, "if there's something foul going on behind our backs, let's allow it to go on. We aren't being asked to contribute or suffer by it. We are living in a nice spot for a nice rent. What are we going to do—look into it and try to spoil it?"

"What if there are designs on us?" Ruth said.

"What designs, hon?" I asked.

"I don't know," she said. "But I sense something."

"Remember the time you sensed the bathroom was haunted?" I said. "It was a mouse."

She started clearing off the dishes. "Are you married to a blind man too?" she asked Marge.

"Men are all blind," Marge said, accompanying my poor man's seer into the kitchen. "We must face it."

Phil and I lit cigarettes.

"No kidding now," I said, so the girls wouldn't hear, "do you think there's anything wrong?"

He shrugged. "I don't know, Rick," he said. "I will say this—it's pretty strange to rent a furnished place for so little."

"Yeah," I said. Yeah, I thought—awake at last. Strange it is.

I stopped for a chat with our strolling cop the next morning. Johnson walks around the neighborhood. There are gangs in the neighborhood, he told me, traffic is heavy and the kids need watching especially after three in the afternoon.

He's a good Joe, lots of fun. I chat with him everyday when I go out for anything.

"My wife suspects foul doings in our apartment house," I told him.

"This is my suspicion too," Johnson said, dead sober. "It is my unwilling conclusion that, within those walls, six-year-olds are being forced to weave baskets by candle light."

"Under the whip hand of a gaunt old hag," I added.

He nodded sadly. Then he looked around, plotter-like.

"You won't tell anyone, will you?" he said. "I want to crack the case all by myself."

I patted his shoulder. "Johnson," I said. "Your secret is locked behind these iron lips."

"I am grateful," he said.

We laughed.

"How's the missus?" he asked.

"Suspicious," I said. "Curious. Investigating."

"Much the same," he said. "Everything normal."

"Right," I said. "I think I'll stop letting her read those science-fiction magazines."

"What is it she suspects?" he asked.

"Oh," I grinned. "Just suppositions. She thinks the rent is too cheap. Everybody around here pays twenty to fifty dollars more, she says."

"Is that right?" Johnson said.

"Yeah," I said, punching his arm. "Don't *you* tell anybody. I don't want to lose a good deal."

Then I went to the store.

"I knew it," Ruth said. "I *knew* it."

She gazed intently at me over a dishpan of soggy clothes.

"You knew what, hon?" I said, putting down the

package of second sheets I'd gone down the street to buy.

"This place is a fluke," she said. She raised her hand. "Don't say a word," she said. "You just listen to me."

I sat down. I waited. "Yes dear," I said.

"I found engines in the basement," she said.

"What kind of engines, dear? Fire engines?"

Her lips tightened. "Come on, now," she said, getting a little burned. "I saw the things."

She meant it.

"I've been down there too, hon," I said. "How come I never saw any engines?"

She looked around. I didn't like the way she did it. She looked as if she really thought someone might be lurking at the window, listening.

"This is *under* the basement," she said.

I looked dubious.

She stood up. "Damn it! You come on and I'll show you."

She held my hand as we went through the hall and into the elevator. She stood grimly by me as we descended, my hand tight in her grip.

"When did you see them?" I asked, trying to be nice.

"When I was washing in the laundry room down there," she said. "In the hallway, I mean, when I was bringing the clothes back. I was coming to the elevator and I saw a doorway. It was a little bit open."

"Did you go in?" I asked.

She looked at me. "You went in," I said.

"I went down the steps and it was light and . . ."

"And you saw engines."

"I saw engines."

"Big ones?"

The elevator stopped and the doors slid open. We went out.

"I'll show you how big," she said.

It was a blank wall. "It's here," she said.

I looked at her. I tapped the wall. "Honey," I said.

"Don't you dare say it!" she snapped. "Have you ever heard of doors in a wall?"

"Was this door in the wall?"

"The wall probably slides over it," she said starting to tap. It sounded solid to me. "Darn it!" she said, "I can just hear what you're going to say."

I didn't say it. I just stood there watching her.

"Lose something?"

The janitor's voice was sort of like Lorre's, low and insinuating. Ruth gasped, caught way off guard. I jumped myself.

"My wife thinks there's a—" I started nervously.

"I was showing him the right way to hang a picture," Ruth interrupted hastily. "*That's* the way, babe." She turned toward me. "You put the nail in at an angle, not straight in. Now, do you understand?" She took my hand.

The janitor smiled.

"See you," I said awkwardly. I felt his eyes on us as we walked back to the elevator.

When the doors shut, Ruth turned quickly.

"Good night!" she stormed. "What are you trying to do, get him on us?"

"Honey. What . . . ?" I was flabbergasted.

"Never mind," she said. "There are engines down there. *Huge* engines. I saw them. And he knows about them."

"Baby," I said. "Why don't . . ."

"Look at me," she said quickly.

I looked. Hard.

"Do you think I'm crazy?" she asked. "Come on, now. Never mind the hesitation."

I sighed. "I think you're imaginative," I said. "You read those . . ."

"Uh!" she muttered. She looked disgusted. "You're as bad as . . ."

"You and Galileo," I said.

"I'll show you those things," she said. "We're going down there again tonight when that janitor is asleep. If he's ever asleep."

I got worried then.

"Honey, cut it out," I said. "You'll get me going too."

"Good," she said. "*Good*. I thought it would take a hurricane."

I sat staring at my typewriter all afternoon, nothing coming out.

But concern.

I didn't get it. Was she actually serious? All right, I thought, I'll take it straight. She saw a door that was left open. Accidentally. That was obvious. If there were really huge engines under the apartment house as she said, then the people who built them darn sure wouldn't want anyone to know about them.

East 7th Street. An apartment house. And huge engines underneath it.

True?

"The janitor has three eyes!"

She was shaking. Her face was white. She stared at me like a kid who'd read her first horror story.

"*Honey*," I said. I put my arms around her. She was scared. I felt sort of scared myself. And not that the janitor had an extra eye either.

I didn't say anything at first. What can you say when your wife comes up with something like that?

She shook a long time. Then she spoke, in a quiet voice, a timid voice.

"I know," she said. "You don't believe me."

I swallowed. "Babe," I said helplessly.

"We're going down tonight," she said. "This is something important now. It's serious."

"I don't think we should . . ." I started.

"I'm going down there," she said. She sounded edgy now, a little hysterical. "I tell you there are engines down there. Goddamn it, there are engines!"

She started crying now, shaking badly. I patted her head, rested it against my shoulder. "All right, baby," I said. "All right."

She tried to tell me through her tears. But it didn't work. Later when she'd calmed down, I listened. I didn't want to get her upset. I figured the safest way was just to listen.

"I was walking through the hall downstairs," she said. "I thought maybe there was some afternoon mail. You know once in a while the mailman will . . ."

She stopped. "Never mind that. What matters is what happened when I walked past the janitor."

"What?" I said, afraid of what was coming.

"He smiled," she said. "You know the way he does. Sweet and murderous."

I let it go. I didn't argue the point. I still didn't think the janitor was anything but a harmless guy who had the misfortune to be born with a face that was strictly from Charles Addams.

"So?" I said. "Then what?"

"I walked past him. I felt myself shiver. Because he looked at me as if he knew something about me *I* didn't even know. I don't care what you say—that's the feeling I got. And then . . ."

She shuddered. I took her hand.

"Then?" I said.

"I felt him looking at me."

I'd felt that too when he found us in the basement. I knew what she meant. You just knew the guy was looking at you.

"All right," I said. "I'll buy that."

"You won't buy this," she said grimly. She sat stiffly a moment, then said, "When I turned around to look he was walking away from me."

I could feel it on the way. "I don't . . ." I started weakly.

"His head was turned but he was looking at me."

I swallowed. I sat there numbly, patting her hand without even knowing I was doing it.

"How, hon?" I heard myself asking.

"There was an eye in the back of his head."

"Hon," I said. I looked at her in—let's face it—fright. A mind on the loose can get awfully confused.

She closed her eyes. She clasped her hands after drawing away the one I was holding. She pressed her lips together. I saw a tear wriggle out from under her left eyelid and roll down her cheek. She was white.

"I saw it," she said quietly. "So help me God, I saw that eye."

I don't know why I went on with it. Self torture, I

guess. I really wanted to forget the whole thing, pretend it never even happened.

"Why haven't we seen it before, Ruth?" I asked. "We've seen the back of the man's head before."

"Have we?" she said. "Have we?"

"Sweetheart, *somebody* must have seen it. Do you think there's never been anyone behind him?"

"His hair parted, Rick," she said, "and before I ran away I saw the hair going back over it, so you couldn't see it."

I sat there silently. What to say now?—I thought. What could a guy possibly say to his wife when she talks to him like that? You're nuts? You're loony? Or the old, tired, "You've been working too hard." She hadn't been working too hard.

Then again maybe she *had* been working overtime. With her imagination.

"Are you going down with me tonight?" she asked.

"All right," I said quietly. "All right, sweetheart. Now will you go and lie down?"

"I'm all right."

"Sweetheart, go and lie down," I said firmly. "I'll go with you tonight. But I want you to lie down now."

She got up. She went into the bedroom and I heard the bedsprings squeak as she sat down, then drew up her legs and fell back on the pillow.

I went in a little later to put a comforter over her. She was looking at the ceiling. I didn't say anything to her. I don't think she wanted to talk to me.

"What can I do?" I said to Phil.

Ruth was asleep. I'd sneaked across the hall.

"Maybe she saw them?" he said. "Isn't it possible?"

"Yeah, sure," I said. "And you know what else is possible too."

"Look, you want to go down and see the janitor. You want to . . ."

"No," I said. "There's nothing we can do."

"You're going down to the basement with her?"

"If she keeps insisting," I said. "Otherwise, no."

"Look," he said. "When you go, come and get us."

I looked at him curiously. "You mean the thing is getting to you, too?" I said.

He looked at me in a funny way. I saw his throat move.

"Don't . . . look, don't tell anyone," he said.

He looked around, then turned back.

"Marge told me the same thing," he said. "She said the janitor has three eyes."

I went down after supper for some ice cream. Johnson was walking around.

"They're working you overtime," I said as he started to walk beside me.

"They expect some trouble from the local gangs," he said.

"I never saw any gangs," I said distractedly.

"They're here," he said.

"Mmmm."

"How's your wife?"

"Fine," I lied.

"She still think the apartment house is a front?" he laughed.

I swallowed. "No," I said. "I've broken her of that. I think she was just kidding me all the time."

He nodded and left me at the corner. And for some reason I couldn't keep my hands from shaking all the way home. I kept looking over my shoulder, too.

"It's time," Ruth said.

I grunted and rolled on my side. She nudged me. I woke up sort of hazy and looked automatically at the clock. The radium numbers told me it was almost four o'clock.

"You want to go *now?*" I asked, too sleepy to be tactful.

There was a pause. That woke me up.

"I'm going," she said quietly.

I sat up. I looked at her in the half darkness, my heart starting to do a drum beat too heavily. My mouth and throat felt dry.

"All right," I said. "Wait till I get dressed."

She was already dressed. I heard her in the kitchen making some coffee while I put on my clothes. There was no noise. I mean it didn't sound as if her hands were shaking. She spoke lucidly too. But when I stared into the bathroom mirror I saw a worried husband. I washed cold water in my face and combed my hair.

"Thanks," I said as she handed me the cup of coffee. I stood there, nervous before my own wife.

She didn't drink any coffee. "Are you awake?" she asked. I nodded. I noticed the flashlight and the screwdriver on the kitchen table. I finished the coffee.

"All right," I said. "Let's get it over with."

I felt her hand on my arm.

"I hope you'll . . ." she started. Then turned her face.

"What?"

"Nothing," she said. "We'd better go."

The house was dead quiet as we went into the hall. We were halfway to the elevator when I remembered Phil and Marge. I told her.

"We can't wait," she said. "It'll be light soon."

"Just wait and see if they're up," I said.

She didn't say anything. She stood by the elevator door while I went down the hall and knocked quietly on the door of their apartment. There was no answer. I glanced up the hall.

She was gone.

I felt my heart lurch. Even though I was sure there was no danger in the basement, it scared me. "Ruth," I muttered and headed for the stairs.

"Wait a second!" I heard Phil call loudly from his door.

"I can't!" I called back, charging down.

When I got to the basement I saw the open elevator door and light streaming from the inside. Empty.

I looked around for a light switch but there wasn't any. I started to move along the dark passage as fast as I could.

"Hon!" I whispered urgently. "Ruth, where are you?"

I found her standing before a doorway in the wall. It was open.

"Now stop acting as if I were insane," she said coldly.

I gaped and felt a hand pressing against my cheek. It was my own. She was right. There were stairs. And it was lighted down there. I heard sounds. Sounds of metallic clickings and strange buzzings.

I took her hand. "I'm sorry," I said. "I'm sorry."

Her hand tightened in mine. "All right," she said.

"Never mind that now. There's something flukey about all this."

I nodded. Then I said, "Yeah," realizing she couldn't see my nod in the darkness.

"Let's go down," she said.

"I don't think we better," I said.

"We've got to know," she said as if the entire problem had been assigned to us.

"But there must be someone down there," I said.

"We'll just peek," she said.

She pulled me. And I guess I felt too ashamed of myself to pull back. We started down. Then it came to me. If she was right about the doorway in the walls and the engines, she must be right about the janitor and he must really have . . .

I felt a little detached from reality. East 7th Street, I told myself again. An apartment house on East 7th Street. It's all real.

I couldn't quite convince myself.

We stopped at the bottom. And I just stared. Engines, all right. Fantastic engines. And, as I looked at them it came to me what kind of engines they were. I'd read about science too, the non-fiction kind.

I felt dizzy. You can't adapt quick to something like that. To be plunged from a brick apartment house into this . . . this storehouse of energy. It got me.

I don't know how long we were there. But suddenly I realized we had to get out of there, report this thing.

"Come on," I said. We moved up the steps, my mind working like an engine itself. Spinning out ideas, fast and furious. All of them crazy—all of them acceptable. Even the craziest one.

It was when we were moving down the basement hall we saw the janitor coming at us.

It was dark still, even with a little light coming from the early morning haze. I grabbed Ruth and we ducked behind a stone pillar. We stood holding our breaths, listening to the thud of his approaching shoes.

He passed us. He was holding a flashlight but he didn't play the beam around. He just moved straight for the open door.

Then it happened.

As he came into the patch of light from the open doorway he stopped. His head was turned away. The guy was facing the stairway.

But he was looking at us.

It knocked out what little breath I had left. I just stood there and stared at that eye in the back of his head. And, although there wasn't any face around it, that damned eye had a smile going with it. A nasty, self-certain and frightening smile. He saw us and he was amused and wasn't going to do anything about it.

He went through the doorway and the door thudded shut behind him, the stone wall segment slid down and shut it from view.

We stood there shivering.

"You saw it," she finally said.

"Yes."

"He knows we saw those engines," she said. "Still he didn't do anything."

We were still talking as the elevator ascended.

"Maybe there's nothing really wrong," I said. "Maybe . . ."

I stopped, remembering those engines. I knew what kind they were.

"What shall we do?" she asked. I looked at her. She was scared. I put my arm around her. But I was scared too.

"We'd better get out," I said. "Fast."

"We have nothing packed though," she said.

"We'll pack them," I said. "We'll leave before morning. I don't think they can do . . ."

"*They?*"

Why did I say that?—I wondered. They. It had to be a group though. The janitor didn't make those engines all by himself.

I think it was the third eye that capped my theory. And when we stopped to see Phil and Marge and they asked us what happened I told them what I thought. I don't think it surprised Ruth much. She undoubtedly thought it herself.

"I think the house is a rocket ship," I said.

They stared at me. Phil grinned; then he stopped when he saw I wasn't kidding.

"*What?*" Marge said.

"I know it sounds crazy," I said, sounding more like my wife than she did. "But those are rocket engines. I don't know how in the hell they got there but . . ." I shrugged helplessly at the whole idea. "All I know is that they're rocket engines."

"That doesn't mean it's a . . . a ship?" Phil finished weakly, switching from statement to question in mid-sentence.

"Yes," said Ruth.

And I shuddered. That seemed to settle it. She'd been right too often lately.

"But . . ." Marge shrugged. "What's the point?"

Ruth looked at us. "I know," she said.

"What, baby?" I asked, afraid to be asking.

"That janitor," she said. "He's not a man. We know that. That third eye makes it . . ."

"You mean the guy *has* one?" Phil asked incredulously.

I nodded. "He has one. I saw it."

"Oh my God," he said.

"But he's not a man," Ruth said again. "Humanoid, yes, but not an earthling. He might look like he does actually—except for the eye. But he might be completely different, so different he had to change his form. Give himself that extra eye just to keep track of us when we wouldn't expect it."

Phil ran a shaking hand through his hair.

"This is crazy," he said.

He sank down into a chair. So did the girls. I didn't. I felt uneasy about sticking around. I thought we should grab our hats and run. They didn't seem to feel in immediate danger though. I finally decided it wouldn't hurt to wait until morning. Then I'd tell Johnson or something. Nothing could happen now.

"This is crazy," Phil said again.

"I saw those engines," I said. "They're really there. You can't get away from it."

"Listen," Ruth said, "they're probably extraterrestrials."

"What are you talking about?" Marge asked irritably. She was good and afraid, I saw.

"Hon," I contributed weakly, "you've been reading an awful lot of science-fiction magazines."

Her lips drew together. "Don't start in again," she said. "You thought I was crazy when I suspected this place. You thought so when I told you I saw those engines. You thought so when I told you the janitor had three eyes. Well, I was right all three times. Now, give me some credit."

I shut up. And she went on.

"What if they're from another planet," she rephrased for Marge's benefit. "Suppose they want some Earth people to experiment on. To *observe*," she amended quickly, I don't know for whose benefit. The idea of being experimented on by three-eyed janitors from another planet had nothing exciting about it.

"What better way," Ruth was saying, "of getting people than to build a rocket ship apartment house, rent it out cheap and get it full of people fast?"

She looked at us without yielding an inch.

"And then," she said, "just wait till some morning early when everybody was asleep and . . . goodbye Earth."

My head was whirling. It was crazy but what could I say? I'd been cleverly dubious three times. I couldn't afford to doubt now. It wasn't worth the risk. And, in my flesh, I sort of felt she was right.

"But the whole house," Phil was saying. "How could they get it . . . in the air?"

"If they're from another planet they're probably centuries ahead of us in space travel."

Phil started to answer. He faltered, then he said, "But it doesn't *look* like a ship."

"The house might be a shell over the ship," I said. "It probably is. Maybe the actual ship includes only the bedrooms. That's all they'd need. That's where everybody would be in the early morning hours if . . ."

"*No*," Ruth said. "They couldn't knock off the shell without attracting much attention."

We were all silent laboring under a thick cloud of confusion and half-formed fears. Half formed because you can't shape your fears of something when you don't even know what it is.

"Listen," Ruth said.

It made me shudder. It made me want to tell her to shut up with her horrible forebodings. Because they made too much sense.

"Suppose it *is* a building," she said. "Suppose the ship is *outside* of it."

"But . . ." Marge was practically lost. She got angry because she was lost. "There's nothing outside the house, that's obvious!"

"Those people would be way ahead of us in science," Ruth said. "Maybe they've mastered invisibility of matter."

We all squirmed at once, I think. "Babe," I said.

"Is it possible?" Ruth asked strongly.

I sighed. "It's possible. *Just* possible."

We were quiet. Then Ruth said, "Listen."

"No," I cut in, "you listen. I think maybe we're going overboard on this thing. But there *are* engines in the basement and the janitor *does* have three eyes. On the basis of that I think we have reason enough to clear out. Now."

We all agreed on that anyway.

"We'd better tell everybody in the building," Ruth said. "We can't leave them here."

"It'll take too long," Marge argued.

"No, we have to," I said. "You pack, babe. I'll tell them."

I headed for the door and grabbed the knob.

Which didn't turn.

A bolt of panic drove through me. I grabbed at it and yanked hard. I thought for a second, fighting down fear, that it was locked on the inside. I checked.

It was locked on the outside.

"What is it?" Marge said in a shaking voice. You could sense a scream bubbling up in her.

"Locked," I said.

Marge gasped. We all stared at each other.

"It's true," Ruth said, horrified. "Oh, my God, it's all true then."

I made a dash for the window. Then the place started to vibrate as if we were being hit by an earthquake. Dishes started to rattle and fall off shelves. We heard a chair crash onto its side in the kitchen.

"What is it!" Marge cried again. Phil grabbed for her as she started to whimper. Ruth ran to me and we stood there, frozen, feeling the floor rock under our feet.

"The engines!" Ruth suddenly cried. "They're starting them!"

"They have to warm up!" I made a wild guess. "We can still get out!"

I let go of Ruth and grabbed a chair. For some reason I felt that the windows had been automatically locked too.

I hurled the chair through the glass. The vibrations were getting worse.

"Quick!" I shouted over the noise. "Out the fire escape! Maybe we can make it!"

Impelled by panic and dread, Marge and Phil came running over the shaking floor. I almost shoved them out through the gaping window hole. Marge tore her skirt. Ruth cut her fingers. I went last, dragging a glass dagger through my leg. I didn't even feel it I was so keyed up.

I kept pushing them, hurrying down the fire escape steps. Marge caught a slipper heel in between two gratings and it snapped off. Her slipper came off. She limped, half fell down the orange-painted metal steps, her face white and twisted with fear. Ruth in her loafers clattered down behind Phil. I came last, shepherding them frantically.

We saw other people at their windows. We heard windows crashing above and below. We saw an older couple crawl hurriedly through their window and start down. They held us up.

"Look out, will you!" Marge shouted at them in a fury.

They cast a frightened look over their shoulders.

Ruth looked back at me, her face drained of color. "Are you coming?" she asked quickly, her voice shaking.

"I'm here," I said breathlessly. I felt as if I were going to collapse on the steps. Which seemed to go on forever.

At the bottom was a ladder. We saw the old lady drop from it with a sickening thud, crying out in pain as her ankle twisted under her. Her husband dropped down and helped her up. The building was vibrating harshly now. We saw dust scaling out from between the bricks.

My voice joined the throng, all crying the same word, *"Hurry!"*

I saw Phil drop down. He half caught Marge, who was sobbing in fright. I heard her half-articulate "Oh, thank God!" as she landed and they started up the alleyway. Phil looked back over his shoulder at us but Marge dragged him on.

"Let me go first!" I snapped quickly. Ruth stepped aside and I swung down the ladder and dropped, feeling a sting in my insteps, a slight pain in my ankles. I looked up, extending my arms for her.

A man behind Ruth was trying to shove her aside so he could jump down.

"Look out!" I yelled like a raging animal, reduced suddenly by fear and concern. If I'd had a gun I'd have shot him.

Ruth let the man drop. He scrambled to his feet, breathing feverishly and ran down the alley. The building was shaking and quivering. The air was filled with the roar of the engines now.

"Ruth!" I yelled.

She dropped and I caught her. We regained our balance and started up the alley. I could hardly breathe. I had a stitch in my side.

As we dashed into the street we saw Johnson moving through the ranks of scattered people trying to herd them together.

"Here now!" he was calling. "Take it easy!"

We ran up to him. "Johnson!" I said. "The ship, it's . . ."

"Ship?" He looked incredulous.

"The house! It's a rocket ship! It's . . ." The ground shook wildly.

Johnson turned away to grab someone running past. My breath caught and Ruth gasped, throwing her hands to her cheeks.

Johnson was still looking at us; with that third eye. The one that had a smile with it.

"No," Ruth said shakily. "No."

And then the sky, which was growing light, grew dark. My head snapped around. Women were screaming their lungs out in terror. I looked in all directions.

Solid walls were blotting out the sky.

"Oh my God," Ruth said. "We can't get out. *It's the whole block.*"

Then the rockets started.

SRL AD

July 5, 1951

DEAR LOOLIE:

I don't know what I'm getting myself in for, but
I'm too tired to care. Ever spend a night on astro-
physical calculus? Well, I just did and I'm groggy.

So I'm taking your ad straight. What the heck, it
doesn't matter. Sat down for a relaxing half hour before sacking out and I feel like shooting off my big fat
typewriter so here I am with a cup of java.

I don't care if you live on Venus or Pluto or in a
little grass shack in Kehalick Kahooey Hawaii. I just
hope you're not selling something.

You know, it *would* be interesting to know if there
really was anyone on Venus, or Mars or any other of
those damn rolling spitballs that circle old Sol for a
good punch.

Okay. I'll assume you know nothing about Earth.
So you don't know a ting. Dat's slang. Don't you jes'
love Earth, LONESOME VENUS GAL?

What's the game old gal? What's the double talk? Socializing? I'll have you investigated, s'blood.

Pretty—yes. What's that?

As for me: pretty—no.

But I'm gay altogether too. I wake up late at night and just gay altogether all over the place. 'Specially if Willy and I (my roommate) have imbibed a few tankards of that mizzible brew they say is squeezed from the waving grain.

You have beer on Venus?

Venus. Venus. One Touch Of. That's a musical show down here. Venus was goddess of Love, I believe. Do you look like Mary Martin? Guess not. If you happen to look like Ava Gardner—hold that rocket ship Sam, I'm packin' mah duds now.

Who am I? This repulsive young lad who communicates in semifacetious vein? Who regales yo poor blinkers wif giddy persiflage?

Name's Todd Baker. Taking the Astronomy Unit here at Fort College in Fort, Indiana. College endowed by a rich old bugger who went off his nut over the Fortean prose.

You know it just struck me that if you were really on Venus (which I keep forgetting because I think that's a load of—*ah* ha ha!)

Anyway if you really were on the misty ghost world out thar yonder you wouldn't be able to make head nor tail of my confused rambling.

So—for regimentation—for mental exercise—I'll pretend you *are* up there: mean distance from the sun 67.2 million miles, eccentricity .0068, inclination to elliptic 3° 23' 38".

Pardon. Carried away by the figures which leap

about my mind like potted sitatungas. That's the way you get after a while. Integration. Differential. Function of a function. Stay away gal! Better to be lonesome on Venus.

I am of the males. I am sane, foregoing epistolary matter to the contrary. I have been here at Fort College these three grotesque years preparing myself for a life of fabulous obscurity studying those pinpoints in yon blackness that someone had the audacity to put there.

Could I not be a plumber? Cry in the night. Not me. I must stick a thermometer in the gullet of stars and diagnose—hmmm, the patient is getting old. He has only 95 billion years to live.

Okay. No distracting and altogether ungay and unsuccessful metaphors and snappy patter.

This is Earth. It has a diameter of 7900 miles. Do not ask why. This is a secret.

I am an Earth man of like fixtures. I am 26. This means that I have been undergoing a process of physical and mental growth (well, physical anyway) for 26 X 365 days. It takes the Earth 365 days to get around the sun, a day being one revolution of said solar handball around its own axis.

On Earth, on this continent, the piece of earth in this hemisphere that Davey Jones has not seen fit to stash away in his everloving locker, there is a country called the United States of America. In it is Indiana. In Indiana is Fort. In Fort is Fort College. In college is me. In me is idiocy for writing to any gal who says she's from Venus.

Tell you what I'm gonna do.

You tell me about Venus. We'uns down hyar can't

see it, you know. Somebody up there is smoking a damnably large cigar.

So, you give me some figures on Venus. Might even send me a few samples of rocks, plants, dirt and so on. How about it? Trapped you, eh?

Anyway, even though you're just a joker from Mother Earth and way back, drop me a line when next you feel the pressure on your brain.

And now to sack. Good night's sleep tonight; all of four hours.

I take it back. Willy is snoring.

Greetings from the wheeling green place.

> Todd Baker
> 1729 "J" Street
> Fort, Indiana

> July 7, 1951

Oh Dear Toddbaker,

Was it nice to hear from you. Am endless grateful. How good. I wish to have a newer translate book there isn't here. You see? "Forgive me dear."

I have got your message. Fast it came fast, picked up by my guardians. So happy am I that you have messaged to Loolie. I got no more than yours. I would not be even happy if there was not an answer at all. I worked in muchness to put the note on me in the place you saw. It was good English what?

There is a lot was not known in your message. Old translate book: see you. Cup of java not there. Not yet

everloving as so common adjective. Or handball. Or
Kehalick Kahooey Hawaii. This is a planet?

I am here. On *CU*. What you call Venus. Nice
ting. Slang. Right? "You are dear to me."

Oh, of yes, I am loving Earth. But most its Toddbaker. I did not plan for me to stay there with you
after—wait now. I must look for the properness word.
After . . . marriage* No.!

No. I had think you come to my planet. But later is
time for that to decide. No worries is there dear?

Socializing. That is wrong now see I. I am soci-able.
I can have many childs. Ten at a time at once. You will
be proud. And pretty—yes. I am. And you I know will
be handsome. I know. We will be so happiness. Oh!
"My dear it is good to know."

I am not goddess of Love. But I love you—any how?
This seems not a question. But in the translate book
is always? after *how*. Is it?

I am glad you own a room-mate. Of natural he can
not stay with us here on *CU*. How ever if Willy,
as you say it, wants another Lonesome Venus Gal I
can do it. I know many. All as pretty—yes as I am
pretty. Yes.

Mary Martian? I did not know that your planet
was in messaging action with the 4th from CU. We
had not thinked it livable. This is good yet. I have told
our skymen. They are glad to know this. Davey Jones
and Ava Gardner is not known. Who is Sam?

Oh dear you are not repulsive. I am know that you
are loveliness. We will be lovely with each other together. How dear. Many babies. Hundred. My*—! I
forget.

Fort, I am not knowing. I picked a spot with a point

and had my guardians to go down to tell of my lone-some. I am the first to try. If it works good and it worked good—yes. Then I will tell the rest of mine. I have two hundred and seven sisters. Nice. All pretty. You will like them when they see you.

Figures you said are all not right. But all right for that. I am giving an extra page of notes. See how they show. Formulas, laws and truths of matter here. In a box I will sending some samples of rock and on so.

I am L-. This means I think 8.5 in your numbers. I am very young. I hope it does not mind you to marriage with such a . . . a child. I can bear already babies. Two hundred at least, of course.

And now I will have to send this message from your Loolie. I will now come soon to get you. You will of real like it more on *сσ* than on your icy colded Earth with so lacking warm and air enough. Here is so fulsome warmth all in the U' U'—*year* in your talk. 224.7 days. Almost.

Now. Dear Toddbaker. Here is fare well for a nonce. Soon come I. How happy will we be? Yes! "My dear it is love I send, A kiss."

LOOLIE

1729 "J" Street
Fort, Indiana
July 10, 1951

Personals Department
The Saturday Review
25 West 45th Street
New York 19, New York

Dear Sir:

I wish to make an inquiry regarding an ad published in your July 3rd issue from a "LONESOME VENUS GAL."

I wrote to this person who claimed to be a resident of the planet Venus. I naturally assumed the claim to be facetious.

Two days after sending my letter I received an answer.

The fact that this letter was written in gibberish does not, in itself, prove anything.

However, with the letter came a sheet of mathematical statistics and a box of mineral and plant samples which this so-called "VENUS GAL" said were from her planet.

A professor at my college—Fort—is now examining the samples and testing the statistics. He has not made any statement.

But I am virtually certain that the samples are of a variety unknown to Earth. They *are*, actually, from another planet. I am almost positive of that.

I would like to know how this person or whatever she is, managed to communicate with you and get such an ad in your magazine.

According to your own written standards, it would seem that this advertisement, by its very nature was far from a communication "of a decorous nature."

This "VENUS GAL" Loolie speaks of *marrying* me—coming down here and getting me.

Please rush a reply. This matter is highly urgent.

Thanking you, I am

Very truly yours
Todd Baker

July 11, 1951

Dear Mr. Baker:

Your letter of the 10th at hand. We must confess
ignorance of its meaning. In our July 3rd issue there
was no such ad as you described placed in our Classified Section.

We are of the opinion that you have been the un-
fortunate butt of some practical joke.

However, we are in communication with one of our
territorial representatives in Fort and he is investigating the matter.

If we can be of further service, please feel free to
call on us.

Sincerely yours
J. Linton Freedhoffer
For the Editor

Mr. Todd Baker
1729 "J" Street
Fort, Indiana

Professor Reed:

Dropped in to see you but you weren't in your office.
Any news?
I'm getting awfully worried. If you find that those

samples are as legitimate as I think they are, I'm sunk. I get the shudders every time I think about what fantastic powers this Loolie must have. How she got that ad in the SRL I'll never figure out.

I certainly hope it *is* a practical joke.

If it isn't . . .

Will you let me know as soon as you reach any definite decision?

Todd Baker

Toddy Lad:;.?!

Prof. Reed called up. Said he found out that the samples (whatever they are) are strictly legit. Really come from some place other than Earth. Who's he kidding? Oops, sorry Charles.

Anyway, the old boy says for you to come over to his house tonight for a big pow-wow. Playing teacher's pet? For shame.

Off to supper.

Adoringly
Your room mate
The Eternal Sophomore
Willy

P.S. Letter came for you.

July 11, 1951

Oh Dear Toddbaker:

Think! How fortunate it is. I have got a special ship. I can come now right away tomorrow. Oh happiness. "Pack your duds, dear." I am coming to bring you back with me. I am so joyfull. Please hurry.

With everything
LOOLIE

LOOLIE!

No! You can't do this! I'm an Earth-man. Let me stay one! Keep away. I'm not going *anywhere* with you. I'm warning you!

Please?
Stay away!

T. Baker

P.S. I got a shotgun! Look out!

(From the *Fort Daily Tribune*, July 13, 1951)

FLOATING GLOBE SIGHTED
OVER COLLEGE CAMPUS

More than thirty students and citizens of Fort claimed to have sighted a floating globe last night.

According to the reports, the globe hovered over the college campus for at least ten minutes. It then headed for the outskirts of the city where it disappeared.

Dear Tell Book:

Well, I'm back. I can't understand it. I've been taken in, I have. It seems so odd.

I went to such trouble to put the insert in that Earth publication. And then this Toddbaker went to all the trouble of writing back. And I thought—here now!—I have a mate at last. He seemed so interested and so nice.

But heavens. When I told him that we were to be co-joined he protested as though this were something terrible. What sense in that? I thought he was just being shy as are all the depleted males up here.

So, on the third phase, I got into the ship (which I had gone to oh! such trouble to get). I was down there in about seven eks.

I stayed there a little less than a half ek, suspended over a green place with tall structures. There with the use of the proto-finder I located the waves of Toddbaker and headed for this "J" street.

I landed behind his personal structure.

I got out and went over to this place. I sensed his presence with my portable proto. The waves were coming freely through a square hole high up on the wall.

I turned on my air belt and floated up there. There I went into this hole. It was a terrible squeeze.

There he was.

Such a shock!

He was holding something long and shiny in his hands and he pointed it at me. But then he dropped it on the floor and said something.

I do not see how these Earth men understand each

other. It was so weird a gurgle and it stuck in him. He stared at me and the voice cavity got large. Then it spread wide across and showed his teeth.

Then the seeing organs in his top part rolled back and disappeared. I suppose it was my air cloud that made it happen. He put out his arms at me and took one step. But then he fell down on the floor with a squeaking noise. He said—*mama*.

I went over and examined him.

My my.

He was not of like fixtures at all. It could not possibly be managed. He was so fragile and pale. It is doubtful that the whole race of them can last. Not with such a form. So little!

So I left him there, poor thing.

And I had been so happy before. Now I'm still lonesome. I want a mate.

And now what? Nothing I guess. Well, maybe one.

July 20, 1951

Dear Mrs. Baker:

I think you'd better come and take Todd home. He's in a sad way.

He's cutting all his classes and he doesn't eat. All he does is sit around the room and stare at things. He hasn't slept more than a few hours all week and when he does fall asleep he keeps talking to himself, calling for "Louie". We don't know any Louie.

I found the enclosed in the basket this afternoon. I don't get it.

But you better get Todd.

In haste,
Willy Haskell

(Enclosure)

Dear Sir:

We regret to inform you that your personal advertisement is not acceptable for our classified section.
We return it herewith.

(Enclosure)

LOOLIE: I'm sorry. I didn't know you were so big and beautiful. Won't you please come back? I'll be waiting. Love, Todd.

> LONESOME VENUS GAL, pretty—yes nice in socializing, tender and gay altogether. Be pleased to write Mars man of like fixtures. Note: am friends with Mary Martian. LOOLIE, GREENER ABODE, VENUS

DEATH SHIP

MASON SAW IT FIRST.

He was sitting in front of the lateral viewer taking notes as the ship cruised over the new planet. His pen moved quickly over the graph-spaced chart he held before him. In a little while they'd land and take specimens. Mineral, vegetable, animal—if there were any. Put them in the storage lockers and take them back to Earth. There the technicians would evaluate, appraise, judge. And, if everything was acceptable, stamp the big, black INHABITABLE on their brief and open another planet for colonization from overcrowded Earth.

Mason was jotting down items about general topography when the glitter caught his eye.

"I saw something," he said.

He flicked the viewer to reverse lensing position.

"Saw what?" Ross asked from the control board.

"Didn't you see a flash?"

Ross looked into his own screen.

"We went over a lake, you know," he said.

"No, it wasn't that," Mason said, "this was in that clearing beside the lake."

"I'll look," said Ross, "but it probably was the lake."

His fingers typed out a command on the board and the big ship wheeled around in a smooth arc and headed back.

"Keep your eyes open now," Ross said. "Make sure. We haven't got any time to waste."

"Yes, sir."

Mason kept his unblinking gaze on the viewer, watching the earth below move past like a slowly rolled tapestry of woods and fields and rivers. He was thinking, in spite of himself, that maybe the moment had arrived at last. The moment in which Earthmen would come upon life beyond Earth, a race evolved from other cells and other muds. It was an exciting thought. 1997 might be the year. And he and Ross and Carter might now be riding a new *Santa Maria* of discovery, a silvery, bulleted galleon of space.

"There!" he said. "There it is!"

He looked over at Ross. The captain was gazing into his viewer plate. His face bore the expression Mason knew well. A look or smug analysis, of impending decision.

"What do you think it is?" Mason asked, playing the strings of vanity in his captain.

"Might be a ship, might not be," pronounced Ross.

Well, for God's sake, let's go down and see, Mason wanted to say, but knew he couldn't. It would have to be Ross's decision. Otherwise they might not even stop.

"I guess it's nothing," he prodded.

He watched Ross impatiently, watched the stubby fingers flick buttons for the viewer. "We might stop," Ross said. "We have to take samples anyway. Only thing I'm afraid of is . . ."

He shook his head. Land, man! The words bubbled up in Mason's throat. For God's sake, let's go down!

Ross evaluated. His thickish lips pressed together appraisingly. Mason held his breath.

Then Ross' head bobbed once in that curt movement which indicated consummated decision. Mason breathed again. He watched the captain spin, push and twist dials. Felt the ship begin its tilt to upright position. Felt the cabin shuddering slightly as the gyroscope kept it on an even keel. The sky did a ninety-degree turn, clouds appeared through the thick ports. Then the ship was pointed at the planet's sun and Ross switched off the cruising engines. The ship hesitated, suspended a split second, then began dropping toward the earth.

"Hey, we settin' down already?"

Mickey Carter looked at them questioningly from the port door that led to the storage lockers. He was rubbing greasy hands over his green jumper legs.

"We saw something down there," Mason said.

"No kiddin'," Mickey said, coming over to Mason's viewer. "Let's see."

Mason flicked on the rear lens. The two of them watched the planet billowing up at them.

"I don't know whether you can . . . oh, yes, there it is," Mason said. He looked over at Ross.

"Two degrees east," he said.

Ross twisted a dial and the ship then changed its downward movement slightly.

"What do you think it is?" Mickey asked.

"Hey!"

Mickey looked into the viewer with even greater interest. His wide eyes examined the shiny speck enlarging on the screen.

"Could be a ship," he said. "Could be."

Then he stood there silently, behind Mason, watching the earth rushing up.

"Reactors," said Mason.

Ross jabbed efficiently at the button and the ship's engines spouted out their flaming gasses. Speed decreased. The rocket eased down on its roaring fire jets. Ross guided.

"What do *you* think it is?" Mickey asked Mason.

"I don't know," Mason answered. "But if it's a ship," he added, half wishfully thinking, "I don't see how it could possibly be from Earth. We've got this run all to ourselves."

"Maybe they got off course," Mickey dampened without knowing.

Mason shrugged. "I doubt it," he said.

"What if it is a ship?" Mickey said. "And it's not ours?"

Mason looked at him and Carter licked his lips.

"Man," he said, "that'd be somethin'."

"Air spring," Ross ordered.

Mason threw the switch that set the air spring into operation. The unit which made possible a landing without them having to stretch out on thick-cushioned couches. They could stand on deck and hardly feel the impact. It was an innovation on the newer government ships.

The ship hit on its rear braces.

There was a sensation of jarring, a sense of slight bouncing. Then the ship was still, its pointed nose straight up, glittering brilliantly in the bright sunlight.

"I want us to stay together," Ross was saying. "No one takes any risks. That's an order."

He got up from his seat and pointed at the wall switch that let atmosphere into the small chamber in the corner of the cabin.

"Three to one we need our helmets," Mickey said to Mason.

"You're on," Mason said, setting into play their standing bet about the air or lack of it on every new planet they found. Mickey always bet on the need for apparatus, Mason for unaided lung use. So far, they'd come out about even.

Mason threw the switch, and there was a muffled sound of hissing in the chamber. Mickey got the helmet from his locker and dropped it over his head. Then he went through the double doors. Mason listened to him clamping the doors behind him. He kept wanting to switch on the side viewers and see if he could locate what they'd spotted. But he didn't. He let himself enjoy the delicate nibbling of suspense.

Through the intercom they heard Mickey's voice.

"Removing helmet," he said.

Silence. They waited. Finally, a sound of disgust.

"I lose again," Mickey said.

"God, did they hit!"

Mickey's face had an expression of dismayed shock

on it. The three of them stood there on the greenish-
blue grass and looked.

It *was* a ship. Or what was left of a ship for, apparently, it had struck the earth at terrible velocity, nose
first. The main structure had driven itself about fifteen feet into the hard ground. Jagged pieces of su-
perstructure had been ripped off by the crash and
were lying strewn over the field. The heavy engines
had been torn loose and nearly crushed the cabin.
Everything was deathly silent, and the wreckage was
so complete they could hardly make out what type of
ship it was. It was as if some enormous child had lost
fancy with the toy model and had dashed it to earth,
stamped on it, banged on it insanely with a rock.

Mason shuddered. It had been a long time since
he'd seen a rocket crash. He'd almost forgotten the
everpresent menace of lost control, of whistling fall
through space, of violent impact. Most talk had been
about being lost in an orbit. This reminded him of the
other threat in his calling. His throat moved unconsciously as he watched.

Ross was scuffing at a chunk of metal at his feet.

"Can't tell much," he said. "But I'd say it's our own."

Mason was about to speak, then changed his mind.

"From what I can see of that engine up there, I'd
say it was ours," Mickey said.

"Rocket structure might be standard," Mason
heard himself say, "everywhere."

"Not a chance," Ross said. "Things don't work
out like that. It's ours all right. Some poor devils from
Earth. Well, at least their death was quick."

"Was it?" Mason asked the air, visualizing the crew
in their cabin, rooted with fear as their ship spun

toward earth, maybe straight down like a fired cannon shell, maybe end-over-end like a crazy, fluttering top, the gyroscope trying in vain to keep the cabin always level.

The screaming, the shouted commands, the exhortations to a heaven they had never seen before, to a God who might be in another universe. And then the planet rushing up and blasting its hard face against their ship, crushing them, ripping the breath from their lungs. He shuddered again, thinking of it.

"Let's take a look," Mickey said.

"Not sure we'd better," Ross said. "We say it's ours. It might not be."

"Jeez, you don't think anything is still alive in there, do you?" Mickey asked the captain.

"Can't say," Ross said.

But they all knew he could see that mangled hulk before him as well as they. Nothing could have survived that.

The look. The pursed lips. As they circled the ship. The head move ment, unseen by them.

"Let's try that opening there," Ross ordered. "And stay together We still have work to do. Only doing this so we can let the base know which ship this is." He had already decided it was an Earth ship.

They walked up to a spot in the ship's side where the skin had been laid open along the welded seam. A long, thick plate was bent over as easily as a man might bend paper.

"Don't like this," Ross said. "But I suppose . . ."

He gestured with his head and Mickey pulled himself up to the opening. He tested each handhold gingerly, then slid on his work gloves as he found some sharp edge. He told the other two and they reached into their jumper pockets. Then Mickey took a long step into the dark maw of the ship.

"Hold *on*, now!" Ross called up. "Wait until I get there."

He pulled himself up, his heavy boot toes scraping up the rocket skin. He went into the hole too. Mason followed.

It was dark inside the ship. Mason closed his eyes for a moment to adjust to the change. When he opened them, he saw two bright beams searching up through the twisted tangle of beams and plates. He pulled out his own flash and flicked it on.

"God, is this thing wrecked," Mickey said, awed by the sight of metal and machinery in violent death. His voice echoed slightly through the shell. Then, when the sound ended, an utter stillness descended on them. They stood in the murky light and Mason could smell the acrid fumes of broken engines.

"Watch the smell, now," Ross said to Mickey who was reaching up for support. "We don't want to get ourselves gassed."

"I will," Mickey said. He was climbing up, using one hand to pull his thick, powerful body up along the twisted ladder. He played the beam straight up.

"Cabin is all out of shape," he said, shaking his head.

Ross followed him up. Mason was last, his flash moving around endlessly over the snapped joints, the wild jigsaw of destruction that had once been a powerful new ship. He kept hissing in disbelief to himself as his beam came across one violent distortion of metal after another.

"Door's sealed," Mickey said, standing on a pretzel-twisted catwalk, bracing himself against the inside rocket wall. He grabbed the handle again and tried to pull it open.

"Give me your light," Ross said. He directed both beams at the door and Mickey tried to drag it open. His face grew red as he struggled. He puffed.

"No," he said, shaking his head. "It's stuck."

Mason came up beside them. "Maybe the cabin is still pressurized," he said softly. He didn't like the echoing of his own voice.

"Doubt it," Ross said, trying to think. "More than likely the jamb is twisted." He gestured with his head again. "Help Carter."

Mason grabbed one handle and Mickey the other. Then they braced their feet against the wall and pulled with all their strength. The door held fast. They shifted their grip, pulled harder.

"Hey, it slipped!" Mickey said. "I think we got it."

They resumed footing on the tangled catwalk and pulled the door open. The frame was twisted, the door held in one corner. They could only open it enough to wedge themselves in sideways.

The cabin was dark as Mason edged in first. He played his light beam toward the pilot's seat. It was empty. He heard Mickey squeeze in as he moved the light to the navigator's seat.

There was no navigator's seat. The bulkhead had been driven in there, the viewer, the table and the chair all crushed beneath the bent plates. There was a clicking in Mason's throat as he thought of himself sitting at a table like that, in a chair like that, before a bulkhead like that.

Ross was in now. The three beams of light searched.

They all had to stand, legs braced, because the deck slanted.

And the way it slanted made Mason think of something. Of shifting weights, of *things* sliding down. . . .

Into the corner where he suddenly played his shaking beam.

And felt his heart jolt, felt the skin on him crawling, felt his unblinking eyes staring at the sight. Then felt his boots thud him down the incline as if he were driven.

"Here," he said, his voice hoarse with shock.

He stood before the bodies. His foot had bumped into one of them as he held himself from going down any further, as he shifted his weight on the incline.

Now he heard Mickey's footsteps, his voice. A whisper. A bated, horrified whisper.

"Mother of God."

Nothing from Ross. Nothing from any of them then but stares and shuddering breaths.

Because the twisted bodies on the floor were theirs, all three of them. And all three . . . dead.

Mason didn't know how long they stood there, wordlessly, looking down at the still, crumpled figures on the deck.

How does a man react when he is standing over his own corpse? The question plied unconsciously at his mind. What does a man say? What are his first words to be? A poser, he seemed to sense, a loaded question.

But it was happening. Here he stood—and there he lay dead at his own feet. He felt his hands grow numb and he rocked unsteadily on the tilted deck.

"*God.*"

Mickey again. He had his flash pointed down at his own face. His mouth twitched as he looked. All three of them had their flash beams directed at their own faces, and the bright ribbons of light connected their dual bodies.

Finally Ross took a shaking breath of the stale cabin air.

"Carter," he said, "find the auxiliary light switch, see if it works." His voice was husky and tightly restrained.

"Sir?"

"The light switch—the light switch!" Ross snapped.

Mason and the captain stood there, motionless, as Mickey shuffled up the deck. They heard his boots kick metallic debris over the deck surface. Mason closed his eyes, but was unable to take his foot away from where it pressed against the body that was his. He felt bound.

"I don't understand," he said to himself.

"Hang on," Ross said.

Mason couldn't tell whether it was said to encourage him or the captain himself.

Then they heard the emergency generator begin its initial whining spin. The lights flickered, went out. The generator coughed and began humming and the lights flashed on brightly.

They looked down now. Mickey slipped down the slight deck hill and stood beside them. He stared down at his own body. Its head was crushed in. Mickey drew back, his mouth a box of unbelieving terror.

"I don't get it," he said. "I don't get it. What *is* this?"

"Carter," Ross said.

"That's *me!*" Mickey said. "God, it's *me!*"

"Hold on!" Ross ordered.

"The three of us," Mason said quietly, "and we're all dead."

There seemed nothing to be said. It was a speechless nightmare. The tilted cabin all bashed in and tangled. The three corpses all doubled over and tumbled into one corner, arms and legs flopped over each other. All they could do was stare.

Then Ross said, "Go get a tarp. Both of you."

Mason turned. Quickly. Glad to fill his mind with simple command. Glad to crowd out tense horror with activity. He took long steps up the deck. Mickey backed up, unable to take his unblinking gaze off the heavy-set corpse with the green jumper and the caved-in, bloody head.

Mason dragged a heavy, folded tarp from the storage locker and carried it back into the cabin, legs and arms moving in robotlike sequence. He tried to numb his brain, not think at all until the first shock had dwindled.

Mickey and he opened up the heavy canvas sheet with wooden motions. They tossed it out and the thick, shiny material fluttered down over the bodies. It settled, outlining the heads, the torsos, the one arm that stood up stiffly like a spear, bent over wrist and hand like a grisly pennant.

Mason turned away with a shudder. He stumbled up to the pilot's seat and slumped down. He stared at his outstretched legs, the heavy boots. He reached out and grabbed his leg and pinched it, feeling almost relief at the flaring pain.

"Come away," he heard Ross saying to Mickey, "I said, *come away!*"

He looked down and saw Ross half dragging Mickey up from a crouching position over the bodies. He held Mickey's arm and led him up the incline.

"We're dead," Mickey said hollowly. "That's us on the deck. *We're dead.*"

Ross pushed Mickey up to the cracked port and made him look out.

"There," he said. "There's our ship over there. Just as we left it. This ship isn't ours. And those bodies. They . . . can't be ours."

He finished weakly. To a man of his sturdy opinionation, the words sounded flimsy and extravagant. His throat moved, his lower lip pushed out in defiance of this enigma. Ross didn't like enigmas. He stood for decision and action. He wanted action now.

"You saw yourself down there," Mason said to him. "Are you going to say it isn't you?"

"That's exactly what I'm saying," Ross bristled. "This may seem crazy, but there's an explanation for it. There's an explanation for everything."

His face twitched as he punched his bulky arm.

"This is me," he claimed. "I'm solid." He glared at them as if daring opposition. "I'm alive," he said.

They stared blankly at him.

"I don't get it," Mickey said weakly. He shook his head and his lips drew back over his teeth.

Mason sat limply in the pilot's seat. He almost hoped that Ross's dogmatism would pull them through this. That his staunch bias against the inexplicable would save the day. He wanted for it to save the day. He tried to think for himself, but it was so much easier to let the captain decide.

"We're all dead," Mickey said.

"Don't be a fool!" Ross exclaimed. "Feel yourself!"

Mason wondered how long it would go on. Actually, he began to expect a sudden awakening, him jolting to a sitting position on his bunk to see the two of them at their tasks as usual, the crazy dream over and done with.

But the dream went on. He leaned back in the seat and it was a solid seat. From where he sat he could run his fingers over solid dials and buttons and switches. All real. It was no dream. Pinching wasn't even necessary.

"Maybe it's a vision," he tried, vainly attempting thought, as an animal mired tries hesitant steps to solid earth.

"That's enough," Ross said.

Then his eyes narrowed. He looked at them sharply. His face mirrored decision. Mason almost felt anticipation. He tried to figure out what Ross was working on. Vision? No, it couldn't be that. Ross would hold no truck with visions. He noticed Mickey staring open-mouthed at Ross. Mickey wanted the consoling of simple explanation, too.

"Time warp," said Ross.

They still stared at him.

"What?" Mason asked.

"Listen," Ross punched out his theory. More than his theory, for Ross never bothered with that link in the chain of calculation. His certainty.

"Space bends," Ross said. "Time and space form a continuum. Right?"

No answer. He didn't need one.

"Remember they told us once in training of the possibility of circumnavigating time. They told us we could leave Earth at a certain time. And when we came back we'd be back a year earlier than we'd calculated. Or a year later.

"Those were just theories to the teachers. Well, I say it's happened to us. It's logical, it could happen. We could have passed right through a time warp. We're in another galaxy, maybe different space lines, maybe different time lines."

He paused for effect.

"I say we're in the future," he said.

Mason looked at him.

"How does that help us?" he asked, "if you're right."

"We're not dead!" Ross seemed surprised that they didn't get it.

"If it's in the future," Mason said quietly, "then we're going to die."

Ross gaped at him. He hadn't thought of that. Hadn't thought that his idea made things even worse. Because there was only one thing worse than dying. And that was knowing you were going to die. And where. And how.

Mickey shook his head. His hands fumbled at his sides. He raised one to his lips and chewed nervously on a blackened nail.

"No," he said weakly, "I don't get it."

Ross stood looking at Mason with jaded eyes. He bit his lips, feeling nervous with the unknown crowding him in, holding off the comfort of solid, rational thinking. He pushed, he shoved it away. He persevered.

"Listen," he said, "we're agreed that those bodies aren't ours."

No answer.

"Use your heads!" Ross commanded. "Feel yourself!"

Mason ran numbed fingers over his jumper, his helmet, the pen in his pocket. He clasped solid hands of flesh and bone. He looked at the veins in his arms. He pressed an anxious finger to his pulse. It's true, he thought. And the thought drove lines of strength back into him. Despite all, despite Ross' desperate advocacy, he was alive. Flesh and blood were his evidence.

His mind swung open then. His brow furrowed in thought as he straightened up. He saw a look almost of relief on the face of a weakening Ross.

"All right then," he said, "we're in the future."

Mickey stood tensely by the port. "Where does that leave us?" he asked.

The words threw Mason back. It was true, where did it leave them?

"How do we know how distant a future?" he said, adding weight to the depression of Mickey's words. "How do we know it isn't in the next twenty minutes?"

Ross tightened. He punched his palm with a resounding smack.

"How do we know?" he said strongly. "We don't go up, we can't crash. That's how we know."

Mason looked at him.

"Maybe if we went up," he said, "we might bypass our death altogether and leave it in this space-time system. We could get back to the space-time system of our own galaxy and . . ."

His words trailed off. His brain became absorbed with twisting thought.

Ross frowned. He stirred restlessly, licked his lips. What had been simple was now something else again. He resented the uninvited intrusion of complexity.

"We're alive now," he said, getting it set in his mind, consolidating assurance with reasonable words, "and there's only one way we can stay alive."

He looked at them, decision reached. "We have to stay here," he said.

They just looked at him. He wished that one of them, at least, would agree with him, show some sign of definition in their minds.

"But . . . what about our orders?" Mason said vaguely.

"Our orders don't tell us to kill ourselves!" Ross said. "No, it's the only answer. If we never go up again, we never crash. We . . . we avoid it, we prevent it!"

His head jarred once in a curt nod. To Ross, the thing was settled.

Mason shook his head.

"I don't know," he said, "I don't . . ."

"I do," Ross stated. "Now let's get out of here. This ship is getting on your nerves."

Mason stood up as the captain gestured toward the door. Mickey started to move, then hesitated. He looked down at the bodies.

"Shouldn't we . . . ?" he started to inquire.

"What, what?" Ross asked, impatient to leave.

Mickey stared at the bodies. He felt caught up in a great, bewildering insanity.

"Shouldn't we . . . bury ourselves?" he said.

Ross swallowed. He would hear no more. He herded

them out of the cabin. Then, as they started down through the wreckage, he looked in at the door. He looked at the tarpaulin with the jumbled mound of bodies beneath it. He pressed his lips together until they were white.

"I'm alive," he muttered angrily.

Then he turned out the cabin light with tight, vengeful fingers and left.

They all sat in the cabin of their own ship. Ross had ordered food brought out from the lockers, but he was the only one eating. He ate with a belligerent rotation of his jaw as though he would grind away all mystery with his teeth.

Mickey stared at the food.

"How long do we have to stay?" he asked, as if he didn't clearly realize that they were to remain permanently.

Mason took it up. He leaned forward in his seat and looked at Ross.

"How long will our food last?" he said.

"There's edible food outside, I've no doubt," Ross said, chewing.

"How will we know which is edible and which is poisonous?"

"We'll watch the animals," Ross persisted.

"They're a different type of life," Mason said. "What they can eat might be poisonous to us. Besides, we don't even know if there are any animals here."

The words made his lips raise in a brief, bitter smile. And he'd actually been hoping to contact another people. It was practically humorous.

Ross bristled. "We'll . . . cross each river as we come

to it," he blurted out as if he hoped to smother all complaint with this ancient homily.

Mason shook his head. "I don't know," he said.

Ross stood up.

"Listen," he said. "It's easy to ask questions. We've all made a decision to stay here. Now let's do some concrete thinking about it. Don't tell me what we can't do. I know that as well as you. Tell me what we can do."

Then he turned on his heel and stalked over to the control board. He stood there glaring at blank-faced gauges and dials. He sat down and began scribbling rapidly in his log as if something of great note had just occurred to him. Later Mason looked at what Ross had written and saw that it was a long paragraph which explained in faulty but unyielding logic why they were all alive.

Mickey got up and sat down on his bunk. He pressed his large hands against his temples. He looked very much like a little boy who had eaten too many green apples against his mother's injunction and who feared retribution on both counts. Mason knew what Mickey was thinking. Of that still body with the skull forced in. The image of himself brutally killed in collision. He, Mason, was thinking of the same thing. And, behavior to the contrary, Ross probably was too.

Mason stood by the port looking out at the silent hulk across the meadow. Darkness was falling. The last rays of the planet's sun glinted off the skin of the crashed rocket ship. Mason turned away. He looked at the outside temperature gauge. Already it was seven degrees and it was still light. Mason moved the thermostat needle with his right forefinger.

Heat being used up, he thought. The energy of our grounded ship being used up faster and faster. The ship drinking its own blood with no possibility of transfusion. Only operation would recharge the ship's energy system. And they were without motion, trapped and stationary.

"How long can we last?" he asked Ross again, refusing to keep silence in the face of the question. "We can't live in this ship indefinitely. The food will run out in a couple of months. And a long time before that the charging system will go. The heat will stop. We'll freeze to death."

"How do we know the outside temperature will freeze us?" Ross asked, falsely patient.

"It's only sundown," Mason said, "and already it's . . . minus thirteen degrees."

Ross looked at him sullenly. Then he pushed up from his chair and began pacing.

"If we go up," he said, "we risk . . . *duplicating* that ship over there."

"But would we?" Mason wondered. "We can only die once. It seems we already have. In this galaxy. Maybe a person can die once in every galaxy. Maybe that's afterlife. Maybe . . ."

"Are you through?" asked Ross coldly.

Mickey looked up.

"Let's go," he said. "I don't want to hang around here."

He looked at Ross.

Ross said, "Let's not stick out our necks before we know what we're doing. Let's think this out."

"I have a wife!" Mickey said angrily. "Just because you're not married—"

"Shut up!" Ross thundered.

Mickey threw himself on the bunk and turned to face the cold bulkhead. Breath shuddered through his heavy frame. He didn't say anything. His fingers opened and closed on the blanket, twisting it, pulling it out from under his body.

Ross paced the deck, abstractedly punching at his palm with a hard fist. His teeth clicked together, his head shook as one argument after another fell before his bullheaded determination. He stopped, looked at Mason, then started pacing again. Once he turned on the outside spotlight and looked to make sure it was not imagination.

The light illumined the broken ship. It glowed strangely, like a huge, broken tombstone. Ross snapped off the spotlight with a soundless snarl. He turned to face them. His broad chest rose and fell heavily as he breathed.

"All right," he said. "It's *your* lives too. I can't decide for all of us. We'll hand vote on it. That thing out there may be something entirely different from what we think. If you two think it's worth the risk of our lives to go up, we'll . . . go up."

He shrugged. "Vote," he said. "I say we stay here."

"I say we go," Mason said.

They looked at Mickey.

"Carter," said Ross, "what's your vote?"

Mickey looked over his shoulder with bleak eyes.

"Vote," Ross said.

"Up," Mickey said. "Take us up. I'd rather die than stay here."

Ross's throat moved. Then he took a deep breath and squared his shoulders.

"All right," he said quietly. "We'll go up."

"God have mercy on us," Mickey muttered as Ross went quickly to the control board.

The captain hesitated a moment. Then he threw switches. The great ship began shuddering as gasses ignited and began to pour like channeled lightning from the rear vents. The sound was almost soothing to Mason. He didn't care anymore; he was willing, like Mickey, to take a chance. It had only been a few hours. It had seemed like a year. Minutes had dragged, each one weighted with oppressive recollections. Of the bodies they'd seen, of the shattered rocket—even more of the Earth they would never see, of parents and wives and sweethearts and children. Lost to their sight forever. No, it was far better to try to get back. Sitting and waiting was always the hardest thing for a man to do. He was no longer conditioned for it.

Mason sat down at his board. He waited tensely. He heard Mickey jump up and move over to the engine control board.

"I'm going to take us up easy," Ross said to them. "There's no reason why we should . . . have any trouble."

He paused. They snapped their heads over and looked at him with muscle-tight impatience.

"Are you both ready?" Ross asked.

"*Take us up*," Mickey said.

Ross jammed his lips together and shoved over the switch that read: *Vertical Rise*.

They felt the ship tremble, hesitate. Then it moved off the ground, headed up with increasing velocity. Mason flicked on the rear viewer. He watched the dark earth recede, tried not to look at the white patch in the corner of the screen, the patch that shone metallically under the moonlight.

"Five hundred," he read. "Seven-fifty . . . one thousand . . . fifteen hundred . . ."

He kept waiting. For explosion. For an engine to give out. For their rise to stop.

They kept moving up.

"Three thousand," Mason said, his voice beginning to betray the rising sense of elation he felt. The planet was getting farther and farther away. The other ship was only a memory now. He looked across at Mickey. Mickey was staring, open-mouthed, as if he were about ready to shout out *"Hurry!"* but was afraid to tempt the fates.

"Six thousand . . . *seven thousand!*" Mason's voice was jubilant. "We're *out* of it!"

Mickey's face broke into a great, relieved grin. He ran a hand over his brow and flicked great drops of sweat on the deck.

"God," he said, gasping, "my God."

Mason moved over to Ross's seat. He clapped the captain on the shoulder.

"We made it," he said. "Nice flying."

Ross looked irritated.

"We shouldn't have left," he said. "It was nothing all the time. Now we have to start looking for another planet." He shook his head. "It wasn't a good idea to leave," he said.

Mason stared at him. He turned away shaking his head, thinking . . . you can't win.

"If I ever see another glitter," he thought aloud, "I'll keep my big mouth shut. To hell with alien races anyway."

Silence. He went back to his seat and picked up his graph chart. He let out a long shaking breath. Let Ross complain, he thought, I can take anything now. Things are normal again. He began to figure casually what might have occurred down there on that planet.

Then he happened to glance at Ross.

Ross was thinking. His lips were pressed together. He said something to himself. Mason found the captain looking at him.

"Mason," he said.

"What?"

"Alien race, you said."

Mason felt a chill flood through his body. He saw the big head nod once in decision. Unknown decision. His hands started to shake. A crazy idea came. No, Ross wouldn't do that, not just to assuage vanity. Would he?

"I don't . . ." he started. Out of the corner of his eye he saw Mickey watching the captain too.

"*Listen*," Ross said. "I'll tell you what happened down there. I'll *show* you what happened!"

They stared at him in paralyzing horror as he threw the ship around and headed back.

"What are you doing!" Mickey cried.

"Listen," Ross said. "Didn't you understand me? Don't you see how we've been tricked?"

They looked at him without comprehension. Mickey took a step toward him.

"Alien race," Ross said. "That's the short of it. That time-space idea is all wet. But I'll tell you what idea isn't all wet. So we leave the place. What's our first instinct as far as reporting it? Saying it's uninhabitable? We'd do more than that. We wouldn't report it at all."

"Ross, you're not taking us back!" Mason said, standing up suddenly as the full terror of returning struck him.

"You bet I am!" Ross said, fiercely elated.

"You're crazy!" Mickey shouted at him, his body twitching, his hands clenched at his sides menacingly.

"Listen to me!" Ross roared at them. "Who would be benefited by us not reporting the existence of that planet?"

They didn't answer. Mickey moved closer.

"Fools!" he said. "Isn't it obvious? There *is* life down there. But life that isn't strong enough to kill us or chase us away with force. So what can they do? They don't want us there. So what can they do?"

He asked them like a teacher who cannot get the right answers from the dolts in his class.

Mickey looked suspicious. But he was curious now, too, and a little timorous as he had always been with his captain, except in moments of greatest physical danger. Ross had always led them, and it was hard to rebel against it even when it seemed he was trying to kill them all. His eyes moved to the viewer where the planet began to loom beneath them like a huge dark ball.

"We're alive," Ross said, "and I say there never *was* a ship down there. We saw it, sure. We *touched* it. But you can see anything if you believe it's there! All your senses can tell you there's something when there's nothing. All you have to do is *believe* it!"

"What are you *getting* at?" Mason asked hurriedly, too frightened to realize. His eyes fled to the altitude gauge. Seventeen thousand . . . sixteen thousand . . . sixteen-fifty . . .

"Telepathy," Ross said, triumphantly decisive. "I say those men or whatever they are, saw us coming. And they didn't want us there. So they read our minds and saw the death fear, and they decided that the best way to scare us away was to show us our ship crashed and ourselves dead in it. And it worked . . . until now."

"So it worked!" Mason exploded. "Are you going to take a chance on killing us just to prove your damn theory?"

"It's *more* than a theory!" Ross stormed, as the ship fell, then Ross added with the distorted argument of injured vanity, "my orders say to pick up specimens from every planet. I've always followed orders before and, by God, I still will!"

"You saw how cold it was!" Mason said. "No one can live there anyway! Use your head, Ross!"

"Damn it, *I'm* captain of this ship!" Ross yelled, "and I give the orders!"

"Not when our lives are in your hands!" Mickey started for the captain.

"Get back!" Ross ordered.

That was when one of the ship's engines stopped and the ship yawed wildly.

"You fool!" Mickey exploded, thrown off balance. "You *did* it, you *did* it!"

Outside the black night hurtled past.

The ship wobbled violently. *Prediction true* was the only phrase Mason could think of. His own vision of the screaming, the numbing horror, the exhortations to a deaf heaven—all coming true. That hulk would be this ship in a matter of minutes. Those three bodies would be . . .

"Oh . . . *damn!*" He screamed it at the top of his lungs, furious at the enraging stubbornness of Ross in taking them back, of causing the future to be as they saw—all because of insane pride.

"No, they're not going to fool us!" Ross shouted, still holding fast to his last idea like a dying bulldog holding its enemy fast in its teeth.

He threw switches and tried to turn the ship. But it wouldn't turn. It kept plunging down like a fluttering leaf. The gyroscope couldn't keep up with the abrupt variations in cabin equilibrium and the three of them found themselves being thrown off balance on the tilting deck.

"Auxiliary engines!" Ross yelled.

"It's no use!" Mickey cried.

"*Damn it!*" Ross clawed his way up the angled deck, then crashed heavily against the engine board as the cabin inclined the other way. He threw switches over with shaking fingers.

Suddenly Mason saw an even spout of flame through the rear viewer again. The ship stopped shuddering and headed straight down. The cabin righted itself.

Ross threw himself into his chair and shot out furious hands to turn the ship about. From the floor Mickey looked at him with a blank, white face. Mason looked at him too, afraid to speak.

"Now shut up!" Ross said disgustedly, not even looking at them, talking like a disgruntled father to his sons. "When we get down there you're going to see that it's true. That ship'll be gone. And we're going to go looking for those bastards who put the idea in our minds!"

They both stared at their captain numbly as the ship headed down backwards. They watched Ross's hands move efficiently over the controls. Mason felt a sense of confidence in his captain. He stood on the deck quietly, waiting for the landing without fear. Mickey got up from the floor and stood beside him, waiting.

The ship hit the ground. It stopped. They had landed again. They were still the same. And . . .

"Turn on the spotlight," Ross told them.

Mason threw the switch. They all crowded to the port. Mason wondered for a second how Ross could possibly have landed in the same spot. He hadn't even appeared to be following the calculations made on the last landing.

They looked out.

Mickey stopped breathing. And Ross' mouth fell open.

The wreckage was still there.

They had landed in the same place and they had found the wrecked ship still there. Mason turned away from the port and stumbled over the deck. He felt lost, a victim of some terrible universal prank, a man accursed.

"You said . . ." Mickey said to the captain.

Ross just looked out of the port with unbelieving eyes.

"Now we'll go up again," Mickey said, grinding his teeth. "And we'll *really* crash this time. And we'll be killed. Just like those . . . those . . ."

Ross didn't speak. He stared out of the port at the refutation of his last clinging hope. He felt hollow, void of all faith in belief in sensible things.

Then Mason spoke.

"We're not going to crash—" he said somberly "—ever."

"What?"

Mickey was looking at him. Ross turned and looked too.

"Why don't we stop kidding ourselves?" Mason said. "We all know what it is, don't we?"

He was thinking of what Ross had said just a moment before. About the senses giving evidence of what was believed. Even if there was nothing there at all . . .

Then, in a split second, with the knowledge, he saw Ross and he saw Carter. As they were. And he took a short shuddering breath, a last breath until illusion would bring breath and flesh again.

"Progress," he said bitterly and his voice was an aching whisper in the phantom ship. "The Flying Dutchman takes to the universe."

THE LAST DAY

HE WOKE UP AND THE FIRST THING HE THOUGHT was—*the last night is gone.*

He had slept through half of it.

He lay there on the floor and looked up at the ceiling. The walls still glowed reddish from the outside light. There was no sound in the living room but that of snoring.

He looked around.

There were bodies sprawled out all over the room. They were on the couch, slumped on chairs, curled up on the floor. Some were covered with rugs. Two of them were naked.

He raised up on one elbow and winced at the shooting pains in his head. He closed his eyes and held them tightly shut for a moment. Then he opened them again. He ran his tongue over the inside of his dry mouth. There was still a stale taste of liquor and food in his mouth.

He rested on his elbow as he looked around the room again, his mind slowly registering the scene.

Nancy and Bill lying in each other's arms, both naked. Norman curled up in an arm chair, his thin face taut as he slept. Mort and Mel lying on the floor, covered with dirty throw rugs. Both snoring. Others on the floor.

Outside the red glow.

He looked at the window and his throat moved. He blinked. He looked down over his long body. He swallowed again.

I'm alive, he thought, and it's all true.

He rubbed his eyes. He took a deep breath of the dead air in the apartment.

He knocked over a glass as he struggled to his feet. The liquor and soda sloshed over the rug and soaked into the dark blue weave.

He looked around at the other glasses, broken, kicked over, hurled against the wall. He looked at the bottles all over, all empty.

He stood staring around the room. He looked at the record player overturned, the albums all strewn around, jagged pieces of records in crazy patterns on the rug.

He remembered.

It was Mort who had started it the night before. He had suddenly rushed to the playing record machine and shouted drunkenly.

"What the hell is music anymore! Just a lot of noise!"

And he had driven the point of his shoe against the front of the record player and knocked it against the wall. He had lurched over and down on his knees. He had struggled up with the player in his beefy arms and heaved the entire thing over on its back and kicked it again.

"The hell with music!" he had yelled. "I hate the crap anyway!"

Then he'd started to drag records out of their jackets and snap them over his kneecap.

"Come on!" he'd yelled to everybody. "Come on!"

And it had caught on. The way all crazy ideas had caught on in these last few days.

Mel had jumped up from making love to a girl. He had flung records out the windows, scaling them far across the street. And Charlie had put aside his gun for a moment to stand at the windows too and try to hit people in the street with thrown records.

Richard had watched the dark saucers bounce and shatter on the sidewalks below. He'd even thrown one himself. Then he'd just turned away and let the others rage. He'd taken Mel's girl into the bedroom and had sex with her.

He thought about that as he stood waveringly in the reddish light of the room.

He closed his eyes a moment.

Then he looked at Nancy and remembered taking her too sometime in the jumble of wild hours that had been yesterday and last night.

She looked vile now, he thought. She'd always been an animal. Before, though, she'd had to veil it. Now, in the final twilight of everything she could revel in the only thing she'd ever really cared about.

He wondered if there were any people left in the world with real dignity. The kind that was still there when it no longer was necessary to impress people with it.

He stepped over the body of a sleeping girl. She had on only a slip. He looked down at her tangled hair, at her red lips smeared, the tight unhappy frown printed on her face.

He glanced into the bedroom as he passed it. There were three girls and two men in the bed.

He found the body in the bathroom.

It was thrown carelessly in the tub and the shower curtain torn down to cover it. Only the legs showed, dangling ridiculously over the front rim of the tub.

He drew back the curtain and looked at the blood-soaked shirt, at the white, still face.

Charlie.

He shook his head, then turned away and washed his face and hands at the sink. It didn't matter. Nothing mattered. As a matter of fact, Charlie was one of the lucky ones now. A member of the legion who had put their heads into ovens, or cut their wrists or taken pills or done away with themselves in the accepted fashions of suicide.

As he looked at his tired face in the mirror he thought of cutting his wrists. But he knew he couldn't. Because it took more than just despair to incite self-destruction.

He took a drink of water. Lucky, he thought, there's still water running. He didn't suppose there was a soul left to run the water system. Or the electric system or the gas system or the telephone system or any system for that matter.

What fool would work on the last day of the world?

Spencer was in the kitchen when Richard went in.

He was sitting in his shorts at the table looking at his hands. On the stove some eggs were frying. The gas was working then too, Richard thought.

"Hello," he said to Spencer.

Spencer grunted without looking up. He stared at his hands. Richard let it go. He turned the gas down a little. He took bread out of the cupboard and put it in the electric toaster. But the toaster didn't work. He shrugged and forgot about it.

"What time is it?"

Spencer was looking at him with the question.

Richard looked at his watch.

"It stopped," he said.

They looked at each other.

"Oh," Spencer said. Then he asked, "What day is it?"

Richard thought. "Sunday, I think," he said.

"I wonder if people are at church," Spencer said.

"Who cares?"

Richard opened the refrigerator.

"There aren't any more eggs," Spencer said.

Richard shut the door.

"No more eggs," he said dully, "No more chickens. No more anything."

He leaned against the wall with a shuddering breath and looked out the window at the red sky.

Mary, he thought. Mary, who I should have married. Who I let go. He wondered where she was. He wondered if she were thinking about him at all.

Norman came trudging in, groggy with sleep and hangover. His mouth hung open. He looked dazed.

"Morning," he slurred.

"Good morning, merry sunshine," Richard said, without mirth.

Norman looked at him blankly. Then he went over to the sink and washed out his mouth. He spit the water down the drain.

"Charlie's dead," he said.

"I know," Richard said.

"Oh. When did it happen?"

"Last night," Richard told him. "You were unconscious. You remember how he kept saying he was going to shoot us all? Put us out of our misery?"

"Yeah," Norman said. "He put the muzzle against my head. He said feel how cool it is."

"Well, he got in a fight with Mort," Richard said. "The gun went off." He shrugged. "That was it."

They looked at each other without expression.

Then Norman turned his head and looked out the window.

"It's still up there," he muttered.

They looked up at the great flaming ball in the sky that crowded out the sun, the moon, the stars.

Norman turned away, his throat moving. His lips trembled and he clamped them together.

"Jesus," he said. "It's *today*."

He looked up at the sky again.

"Today," he repeated. "*Everything*."

"Everything," said Richard.

Spencer got up and turned off the gas. He looked down at the eggs for a moment. Then he said, "What the hell did I fry these for?"

He dumped them into the sink and they slid greasily over the white surface. The yolks burst and spurted smoking, yellow fluid over the enamel.

Spencer bit his lips. His face grew hard.

"I'm taking her again," he said, suddenly.

He pushed past Richard and dropped his shorts off as he turned the corner into the hallway.

"There goes Spencer," Richard said.

Norman sat down at the table. Richard stayed at the wall.

In the living room they heard Nancy suddenly call out at the top of her strident voice.

"Hey, wake up everybody! Watch me do it! Watch me everybody, *watch me!*"

Norman looked at the kitchen doorway for a moment. Then something gave inside of him and he slumped his head forward on his arms on the table. His thin shoulders shook.

"I did it too," he said brokenly. "I did it too. Oh God, what did I come here for?"

"Sex," Richard said. "Like all the rest of us. You thought you could end your life in carnal, drunken bliss."

Norman's voice was muffled.

"I can't die like that," he sobbed. "I can't."

"A couple of billion people are doing it," Richard said. "When the sun hits us, they'll still be at it. What a sight."

The thought of a world's people indulging themselves in one last orgy of animalism made him shudder. He closed his eyes and pressed his forehead against the wall and tried to forget.

But the wall was warm.

Norman looked up from the table.

"Let's go home," he said.

Richard looked at him. "Home?" he said.

"To our parents. My mother and father. Your mother."

Richard shook his head.

"I don't want to," he said.

"But I can't go alone."

"Why?"

"Because . . . I can't. You know how the streets are full of guys just *killing* everybody they meet."

Richard shrugged.

"Why don't you?" Norman asked.

"I don't want to see her."

"Your *mother*?"

"Yes."

"You're crazy," Norman said. "Who else is there to . . ."

"No."

He thought of his mother at home waiting for him. Waiting for him on the last day. And it made him ill to think of him delaying, of maybe never seeing her again.

But he kept thinking—How can I go home and have her try to make me pray? Try to make me read from the Bible, spend these last hours in a muddle of religious absorption?

He said it again for himself.

"*No.*"

Norman looked lost. His chest shook with a swallowed sob.

"I want to see my mother," he said.

"Go ahead," Richard said, casually.

But his insides were twisting themselves into knots. To never see her again. Or his sister and her husband and her daughter.

Never to see any of them again.

He sighed. It was no use fighting it. In spite of everything, Norman was right. Who else was there in the world to turn to? In a wide world, about to be burned, was there any other person who loved him above all others?

"Oh . . . all right," he said. "Come on. Anything to get out of this place."

The apartment house hall smelled of vomit. They found the janitor dead drunk on the stairs. They found a dog in the foyer with its head kicked in.

They stopped as they came out the entrance of the building.

Instinctively they looked up.

At the red sky, like molten slag. At the fiery wisps that fell like hot rain drops through the atmosphere. At the gigantic ball of flame that kept coming closer and closer that blotted out the universe.

They lowered their watering eyes. It hurt to look. They started walking along the street. It was very warm.

"December," Richard said. "It's like the tropics."

As they walked along in silence, he thought of the tropics, of the poles, of all the world's countries he would never see. Of all the things he would never do.

Like hold Mary in his arms and tell her, as the world was ending, that he loved her very much and was not afraid.

"*Never*," he said, feeling himself go rigid with frustration.

"What?" Norman said.

"Nothing. Nothing."

As they walked, Richard felt something heavy in his jacket pocket, It bumped against his side. He reached in and drew out the object.

"What's that?" Norman asked.

"Charlie's gun," Richard said. "I took it last night so nobody else would get hurt."

His laughter was harsh.

"So nobody else would get hurt," he said bitterly. "Jesus, I ought to be on the stage."

He was about to throw it away when he changed his mind. He slid it back into his pocket.

"I may need it," he said.

Norman wasn't listening.

"Thank God nobody stole my car. Oh . . . !"

Somebody had thrown a rock through the windshield.

"What's the difference?" Richard said.

"I . . . none, I suppose."

They got into the front seat and brushed the glass off the cushion. It was stuffy in the car. Richard pulled off his jacket and threw it out. He put the gun in his side pants pocket.

As Norman drove downtown, they passed people in the street.

Some were running around wildly, as if they were searching for something. Some were fighting with each other. Strewn all over the sidewalks were bodies of people who had leaped from windows and been struck down by speeding cars. Buildings were on fire, windows shattered from the explosions of unlit gas jets.

There were people looting stores.

"What's the matter with them?" Norman asked, miserably. "Is that how they want to spend their last day?"

"Maybe that's how they spent their whole life," Richard answered.

He leaned against the door and gazed at the people they passed. Some of them waved at him. Some cursed and spat. A few threw things at the speeding car.

"People die the way they lived," he said. "Some good, some bad."

"Look out!"

Norman cried out as a car came careening down the street on the wrong side. Men and women hung out of the window shouting and singing and waving bottles.

Norman twisted the wheel violently and they missed the car by inches.

"Are they crazy!" he said.

Richard looked out through the back window. He saw the car skid, saw it get out of control and go crashing into a store front and turn over on its side, the wheels spinning crazily.

He turned back front without speaking. Norman kept looking ahead grimly, his hands on the wheel, white and tense.

Another intersection.

A car came speeding across their path. Norman jammed on the brakes with a gasp. They crashed against the dashboard, getting their breath knocked out.

Then, before Norman could get the car started again, a gang of teenage boys with knives and clubs came dashing into the intersection. They'd been chasing the other car. Now they changed direction and flung themselves at the car that held Norman and Richard.

Norman threw the car into first and gunned across the street.

A boy jumped on the back of the car. Another tried

for the running board, missed and went spinning over the street. Another jumped on the running board and grabbed the door handle. He slashed at Richard with a knife.

"Gonna kill ya bastids!" yelled the boy. "Sonsabitches!"

He slashed again and tore open the back of the seat as Richard jerked his shoulder to the side.

"Get out of here!" Norman screamed, trying to watch the boy and the street ahead at the same time.

The boy tried to open the door as the car wove wildly up Broadway. He slashed again but the car's motion made him miss.

"I'll *get ya!*" he screamed in a fury of brainless hate.

Richard tried to open the door and knock the boy off, but he couldn't. The boy's twisted white face thrust in through the window. He raised his knife.

Richard had the gun now. He shot the boy in the face.

The boy flung back from the car with a dying howl and landed like a sack of rocks. He bounced once, his left leg kicked and then he lay still.

Richard twisted around.

The boy on the back was still hanging on, his crazed face pressed against the back window. Richard saw his mouth moving as the boy cursed.

"Shake him off!" he said.

Norman headed for the sidewalk, then suddenly veered back into the street. The boy hung on. Norman did it again. The boy still clung to the back.

Then on the third time he lost his grip and went off. He tried to run along the street but his momentum was too great and he went leaping over the curb and crashing into a plate glass window, arms stuck up in front of him to ward off the blow.

They sat in the car, breathing heavily. They didn't talk for a long while. Richard flung the gun out the window and watched it clatter on the concrete and bounce off a hydrant. Norman started to say something about it, then stopped.

The car turned onto Fifth Avenue and started downtown at sixty miles an hour. There weren't many cars.

They passed churches. People were packed inside them. They overflowed out onto the steps.

"Poor fools," Richard muttered, his hands still shaking.

Norman took a deep breath.

"I wish I was a poor fool," he said. "A poor fool who could believe in something."

"Maybe," Richard said. Then he added, "I'd rather spend the last day believing what I think is true."

"The last day," Norman said, "I . . ."

He shook his head. "I can't believe it," he said. "I read the papers. I see that . . . thing up there. I know it's going to happen. But, God! The *end?*"

He looked at Richard for a split second.

"Nothing afterward?" he said.

Richard said, "I don't know."

At 14th Street, Norman drove to the East Side, then sped across the Manhattan Bridge. He didn't stop for anything, driving around bodies and wrecked cars. Once he drove over a body and Richard saw his face twitch as the wheel rolled over the dead man's leg.

"They're all lucky," Richard said. "Luckier than we are."

They stopped in front of Norman's house in downtown Brooklyn. Some kids were playing ball in the street. They didn't seem to realize what was happening. Their shouts sounded very loud in the silent street. Richard wondered if their parents knew where the children were. Or cared.

Norman was looking at him.

"Well . . . ?" he started to say.

Richard felt his stomach muscles tightening. He couldn't answer.

"Would you . . . like to come in for a minute?" Norman asked.

Richard shook his head.

"No," he said. "I better get home. I . . . should see her. My mother, I mean."

"Oh."

Norman nodded. Then he straightened up. He forced a momentary calm over himself.

"For what it's worth, Dick," he said, "I consider you my best friend and . . ."

He faltered. He reached out and gripped Richard's hand. Then he pushed out of the car, leaving the keys in the ignition.

"So long," he said hurriedly.

Richard watched his friend run around the car and move for the apartment house. When he had almost reached the door, Richard called out.

"Norm!"

Norman stopped and turned. The two of them looked at each other. All the years they had known each other seemed to flicker between them.

Then Richard managed to smile. He touched his forehead in a last salute.

"So long, Norm," he said.

Norman didn't smile. He pushed through the door and was gone.

Richard looked at the door for a long time. He started the motor. Then he turned it off again thinking that Norman's parents might not be home.

After a while he started it again and began the trip home.

As he drove, he kept thinking.

The closer he got to the end, the less he wanted to face it. He wanted to end it now. Before the hysterics started.

Sleeping pills, he decided. It was the best way. He had some at home. He hoped there were enough left. There might not be any left in the corner drug store. There'd been a rush for sleeping pills during those last few days. Entire families took them together.

He reached the house without event. Overhead the sky was an incandescent crimson. He felt the heat on his face like waves from a distant oven. He breathed in the heated air.

He unlocked the front door and walked in slowly.

I'll probably find her in the front room, he thought. Surrounded by her books, praying, exhorting invisible powers to succor her as the world prepared to fry itself.

She wasn't in the front room.

He searched the house. And, as he did so, his heart began to beat quickly and when he knew she really wasn't there he felt a great hollow feeling in his stomach. He knew that his talk about not wanting to see her had been just talk. He loved her. And she was the only one left now.

He searched for a note in her room, in his, in the living room.

"Mom," he said, "Mom, where are you?"

He found the note in the kitchen. He picked it up from the table.

Richard, Darling.

I'm at your sister's house. Please come there. Don't make me spend the last day without you. Don't make me leave this world without seeing your dear face again. Please.

The last day.

There it was in black and white. And, of all people, it had been his mother to write down the words. She who had always been so skeptical of his taste for material science. Now admitting that science's last prediction.

Because she couldn't doubt anymore. Because the sky was filled with flaming evidence and no one could doubt anymore.

The whole world going. The staggering detail of evolutions and revolutions, of strifes and clashes, of endless continuities of centuries streaming back into the clouded past, of rocks and trees and animals and men. All to pass. In a flash, in a moment. The pride, the vanity of man's world incinerated by a freak of astronomical disorder.

What point was there to all of it then? None, none at all. Because it was all ending.

He got some sleeping pills from the medicine cabinet

and left. He drove to his sister's house thinking about his mother as he passed through the streets littered with everything from empty bottles to dead people.

If only he didn't dread the thought of arguing with his mother on this last day. Of disputing with her about her God and her conviction.

He made up his mind not to argue. He'd force himself to make their last day a peaceful one. He would accept her simple devotion and not hack at her faith anymore.

The front door was locked at Grace's house. He rang the bell and, after a moment, heard hurried steps inside.

He heard Ray shout inside, "Don't open it Mom! It may be that gang again!"

"It's Richard, I know it is!" his mother called back.

Then the door was open and she was embracing him and crying happily.

He didn't speak. Finally he said softly,

"Hello Mom."

His niece Doris played all afternoon in the front room while Grace and Ray sat motionless in the living room looking at her.

If I were with Mary, Richard kept thinking. If only we were together today. Then he thought they might have had children. And he would have to sit like Grace and know that the few years his child had lived would be its only years.

The sky grew brighter as evening approached. It flowed with violent crimson currents. Doris stood quietly at the window and looked at it. She hadn't laughed all day or cried. And Richard thought to himself—she *knows*.

And thought too that at any moment his mother would ask them all to pray together. To sit and read the Bible and hope for divine charity.

But she didn't say anything. She smiled. She made supper. Richard stood with her in the kitchen as she made supper.

"I may not wait," he told her. "I . . . may take sleeping pills."

"Are you afraid, son?" she asked.

"Everybody is afraid," he said.

She shook her head. "Not everybody," she said.

Now, he thought, it's coming. That smug look, the opening line.

She gave him a dish with the vegetable and they all sat down to eat.

During supper none of them spoke except to ask for food. Doris never spoke once. Richard sat looking at her from across the table.

He thought about the night before. The crazy drinking, the fighting, the carnal abuses. He thought of Charlie dead in the bathtub. Of the apartment in Manhattan. Of Spencer driving himself into a frenzy of lust at the climax to his life. Of the boy lying dead in the New York gutter with a bullet in his brain.

They all seemed very far away. He could almost believe it had all never happened. Could almost believe that this was just another evening meal with his family.

Except for the cherry glow that filled the sky and flooded in through the windows like an aura from some fantastic fireplace.

Near the end of the meal Grace went and got a box. She sat down at the table with it and opened it. She took out white pills. Doris looked at her, her large eyes searching.

"This is dessert," Grace told her. "We're all going to have white candy for dessert."

"Is it peppermint?" Doris asked.

"Yes," Grace said. "It's peppermint."

Richard felt his scalp crawling as Grace put pills in front of Doris. In front of Ray.

"We haven't enough for all of us," she said to Richard.

"I have my own," he said.

"Have you enough for Mom?" she asked.

"I won't need any," her mother said.

In his tenseness, Richard almost shouted at her. Shouted—Oh stop being so damned noble! But he held himself. He stared in fascinated horror at Doris holding the pills in her small hand.

"This isn't peppermint," she said. "Momma this isn't . . ."

"*Yes it is.*" Grace took a deep breath. "Eat it, darling."

Doris put one in her mouth. She made a face. Then she spit it into her palm.

"It *isn't* peppermint," she said, upset.

Grace threw up her hand and buried her teeth in the white knuckles. Her eyes moved frantically to Ray.

"Eat it, Doris," Ray said. "Eat it, it's good."

Doris started to cry. "No, I don't like it."

"*Eat it!*"

Ray turned away suddenly, his body shaking.

Richard tried to think of some way to make her eat the pills but he couldn't.

Then his mother spoke.

"We'll play a game, Doris," she said. "We'll see if you can swallow all the candy before I count ten. If you do I'll give you a dollar."

Doris sniffed. "A dollar?" she said.

Richard's mother nodded.

"One," she said.

Doris didn't move.

"Two," said Richard's mother. "A *dollar* . . ."

Doris brushed aside a tear. "A . . . whole dollar?"

"Yes, darling. Three, four, hurry up."

Doris reached for the pills.

"Five . . . six . . . seven . . ."

Grace had her eyes shut tightly. Her cheeks were white.

"Nine . . . ten . . ."

Richard's mother smiled but her lips trembled and there was a glistening in her eyes.

"There," she said cheerfully. "You've won the game."

Grace suddenly put pills into her mouth and swallowed them in fast succession. She looked at Ray. He reached out one trembling hand and swallowed his pills. Richard put his hand in his pocket for his pills but took it out again. He didn't want his mother to watch him take them.

Doris got sleepy almost immediately. She yawned and couldn't keep her eyes open. Ray picked her up and she rested against his shoulder, her small arms around his neck. Grace got up and the three of them went back into the bedroom.

Richard sat there while his mother went back and said goodbye to them. He sat staring at the white table cloth and the remains of food.

When his mother came back she smiled at him.

"Help me with the dishes," she said.

"The . . . ?" he started. Then he stopped. What difference did it make what they did?

He stood with her in the redlit kitchen, feeling a sense of sharp unreality as he dried the dishes they would never use again and put them in the closet that would be no more in a matter of hours.

He kept thinking about Ray and Grace in the bedroom. Finally he left the kitchen without a word and went back. He opened the door and looked in. He looked at the three of them for a long time. Then he shut the door again and walked slowly back to the kitchen. He stared at his mother.

"They're . . ."

"All right," his mother said.

"Why didn't you say anything to them?" he asked her. "How come you let them do it without saying anything?"

"Richard," she said, "everyone has to make his own way on this day. No one can tell others what to do. Doris was their child."

"And I'm yours . . . ?"

"You're not a child any longer," she said.

He finished up the dishes, his fingers numb and shaking.

"Mom, about last night," he said.

"I don't care about it," she said.

"But . . ."

"It doesn't matter," she said. "This part is ending."

Now, he thought, almost with pain. *This* part. Now she would talk about afterlife and heaven and reward for the just and eternal penitence for the sinning.

She said, "Let's go out and sit on the porch."

He didn't understand. He walked through the quiet house with her. He sat next to her on the porch steps and thought. I'll never see Grace again. Or Doris. Or Norman or Spencer or Mary or anybody . . .

He couldn't take it all in. It was too much. All he could do was sit there woodenly and look at the red sky and the huge sun about to swallow them. He couldn't even feel nervous any more. Fears were blunted by endless repetition.

"Mom," he said after a while, "why . . . why haven't you spoken about religion to me? I know you must want to."

She looked at him and her face was very gentle in the red glow.

"I don't have to, darling," she said. "I know we'll be together when this is over. You don't have to believe it. I'll believe for both of us."

And that was all. He looked at her, marveling at her confidence and her strength.

"If you want to take those pills now," she said, "it's all right. You can go to sleep in my lap."

He felt himself tremble. "You wouldn't mind?"

"I want you to do what you think is best."

He didn't know what to do until he thought of her sitting there alone when the world ended.

"I'll stay with you," he said impulsively.

She smiled.

"If you change your mind," she said, "you can tell me."

They were quiet for a while. Then she said,

"It *is* pretty."

"*Pretty?*" he asked.

"Yes," she said, "God closes a bright curtain on our play."

He didn't know. But he put his arm around her shoulders and she leaned against him. And he did know one thing.

They sat there in the evening of the last day. And, though there was no actual point to it, they loved each other.

LITTLE GIRL LOST

TINA'S CRYING WOKE ME UP IN A SECOND. IT was pitch black, middle of the night. I heard Ruth stir beside me in bed. In the front room Tina caught her breath, then started in again, louder.

"Oh, gawd," I muttered groggily.

Ruth grunted and started to push back the covers.

"I'll get it," I said wearily and she slumped back on the pillow. We take turns when Tina has her nights; has a cold or a stomachache or just takes a flop out of bed.

I lifted up my legs and dropped them over the edge of the blankets. Then I squirmed myself down to the foot of the bed and slung my legs over the edge. I winced as my feet touched the icy floor boards. The apartment was arctic, it usually is these winter nights, even in California.

I padded across the cold floor threading my way between the chest, the bureau, the bookcase in the hall and then the edge of the TV set as I moved into the living room. Tina sleeps there because we could only get a one bedroom apartment. She sleeps on a couch that breaks down into a bed. And, at that moment, her crying was getting louder and she started calling for her mommy.

"All right. Tina. Daddy'll fix it all up," I told her.

She kept crying. Outside, on the balcony, I heard our collie Mack jump down from his bed on the camp chair.

I bent over the couch in the darkness. I could feel that the covers were lying flat. I backed away, squinting at the floor but I didn't see any Tina moving around.

"Oh, my God," I chuckled to myself, in spite of irritation, "the poor kid's under the couch."

I got down on my knees and looked, still chuckling at the thought of little Tina falling out of bed and crawling under the couch.

"Tina, where are you?" I said, trying not to laugh.

Her crying got louder but I couldn't see her under the couch. It was too dark to see clearly.

"Hey, where are you, kiddo?" I asked. "Come to papa."

Like a man looking for a collar button under the bureau I felt under the couch for my daughter, who was still crying and begging for mommy, mommy.

Came the first twist of surprise. I couldn't reach her no matter how hard I stretched.

"Come *on*, Tina," I said, amused no longer, "stop playing games with your old man."

She cried louder. My outstretched hand jumped back as it touched the cold wall.

"Daddy!" Tina cried.

"Oh for . . . !"

I stumbled up and jolted irritably across the rug. I turned on the lamp beside the record player and turned to get her, and was stopped dead in my tracks, held there, a half-asleep mute, gaping at the couch, ice water plaiting down my back.

Then, in a leap, I was on my knees by the couch and my eyes were searching frantically, my throat getting tighter and tighter. I heard her crying under the couch, but I couldn't see her.

My stomach muscles jerked in as the truth of it struck me. I ran my hands around wildly under the bed but they didn't touch a thing. I heard her crying and by God, she wasn't there!

"Ruth!" I yelled. "Come here!"

I heard Ruth catch her breath in the bedroom and then there was a rustle of bedclothes and the sound of her feet rushing across the bedroom floor. Out of the corners of my eyes I saw the movement of her light blue nightgown.

"What is it?" she gasped.

I backed to my feet, hardly able to breathe much less speak. I started to say something but the words choked up in my throat. My mouth hung open. All I could do was point a shaking finger at the couch.

"Where is she!" Ruth cried.

"I don't know!" I finally managed. "See . . ."

"*What!*"

Ruth dropped to her knees beside the couch and looked under.

"Tina!" she called.

"Mommy."

Ruth recoiled from the couch, color draining from

her face. The eyes she turned to me were horrified. I suddenly heard the sound of Mack scratching wildly at the door.

"Where *is* she?" Ruth asked again, her voice hollow.

"I don't know," I said, feeling numb. "I turned on the light and . . ."

"But she's *crying*," Ruth said as if she felt the same distrust of sight that I did. "I . . . Chris, *listen*."

The sound of our daughter crying and sobbing in fright.

"Tina!" I called loudly, pointlessly, "Where *are* you, angel?"

She just cried. "Mommy!" she said. "Mommy, pick me up!"

"No, no, this is crazy," Ruth said, her voice tautly held as she rose to her feet, "she's in the kitchen."

"But . . ."

I stood there dumbly as Ruth turned on the kitchen light and went in. The sound of her agonized voice made me shudder.

"Christ! *She's not in here.*"

She came running in, her eyes stark with fear. She bit her teeth into her lip.

"But, where *is* . . . ?" she started to say, then stopped.

Because we both heard Tina crying and the sound of it was coming from under the couch.

But there wasn't anything under the couch.

Still Ruth couldn't accept the crazy truth. She jerked open the hall closet and looked in it. She looked behind the TV set, even behind the record player, a space of maybe two inches.

"Honey, *help* me," she begged, "we can't just leave her this way."

I didn't move.

"Honey, she's under the couch," I said.

"But she's not!"

Once more, like the crazy, impossible dream it was, me on my knees on the cold floor, feeling under the couch, I got *under* the couch. I touched every inch of floor space there. But I couldn't touch her, even though I heard her crying—*right in my ear.*

I got up, shivering from the cold and something else. Ruth stood in the middle of the living room rug staring at me. Her voice was weak, almost inaudible.

"Chris," she said, "Chris, what *is* it?"

I shook my head. "Honey, I don't know," I said, "I don't know what it is."

Outside, Mack began to whine as he scratched. Ruth glanced at the balcony door, her face a white twist of fear. She was shivering now in her silk gown as she looked back at the couch. I stood there absolutely helpless, my mind racing a dozen different ways, none of them toward a solution, not even toward concrete thought.

"What are we going to do?" she asked, on the verge of a scream I knew was coming.

"Baby, I . . ."

I stopped short and suddenly we were both moving for the couch.

Tina's crying was fainter.

"Oh, no," Ruth whimpered. "No. *Tina.*"

"Mommy," said Tina, further away. I could feel the chills lacing over my flesh.

"Tina, come back here!" I heard myself shouting,

the father yelling at his disobedient child, who can't be seen.

"TINA!" Ruth screamed.

Then the apartment was dead silent and Ruth and I were kneeling by the couch looking at the emptiness underneath. Listening.

To the sound of our child, peacefully snoring.

"Bill, can you come right over?" I said frantically.

"What?" Bill's voice was thick and fuzzy.

"Bill, this is Chris. Tina has disappeared!"

He woke up.

"She's been kidnaped?" he asked.

"No," I said. "She's here but . . . she's not here."

He made a confused sound. I grabbed in a breath.

"Bill, for God's sake get over here!"

A pause.

"I'll be right over," he said. I knew from the way he said it he didn't know why he was coming.

I dropped the receiver and went over to where Ruth was sitting on the couch shivering and clasping her hands tightly in her lap.

"Hon, get your robe," I said. "You'll catch cold."

"Chris, I . . ." Tears running down her cheeks. "Chris where *is* she?"

"Honey."

It was all I could say, hopelessly, weakly. I went into the bedroom and got her robe. On the way back, I stooped over and twisted hard on the wall heater.

"There," I said, putting the robe over her back, "put it on."

She put her arms through the sleeves of the robe, her eyes pleading with me to do something. Knowing very well I couldn't do it, she was asking me to bring her baby back.

I got on my knees again, just to be doing something. I knew it wouldn't help any. I remained there a long time just staring at the floor under the couch. Completely in the dark.

"Chris, she's s-sleeping on the floor," Ruth said, her words faltering from colorless lips. "Won't she catch *cold?*"

"I . . ."

That was all I could say. What could I tell her? No, she's not on the floor? How did I know? I could hear Tina breathing and snoring gently on the floor but she wasn't there to touch. She was gone but she wasn't gone. My brain twisted back and forth on itself trying to figure out that one. Try adjusting to something like that sometime. It's a fast way to a breakdown.

"Honey, she's . . . she's not here," I said. "I mean . . . not on the floor."

"But . . ."

"I know, I know . . ." I raised my hands and shrugged in defeat. "I don't think she's cold, honey," I said as gently and persuasively as I could.

She started to say something too but then she stopped. There was nothing to say. It defied words.

We sat in the quiet room waiting for Bill to come. I'd called him because he's an engineering man, Cal Tech, top man with Lockheed over in the valley. I don't know why I thought that would help but I called him. I'd have called anyone just to have another mind to help. Parents are useless beings when they're afraid for their children.

Once, before Bill came, Ruth slipped to her knees

by the couch and started slapping her hands over the floor.

"Tina, wake up!" she cried in newborn terror. *"Wake up!"*

"Honey, what good is that going to do?" I asked.

She looked up at me blankly and knew. It wasn't going to do any good at all.

I heard Bill on the steps and reached the door before he did. He came in quietly, looking around and giving Ruth a brief smile. I took his coat. He was still in pajamas.

"What is it, kid?" he asked hurriedly.

I told him as briefly and as clearly as I could. He got down on his knees and checked for himself. He felt around underneath the couch and I saw his brow knit into lines when he heard Tina's calm and peaceful breathing.

He straightened up.

"Well?" I asked.

He shook his head. "My *God*," he muttered.

We both stared at him. Outside Mack was still scratching and whining at the door.

"Where *is* she?" Ruth asked again. "Bill, I'm about to lose my mind."

"Take it easy," he said. I moved beside her and put my arm around her. She was trembling.

"You can hear her breathing," Bill said. "It's normal breathing. She must be all right."

"But where is she?" I asked. "You can't see her, you can't even *touch* her."

"I don't know," Bill said and was on his knees by the bed again.

"Chris, you'd better let Mack in," Ruth said, worried about that for a moment, "he'll wake all the neighbors."

"All right, I will," I said and kept watching Bill.

"Should we call the police?" I asked. "Do you . . . ?"

"No, no, that wouldn't do any good," Bill said, "this isn't . . ." He shook his head as if he were shaking away everything he'd ever accepted. "It's not a police job," he said.

"Chris, he'll wake up all the . . ."

I turned for the door to let Mack in.

"*Wait a minute,*" Bill said and I was turned back, my heart pounding again.

Bill was half under the couch, listening hard.

"Bill, what is . . . ?" I started.

"*Shhh!*"

We were both quiet. Bill stayed there a moment longer. Then he straightened up and his face was blank.

"I can't hear her," he said.

"Oh, *no!*"

Ruth fell forward before the couch.

"Tina! Oh, God, where *is* she!"

Bill was up on his feet, moving quickly around the room. I watched him, then looked back at Ruth slumped over the couch, sick with fear.

"Listen," Bill said, "do you hear anything?"

Ruth looked up. "*Hear* . . . anything?"

"Move around, move around," Bill said. "See what you hear."

Like robots Ruth and I moved around the living room having no idea what we were doing. Everything was quiet except for the incessant whining and scratching of Mack. I gritted my teeth and muttered a terse—"*Shut up!*"—as I passed the balcony door. For a second the vague idea crossed my mind that Mack knew about Tina. He'd always worshiped her.

Then there was Bill standing in the corner where the closet was, stretching up on his toes and listening. He noticed us watching him and gestured quickly for us to come over. We moved hurriedly across the rug and stood beside him.

"Listen," he whispered. We did.

At first there was nothing. Then Ruth gasped and none of us were letting out the noise of breath.

Up in the corner, where the ceiling met the walls, we could hear the sound of Tina sleeping.

Ruth stared up there, her face white, totally lost.

"Bill, what the . . ." I gave up.

Bill just shook his head slowly. Then suddenly he held up his hand and we all froze, jolted again.

The sound was gone.

Ruth started to sob helplessly. "*Tina.*"

She started out of the corner.

"We have to find her," she said despairingly. "*Please.*"

We ran around the room in unorganized circles, trying to hear Tina. Ruth's tear-streaked face was twisted into a mask of fright.

I was the one who found her this time.

Under the television set.

We all knelt there and listened. As we did, we heard her murmur a little to herself and the sound of her stirring in sleep.

"Want my dolly," she muttered.

"*Tina!*"

I held Ruth's shaking body in my arms and tried to stop her sobbing. Without success. I couldn't keep my own throat from tightening, my heart from pounding slow and hard in my chest. My hands shook on her back, slick with sweat.

"For God's sake, *what is it?*" Ruth said but she wasn't asking us.

Bill helped me take her to a chair by the record player. Then he stood restlessly on the rug, gnawing furiously on one knuckle, the way I'd seen him do so often when he was engrossed in a problem.

He looked up, started to say something then gave it up and turned for the door.

"I'll let the pooch in," he said. "He's making a hell of a racket."

"Don't you have any idea what might have happened to her?" I asked.

"*Bill . . . ?*" Ruth begged.

Bill said, "I think she's in another dimension," and he opened the door.

What happened next came so fast we couldn't do a thing to stop it.

Mack came bounding in with a yelp and headed straight for the couch.

"He *knows!*" Bill yelled and dived for the dog.

Then the crazy part happened. One second Mack was sliding under the couch in a flurry of ears, paws and tail. Then he was gone—*just like that*. Blotted up. The three of us gaped.

Then I heard Bill say, "Yes. *Yes.*"

"Yes, *what?*" I didn't know where *I* was by then.

"The kid's in another dimension."

"What are you talking about?" I said in worried, near-angry tones. You don't hear talk like that everyday.

"Sit down," he said.

"Sit down? Isn't there anything we can do?"

Bill looked hurriedly at Ruth. She seemed to know what he was going to say.

"I don't know if there is," was what he said.

I slumped back on the couch.

"Bill," I said. Just speaking his name.

He gestured helplessly.

"Kid," he said, "this has caught me as wide open as you. I don't even know if I'm right or not but I can't think of anything else. I think that in some way, she's gotten herself into another dimension, probably the fourth. Mack, sensing it, followed her there. But how did they get there?—I don't know. I was under that couch, so were you. Did you see anything?"

I looked at him and he knew the answer.

"Another . . . *dimension?*" Ruth said in a tight voice. The voice of a mother who has just been told her child is lost forever.

Bill started pacing, punching his right fist into his palm.

"Damn, damn," he muttered. "How do things like this happen?"

Then while we sat there numbly, half listening to him, half for the sound of our child, he spoke. Not to us really. To himself, to try and place the problem in the proper perspective.

"One dimensional space, a line," he threw out the words quickly. "Two dimensional space, an infinite number of lines—an infinite number of one dimen-

sional spaces. Three dimensional space an infinite number of planes—an infinite number of two dimensional
spaces. Now the basic factor . . . the *basic* factor . . ."

He slammed his palm and looked up at the ceiling.
Then he started again, more slowly now.

"Every point in each dimension a *section* of a line
in the next higher dimension. All points in line are *sections* of the perpendicular lines that make the line a
plane. All points in plane are sections of perpendicular lines that make the plane a solid.

"That means that in the third dimension . . ."

"Bill, for God's sake!" Ruth burst out. "Can't we *do*
something? My *baby* is in . . . in *there*."

Bill lost his train of thought. He shook his head.

"Ruth, I don't . . ."

I got up then and was down on the floor again,
climbing under the couch. I *had* to find it! I felt, I
searched. I listened until the silence rang. Nothing.

Then I jerked up suddenly and hit my head as Mack
barked loudly in my ear.

Bill rushed over and slid in beside me, his breath
labored and quick.

"God's sake," he muttered, almost furiously. "Of
all the damn places in the world . . ."

"If the . . . the *entrance* is here," I muttered, "why
did we hear her voice and breathing all over the
room?"

"Well, if she moved beyond the effect of the third
dimension and was entirely in the fourth—then her
movement, for us, would seem to spread over all space.
Actually she'd be in one spot in the fourth dimension
but to us . . ."

He stopped.

Mack was whining. But more importantly Tina started in again. Right by our ears.

"He brought her back!" Bill said excitedly. "Man, what a mutt!"

He started twisting around, looking, touching, slapping at empty air.

"We've got to find it!" he said. "We've got to reach in and pull them out. God knows how long this dimension pocket will last."

"What?" I heard Ruth gasp, then suddenly cry, "Tina, where are you? This is mommy."

I was about to say something about it being no use but then Tina answered.

"Mommy, mommy! Where are you, mommy?"

Then the sound of Mack growling and Tina crying angrily.

"She's trying to run around and find Ruth," Bill said. "But Mack won't let her. I don't know *how* but he seems to know where the joining place is."

"Where *are* they for God's sake!" I said in a nervous fury.

And backed right into the damn thing.

To my dying day I'll never really be able to describe what it was like. But here goes.

It was black, yes—to *me*. And yet there seemed to be a million lights. But as soon as I looked at one it disappeared and was gone. I saw them out of the sides of my eyes.

"Tina," I said, "where are you? Answer me! Please!"

And heard my voice echoing a million times, the words echoing endlessly, never ceasing but moving off as if they were alive and traveling. And when I moved my hand the motion made a whistling sound that echoed and reechoed and moved away like a swarm of insects flowing into the night.

"Tina!"

The sound of the echoing hurt my ears.

"Chris, can you hear her?" I heard a voice. But was it a voice—or more like a thought?

Then something wet touched my hand and I jumped.

Mack.

I reached around furiously for them, every motion making whistling echoes in vibrating blackness until I felt as if I were surrounded by a multitude of birds flocking and beating insane wings around my head. The pressure pounded and heaved in my brain.

Then I felt Tina. I say I felt her but I think if she wasn't my daughter and if I didn't *know* somehow it was her, I would have thought I'd touched something else. Not a shape in the sense of third dimension shape. Let it go at that, I don't want to go into it.

"Tina," I whispered. "Tina, baby."

"Daddy, I'm scared of dark," she said in a thin voice and Mack whined.

Then I was scared of dark too, because a thought scared my mind.

How could I get us all out?

Then the other thought came—Chris, have you got them?

"I've got them!" I called.

And Bill grabbed my legs (which, I later learned, were still sticking out in the third dimension) and jerked me back to reality with an armful of daughter and dog and memories of something I'd prefer having no memories about.

We all came piling out under the couch and I hit my head on it and almost knocked myself out. Then I was being alternately hugged by Ruth, kissed by the dog and helped to my feet by Bill. Mack was leaping on all of us, yelping and drooling.

When I was in talking shape again I noticed that Bill had blocked off the bottom of the couch with two card tables.

"Just to be safe," he said.

I nodded weakly. Ruth came in from the bedroom.

"Where's Tina?" I asked automatically, uneasy left-overs of memory still cooking in my brain.

"She's in our bed," she said. "I don't think we'll mind for one night."

I shook my head.

"I don't think so," I said.

Then I turned to Bill.

"Look," I said. "What the hell happened?"

"Well," he said, with a wry grin, "I told you. The third dimension is just a step below the fourth. In particular, every point in our space is a section of a perpendicular to every point in the fourth dimension. They wouldn't be parallel—to us. But if enough of them *in one area* happened to be parallel in *both* dimensions—it might form a connecting corridor."

"You mean . . . ?"

"That's the crazy part," he said. "Of all the places in the world—under the couch—there's an area of points that are sections of parallel lines—parallel in both dimensions. They make a corridor into the next space.

"Or a hole," I said.

Bill looked disgusted.

"Hell of a lot of good my reasoning did," he said. "It took a *dog* to get her out."

I groaned softly.

"You can have it," I said.

"Who wants it?" he answered.

"What about the sound?"

"You're asking me?" he said.

That's about it. Oh, naturally, Bill told his friends at Cal Tech, and the apartment was overrun with research physicists for a month. But they didn't find anything. They said the thing was gone. Some said worse things.

But, just the same, when we got back from my mother's house where we stayed during the scientific siege—we moved the couch across the room and stuck the television where the couch was.

So some night we may look up and hear Arthur Godfrey chuckling from another dimension. Maybe he belongs there.

TRESPASS

IN THE HALL HE PUT DOWN HIS SUITCASE. "HOW have you been?" he asked.

"Fine" she said, with a smile.

She helped him off with his coat and hat and put them in the hall closet.

"This Indiana January sure feels cold after six months in South America."

"I bet it does," she said.

They walked into the living room, arms around each other.

"What have you been doing with yourself?" he asked.

"Oh . . . not too much," she said. "Thinking about you."

He smiled and hugged her.

"That's a lot," he said.

Her smile flickered a moment, then returned. She held his hand tightly. And, suddenly, although he didn't realize it at first, she was wordless. He'd gone over this moment in his mind so often that the sharpness of its anticlimax later struck him. She smiled and looked into his eyes while he spoke but the smile kept fading and her eyes kept evading his at the very moments he wanted their attention most.

Later in the kitchen she sat across from him as he drank the third cup of her hot, rich coffee.

"I won't sleep tonight," he said, grinning, "but I don't want to."

Her smile was only obliging. The coffee burned his throat and he noticed she wasn't drinking any of the first cup she'd poured for herself.

"No coffee for you?" he asked.

"No, I . . . I don't drink it anymore."

"On a diet or something?"

He saw her throat move.

"Sort of," she said.

"That's silly," he said. "Your figure is perfect."

She seemed about to say something. Then she hesitated. He put down his cup.

"Ann, is . . ."

"Something wrong?" she finished.

He nodded.

She lowered her eyes. She bit her lower lip and clasped her hands before her on the table. Then her eyes closed and he got the feeling that she was shutting herself away from something hopelessly terrible.

"Honey, what is it?"

"I guess . . . the best way is to just . . . just up and tell you."

"Well, of course, sweetheart," he said anxiously. "What is it? Did something happen while I was gone?"

"Yes. And no."

"I don't understand."

She was looking at him suddenly. The look was haunted and it made him shudder.

"I'm going to have a baby," she said.

He was about to cry out—but that's wonderful. He was about to jump up and embrace her and dance her around the room.

Then it hit him, driving the color from his face.

"What?" he said.

She didn't answer because she knew he'd heard.

"How . . . long have you known this?" he asked, watching her eyes hold motionless on his face.

She drew in a shaking breath and he knew her answer would be the wrong one. It was.

"Three weeks," she said.

He sat there looking blankly at her and stirring the coffee without realizing. Then he noticed and, slowly, he drew out the spoon and put it down beside the cup.

He tried to say the word but he couldn't. It trembled in his vocal cords. He tensed himself.

"Who?" he asked her, his voice toneless and weak.

Her eyes were back on him, her face ashen. Her lips trembled when she told him.

She said, "No one."

"*What?*"

"David," she said carefully, "I . . ."

Then her shoulders slumped.

"No one, David. No one."

It took a moment for the reaction to hit him. She saw it on his face before he turned it away from her. Then she stood up and looked down at him, her voice shaking.

"David, I swear to God I never had anything to do with any man while you were gone!"

He sank back numbly against the chair back. God, Oh God, what could he say? A man comes back from six months in the jungle and his wife tells him she's pregnant and asks him to believe that . . .

His teeth set on edge. He felt as if he were involved in the beginning of some hideously smutty joke. He swallowed and looked down at his trembling hands. Ann, Ann! He wanted to pick up his cup and hurl it against the wall.

"David, you've got to bel—"

He stumbled up and out of the room. She was behind him quickly, clutching for his hand.

"David, you've *got* to believe me. I'll go insane if you don't. It's the only strength that's kept me going—the hope that you'd believe me. If you don't . . ."

Her words broke off and they stared bleakly at each other. He felt her hand holding his. Cold.

"Ann, what do you want me to believe? That my child was conceived five months after I left you?"

"David, if I were guilty would I . . . be so *open* in telling you? You know how I feel about our marriage. About you."

Her voice lowered.

"If I'd done what you think I've done, I wouldn't tell you," she said, "I'd kill myself."

He kept looking helplessly at her, as if the answer lay in her anxious face. Finally he spoke.

"We'll . . . go to Doctor Kleinman," he said. "We'll . . ."

Her hand dropped away from his.

"You don't believe me, do you?"

His voice was tortured.

"You know what you're asking of me, don't you?"

he said. "Don't you, Ann? I'm a scientist. I can't accept the incredible . . . just like that. Don't you think I *want* to believe you? But . . ."

She stood before him a long time. Then she turned away a little and her voice was well controlled.

"All right," she said quietly, "do what you think is best."

Then she walked out of the room. He watched her go. Then he turned and walked slowly to the mantel. He stood looking at the kewpie doll sitting there with its legs hanging down over the edge. *Coney Island* read the words on her dress. They'd won it on their honeymoon trip eight years before.

His eyes fell shut suddenly.

Homecoming.

The word was a dead word now.

"Now that the welcomes are done for," said Doctor Kleinman, "what are you doing here? Catch a bug in the jungle?"

Collier sat slumped in the chair. For a few seconds he glanced out the window. Then he turned back to Kleinman and told him quickly.

When he'd finished they looked at each other for a silent moment.

"It's *not* possible, is it?" Collier said then.

Kleinman pressed his lips together. A grim smile flickered briefly on his face.

"What can I say?" he said. "No, it's impossible? No, not as far as observation goes? I do not know, David. We assume that the sperm survives in the cervix canal no more than three to five days, maybe a little longer. But, even if they do . . ."

"They can't fertilize?" Collier finished.

Kleinman didn't nod or answer but Collier knew the answer. Knew it in simple words that were pronouncing doom on his life.

"There's no hope then," he said quietly.

Kleinman pressed his lips together again and ran a reflective finger along the edge of his letter opener.

"Unless," he said, "it is to speak to Ann and make her understand you will not desert her. It is probably fear which makes her speak as she does."

". . . will not desert her," Collier echoed in an inaudible whisper and shook his head.

"I suggest nothing, mind you," Kleinman went on. "Only that it is possible Ann is too hysterically frightened to tell you the truth."

Collier rose, drained of vitality.

"All right," he said indecisively, "I'll speak to her again. Maybe we can . . . work it out."

But when he told her what Kleinman had said she just sat in the chair and looked at him without expression on her face.

"And that's it," she said. "You've decided."

He swallowed.

"I don't think you know what you're asking of me," he said.

"Yes, I know what I'm asking," she answered. "Just that you believe in me."

He started to speak in rising anger, then checked himself.

"Ann," he said, "just *tell* me. I'll do my best to understand."

Now she was losing temper too. He watched her hands tighten, then tremble on her lap.

"I hate to spoil your noble scene," she said, "but I'm not pregnant by another man. Do you understand me—believe me?"

She wasn't hysterical now or frightened or on the defensive. He stood there looking down at her, feeling numb and confused. She never had lied to him before and yet . . . what was he to think?

She went back to her reading then and he kept standing and watching her. These are the facts, his mind insisted. He turned away from her. Did he really know Ann? Was it possible she was something entirely strange to him now? Those six months?

What had happened during those six months?

He stood making up the living-room couch with sheets and the old comforter they had used when they were first married. As he looked down at the thick quilting and the gaudy patterns now faded from *innumerable* washings, a grim smile touched his lips.

Homecoming.

He straightened up with a tired sigh and walked over to where the record player scratched gently. He lifted the arm up and put on the next record. He looked at the inside cover of the album as Tchaikovsky's *Swan Lake* started.

To my very own darling. Ann.

They hadn't spoken all afternoon or evening. After supper she'd gotten a book from the case and gone upstairs. He'd sat in the living room trying to read *The Fort Tribune,* trying even harder to relax. Yet how could he? Could a man relax in his home with his wife who carried a child that wasn't his? The newspaper had finally slipped from his lax fingers and fallen to the floor.

Now he sat staring endlessly at the rug, trying to figure it out.

Was it possible the doctors were wrong? Could the life cell exist and maintain its fertilizing capacity for, not days, but months? Maybe, he thought, he'd rather believe that than believe Ann could commit adultery. Theirs had always been an ideal relationship, as close an approximation of The Perfect Marriage as one could allow possible. Now this.

He ran a shaking hand through his hair. Breath shuddered through him and there was a tightness in his chest he could not relieve. A man comes home from six months in the . . .

Put it out of your mind!—he ordered himself, then forced himself to pick up the paper and read every word in it including comics and the astrology column. *You will receive a big surprise today*, the syndicated seer told him.

He flung down the paper and looked at the mantel clock. After ten. He'd been sitting there over an hour while Ann sat up in bed reading. He wondered what book was taking the place of affection and understanding.

He rose wearily. The record player was scratching again.

After brushing his teeth he went out into the hall and started for the stairs. At the bedroom door he hesitated, glanced in. The light was out. He stopped and listened to her breathing and knew she wasn't asleep.

He almost started in as a rushing sense of need for

her covered him. But then he remembered that she was going to have a baby and it couldn't possibly be his baby. The thought made him stiffen. It turned him around, thin-lipped, and took him down the stairs and he slapped down the wall switch to plunge the living room into darkness.

He felt for the couch and sank down on it. He sat for a while in the dark, smoking a cigarette. Then he pressed the stub into an ashtray and lay back. The room was cold. He climbed under the sheets and comforter and lay there shivering. *Homecoming*. The word oppressed him again.

He must have slept a little while, he thought, staring up at the black ceiling. He held up his watch and looked at the luminous hands. Three-twenty. He grunted and rolled onto his side. Then he raised up and shook the pillow to puff it up.

He lay there thinking of her. Six months away and here, on the first night home, he was on the living room couch while she lay upstairs in bed. He wondered if she were frightened. She still had a little fear of the darkness left over from her childhood. She used to hug against him and press her cheek against his shoulder and go to sleep with a happy sigh.

He tortured himself thinking about it. More than anything else he wanted to rush up the stairs and crawl in beside her, feel her warm body against him. Why don't you? asked his sleepy mind. Because she's carrying someone else's child, came the obedient answer. Because she's sinned.

He twisted his head impatiently on the pillow. *Sinned*. The word sounded ridiculous. He rolled onto his back again and reached for a cigarette. He lay there smoking slowly, watching the glowing tip move in the blackness.

It was no use. He sat up swiftly and fumbled for the ashtray. He had to have it out with her, that was all. If he reasoned with her, she'd tell him what had happened. Then they'd have something to go on. It was better that way.

Rationalization, said his mind. He ignored it as he trudged up the icy steps and hesitated outside the bedroom.

He went in slowly, trying to remember how the furniture was placed. He found the small nightlamp on the bureau and turned the knob. The tiny glow pushed away darkness from itself.

He shivered under his heavy robe. The room was freezing, all the windows open wide. But, as he turned, he saw Ann lying there clad only in a thin nightgown. He moved quickly to the bed and pulled the bedclothes up over her, trying not to look at her body. Not now, he thought, not at a time like this. It would distort everything.

He stood over the bed and watched her sleep. Her hair was spread darkly over the pillow. He looked at her white skin, her soft red lips. She's a beautiful woman, he almost spoke the words aloud.

He turned his head away. All right, the word was ridiculous but it was true. What else would you call the betrayal of marriage? Was there a better word than sinned?

His lips tightened. He was remembering how she'd always wanted a baby. Well, she had one now.

He noticed the book next to her on the bed and

picked it up. *Basic Physics.* What on earth was she reading that for? She'd never shown the remotest interest in the sciences except for perhaps a little sociology, a smattering of anthropology. He looked down curiously at her.

He wanted to wake her up but he couldn't. He knew he'd be struck dumb as soon as her eyes opened. I've been thinking, I want to discuss this sensibly, his mind prompted. It sounded like a soap opera line.

That was the crux of it, the fact that he was incapable of discussing it with her sensibly or not. He couldn't leave her, neither could he thrash it out as he'd planned. He felt a tightening of anger at his vacillation. Well, he defended angrily, how can a man adjust to such a circumstance? A man comes home from six months in . . .

He moved back from the bed and sank down on the small chair that stood beside the bureau. He sat there shivering a little and watching her face. It was such a childlike face, so innocent.

As he watched, she stirred in her sleep, writhing uncomfortably under the blankets. A whimper moved her lips, then suddenly, her right hand reached up and heaved the blankets aside so that they slid off the edge of the bed. Her feet kicked them away completely. Then a great sigh trembled her body and she rolled onto her side and slept, despite the shivering that began almost immediately.

Again he stood, dismayed at her actions. She'd never been a restless sleeper. Was it a habit she'd acquired while he was gone? It's guilt—his mind said, disconcertingly. He twitched at the infuriating idea and, walking over to the bed, he tossed the blankets over her roughly.

When he straightened up he saw that her eyes were on him. He started to smile, then wrenched it from his lips.

"You're going to get pneumonia if you keep throwing off the bedclothes," he said irritably.

She blinked. "What?" she said.

"I *said* . . ." he started, then stopped. There was too much anger piling up in him. He fought it off.

"You're kicking off the blankets," he said, in a flat voice.

"Oh," she said, "I . . . I've been doing it for about a week now."

He looked at her. What now?—the thought came.

"Would you get me a drink of water?" she asked.

He nodded, glad for the excuse to take his eyes from her. He padded into the hall and bathroom and ran the water until it got cold, then filled up the glass.

"Thank you," she said softly as he handed it to her.

"Welcome."

She drank all of it in one swallow then looked up guiltily.

"Would you . . . mind getting me another one?"

He looked at her for a moment, then took the glass and brought her another drink. She drank it just as quickly.

"What have you been eating?" he asked, feeling a strange tightness at finally talking to her about such an irrelevant topic.

"Salt . . . I guess," she said.

"You must have had an awful lot."

"I have, David."

"That's not good."

"I know." She looked at him imploringly.

"What do you want—*another* glass?" he asked.

She lowered her eyes. He shrugged. He didn't think it was right but he didn't care to argue about it. He went to the bathroom and got her the third drink. When he got back her eyes were closed. He said, "Here's your water," but she was asleep. He put down the glass.

As he watched her he felt an almost uncontrollable desire to lie beside her, hold her close and kiss her lips and face. He thought of all the nights he'd lain awake in the sweltering tent thinking about Ann. Rolling his head on the pillow almost in agony because she was so far away. He had the same feeling now. And yet, although he stood beside her, he couldn't touch her.

Turning abruptly, he snapped off the nightlamp and left the bedroom. He went downstairs and threw himself down on the couch and dared his brain not to fall asleep. His brain conceded and he fell into a blank, uneasy slumber.

When she came into the kitchen the next morning she was coughing and sneezing.

"What did you do, throw off the blankets again?" he said.

"Again?" she asked.

"Don't you remember me coming up there?"

She looked at him blankly.

"No," she said.

They looked at each other for a moment. Then he went to the cupboard and took out two cups.

"Can you drink coffee?" he asked.

She hesitated a moment. Then she said, "Yes."

He put the cups down on the table, then sat down and waited. When the coffee started spurting up into the glass dome of the pot, Ann stood and picked up a potholder. Collier watched her pour the black, steaming fluid into the cups. Her hand shook a little as she poured his cup and he shrank back to avoid getting splashed.

He waited until she was sitting down, then asked grumpily, "What are you reading *Basic Physics* for?"

Again the blank, uncertain look.

"I don't know," she said. "It just . . . caught my interest for some reason."

He spooned sugar into his coffee and stirred, hearing her pour cream into hers.

"I . . . thought you . . ." He took a breath. "I thought you had to drink skimmed milk. Or something," he said.

"I felt like a cup of coffee."

"I see."

He sat there, looking morosely at the table, drinking the burning coffee in slow sips. He forced himself to sink into a dull, edgeless cloud. He almost forgot she was there. The room disappeared, all its sights and sounds falling away.

Then her cup banged down. He started.

"If you're not going to talk to me, we might as well end it right now!" she said angrily. "If you think I'm going to stick around until you feel like talking to me, you're wrong!"

"What would you like me to do!" he flared back. "If you found out I'd fathered some other woman's child, how would you feel?"

She closed her eyes and a look of strained patience held her face tautly.

"Listen, David," she said, "for the last time, *I have not committed adultery.* I know it spoils your role of the injured spouse but I can't help that. You can make me swear on a hundred Bibles and I'll still tell you the same thing. You can put truth serum in me and I'll tell you the same thing. You can strap me to a lie detector and my story will still be the same. David, I'm . . . !"

She couldn't finish. A spasm of coughing began shaking her body. Her face darkened and tears ran down her cheeks as she gripped the side of the table with whitened fingers, gasping for breath.

For a moment he forgot everything except that she was in pain. He jumped up and ran to the sink for water. Then he patted her back gently while she drank. She thanked him in a choking voice. He patted her back once more, almost longingly.

"You'd better stay in bed today," he said, "that's a bad cough you have. And I'd . . . you'd better pin down the blankets so you don't . . ."

"David, what are you going to do?" she asked unhappily.

"Do?"

She didn't explain.

"I'm . . . not sure, Ann," he said. "I want with all my heart to believe you. But . . ."

"But you can't. Well, that's that."

"Oh, stop jumping to conclusions! Can't you give me some time to work it out? For God's sake, I've only been home one day."

For a brief moment he thought he saw something of the old warmth in her eyes. Maybe she could see, behind his anger, how much he wanted to stay. She picked up her coffee.

"Work it out then," she said. "*I* know what the truth is. If you don't believe me . . . then work it out your own clever way."

"Thank you," he said.

When he left the house she was back in bed, bundled up warmly, coughing and reading *An Introduction To Chemistry*.

"Dave!"

Professor Mead's studious face broke into a grin. He put down the tweezers he'd been moving the microscope slide with and shoved out his right hand. Johnny Mead, former All-American quarterback, was twenty-seven, tall and broad, sporting a perpetual crewcut. He held Collier's hand in a firm grip.

"How's it been, boy?" he asked. "Had enough of those Matto Grosso vermin?"

"More than enough," Collier said, smiling.

"You're looking good, Dave," Mead said. "Nice and tan. You must make quite a sight around this campus of leprous-skinned faculty."

They moved across the wide laboratory toward Mead's office, passing students bent over their microscopes and working the testing instruments. Collier got a momentary feeling of return, then lost it in the irony that he should get the feeling here and not at home.

Mead closed the door and waved Collier to a chair.

"Well, tell me all about it, Dave," he said. "Your daring exploits in the tropics."

Collier cleared his throat.

"Well, if you don't mind, Johnny," he said, "there's something else I want to talk to you about now."

"Fire away, boy."

Collier hesitated.

"Understand now," he said, "I'm telling you this under strictest confidence and only because I consider you my best friend."

Mead leaned forward in his chair, the look of youthful exuberance fading as he saw that Collier was worried.

Collier told him.

"No, Dave," Johnny said when he was finished.

"Listen, Johnny," Collier went on, "I know it sounds crazy. But she's insisted so forcibly that she's innocent that . . . well, frankly, I'm at a loss. Either she's had such an emotional breakdown that her mind has rejected the memory of . . . of . . ."

His hands stirred helplessly in his lap.

"Or?" Johnny said.

Collier took a deep breath.

"Or else she's telling the truth," he said.

"But . . ."

"I know, I know," Collier said. "I've been to our doctor. Kleinman, you know him."

Johnny nodded.

"Well, I've been to him and he said the same thing you don't have to say. That it's impossible for a woman to become pregnant five months after intercourse. I know that but . . ."

"What?"

"Isn't there some other way?"

Johnny looked at him without speaking. Collier's

head dropped forward and his eyes closed. After a moment he made a sound of bitter amusement.

"Isn't there some other way," he mocked himself. "What a stupid question."

"She insists she's had no . . ."

Collier nodded wearily.

"Yes," he said. "She . . . yes."

"I don't know," Johnny said, running the tip of a forefinger over his lower lip. "Maybe she's hysterical. Maybe . . . David, *maybe she isn't pregnant at all.*"

"What!"

Collier's head snapped up, his eyes looking eagerly into Johnny's.

"Don't jump the gun, Dave. I don't want that on my conscience. But, well . . . hasn't Ann always wanted a baby? I think she has—wanted it bad. Well . . . it may be just a crazy theory but I think it's possible that the emotional . . . *drain* of being separated from you for six months could cause a false pregnancy."

A wild hope began to surge in Collier, irrational he knew but one he clutched at, desperately.

"I think you should talk to her again," Johnny said. "Try to get more information from her. Maybe even do what she suggests and try hypnosis, truth serum, anything. But . . . *boy,* don't give up! I *know* Ann. And I trust her."

As he half ran down the street he kept thinking how little credit was due him for finding the trust he needed. But, at least, thank God, he had it for now. It filled him with hope, it made him want to cry out—it has to be true, it *has* to be!

Then, as he turned into the path of the house, he stopped so quickly that he almost fell forward and his breath drew in with a gasp.

Ann was standing on the porch in her nightgown, an icy January wind whipping the fragile silk around the full contours of her body. She stood on the frost-covered boards in her bare feet, one hand on the railing.

"*Oh, my God,*" muttered Collier in a strangled voice as he raced up the path to grab her.

Her flesh was bluish and like ice when he caught her and when he looked into her wide, staring eyes, a bolt of panic drove through him.

He half led, half dragged her into the warm living room and set her down in the easy chair before the fireplace. Her teeth were chattering and breath passed her lips in wheezing gasps. His hands shook as he ran around frantically getting blankets, plugging in the heating pad and placing it under her icy feet, breaking up wood with frenzied motions and starting a fire, making hot coffee.

Finally, when he'd done everything he could, he knelt before her and held her frigid hands in his. And, as he listened to the shivering of her body reflected in her breath, a sense of utter anguish wrenched at his insides.

"Ann, Ann, what's the *matter* with you?" he almost sobbed. "Are you out of your mind?"

She tried to answer but could not. She huddled beneath the blankets, her eyes pleading with him.

"You don't have to talk, sweetheart," he said. "It's all right."

"I . . . I . . . I . . . h-*had to go out,*" she said.

And that was all. He stayed there before her, his eyes never leaving her face. And, even though she was shaking and gripped by painful seizures of coughing, she seemed to realize his faith in her because she smiled at him and, in her eyes, he saw that she was happy.

By supper time she had a raging fever. He put her in bed and gave her nothing to eat but all the water she wanted. Her temperature fluctuated, her flushed burning skin becoming cold and clammy in almost seconds.

Collier called Kleinman about six and the doctor arrived fifteen minutes later. He went directly to the bedroom and checked Ann. His face became grave and he motioned Collier into the hall.

"We must get her to the hospital," he said quietly.

Then he went downstairs and phoned for an ambulance. Collier went back in to the bedside and stood there holding her limp hand, looking down at her closed eyes, her feverish skin. Hospital, he thought, oh my God, the hospital.

Then a strange thing happened.

Kleinman returned and beckoned once more for Collier to come out in the hall. They stood there talking until the downstairs bell rang. Then Collier went down to let them in and the two orderlies and the intern followed him up the stairs carrying their stretcher.

They found Kleinman standing by the bed staring down at Ann in speechless amazement.

Collier ran to him.

"What is it!" he cried.

Kleinman lifted his head slowly.

"She is cured," he said in awed tones.

"What?"

The intern moved quickly to the bed. Kleinman spoke to him and to Collier.

"The fever is gone," he said. "Her temperature, her respiration, her pulse beat—all are normal. She has been completely cured of pneumonia in . . ."

He checked his pocket watch.

"*In seventeen minutes,*" he said.

Collier sat in Kleinman's waiting room staring sightlessly at the magazine in his lap. Inside, Ann was being x-rayed.

There was no doubt anymore, Ann was pregnant. X-rays at six weeks had shown the fetus inside her. Once more their relationship suffered from doubt. He was still concerned for her health but, once more, was unable to speak to her and tell her that he believed in her. And, though he'd never actually told her of his renewed doubt, Ann had felt it. She avoided him at home, sleeping half the time, the other half reading omniverously. He still couldn't understand that. She'd gone through all his books on the physical sciences, then his texts on sociology, anthropology, philosophy, semantics, history and now she was reading geography books. There seemed no sense to it.

And, all during this period, while the form in her body changed from a small lump to a pear shape, to a globe, then an ovoid—she'd been eating an excess of salt. Doctor Kleinman kept warning her about it. Collier had tried to stop her but she wouldn't stop. Eating salt seemed a compulsion.

As a result she drank too much water. Now her weight

had come to the point where the over-size fetus was pressing against her diaphragm causing breathing difficulty.

Just yesterday Ann's face had gone blue and Collier had rushed her to Kleinman's office. The doctor had done something to ease the condition. Collier didn't know what. Then Ann had been x-rayed and Kleinman told Collier to bring her back the next day.

The door opened and Kleinman led Ann out of his office.

"Sit, my dear," he told her. "I want to talk to David."

Ann walked past Collier without looking at him and sat down on the leather couch. As he stood, he noticed her reaching for a magazine. *The Scientific American.* He sighed and shook his head as he walked into Kleinman's office.

As he moved for the chair, he thought, for what seemed the hundredth time, of the night she'd cried and told him she had to stay because there was no place else to go. Because she had no money of her own and her family was dead. She'd told him that if it wasn't for the fact that she was innocent she'd probably kill herself for the way he was treating her. He had stood beside the bed, silent and tense, while she cried, unable to argue, to console, even to reply. He'd just stood there until he could bear it no longer and then walked out of the room.

"What?" he said.

"I say look at these," Kleinman said grimly.

Kleinman's behavior had changed too in the past months, declining from confidence to a sort of confused anger.

Collier looked down at the two x-ray plates, glanced at the dates on them. One was from the day before, the other was the plate Kleinman had just taken.

"I don't . . ." Collier stared.

Kleinman told him, "Look at the size of the child."

Collier compared the plates more carefully. At first he didn't see. Then his startled eyes flicked up suddenly.

"Is it possible?" he said, feeling a crushing sense of the unreal on him.

"It has happened," was all Kleinman said.

"But . . . *how?*"

Kleinman shook his head and Collier saw the doctor's left hand on the desk grip into a fist as if he were angered by this new enigma.

"I have never seen the like of it," Kleinman said. "Complete bone structure by the seventh week. Facial form by the eighth week. Organs complete and functioning by the end of the second month. The mother's insane desire for salt. And now this. . . ."

He picked up the plates and looked at them almost in belligerence.

"How can a child decrease its size?" he said.

Collier felt a pang of fear at the mystified tone in Kleinman's voice.

"It is clear, it is clear," Kleinman shook his head irritably. "The child had grown to excess proportions because of the mother drinking too much water. To such proportions that it was pressing dangerously against her diaphragm. And now, in *one* day, the pressure is gone, the size of the child markedly decreased."

Kleinman's hands snapped into hard fists.

"It is almost," he said nervously, "as if the child knows what is going on."

"No more salt!"

His voice rose in pitch as he jerked the salt shaker from her hand and stamped over to the cupboard. Then he took her glass of water and emptied most of it into the sink. He sat down again.

She sat with her eyes shut, her body trembling. He watched as tears ran slowly from her eyes and down her cheeks. Her teeth bit into her lower lip. Then her eyes opened; they were big, frightened eyes. She caught a sob in the middle and hastily brushed her tears aside. She sat there quietly.

"Sorry," she murmured and, for some reason, Collier got the impression that she wasn't talking to him.

She finished the remaining water in a gulp.

"You're drinking too much water again," he said. "You know what Doctor Kleinman said."

"I . . . try," she said, "but I can't help it. I feel such a need for salt and it makes me so thirsty."

"You'll have to quit drinking so much water," he said coldly. "You'll endanger the child."

She looked startled as her body twitched suddenly. Her hands slipped from the table to press against her swollen stomach. Her look implored him to help her.

"What is it?" he asked hurriedly.

"I don't know," she said. "The baby kicked."

He leaned back, muscles unknotted.

"That's to be expected," he said.

They sat quietly a while. Ann toyed with her food.

Once he saw her reach out automatically for the salt, then raise her eyes in slight alarm when her fingers didn't find the shaker.

"David," she said after a few minutes.

He swallowed his food.

"What?"

"Why have you stayed with me?"

He couldn't answer.

"Is it because you believe me?"

"I don't know, Ann. I don't know."

The look of slight hope on her face left and she lowered her head.

"I thought," she said, "maybe . . . because you were staying . . ."

The crying again. She sat there not even bothering to brush aside the tears that moved slowly down her cheeks and over her lips.

"Oh, *Ann,*" he said, half irritably, half in sorrow.

He got up to go to her. As he did her body twitched again, this time more violently, and her face went blank. Again she cut off her sobs and rubbed at her cheeks with almost angry fingers.

"I can't *help* it," she said slowly and loudly.

Not to him. Collier was sure it was not to him.

"What are you talking about?" he said nervously.

He stood there looking down at his wife. She looked so helpless, so afraid. He wanted to pull her against himself and comfort her. He wanted to . . .

Still sitting, she leaned against his chest while he stroked her soft brown hair.

"Poor little girl," he said. "My poor little girl."

"Oh David, *David*, if only you'd believe me. I'd do anything to make you believe me, anything. I can't stand to have you so cold to me. Not when I know I haven't done anything wrong."

He stood there silently and his mind spoke to him. There is a chance, it said, a chance.

She seemed to guess what he was thinking. Because she looked up at him and there was absolute trust in her eyes.

"Anything, David, *anything*."

"Can you hear me, Ann?" he said.

"Yes," she said.

They were in Professor Mead's office. Ann lay on the couch, her eyes closed. Mead took the needle from Collier's fingers and put it on the desk. He sat on the corner of the desk and watched in grim silence.

"Who am I, Ann?"

"David."

"How do you feel, Ann?"

"Heavy. I feel heavy."

"Why?"

"The baby is so heavy."

Collier licked his lips. Why was he putting it off, asking these extraneous questions? He knew what he wanted to ask. Was he too afraid? What if, despite her insistence on this, she gave the wrong answer?

He gripped his hands together tightly and his throat seemed to become a column of rock.

"Dave, not too long," Johnny cautioned.

Collier drew in a rasping breath.

"Is it . . ." he started, then swallowed with difficulty, "is it . . . *my* child, Ann?"

She hesitated. She frowned. Her eyes flickered open for a second, then shut. Her entire body writhed. She seemed to be fighting the question. Then the color drained from her face.

"*No*," she said through clenched teeth.

Collier felt himself stiffening as if all his muscles and tendons were dough expanding and pushing out his flesh.

"Who's the father?" he asked, not realizing how loud and unnatural his voice was.

At that, Ann's body shuddered violently. There was a clicking sound in her throat and her head rolled limply on the pillow. At her sides, the white fists opened slowly.

Mead jumped over and put his fingers to her wrist. His face was taut as he felt for the pulsebeat. Satisfied, he lifted her right eyelid and peered at the eye.

"She's really out," he said. "I told you it wasn't a good idea to give serum to such a heavily pregnant woman. You should have done it months ago. Klein-man won't like this."

Collier sat there not hearing a word, his face a mask of hopeless distress.

"Is she all right?" he asked.

But the words hardly came out. He felt something shake in his chest. He didn't realize what it was until it was too late. Then he ran shaking hands over his cheeks and stared at the wet fingers with incredulous eyes. His mouth opened, closed. He tried to cut off the sobs but he could not.

He felt Johnny's arm around his shoulders.

"It's all right, boy," Johnny said.

Collier jammed his eyes shut, wishing that his whole body could be swallowed up in the swimming darkness before his gaze. His chest heaved with trembling breaths and he couldn't swallow the lump in his throat. His head kept shaking slowly. My life is ended, he thought, I loved and trusted her and she has betrayed me.

"Dave?" he heard Johnny say.

Collier grunted.

"I don't want to make things worse. But . . . well, there's still a hope, I think."

"Huh?"

"Ann didn't answer your question. She didn't say the father was . . . another man," he finished weakly.

Collier pushed angrily to his feet.

"Oh *shut up*, will you?" he said.

Later they carried her to the car and Collier drove her home.

Slowly he took off his coat and hat and let them drop on the hall chest. Then he shuffled into the living room and sank down on his chair. He lifted his feet to the ottoman with a weary grunt. He sat there, slumped over, staring at the wall.

Where was she?—he wondered. Upstairs reading probably, just as he'd left her this morning. She had a pile of library books by the bed. Rousseau, Locke, Hegel, Marx, Descartes, Darwin, Bergson, Freud, Whitehead, Jeans, Eddington, Einstein, Emerson, Dewey, Confucius, Plato, Aristotle, Spinoza, Kant, Schopenhauer, James—an endless assortment of books.

And the way she read them. As if she were sitting there and rapidly turning the pages without even looking at what was written on them. Yet he knew she was getting it all. Once in a while she'd let a phrase drop, a concept, an idea. She was getting every word.

But why?

Once he had gotten the wild idea that Ann had read something about acquired characteristics and was trying to pass along this knowledge to her unborn child. But he had quickly put aside that idea. Ann was intelligent enough to know that such a thing was patently impossible.

He sat there shaking his head slowly, a habit he'd acquired in the past few months. Why was he still with her? He kept asking himself the question. Somehow the months had slipped by and still he was living in this house. A hundred times he'd started to leave and changed his mind. Finally he'd given up and moved into the back bedroom. They lived now like landlord and tenant.

His nerves were starting to go. He found himself obsessed with an overwhelming impatience. If he was walking from one place to another he would suddenly feel a great rush of anger that he had not already completed the trip. He resented all transport, he wanted things done immediately. He snapped at his pupils whether they rated it or not. His classes were being so poorly conducted that he'd been called before Doctor Peden, the head of the Geology Department. Peden hadn't been too hard on him because he knew about Ann but Collier knew he couldn't go on like this.

His eyes moved over the room. The rug was thick with dust. He'd tried going over it with the vacuum whenever he thought of it, but it piled up too fast to keep pace with. The whole house was going to pot. He had to take care of his laundry. The machine in the basement hadn't been used for months. He didn't want to know how to operate it and Ann never touched it now. He took the clothes to the laundromat downtown.

When he'd commented once on the slovenliness of the house, Ann had looked hurt and started to cry. She cried all the time now and always the same way. First, as if she were going to continue for an hour straight. Then, suddenly, with lurching abruptness, she would stop crying and wipe away the tears. He got the impression sometimes that it had something to do with the child, that she stopped for fear the crying would affect the baby. Or else it was the other way around, he thought, that the baby didn't like . . .

He closed his eyes as if to shut out the thought. His right hand tapped nervously and impatiently on the arm of the chair. He got up restlessly and walked around the room running a forefinger over flat surfaces, wiping the dust off on his handkerchief.

He stood staring malignantly at the heap of dishes in the sink, the unkempt condition of the curtains, the smeared linoleum. He felt like rushing upstairs and letting her know that, pregnancy or no pregnancy, she was going to snap out of this doldrum and act like a wife again or he was leaving.

He started through the dining room, then halfway to the stairs he hesitated, halted completely. He went back to the stove slowly and put the flame on underneath the coffee pot. The coffee would be stale but he'd rather drink it that way than make more.

What was the use? She'd try to talk to him and tell him she understood but then, as if she were under a spell, she'd start to cry. And, after a few moments, she'd get that startled look and stop crying. As a matter of fact she was even beginning to control her tears from the outset. As if she knew that the crying was not going to work so she may as well not start at all.

It was eerie.

The word brought him up short. That was it—eerie. The pneumonia. The decrease in fetal size. The reading. The desire for salt. The crying and the stopping of it.

He found himself staring at the white wall over the stove. He found himself shuddering.

Ann didn't tell us the father was another man.

When he came in she was in the kitchen drinking coffee. Without a word he took the cup from her and poured the remainder of it into the sink.

"You're not supposed to drink coffee," he said.

He looked into the coffee pot. He'd left it almost full that morning.

"Did you drink *all* of it?" he asked angrily.

She lowered her head.

"For God's sake, don't cry," he rasped.

"I . . . I won't," she said.

"Why do you drink coffee when you know you're not supposed to?"

"I just couldn't stand it anymore."

"*Oh-h,*" he said, clenching his teeth. He started out of the room.

"David, I can't help it," she called after him, "I can't drink water. I have to drink *something.* David, can't—can't you! . . ."

He went upstairs and took a shower. He couldn't concentrate on anything. He put down the soap and then forgot where. He stopped shaving before he was done and wiped off the lather. Then, later, while he was combing his hair, he noticed half his face still bearded and, with a muffled curse, he lathered again and finished.

The night was like all the others except for one thing. When he went into the bedroom for clean pajamas he saw that she was having difficulty focusing her eyes. And, while he lay in the back bedroom correcting test papers, he heard her giggling. Later he tossed around for several hours before he slept and all that time she kept giggling at something. He wanted to slam the door shut and drown out the sound but he couldn't. He had to leave the door open in case she needed him during the night.

At last he slept. For how long he didn't know. It seemed only a moment before he lay there blinking up at the dark ceiling.

"Now am I alien and forgotten, 0 lost of traveled night."

First he thought he was dreaming.

"Murk and strangeness, here am I in ever night, hot, hot."

He sat up suddenly then, his heart jolting.

It was Ann's voice.

He threw his legs over the side of the bed and found his slippers. He pushed up quickly and padded to the door, shivering as the cold air chilled the rayon thinness of his pajamas. He moved into the hall and heard her speaking again.

"Dream of goodbyes, forsaken, plunged in swelling liquors, cry I for light, release me from torment and trial."

All spoken in a singsong rhythm, in a voice that was Ann's and not Ann's, more high-pitched, more tense.

She was lying there on her back, her hands pressed to her stomach. It was moving. He watched the flesh ripple under the thinness of her nightgown. She should have been chilled without any blankets but she seemed warm. The bedside lamp was still on, the book—*Science and Sanity, Korzybski*—fallen from her fingers and lying half open on the mattress.

It was her face. Sweat drops dotted it like hundreds of tiny crystals. Her lips were drawn back from her teeth.

Her eyes wide open.

"Kin of the night, sickened of this pit, O send me not to make the way!"

He felt a horrible fascination in standing there listening to her. But she was in pain. It was obvious from her whitened skin, the way her hands, like claws, raked the sheet at her sides into mounds of wadded, sweat-streaked cotton.

"I cry, I cry," she said. *"Rhyuio Gklemmo Fglwo!"*

He slapped her face and her body lurched on the bed.

"He again, the hurting one!"

Her lips spread wide in a scream. He slapped her again and focus came to her eyes. She lay there staring up at him in complete horror. Her hands jumped to her cheeks, pressing against them. She seemed to recoil into the bed. Her pupils shrank to pinpoints in the milk-white of her eyes.

"No," she said. "*No!*"

"Ann, it's me, David! You're all right!"

She looked uncomprehendingly at him for a long moment, her breasts heaving with tortured breaths.

Then, suddenly, she was relaxed and recognized

him. Her lower jaw went slack and a moan of relief filled her throat.

He sat down beside her and took her in his arms. She clung to him, crying, her face into his chest.

"All right, baby, let it out, let it out."

Again. The choking off of sobs, the suddenly dried eyes, the pulling away from him, the blank look.

"What is it?" he asked.

No answer. She stared at him.

"Baby, what *is* it? Why can't you cry?"

Something crossed her face, then slipped away.

"Baby, you should cry."

"I don't want to cry."

"Why not?"

"He won't let me," she blurted out.

Suddenly, they were both silent, staring at each other and, he knew, in an instant, that they were very close to the answer.

"*He?*" he asked.

"No," she said suddenly, "I don't mean it. I don't mean that. I don't mean *he*, I mean something else."

For a long time they sat there looking at each other. Then speaking no more, he made her lie down and covered her up. He got a blanket and stayed the rest of the night in the chair by the bureau. When he woke up in the morning, cramped and cold, he saw that she'd thrown off the blankets again.

Kleinman told him that Ann had adjusted to cold. There seemed to be something added to her system which was sending out heat to her when she needed it.

"And all this salt she takes." Kleinman threw up his hands. "It is beyond sense. You would think the child thrives on a saline diet. Yet she no longer gains excess weight. She does not drink water to combat the thirst. What does she do to ease the thirst?"

"Nothing," Collier said. "She's always thirsty."

"And the reading, it goes on?"

"Yes," said Collier.

"And the talking in her sleep?"

"Yes."

Kleinman shook his head.

"Never in my life," he said, "have I seen a pregnancy like this."

She finished up the last of the huge pile she'd been constantly augmenting. She took all the books back to the library.

A new development began.

She was seven months pregnant. It was May and Collier noticed that the car's oil was filthy, the tires were unnaturally worn, and a dent was in the left rear fender.

"Have you been using the car?" he asked her one Saturday morning. It was in the living room, the phonograph was playing Brahms.

"Why?" she asked. He told her and she said irritably, "If you already know, why do you ask me?"

"Have you?"

"Yes. I've been using the car. Is that permissible?"

"You needn't be sarcastic."

"Oh no," she said angrily. "I needn't get sarcastic. I've been pregnant seven months and not once have you believed that some other man isn't the father. No matter how many times I've told you that I'm innocent, you still won't say—I believe you. And *I'm* sarcastic. Oh, honest, David, you're a panic, a real panic."

She stamped over to the phonograph and turned it off.

"I'm *listening* to it," he said.

"That's too bad. I don't like it."

"Since when?"

"Oh, leave me alone."

He caught her by the wrist as she turned away.

"Listen," he said, "maybe you think the whole thing has been a vacation for me. I come home from six months research and find you pregnant. Not by me! I don't care what you say, I'm *not* the father and I nor anyone else knows any way but one for a woman to get pregnant. Still I haven't left. I've watched you turn into a book-reading machine. I've had to clean the house when I could, cook most of the meals, take care of our clothes—as well as teach every day at the college. I've had to look over you as I would a child, keeping you from kicking off the blankets, keeping you from eating too much salt, from drinking too much water, too much coffee, from smoking too much . . ."

"I've stopped smoking myself," she said, pulling away.

"Why?" he threw at her suddenly. She looked blank.

"Go ahead," he said, "say it. Because *he* doesn't like it."

"I stopped smoking myself," she repeated. "I can't stand them."

"And now you don't like music."

"It . . . hurts my stomach," she said, vaguely.

"Nonsense," he said.

Before he could stop her, she'd gone out the front door into the blazing sunlight. He went to the door and watched her get into the car clumsily. He started to call to her but she'd started the motor and couldn't hear him. He watched the car disappear up the block doing fifty in second gear.

"How long has she been gone now?" Johnny asked.

Collier glanced nervously at his watch.

"I don't know exactly," he said. "Since around nine-thirty, I guess. We'd argued, as I said . . ."

He broke off nervously and checked his watch again. It was past midnight.

"How long has she been driving like this?" Johnny asked.

"I don't know, Johnny. I told you I just found out."

"Doesn't her size . . . ?" started Johnny.

"No, the baby isn't big anymore." Collier spoke the astounding now in a matter-of-fact voice. He ran a shaky hand through his hair.

"You think we should call the police?" he asked.

"Wait a little."

"What if she's had an accident?" Collier said. "She's not the best driver in the world. Why in God's name did I let her go? Seven months pregnant and I let her go driving. Oh, I ought to be . . ."

He felt himself getting ready to crack. All this tension in his house, this strange and endlessly distressing pregnancy—it was getting to him. A man couldn't hold onto tension for seven months and not feel it. He could not keep his hands from shaking anymore. He'd developed a habit of persistent blinking to use up some of the nervous energy.

He paced across the rug to the fireplace and stood there tapping his nails nervously on the shelf.

"I think we should call the police," he said.

"Take it easy," Johnny warned.

"What would you advise?" Collier snapped.

"Sit down. Right there. That's it. Now, relax. She's all right, believe me. I'm not worried about Ann. She's probably had a flat or an engine failure somewhere in the middle of nowhere. How many times have I heard you go on about needing a new battery? It probably died, that's all."

"Well . . . wouldn't the police be able to find her a lot quicker?"

"All right, boy, if it'll make you happier, I'll call them."

Collier nodded, then started up as a car passed in the street. He rushed to the window and drew back the blinds. Then he bit his lips and turned back. He went back to the fireplace while Johnny moved for the hall phone. He listened to Johnny dialing, then twitched as the receiver was put down hurriedly.

"Here she is," Johnny said.

They led her into the front room, dizzy and confused. She didn't answer Collier's frantic questions. She headed straight for the kitchen as if she didn't notice them.

"Coffee," she said in a guttural voice.

At first Collier tried to stop her, then he felt Johnny's hand on his arm.

"Let her go," Johnny said. "It's time we got to the bottom of this."

She stood in front of the stove and turned the flame up high under the coffee pot. She ladled in careless spoonfuls, then slammed on the lid, and stood looking down at it studiedly.

Collier started to say something but, once more,

Johnny restrained him. Collier stood restively in the kitchen doorway, watching his wife.

When the brown liquid started popping up into the dome, Ann grabbed the pot off the stove without using a potholder. Collier drew in his breath and gritted his teeth.

She poured out the steaming liquid and it sloshed up the sides of the used cup on the table. Then she slammed down the pot and reached hungrily for the cup.

She finished the whole pot in ten minutes.

She drank without cream or sugar, as if she didn't care what it tasted like. As if she didn't taste it at all.

Only when she'd finished did her face relax. She slumped back in the chair and sat there a long time. They watched her in silence.

Then she looked up at them and giggled.

She pushed up and fell against the table. Collier heard Johnny draw in sudden breath.

"My God," he said, "she's *drunk!*"

She was a heavy unwieldy form to get up the stairs, especially since she gave them no assistance. She kept humming to herself—a strange, discordant melody that seemed to move in indefinable tone steps, repeated and repeated like the sound of low wind. There was a beatific smile on her face.

"A lot of good that did," Collier muttered.

"Be patient, be patient," Johnny whispered back.

"Easy enough for you to . . ."

"Shhh," Johnny quieted him but Ann didn't hear a word they said.

She stopped humming as soon as they put her down on the bed and fell into a deep sleep before they straightened up. Collier drew a thin blanket over her and put a pillow under her head. She didn't stir as he lifted her head.

Then the two men stood in silence beside the bed. Collier looked down at the wife he no longer understood. His mind swam with painful discordances and, through them all, burned the horrible strain of doubt that had never left him. Who was the father of her child? Even though he couldn't leave her, even though he felt a great loving pity for her—they could never be close again until he knew.

"I wonder where she goes?" Johnny asked. "When she drives, I mean."

"I don't know." Sullenly.

"She must have gone pretty far to wear down the tires so much. I wonder if . . ."

That was when she started again.

"*Send me not,*" she said.

Johnny gripped Collier's arm.

"Is that it?" he asked.

"I don't know yet."

"*Black, black, drive me out, horror in these shores, heavy, heavy.*"

Collier shuddered.

"That's it," he said.

Johnny knelt hurriedly beside the bed and listened carefully.

"*Breathe me, implore my fathers, seek me out in washing pain, send me not to make the way.*"

Johnny stared at Ann's taut features. She looked as if she were in pain again. And yet it was not her face, Collier suddenly realized. The expression wasn't hers.

Ann threw off the blanket and thrashed on the bed, sweat breaking out on her face.

"*To walk on shores of orange sea, cool, to tread the crimson fields, cool, to raft on silent waters, cool, to ride upon the desertland, cool, return me fathers of my fathers, Rhyuio Gklemmo Fglwo.*"

Then she was silent except for tiny groans. At her sides, her hands clutched the sheets and her breaths were labored and uneven.

Johnny straightened up and looked at Collier. Neither of them spoke a word.

They sat with Kleinman.

"What you suggest is fantastic," the doctor said.

"Listen," Johnny said. "Let's run it down. One—the excess saline requirements, not the requirements of a normal pregnancy. Two—the cold, the way Ann's body adjusted to it, the way she was cured of pneumonia in minutes."

Collier sat staring numbly at his friend.

"All right," Johnny said, "first the salt. In the beginning it made Ann drink too much water. She gained weight and then her weight endangered the child. What happened? She no longer was allowed to drink water."

"Allowed?" Collier asked.

"Let me finish," Johnny said. "About the cold; it was as if the child needed cold and forced Ann to stay cold—until it realized that by acquiring itself some comfort it was endangering the very vessel it lived in. So it cured the vessel of pneumonia. It adjusted the vessel to cold."

"You talk as though . . ." Kleinman started.

"The effects of cigarettes," Johnny said. "Excuse me, doctor. Ann might have smoked in moderation without endangering herself or the child. Yet she stopped altogether. It might have been an ethical point, true. Again, it might be that the child reacted violently to nicotine, and, in a sense, forbade her to . . ."

Kleinman interrupted irritably.

"You talk as if the child were directing its mother rather than being helpless, subject to its mother's actions."

"Helpless?" was all Johnny said.

Kleinman didn't go on. He pressed his lips together in annoyed surrender and tapped nervously on his desk. Johnny waited a moment and then, seeing that Kleinman wasn't going to continue, he went on.

"Three—the aversion to music which she once loved. Why? Because it was music? I don't think so. *Because of the vibrations.* Vibrations which a normal child wouldn't even notice being so insulated from sound not only by the layers of its mother's epidermis and the amniotic fluid but by the very structure of its own hearing apparatus. Apparently, this . . . child . . . has much keener hearing.

"The coffee," he said. "It made her drunk. Or—it made *it* drunk."

"Now wait," Collier started, then broke off.

"And now," Johnny said, "as to her reading. It fits in too. All those books—more or less the basic works in every field of knowledge, a seemingly calculated study of mankind and his every thought."

"What are you driving at?" Collier spoke nervously.

"Think, Dave! All these things. The reading, the trips in the car. As if she were trying to get as much information as she could about life in our civilization. As if the child were . . ."

"You are not implying that the child was . . ." Kleinman began.

"Child?" Johnny said grimly. "I think we can stop referring to it as a child. Perhaps the body is childlike. But the mind—*never.*"

They were deadly silent. Collier felt his heart pulsing strangely in his chest.

"Listen," Johnny said. "Last night Ann—or the . . . *it*—was drunk. Why? Maybe because of what it's learned, what it's seen. I hope so. Maybe it was sick and wanted to forget."

He leaned forward.

"Those visions Ann had; I think they tell the story—as crazy as it is. The deserts, the marshes, the crimson fields. Add the cold. Only one thing wasn't mentioned and I think that's probably because they don't exist."

"What?" Collier asked, reality scaling away from him.

"The canals," Johnny said. "*Ann has a Martian in her womb.*"

For a long time they looked at him in incredulous silence. Then both started talking at once, protesting with nervous horror in their voices. Johnny waited until the first spasm of their words had passed.

"Is there a better answer?" he asked.

"But . . . *how*?" Kleinman asked heatedly. "How could such a pregnancy be effected?"

"I don't know," Johnny said. "But why? I think I know."

Collier was afraid to ask.

"All through the years," Johnny said, "There's been

no end of talk and writing about the Martians, about flying saucers. Books, stories, movies, articles—always with the same theme."

"I don't . . ." Collier began.

"I think the invasion has finally come," Johnny said. "At least a tryout. I think this is their first attempt, an insidious, cruel attempt—invasion by flesh. To place an adult life cell from their own planet into the body of an Earth woman. Then, when this fully matured Martian mind is coupled to the form of an Earth child—the process of conquest begins. This is their experiment, I think, their test. If it works . . ."

He didn't finish.

"But . . . oh, that's *insane*," Collier said, trying to push away the fear that was crowding him in.

"So is her reading," said Johnny. "So are her trips in the car. So is her coffee drinking and her dislike of music and her pneumonia healing and her standing out in the cold and the reduction of body size and the visions and that crazy toneless song she sang. What do you want, Dave . . . a blueprint?"

Kleinman stood up and went to his filing cabinets. He pulled out a drawer and came back to the desk with a folder in his hand.

"I have had this in my files for three weeks now," he said. "I have not told you. I did not know how. But this information, this *theory*," he quickly amended, "compels me to . . ."

He pushed the x-ray slide across the desk to them.

They looked at it and Collier gasped. Johnny's voice was awed.

"A *double heart*," he said.

Then his left hand bunched into a fist.

"That clinches it!" he said. "Mars has two-fifths the gravity of Earth. They'd need a double heart to drive their blood or whatever it is they have in their veins."

"But . . . it does not need this here," Kleinman said.

"Then there's some hope," Johnny said. "There are rough spots in this invasion. The Martian cell would, of genetic necessity, cause certain Martian characteristics in the child—the double heart, the acute hearing, the need for salt, I don't know why, the need for cold. In time—and if this experiment works— they may iron out these difficulties and be able to create a child with only the Martian mind and every physical characteristic Earthlike. I don't know but I suspect the Martian is also telepathic. Otherwise how would it have known it was in danger when Ann had pneumonia?"

The scene flitted suddenly across Collier's mind— him standing beside the bed, the thought—*the hospital, oh God, the hospital*. And, under Ann's flesh, a tiny alien brain, well versed by then in the terms of Earth, plucking at his thought. Hospital, investigation, discovery. . . . He shuddered convulsively.

". . . we to do?" he caught the tail end of Kleinman's question. "Kill the . . . the *Martian* after it is born?"

"I don't know," Johnny said. "But if this . . ." he shrugged, "this *child* is born alive and born normal—I don't think killing would help. I'm sure they must be watching. If the birth is normal—they might assume their experiment is a success whether we killed the child or not."

"A Caesarean?" Kleinman said.

"Maybe," Johnny said. "But . . . would they be

sure they've failed if we had to use artificial means to destroy . . . their first invader? No, I don't think it's good enough. They'd try again, this time somewhere where no one could check on it—in an African village, in some unavailable town, in . . ."

"We can't leave that . . . that *thing* in her!" Collier said in horror.

"How do we know we can remove it," Johnny said grimly, "and not kill Ann?"

"What?" Collier asked, feeling as if he were some brainless straight man for horror.

Johnny exhaled raggedly.

"I think we have to wait," he said. "I don't think we have any choice."

Then, seeing the look on Collier's face, he hurriedly added,

"It's not hopeless, boy. There are things in our favor. The double heart which might drive the blood too fast. The difficulties of combining alien cells. The fact that it's July and the heat might destroy the Martian. The fact that we can cut off all its salt supply. It can all help. But, most of all, because the Martian isn't happy. It drank to forget and—what were its words? *O, send me not to make the way.*"

He looked grimly at them.

"Let's hope it dies of despair," he said.

"Or?" Collier asked hollowly.

"Or else this . . . miscegenation from space succeeds."

Collier dashed up the stairs, his heart pounding with a strange ambivalent beat. Knowing at last she was innocent was horribly balanced by knowledge of the danger she was in.

At the top of the stairs he stopped. The house was silent and hot in the late afternoon.

They were right, he suddenly realized, right in advising him not to tell her. It hadn't actually struck him until then, he'd thought it wrong not to let her know. He'd thought she wouldn't mind as long as she knew what it was, as long as she had his faith again.

But now he wondered. It was a terrifying thing, the import of it made him tremble. Might not the knowledge of this horror drive her into hysterics; she'd been bordering on breakdown for the past three months.

His mouth tightened and he walked into the room.

She lay on her back, her hands resting limply on her swollen stomach, her lifeless eyes staring up at the ceiling. He sat down, on the edge of the bed. She didn't look at him.

"Ann."

No answer. He felt himself shiver. I can't blame you, he thought, I've been harsh and thoughtless.

"Sweetheart," he said.

Her eyes moved slowly over and their gaze on him was cold and alien. It was the creature in her, he thought, she didn't realize how it controlled her. She must never realize. He knew that then, clearly.

He leaned over and pressed his cheek against hers.

"Darling," he said.

A dull, tired voice audible. "What?"

"Can you hear me?" he said.

She didn't reply.

"Ann, about the baby."

There was a slight sign of life in her eyes.

"What about the baby?"

He swallowed.

"I . . . I know that . . . that it isn't the baby of . . . another man."

For a moment she stared at him. Then she muttered, "Bravo," and turned her head away.

He sat there, hands gripped into tight fists, thinking—well, that's that, I've killed her love completely.

But then her head turned back. There was something in her eyes, a tremulous question.

"What?" she said.

"I believe you," he said. "I know you've told me the truth. I'm apologizing with all my heart . . . if you'll let me."

For a long moment nothing seemed to register. Then she took her hands from her stomach and pressed them against her cheeks. Her wide brown eyes began to glisten as they looked at him.

"You're not . . . fooling me?" she asked him.

For a moment he hung suspended, then he threw himself against her.

"Oh, Ann, Ann," he said, "I'm sorry. I'm so sorry, Ann."

Her arms slid around his neck and held him. He felt her breasts shake with inner sobs. Her right hand caressed his hair.

"David, David . . ." She said it over and over.

For a long time they remained there, silent and at peace. Then she asked:

"What made you change your mind?"

His throat moved.

"I just did," he said.

"But why?"

"No reason, honey. I mean, of course, there was a reason. I just realized that . . ."

"You've doubted me for seven months, David. Why did you change your mind now?"

He felt a burst of rage at himself. Was there nothing he could tell her that would satisfy her?

"I think I've misjudged you," he said.

"Why?"

He sat up and looked at her without the answer. The look of soft happiness was leaving her face. Her expression was taut and unyielding.

"*Why*, David?"

"I told you, sweet . . ."

"You didn't tell me."

"Yes, I did. I said I think I've misjudged you."

"That's no reason."

"Ann, don't let's argue now. Does it matter if . . ."

"Yes, it matters a lot!" she said, her voice breaking, as her breath caught.

"And what about your biological assurances?" she said. "No woman can have a baby without being impregnated by a man. You always made that very clear. What about that? Have you given up your faith in biology and transferred it to me?"

"No, darling," he said. "I simply know things I didn't know before."

"What things?"

"I can't tell you."

"More secrets! Is this Kleinman's advice, just a trick to make my last month cozy? Don't lie to me, I know when you're lying to me."

"Ann, don't get so excited."

"I'm not excited!"

"You're shouting. Now stop it."

"I will not stop it! You toy with my feelings for more than half a year and now you want me to be calmly rational! Well, I won't be! I'm sick of you and your pompous attitude! I'm tired of . . . *Uhhh*!"

She lurched on the bed, her head snapping as she jerked her head from the pillow, all the color drained from her face in an instant. Her eyes on him were the eyes of a wounded child, dazed and shocked.

"*My insides!*" she gasped.

"Ann!"

She was half sitting now, her body shaking, a wild, despairing groan starting up in her throat. He grabbed her shoulders and tried to steady her. The Martian!— the thought clutched at his mind—it doesn't like her angry!

"It's all right baby, all r . . ."

"He's hurting me!" she cried. "He's hurting me, David! *Oh God!*"

"He can't hurt you," he heard himself say.

"No, no, no, I can't stand it," she said between clenched teeth. "*I can't stand it.*"

Then, as abruptly as the attack had come, her face relaxed utterly. Not so much with actual relaxation as with a complete absence of all feeling. She looked dizzily at David.

"I'm numb," she said quietly, "I . . . can't . . . feel . . . a . . ."

Slowly she sank back on the pillow and lay there a second with her eyes open. Then she smiled drowsily at Collier.

"Good night, David," she said.

And closed her eyes.

Kleinman stood beside the bed.

"She is in perfect coma," he said, quietly. "More accurately I should say under hypnotic trance. Her body functions normally but her brain has been . . . frozen."

Johnny looked at him.

"Suspended animation?"

"No, her body functions. She is just asleep. I cannot wake her."

They went downstairs to the living room.

"In a sense," Kleinman said, "she is better off. There will be no upsets now. Her body will function painlessly, effortlessly."

"The Martian must have done it," Johnny said, "to safeguard its . . . home."

Collier shuddered.

"I'm sorry, Dave," Johnny said.

They sat silent a moment.

"It must realize we know about it," Johnny said.

"Why?" asked Collier.

"It wouldn't be tipping off its hand completely if it thought there was still a chance of secrecy."

"Maybe it could not stand the pain," said Kleinman.

Johnny nodded. "Yes, maybe."

Collier sat there, his heart beating strainedly. Suddenly he clenched his fists and drove them down on his legs.

"Meanwhile, what are we supposed to do!" he said. "Are we helpless before this . . . this *trespasser*?"

"We can't take risks with Ann," was all Johnny said and Kleinman nodded once.

Collier sank back in the chair. He sat staring at the kewpie doll on the mantel. *Coney Island* read the doll's dress and on the belt—*Happy Days*.

"Rhyuio Gklemmo Fglwo!"

Ann writhed in unconscious labor on the hospital bed. Collier stood rigidly beside her, his eyes fastened to her sweat-streaked face. He wanted to run for Kleinman but he knew he shouldn't. She'd been like this twenty hours now—twenty hours of twisting, teeth-clenching agony. When it had started he'd cut his classes completely to stay with her.

He reached down trembling fingers to hold her damp hand. Her fingers clamped on his until the grip almost hurt. And, as he watched in numbed horror, he saw the face of the Earth-formed Martian passing across his wife's features—the slitted eyes, the thin, drawn-back lips, the white skin pulled rigidly over facial bones.

"Pain! Pain! Spare me, fathers of my fathers, send me not to . . . !"

There was a clicking in her throat, then silence. Her face suddenly relaxed and she lay there shivering weakly. He began to pat her face with a towel.

"In the yard, David," she muttered, still unconscious.

He bent over suddenly, his heart jolting.

"In the yard, David," she said. "I heard a sound and I went out. The stars were bright and there was a crescent moon. While I stood there I saw a white light come over the yard. I started to run back to the house but something hit me. Like a needle going into my back and my stomach. I cried out but then it was black and I couldn't remember. Anything. I tried to tell you David, but I couldn't remember, I couldn't remember, I couldn't . . ."

A hospital. In the corridor the father paces, his eyes feverish and haunted. The hall is hot and silent in the early August morning. He walks back and forth restlessly and his hands are white fists at his sides.

A door opens. The father whirls as a doctor comes out. The doctor draws down the cloth which has covered his mouth and nose. He looks at the man.

"Your wife is well," says the doctor.

The father grabs the doctor's arm.

"And the baby?" he asks.

"The baby is dead."

"Thank God," the father says.

Still wondering if in Africa, in Asia . . .

BEING

In darkness hovering. A soundless shell of metals glistening pale—held aloft by threads of anti-gravity. Below, the planet, shrouded with night, turning from the moon. On its blackswept face, an animal staring up with bright-eyed panic at the dully phosphorescent globe suspended overhead. A twitch of muscle. The hard earth drums delicately beneath fleeing pawbeats. Silence again, wind-soughed and lone. Hours. Black hours passing into gray, then mottled pink. Sunlight sprays across the metal globe. It shimmers with unearthly light.

IT WAS LIKE PUTTING HIS HAND INTO A SCORCHING oven.

"Oh my *God*, it's hot," he said, grimacing, jerking back his hand and closing it once more, gingerly, over the sweat-stained steering wheel.

"It's your imagination." Marian lay slumped against the warm, plastic-covered seat. A mile behind, she'd stuck her sandaled feet out the window. Her eyes were closed, breath fell in fitful gasps from her drying lips. Across her face, the hot wind fanned bluntly, ruffling the short blonde hair.

"It's not hot," she said, squirming uncomfortably, tugging at the narrow belt on her shorts. "It's cool. As a cucumber."

"Ha," Les grunted. He leaned forward a little and clenched his teeth at the feel of his sport shirt clinging damply to his back. "What a month for driving," he growled.

They'd left Los Angeles three days before on their way to visit Marian's family in New York. The weather had been equatorial from the start, three days of blazing sun that had drained them of energy.

The schedule they were attempting to maintain made things even worse. On paper, four hundred miles a day didn't seem like much. Converted into practical traveling it was brutalizing. Traveling over dirt cutoffs that sent up spinning, choking dust clouds. Traveling over rut-pocked stretches of highway under repair; afraid to hit more than twenty miles an hour on them for fear of snapping an axle or shaking their brains loose.

Worst of all, traveling up twenty to thirty mile grades that sent the radiator into boiling frenzies every half hour or so. Then sitting for long, sweltering minutes, waiting for the motor to cool off, pouring in fresh water from the water bag, sitting and waiting in the middle of an oven.

"I'm done on one side," Les said, breathlessly. "Turn me."

"And ha to you," Marian sotto voced.

"Any water left?"

Marian reached down her left hand and tugged off the heavy top of the portable ice box. Feeling inside its coolish interior, she pulled up the thermos bottle. She shook it.

"Empty," she said, shaking her head.

"As my *head*," he finished in a disgusted voice, "for ever letting you talk me into driving to New York in August."

"Now, now," she said, her cajoling a trifle worn, "don't get heated up."

"*Damn!*" he snapped irritably. "When is this damn cutoff going to get back to the damn highway?"

"Damn," she muttered lightly. "Damn damn."

He said no more. His hands gripped tighter on the wheel. HWY. 66, ALT. RTE.—they'd been on the damn thing for hours now, shunted aside by a section of the main highway undergoing repair. For that matter, he wasn't even sure they were on the alternate route. There had been five crossroads in the past two hours. In speeding along to get out of the desert, he hadn't looked too carefully at the crossroad signs.

"Honey, there's a station," Marian said, "let's see if we can get some water."

"And some gas," he added, glancing at the gauge, "*and* some instructions on how to get back to the highway."

"The damn highway," she said.

A faint smile tugged at Les's mouth corners as he pulled the Ford off the road and braked up beside the two paint-chipped pumps that stood before an old sagging shack.

"This is a hot looking spot," he said dispassionately. "Ripe for development."

"For the right party." Marian's eyes closed again. She drew in a heavy breath through her open mouth.

No one came out of the shack.

"Oh, don't tell me it's *deserted,*" Les said disgustedly, looking around.

Marian drew down her long legs. "Isn't there anybody here?" she asked, opening her eyes.

"Doesn't look like it."

Les pushed open the door and slid out. As he stood, an involuntary grunt twitched his body and his knees almost buckled. It felt as if someone had dropped a mountain of heat on his head.

"*God!*" He blinked away the waves of blackness lapping at his ankles.

"What is it?"

"This *heat.*" He stepped between the two rusty-handled pumps and crunched over the hot, flaky ground for the doorway of the shack.

"And we're not even a third of the way," he muttered grimly to himself. Behind him, he heard the car door slam on Marian's side and her loose sandals flopping on the ground.

Dimness gave the illusion of coolness only for a second. Then the muggy, sodden air in the shack pressed down on Les and he hissed in displeasure.

There was no one in the shack. He looked around its small confines at the uneven-legged table with the scarred surface, the backless chair, the cobwebbed coke machine, the price lists and calendars on the wall, the threadbare shade on the small window, drawn down to the sill, shafts of burnished light impaling the many rents.

The wooden floor creaked as he stepped back out into the heavy sunlight.

"No one?" Marian asked and he shook his head. They looked at each other without expression a moment and she patted at her forehead with a damp handkerchief.

"Well, onward," she said wryly.

That was when they heard the car come rattling down the rutted lane that led off the road into the desert. They walked to the edge of the shack and watched the old, home-made tow truck make its wobbling, noisy approach toward the station. Far back from the road was the low form of the house it had come from.

"To the rescue," Marian said. "I hope he has water."

As the truck groaned to a halt beside the shack, they could see the heavily tanned face of the man behind the wheel. He was somewhere in his thirties, a dour looking individual in a T-shirt and patched and faded blue overalls. Lank hair protruded from beneath the brim of his grease-stained Stetson.

It wasn't a smile he gave them as he slid out of the truck. It was more like a reflex twitching of his lean, humorless mouth. He moved up to them with jerky boot strides, his dark eyes moving from one to the other of them.

"You want gas?" he asked Les in a hard, thick-throated voice.

"Please."

The man looked at Les a moment as if he didn't understand. Then he grunted and headed for the Ford, reaching into his back overall pocket for the pump key. As he walked past the front bumper, he glanced down at the license plate.

He stood looking dumbly at the tank cap for a moment, his calloused fingers trying vainly to unscrew it.

"It locks," Les told him, walking over hurriedly with the keys. The man took them without a word and unlocked the cap. He put the cap on top of the trunk door.

"You want ethyl?" he asked, glancing up, his eyes shadowed by the wide hat brim.

"Please," Les told him.

"How much?"

"You can fill it."

The hood was burning hot. Les jerked back his fingers with a gasp. He took out his handkerchief, wrapped it around his hand and pulled up the hood. When he unscrewed the radiator cap, boiling water frothed out and splashed down smoking onto the parched ground.

"Oh, fine," he muttered to himself.

The water from the hose was almost as hot. Marian came over and put one finger in the slow gush as Les held it over the radiator.

"Oh . . . *gee*," she said in disappointment. She looked over at the overalled man. "Have you got any *cool* water?" she asked.

The man kept his head down, his mouth pressed into a thin, drooping line. She asked again, without result.

"The hair-triggered Arizonian," she muttered to Les as she started back toward the man.

"I beg your pardon," she said.

The man jerked up his head, startled, the pupils of his dark eyes flaring. "Ma'am?" he said quickly.

"Can we get some cool drinking water?"

The man's rough-skinned throat moved once. "Not here, ma'am," he said, "but . . ."

His voice broke off and he looked at her blankly.

"You . . . you're from California, ain't you?" he said.

"That's right."

"Goin' . . . far?"

"New York," she said impatiently. "But what about—"

The man's bleached eyebrows moved together. "New York," he repeated. "Pretty far."

"What about the water?" Marian asked him.

"Well," the man said, his lips twitching into the outline of a smile, "I ain't got none here but if you want to drive back to the house, my wife'll get you some."

"Oh." Marian shrugged slightly. "All right."

"You can look at my zoo while my wife gets the water," the man offered, then crouched down quickly beside the fender to listen and hear if the tank was filling up.

"We have to go back to his house to get water," Marian told Les as he unscrewed one of the battery caps.

"Oh? Okay."

The man turned off the pump and replaced the cap.

"New York, haah?" he said, looking at them. Marian smiled politely and nodded.

After Les had pushed the hood back down, they got into the car to follow the man's truck back to the house.

"He has a zoo," Marian said, expressionlessly.

"How nice," Les said as he let up the clutch and the car rolled down off the slight rise on which the gas pumps stood.

"They make me mad," Marian said.

They'd seen dozens of the zoos since they'd left Los Angeles. They were usually located beside gas stations—designed to lure extra customers. Invariably, they were pitiful collections—barren little cages in which gaunt foxes cringed, staring out with sick, glazed eyes, rattlesnakes coiled lethargically, maybe a feather-molted eagle glowered from a dark cage corner. And, usually, in the middle of the so-called zoo would be a chained-up wolf or coyote; a straggly woe-be-gone creature who paced constantly in a circle whose radius was the length of the chain; who never looked at the people but stared straight ahead with red-rimmed eyes, pacing endlessly on thin stalks of legs.

"I hate them," Marian said bitterly.

"I know, baby," Les said.

"If we didn't need water, I'd never go back to his damned old house."

Les smiled. "Okay ma," he said quietly, trying to avoid the holes in the lane. "*Oh*." He snapped two fingers. "I forgot to ask him how to get back to the highway."

"Ask him when we get to his house," she said.

The house was faded brown, a two-story wooden structure that looked a hundred years old. Behind it stood a row of low, squarish huts.

"The zoo," Les said. "Lions 'n tigers 'n everything."

"Nuts," she said.

He pulled up in front of the quiet house and saw the man in the Stetson slide off the dusty seat of his truck and jump down off the running board.

"Get you the water," he said quickly and started for the house. He stopped a moment and looked back. "Zoo's in the back," he said, gesturing with his head.

They watched him move up the steps of the old house. Then Les stretched and blinked at the glaring sunlight.

"Shall we look at the zoo?" he asked, trying not to smile.

"No."

"Oh, come on."

"No, I don't want to see *that*."

"I'm going to take a look."

"Well . . . all right," she said, "but it's going to make me mad."

They walked around the edge of the house and moved along its side in the shade.

"Oh, does that feel good," Marian said.

"Hey, he forgot to ask for his money."

"He will," she said.

They approached the first cage and looked into the dim interior through the two-foot-square window that was barred with thick doweling.

"Empty," Les said.

"Good."

"Some zoo."

They walked slowly toward the next cage. "Look how *small* they are," Marian said unhappily. "How would *he* like to be cooped up in one of them?"

She stopped walking.

"No, I'm not going to look," she said angrily, "I don't want to see how the poor things are suffering."

"I'll just take a look," he said.

"You're a fiend."

She heard him chuckle as she stood watching him walk up to the second of the cages. He looked in.

"*Marian!*" His cry made her body twitch.

"What is it?" she asked, running to him anxiously.

"*Look.*"

He stared with shocked eyes into the cage.

Her whisper trembled. "*Oh my God.*"

There was a man in the cage.

She looked at him with unbelieving eyes, unconscious of the large drops of sweat trickling across her brow and down her temples.

The man was lying on the floor, sprawled like a broken doll across a dirty army blanket. His eyes were open but the man saw nothing. His pupils were dilated, he looked doped. His grimy hands rested limply on the thinly-strawed floor, motionless twists of flesh and bone. His mouth hung open like a yellow-toothed wound, edged with dry, cracking lips.

When Les turned, he saw that Marian was already looking at him, her face blank, the skin drawn tautly over her paling cheeks.

"What *is* this?" she asked in a faint tremor of voice.

"I don't know."

He glanced once more into the cage as if he already doubted what he'd seen. Then he was looking at Marian again. "I don't know," he repeated, feeling the heartbeats throb heavily in his chest.

Another moment they looked at each other, their eyes stark with uncomprehending shock.

"What are we going to do?" Marian asked, almost whispering the words.

Les swallowed the hard lump in his throat. He looked into the cage again. "Hel-*lo*," he heard himself say, "can you—"

He broke off abruptly, throat moving again. The man was comatose.

"Les, what if—"

He looked at her. And, suddenly, his scalp was crawling because Marian was looking in wordless apprehension at the next cage.

His running footsteps thudded over the dry earth, raising the dust.

"*No,*" he murmured, looking into the next cage. He felt himself shudder uncontrollably as Marian ran up to him.

"Oh my God, this is *hideous,*" she cried, staring with sick fright at the second caged man.

They both started as the man looked up at them with glazed, lifeless eyes. For a moment, his slack body lurched up a few inches and his dry lips fluttered as though he were trying to speak. A thread of saliva ran from one corner of his mouth and dribbled down across his beard-blackened chin. For a moment his sweaty, dirt-lined face was a mask of impotent entreaty.

Then his head rolled to one side and his eyes rolled back.

Marian backed away from the cage, shaking hand pressed to her cheek.

"The man's *insane,*" she muttered and looked around abruptly at the silent house.

Then Les had turned too and both of them were suddenly aware of the man in the house who had told them to go and look at his zoo.

"Les, what are we going to do?" Marian's voice shook with rising hysteria.

Les felt numb, devoured by the impact of what they'd seen. For a long moment he could only stand shivering and stare at his wife, feeling immersed in some fantastic dream.

Then his lips jammed together and the heat seemed to flood over him.

"Let's get out of here," he snapped and grabbed her hand.

The only sound was their harsh panting and the quick step of Marian's sandals on the hard ground. The air throbbed with intense heat, smothering their breath, making perspiration break out heavily across their faces and bodies.

"Faster," Les gasped, tugging at her hands.

Then, as they turned the edge of the house, they both recoiled with a violent contracting of muscles.

"*No!*" Marian's cry contorted her face into a twisted mask of terror.

The man stood between them and their car, a long double-barreled shotgun leveled at them.

Les didn't know why the idea flooded through his brain. But, suddenly, he realized that no one knew where he and Marian were, no one could even know where to begin searching for them. In rising panic, he thought of the man asking them where they were going, he thought of the man looking down at their California license plate.

And he heard the man, the hard, emotionless voice of the man.

"Now go on back," the man said, "to the zoo."

After he'd locked the couple in one of the cages, Merv Ketter walked slowly back to the house, the heavy shotgun pulling down his right arm. He'd felt no pleasure in the act, only a draining relief that had, for a moment, loosened the tightness in his body. But, already, the tightness was returning. It never went away for more than the few minutes it took him to trap another person and cage him.

If anything, the tightness was worse now. This was the first time he'd ever put a woman in one of his cages. The knowledge twisted a cold knot of despair in his chest. A woman—he'd put a *woman* in his cage. His chest shuddered with harsh breath as he ascended the rickety steps of the back porch.

Then, as the screen door slapped shut behind him, his long mouth tightened. Well, what was he supposed to do? He slammed the shotgun down on the yellow oil-clothed surface of the kitchen table, another forced breath wracking his chest. What *else* could I do—he argued with himself. His boots clacked sharply across the worn linoleum as he walked to the quiet, sunlanced living room.

Dust rose from the old arm chair as he dropped down heavily, spiritlessly. What *was* he supposed to do? He'd had no choice.

For the thousandth time, he looked down at his left forearm, at the slight reddish bulge just under the elbow joint. Inside his flesh, the tiny metal cone was still humming delicately. He knew it without listening. It never stopped.

He slumped back exhaustedly with a groan and lay his head on the high back of the chair. His eyes stared dully across the room, through the long slanting bar of sunlight quivering with dust motes. At the mantelpiece.

The Mauser rifle—he stared at it. The Luger, the bazooka shell, the hand grenade, all of them still active. Vaguely, through his tormented brain, curled the idea of putting the Luger to his temple, holding the Mauser against his side, even of pulling out the pin and holding the grenade against his stomach.

War hero. The phrase scraped cruelly at his mind. It had long lost its meaning, its comfort. Once, it had meant something to him to be a medaled warrior, ribboned, lauded, admired.

Then Elsie had died, then the battles and the pride were gone. He was alone in the desert with his trophies and with nothing else.

And then one day he'd gone into the desert to hunt.

His eyes shut, his leathery throat moved convulsively. What was the use of thinking, of regretting? The will to live was still in him. Maybe it was a stupid, a pointless will but it was there just the same; he couldn't rid himself of it. Not after two men were gone, not after five, no, not even after seven men were gone.

The dirt-filled nails dug remorselessly into his palms until they broke the skin. But a woman, a *woman*. The thought knifed at him. He'd never planned on caging a woman.

One tight fist drove down in futile rage on his leg. He couldn't help it. Sure, he'd seen the California plate. But he wasn't going to do it. Then the woman had asked for water and he suddenly had known that he had no choice, he *had* to do it.

There were only two men left.

And he'd found out that the couple was going to New York and the tension had come and gone, loosened and tightened in a spastic rhythm as he knew, in his very flesh, that he was going to tell them to come and look at his zoo.

I should have given them an injection, he thought. They might start screaming. It didn't matter about the man, he was used to men screaming. But a woman . . .

Merv Ketter opened his eyes and stared with hopeless eyes at the mantelpiece, at the picture of his dead wife, at the weapons which had been his glory and now were meaningless—steel and wood without worth, without substance.

Hero.

The word made his stomach turn.

The glutinous pulsing slowed, paused a moment's fraction, then began again, filling the inner shell with its hissing, spumous sound. A flaccid wave of agitation rippled down along the rows of muscle coils. The being stirred. It was time.

Thought. The shapeless, gauzelike airbubble, coalesced; surrounded. The being moved, an undulation, a gelatinous worming within the shimmering bubble. A bumping, a slithering, a rocking flow of viscous tissues.

Thought again—a wave directing. The hiss of entering atmosphere, the soundless swinging of metal.

Open. Shutting with a click. Sunset blood edged the horizon. A slow and noiseless sinking in the air, a colorless balloon filled with something formless, something alive.

Earth, cooling. The being touched it, settled. It moved across the ground and every living thing fled its scouring approach. In its ropy wake, the ground was left a green and yellow iridescence.

"Look out."

Marian's sudden whisper almost made him drop the nail file. He jerked back his hand, his sweat-grimed cheek twitching and drew back quickly into the shadows. The sun was almost down.

"Is he coming this way?" Marian asked, her voice husky with dryness.

"I don't know." He stood tensely, watching the overalled man approach, hearing the fast crunch of his boot heels on the baked ground. He tried to swallow but all the moisture in him had been blotted up by the afternoon heat and only a futile clicking sounded in his throat. He was thinking about the man seeing the deeply filed slit in the window bar.

The man in the Stetson walked quickly, his face blank and hard, his hands swinging in tense little arcs at his sides.

"What's he going to do?" Marian's voice rasped nervously, her physical discomfort forgotten in the sudden return of fear.

Les only shook his head. All afternoon he'd been asking himself the same question. After they'd been locked up, after the man had gone back to his house, during the first terrifying minutes and for the rest of the time when Marian had found the nail file in the pocket of her shorts and shapeless panic had gained the form of hoping for escape. All during that time the question had plagued him endlessly. *What was the man going to do with them?*

But it wasn't their cage the man was headed for. A loosening of relief made them both go slack. The man hadn't even looked toward the cage they were in. He seemed to avoid looking toward it.

Then the man had passed out of their sight and they heard the sound of him unlocking one of the cages. The squeaking rasp of the rusty door hinges made Les's stomach muscles draw taut.

The man appeared again.

Marian caught her breath. They both stared at the unconscious man being dragged across the ground, his heels raking narrow gouges in the dust.

After a few feet, the man let go of the limp arms and the body fell with a heavy thud. The man in the overalls looked behind him then, his head jerking around suddenly. They saw his throat move with a convulsive swallow. The man's eyes moved quickly, looking in all directions.

"What's he *looking* for?" Marian asked in a shaking whisper.

"Marian, I don't *know*."

"He's *leaving* him there!" She almost whimpered the word.

Their eyes filled with confused fear, they watched the overalled man move for the house again, his long legs pumping rapidly, his head moving jerkily as he looked from side to side. Dear God, what *is* he looking for?—Les thought in rising dread.

The man suddenly twitched in mid-stride and clutched at his left arm. Then, abruptly, he broke into a frightened run and leaped up the porch steps two at a time. The screen door slapped shut behind him with a loud report and then everything was deadly still.

A sob caught in Marian's throat. "I'm *afraid*," she said in a thin, shuddering voice.

He was afraid too; he didn't know of what but he was terribly afraid. Chilling uneasiness crawled up his back and rippled coldly on his neck. He kept staring at the body of the man sprawled on the ground, at the still, white face looking up sightlessly at the darkening sky.

He jolted once as, across the yard, he heard the back door of the house being slammed shut and locked.

Silence. A great hanging pall of it that pressed down on them like lead. The man slumped motionless on the ground. Their breaths quick, labored. Their lips trembling, their eyes fastened almost hypnotically on the man.

Marian drew up one fist and dug her teeth into the knuckles. Sunlight rimmed the horizon with a scarlet ribbon. Soundlessness. Heavy soundlessness.

Soundlessness.

Sound.

Their breath stopped. They stood there, mouths open, ears straining at the sound they'd never heard before. Their bodies went rigid as they listened to—

A bumping, a slithering, a rocking flow of—

"Oh *God!*" Her voice was a gasping of breathless

horror as she spun away, shaking hands flung over her eyes.

It was getting dark and he couldn't be sure of what he saw. He stood paralyzed and numb in the fetid air of the cage, staring with blood-drained face at the thing that moved across the ground toward the man's body; the thing that had shape yet not shape, that crept like a current of shimmering jellies.

A terrified gagging filled his throat. He tried to move back but he couldn't. He didn't want to see. He didn't want to hear the hideous gurgling sound like water being sucked into a great drain, the turbid bubbling that was like vats of boiling tallow.

No, his mind kept repeating, unable to accept, no, no, no, *no*!

Then the scream made them both jerk like bone-less things and drove Marian against one of the cage walls, shaking with nauseous shock.

And the man was gone from the earth. Les stared at the place where he had been, stared at the luminous mass that pulsated there like a great mound of balloon-encased plankton undulating palely in their fluids.

He stared at it until the man had been completely eaten.

Then he turned away on deadened legs and stumbled to Marian's side. Her shaking fingers clutched like talons at his back and he felt her tear-streaked, twisted face press into his shoulder. Unfeelingly, he slid his arms around her, his face stiff with spent horror. Vaguely, through the body-clutching horror, he felt the need to comfort her, to erase her fright.

But he couldn't. He felt as if a pair of invisible claws had reached into his chest and ripped out all his insides. There wasn't anything left, just a cold frost-edged hollow in him. And, in the hollow, a knife jabbing its razor tip each time he realized again why they were there.

When the scream came, Merv slammed both hands across his ears so hard it made his head ache.

He couldn't seem to cut off the sound anymore. Doors wouldn't shut tightly enough, windows wouldn't seal away the world, walls were too porous—the screams always reached him.

Maybe it was because they were really in his mind where there were no doors to lock, no windows to shut and close away the screaming of terror. Yes, maybe they *were* in his mind. It would explain why he still heard them in his sleep.

And, when it was over and Merv knew that the thing had gone, he trudged slowly into the kitchen and opened the door. Then, like a robot driven by remorseless gears, he went to the calendar and circled the date. Sunday, August 22nd.

The eighth man.

The pencil dropped from his slack fingers and rolled across the linoleum. Sixteen days—one man each two days for sixteen days. The mathematics of it were simple. The truth was not.

He paced the living room, passing in and out of the lamplight aura which cast a buttery glow across his exhausted features, then melted away as he moved into shadow again. Sixteen days. It seemed like sixteen years since he'd gone out into the desert to hunt for jackrabbits. Had it only been sixteen days ago?

Once again he saw the scene within his mind; it never left. Him scuffing across late afternoon sands, shotgun cradled against his hip, head slowly turning, eyes searching beneath the brim of his hat.

Then, moving over the crest of a scrub-grown dune, stopping with a gasp, his eyes staring up at the globe which shimmered like a light immersed in water. His heartbeat jolting, every muscle tensing abruptly at the sight.

Approaching then, standing almost below the luminescent sphere that caught the lowering sun rays redly.

A gasp tearing back his lips at the circular cavity appearing on the surface of the globe. And out of the cavity floating—

He'd spun then and run, his breath whistling as he scrambled frantically up the rise again, his boot heels gouging at the sand. Topping the rise, he'd started to run in long, panic-driven strides, the gun held tautly in his right hand, banging against his leg.

Then the sound overhead—like the noise of gas escaping. Wild-eyed, he'd looked up over his shoulder. A terrified cry had wrenched his face into a mask of horror.

Ten feet over his head, the bulbous glow floated.

Merv lunged forward, his legs rising high as he fled. A fetid heat blew across his back. He looked up again with terrified eyes to see the thing descending on him. Seven feet above him—six—five—

Merv Ketter skidded to his knees, twisted around,

jerked up the shotgun. The silence of the desert was shattered by the blast.

A gagging scream ripped from his throat as shot sprayed off the lucent bubble like pebbles off a rubber ball. He felt some of it burrow into his shoulder and arm as he flung over to one side, the gun falling from his nerveless grip. Four feet—three—the heat surrounded him, the choking odor made the air swim before his eyes.

His arms flung up. "*NO!*"

Once he had jumped into a water hole without looking and been mired on the shallow bottom by hot slime. It felt like that now, only this time the ooze was jumping onto him. His screams were lost in the crawling sheath of gasses and his flailing limbs caught fast in glutinous tissue. Around his terror-frozen eyes, he saw an agitating gelatine filled with gyrating spangles. Horror pressed at his skull, he felt death sucking at his life.

But he didn't die.

He inhaled and there was air even though the air was grumous with a stomach-wrenching stench. His lungs labored, he gagged as he breathed.

Then something moved in his brain.

He tried to twist and tried to scream but he couldn't. It felt like vipers threading through his brain, gnawing with poisoned teeth on tissues of his thought.

The serpents coiled and tightened. *I could kill you now*—the words scalded like acid. The muscle cords beneath his face tensed but even they couldn't move in the putrescent glue.

And then more words had formed and were burning, were branding themselves indelibly into his mind.

You will get me food.

He was still shuddering now, standing before the calendar, staring at the penciled circles.

What else could he have done? The question pleaded like a groveling suppliant. The being had picked his mind clean. It knew about his home, his station, his wife, his past. It told him what to do, it left no choice. He had to do it. Would anyone have let themselves die like that if they had an alternative; would *anyone*? Wouldn't anyone have promised the world itself to be freed of that horror?

Grim-faced, trembling, he went up the stairs on feeble legs, knowing there would be no sleep, but going anyway.

Slumped down on the bed, one shoe off, he stared with lifeless eyes at the floor, at the hooked rug that Elsie had made so long ago.

Yes, he'd promised to do what the being had ordered. And the being had sunk the tiny, whirring cone deep into his arm so that he could only escape by cutting open his own flesh and dying.

And then the hideous gruel had vomited him onto the desert sands and he had lain there, mute and palsied while the being had raised slowly from the earth. And he had heard in his brain the last warning—

In two days . . .

And it had started, the endless, enervating round of trapping innocent people in order to preserve himself from the fate he knew awaited them.

And the horrible thing, the truly horrible thing was that he knew he would do it again. He knew he'd do anything to keep the being away from him. Even if it meant that the woman must—

His mouth tightened. His eyes shut and he sat trembling without control on the bed.

What would he do when the couple were gone? What would he do if no one else came to the station? What would he do if the police came checking on the disappearances of eleven people?

His shoulders twisted and an anguished sobbing pulsed in his throat.

Before he lay down he took a long swallow from the dwindling whiskey bottle. He lay in the darkness, a nerve-scraped coil, waiting, the small pool of heat in his stomach unable to warm the coldness and the emptiness of him.

In his arm the cone whirled.

Les jerked out the last bar and stood there for a moment, head slumped forward on his chest, panting through clenched teeth, his body heaving with exhausted breath. Every muscle in his back and shoulders and arms ached with throbbing pain.

Then he sucked in a rasping breath. "Let's go," he gasped.

His arms vibrated as he helped Marian clamber through the window.

"Don't make any noise." He could hardly speak he was so tired from the combination of thirst, hunger, heat exhaustion and seemingly endless, muscle-cramped filing.

He couldn't get his leg up, he had to go through the rough-edged opening head first, pushing and squirming, feeling splinters jab into his sweat-greased flesh. When he thudded down, the pain of impact ran jaggedly along his extended arms and, for a second, the darkness swam with needles of light.

Marian helped him up.

"Let's go," he said again, breathlessly and they started to run across the ground toward the front of the house.

Abruptly, he grabbed her wrist and jerked her to a halt.

"Get those *sandals* off," he ordered hoarsely. She bent over quickly and unbuckled them.

The house was dark as they hurried around the back corner of it and dashed along the side beneath the moon-reflecting windows. Marian winced as her right foot jarred down on a sharp pebble.

"Thank God," Les gasped to himself as they reached the front of the house.

The car was still there. As they ran toward it, he felt into his back pocket and took out his wallet. His shaking fingers reached into the small change purse and felt the coolness of the extra ignition key. He was sure the other keys wouldn't be in the car.

They reached it.

"*Quick,*" he gasped and they pulled open the doors and slid in. Les suddenly realized that he was shivering in the chilly night air. He took out the key and fumbled for the ignition slot. They'd left the doors open, planning to close them when the motor started.

Les found the slot and slid in the key, then drew in a tense, shuddering breath. If the man had done anything to the motor, they were lost.

"Here goes," he murmured and jabbed at the starter button.

The motor coughed and turned over once with a groan. Les's throat clicked convulsively, he jerked back his hand and threw an apprehensive look at the dark house.

"Oh God, won't it start?" Marian whispered, feeling her legs and arms break out in gooseflesh.

"I don't know, I hope it's just cold," he said hurriedly. He caught his breath, then pushed in the button again, pumping at the choke.

The motor turned again lethargically. Oh God, he *has* done something to it!—the words exploded in Les's mind. He jammed in the button feverishly, his body tense with fear. Why didn't we *push* it to the main road!—the new thought came, deepening the lines on his face.

"*Les!*"

He felt her hand clutch at his arm and, almost instinctively, his gaze jerked over to the house.

A light had flared up at a second story window.

"Oh Jesus, *start!*" he cried in a broken frenzy and pushed at the button with a rigid thumb.

The motor coughed into life and a wave of relief covered him. Simultaneously, he and Marian pulled at the doors and slammed them shut while he gunned the engine strongly to get it warm.

As he threw the gears into first, the head and trunk of the man appeared in the window. He shouted something but neither of them heard it over the roar of the motor.

The car jerked forward and stalled.

Les hissed in impotent fury as he jabbed in the button again. The motor caught and he eased up the clutch. The tires bumped over the uneven ground. Upstairs, the man was gone from the window and Marian, her eyes fastened to the house, saw a downstairs light go on.

"*Hurry!*" she begged.

The car picked up speed and Les, shoving the gears into second, jerked the car into a tight semicircle. The tires skidded on the hard earth and, as the car headed for the lane, Les threw it into third and jerked at the knob that sent the two headlights splaying out brightly into the darkness.

Behind them, something exploded and they both jerked their shoulders forward convulsively as something gouged across the roof with a grating shriek. Les shoved the accelerator to the floor and the car leaped forward, plunging and rocking into the rutted lane.

Another shotgun blast tore open the night and half of the back window exploded in a shower of glass splinters. Again, their shoulders twitched violently and Les grunted as a sliver gouged its razor edge across the side of his neck.

His hands jerked on the wheel, the car hit a small ditch and almost veered into a bank on the left side of the lane. His fingers tightened convulsively and, with arms braced, he pulled the car back into the center of the lane, crying to Marian.

"Where is he?"

Her white face twisted around.

"I can't see him!"

His throat moved quickly as the car bucked and lurched over the holes, the headlights jerking wildly with each motion.

Get to the next town, he thought wildly, tell the

sheriff, try and save that other poor devil. His foot
pressed down on the pedal as the lane smoothed out.
Get to the next town and—

She screamed it. "*Look out!*"

He couldn't stop in time. The hood of the Ford
drove splintering into the heavy gate across the lane
and the car jolted to a neck-jerking halt. Marian
went flailing forward against the dashboard, the side
of her head snapping against the windshield. The engine stalled and both headlights smashed out in an
instant.

Les shoved away from the steering wheel, knocked
breathless by the impact.

"Honey, *quick*," he gasped.

A choking sob shook in Marian's throat. "My head,
my *head*." Les sat in stunned muteness a moment, staring at her as she twisted her head around in an agony
of pain, one hand pressed rigidly to her forehead.

Then he shoved open the door at his side and grabbed
for her free hand. "Marian, we have to get *out* of
here!"

She kept crying helplessly as he almost dragged
her from the car and threw his arm around her waist
to support her. Behind him, he heard the sound of
heavy boots running down the lane and saw, over his
shoulder, a bright flashlight eye bobbing as it bore
down on them.

Marian collapsed at the gate. Les stood there holding her, trembling impotently as the man came running up, a .45 clutched in his right hand, a flashlight
in his left. Les winced at the beam flaring into his
eyes.

"Back," was all the man said, panting heavily and

Les saw the barrel of the gun wave once toward the house.

"But my wife is *hurt!*" he said. "She hit her head against the windshield. You can't just put her back in a *cage!*"

"I said get *back!*" The man's shout made Les start.

"But she can't walk, she's unconscious!"

He heard a rasping breath shudder through the man's body and saw that he was stripped to the waist and shivering.

"Carry her then," the man said.

"But—"

"Shall I blast ya where ya stand!" the man yelled in a frenzied anger.

"*No.* No." Les shook nervously as he lifted up Marian's slack body. The man stepped aside and Les started back up the lane, trying to watch Marian's face and his footing at the same time.

"Honey," he whispered. "Marian?"

Her head hung limply over his left forearm, the short blonde hair ruffling against her temples and brow as he walked. Tension kept building up in him until he felt like screaming.

"Why are you *doing* this?" he suddenly blurted out over his shoulder.

No answer, just the rhythmic slogging of the man's boots over the pocked ground.

"How can you *do* this to anyone?" Les asked brokenly. "Trapping your own kind and giving them to that—that God only knows what it is!"

"*Shut* up!" But there was more defeat than anger in the man's voice.

"Look," Les said suddenly, impulsively, "let my wife

go. Keep me here if you have to but . . . but let *her* go. *Please!*"

The man said nothing and Les bit his lips in frustrated anguish. He looked down at Marian with sick, frightened eyes.

"Marian," he said, "*Marian*." He shivered violently in the cold night air.

The house loomed up bleakly out of the flat darkness of the desert.

"For God's sake, don't put her in a cage!" he cried out desperately.

"*Get back*." The man's voice was flat, there was nothing in it, neither promise nor emotion.

Les stiffened. If it had been just him, he would have whirled and leaped at the man, he knew it. He wouldn't, willingly, walk back past the edge of the house again, back toward the cages, toward that *thing*.

But there was Marian.

He stepped over the thrown-down shotgun on the ground and heard, behind him, the grunt of the man as he bent over and picked it up. I have to get her out of here, he thought, I *have* to!

It happened before he could do anything. He heard the man step up suddenly behind him and then felt a pinprick on his right shoulder. He caught his breath at the sudden sting and turned as quickly as he could, weighed down by Marian's dead limpness.

"What are you—"

He couldn't even finish the sentence. It seemed suddenly as if hot, numbing liquors were being hosed through his veins. An immense lassitude covered his limbs and he hardly felt it when the man took Marian from his arms.

He stumbled forward a step, the night alive with glittering pinpoints of light. The earth ran like water beneath his feet, his legs turned to rubber.

"*No.*" He said it in a lethargic grumble.

Then he toppled. And didn't even feel the impact of the ground against his falling body.

> *The belly of the globe was warm. It undulated with a thick and vaporous heat. In the humid dimness, the being rested, its shapeless body quivering with monotonous pulsations of sleep. The being was comfortable, it was content, coiled grotesquely like some cosmic cat before a hearth.*
>
> *For two days.*

Piercing screams woke him. He stirred fitfully and moved his lips as though to speak. But his lips were made of iron. They sagged inertly and he couldn't move them. Only a great forcing of will would raise his leaden eyelids.

The cage air fluttered and shimmered with strange convections. His eyes blinked slowly; glazed, uncomprehending eyes. His hands flopped weakly at his sides like dying fish.

It was the man in the other cage screaming. The poor devil had come out of his drugged state and was hysterical because he knew.

Les's sweat-grimed brow wrinkled slowly, evenly. *He could think.* His body was like a massive stone, unwieldy and helpless. But, behind its flint, immobile surface, his brain was just as sure.

His eyes fell shut. That made it all the more horrible.

To know what was coming. To lie there helpless and know what was going to happen to him.

He thought he shuddered, but he wasn't sure. That thing, what *was* it? There was nothing in his knowledge to construct from, no foundation of rational acceptance to build upon. What he'd seen that night was something beyond all—

What day was it? Where was—

Marian!

It was like rolling a boulder to turn his head. Clicking filled his throat, saliva dribbled unnoticed from the corners of his mouth. Again, he forced his eyes open with a great straining of will.

Panic drove knife blades into his brain even though his face changed not at all.

Marian wasn't there.

She lay, limply drugged, on the bed. He'd laid another cool, wet cloth across her brow, across the welt on her right temple.

Now he stood silently, looking down at her. He'd just gotten back from the cages where he'd injected the screaming man again to quiet him. He wondered what was in the drug the being had given him, he wondered what it did to the man. He hoped it made him completely insensible.

It was the man's last day.

No, it's dumb imagination, he told himself suddenly. She didn't look like Elsie, she didn't look at all like Elsie.

It was his mind. He *wanted* her to look like Elsie,

that was what it was. His throat twitched as he swallowed. Stupid. The word slapped dully at his brain. She *didn't* look like Elsie.

For a moment, he let his gaze move once more over the woman's body, at the smooth rise of her bust, the willowy hips, the long, wellformed legs. Marian. That was what the man had called her. Marian.

It was a nice name.

With an angry twist of his shoulders, he turned away from the bed and strode quickly from the room. What was the *matter* with him anyway? What did he think he was going to do—let her go? There had been no sense in taking her into the house the night before last, in putting her in the spare bedroom. No sense in it at all. He couldn't let himself feel sympathy for her, for anyone. If he did, he was lost. That was obvious.

As he moved down the steps, he tried to remind himself once more of the horror of being absorbed into that gelatinous mass. He tried to remember the brain-searing terror of it. But, somehow, the memory kept disappearing like a wind-blown cloud and he kept thinking instead of the woman. *Marian.* She did look like Elsie; the same color hair, the same mouth.

No!

He'd leave her in the bedroom until the drug wore off. Then he'd put her back in the cage again. *It's me or them*!—he argued furiously with himself. I ain't going to die like *that*! Not for anyone.

He kept arguing with himself all the way down to the station.

I must be crazy, he thought, taking her in the house

like that, feeling sorry for her. I can't afford it. I *can't*. She's just two days to me, that's all, just a two-day reprieve from—

The station was empty, silent. Merv braked the truck and got out.

His boots crunched over the hot earth as he paced restlessly around the pumps. I *can't* let her go! he lashed out at himself, his face taut with fury. He shuddered then at the realization that he had been entertaining the thought for two days now.

"Why wasn't she a *man*?" he muttered to himself, fists tight and blood-drained at his sides. He raised his left arm and looked at the reddish lump. Why couldn't he tear it out of his flesh? *Why*?

The car came then. A salesman's car, dusty and hot.

As Merv pumped gas in, as he checked the oil and water, he kept glancing from under his hat brim at the hot-faced little man in the linen suit and panama hat. Replace *her*. Merv wouldn't let the thought out yet he knew it was there. He found himself glancing down at the license plate.

Arizona.

His face tightened. No. No, he'd always gotten out-of-state cars, it was safer that way. I'll have to let him go, he thought miserably, I'll *have* to. I can't afford to . . .

But when the little man was reaching into his wallet, Merv felt his hand slide back to his back overall pocket, he felt his fingers tighten over the warm butt of the .45.

The little man stared, slack-jawed, at the big gun.

"What *is* this?" he asked weakly. Merv didn't tell him.

* * *

Night brushed its black iced fingers across the moving bubble. Earth flowed beneath its liquid coming.

Why was the air so faint with nourishment, why did the atmosphere press so feebly in? This land, it was a weak, a dying land, its life-administering gasses almost spent.

Amidst slithering, amidst scouring approach, the being thought of escape.

How long now had it been here in this barren place? There was no way of telling for the planet's sun appeared and disappeared with insane rapidity, darkness and light flickering in alternation like the wink of an eye.

And, on the ship, the instruments of chronometry were shattered, they were irreparable. There was no context any more, no customed metric to adjust by. The being was lost upon this tenuous void of living rock, unable to do more than forage for its sustenance.

Off in the black distance, the dwelling of the planet's animal appeared, grotesquely angular and peaked. It was a stupid animal, this brainless beast incapable of rationality, able only to emit wild squawking cries and flap its tendrils like the night plants of his own world. And its body—it was too hard with calciumed rigidity, providing scant nutriment, making it necessary for the being to eat twice as often so violent an energy did digestion take.

Closer. The clicking grew louder.

The animal was there, as usual, lying still upon the ground, its tendrils curled and limp. The being shot out threads of thought and sapped the sluggish juices *of thought from the animal. It was a barbaric place if this was its intelligence. The being heaved closer, swelling and sucking along the windswept earth.*

The animal stirred and deep revulsion quivered in the being's mind. If it were not starving and helpless it could never force itself to absorb this twitching, stiff-ribbed beast.

Bubble touched tendril. The being flowed across the animal form and trembled to a stop. Visual cells revealed the animal looking up, distended eyed. Audial cells transferred the wild and strangling noise the dying animal made. Tactile cells absorbed the flimsy agitations of its body.

And, in its deepest center, the being sensed the tireless clicking that emanated from the dark lair where, hidden and shaking, the first animal was—the animal in whose flaccid tendril was imbedded the location cone.

The being ate. And, eating, wondered if there would ever be enough food to keep it alive—

—for the thousand earth years of its life.

He lay slumped across the cage floor, his heartbeat jolting as the man looked in at him.

He'd been testing the walls when he heard the slap of the screen door and the sound of the man's boots descending the porch steps. He'd lunged down and rolled over quickly onto his back, trying desperately to remember what position he'd been in while he was still drugged, arranging his hands limply at his sides, drawing up his right leg a little, closing his eyes. The man mustn't know that he was conscious. The man had to open the door without caution.

Les forced himself to breathe slowly and evenly even though it made his stomach hurt. The man made no sound as he gazed in. When he opens the lock, Les kept telling himself—as soon as I hear the door pulled open, I'll jump.

His throat moved once as a nervous shudder rippled through him. Could the man tell he was faking? His muscles tensed, waiting for the sound of the door opening. He *had* to get away now.

There would be no other time. *It* was coming tonight.

Then the sound of the man's boots started away. Abruptly, Les opened his eyes, a look of shocked disbelief contorting his features. The man wasn't going to open the cage!

For a long time he lay there, shivering, staring up mutely at the barred window where the man had stood. He felt like crying aloud and beating his fists against the door until they were bruised and bleeding.

"No . . . *no*." His voice was a lifeless mumble.

Finally, he pushed up and got on his knees. Cautiously, he looked over the rim of the window. The man was gone.

He crouched back down and went through his pockets again.

His wallet—nothing there to help him. His handkerchief, the stub of pencil, forty-seven cents, his comb.

Nothing else.

He held the articles in his palms and stared down at them for long moments as if, somehow, they held the answer to his terrible need. There *had* to be an answer, it was inconceivable that he should actually end up out there on the ground like that other man, put there for that thing to—

"*No!*"

With a spasmodic twitch of his hands, he flung the articles onto the dirt floor of the cage, his lips drawn back in a dull cry of frightened outrage. It can't be real, it had to be a dream!

He fell to his knees desperately and once more began running shaking fingers over the sides of the cage, looking for a crack, a weak board, anything.

And, while he searched in vain, he tried not to think about the night coming and what the night was going to bring.

But that was all he could think about.

She sat up, gasping, as the man's calloused fingers stroked at her hair. Her widened eyes stared at him in horror as he jerked back his hand.

"Elsie," he muttered.

The whiskey-heavy cloud of his breath poured across her face and she drew back, grimacing, her hands clutching tensely at the bedspread.

"Elsie." He said it again, thick voiced, his glazed eyes looking at her drunkenly.

The bedspread rustled beneath her as she pushed back further until her back bumped against the wooden headboard.

"Elsie, I didn't mean to," the man said, dark blades of hair hanging down over his temples, breath falling hotly from his open mouth. "Elsie, don't . . . don't be scared of me."

"W-where's my husband?"

"Elsie, you look like Elsie," the man slurred the words, his blood-streaked eyes pleading. "You look like Elsie, oh . . . *God*, you look like Elsie."

"Where's my husband!"

His hand clamped over her wrist and she felt herself jerked like a flimsy doll against the man's chest. His stale breath surrounded her.

"*No,*" she gasped, her hands pushing at his shoulders.

"I love ya, Elsie, I *love* ya!"

"*Les!*" Her scream rang out in the small room.

Her head snapped to the side as the man's big palm drove across her cheek.

"He's *dead!*" the man shouted hoarsely. "It *ate* him, it *ate* him! You *hear!*"

She fell back against the headboard, her eyes stark with horror. "*No.*" She didn't even know she'd spoken.

The man struggled up to his feet and stood there weaving, looking down at her blank face.

"You think I wanted to?" he asked brokenly, a tear dribbling down his beard-darkened cheek. "You think I *liked* to do it?" A sob shuddered in his chest. "I *didn't* like to do it. But you don't know, y-you don't *know*. I was in it, I was *in* it! Oh God . . . you don't know what it was like. You don't *know!*"

He sank down heavily on the bed, his head slumped forward, his chest racked with helpless sobs.

"I didn't want to. God, do you think I w-*wanted* to?"

Her left fist was pressed rigidly against her lips. She couldn't seem to breathe. No. Her mind struggled to disbelieve. No, it's not true, it isn't true.

Suddenly, she threw her legs over the side of the

bed and stood. Outside, the sun was going down. It doesn't come till dark, her mind argued desperately, not until dark. But how long had she been unconscious?

The man looked up with red-rimmed eyes. "What are ya doing?"

She started running for the door.

As she jerked open the door, the man collided with her and the two of them went crashing against the wall. Breath was driven from her body and the ache in her head flared up again. The man clutched at her; she felt his hands running wildly over her chest and shoulders.

"Elsie, Elsie . . ." the man gasped, trying to kiss her again.

That was when she saw the heavy pitcher on the table beside them. She hardly felt his tightening fingers, his hard, brutal mouth crushed against hers. Her stretching fingers closed over the pitcher handle, she lifted . . .

Great chunks of the white pottery showered on the floor as the man's cry of pain filled the room.

Then Marian was leaning against the wall, gasping for breath and looking down at his crumpled body, at his thick fingers still twitching on the rug.

Suddenly her eyes fled to the window. Almost sunset.

Abruptly, she ran back to the man and bent over his motionless body. Her shaking fingers felt through his overall pockets until they found the ring of keys.

As she fled from the room, she heard the man groan

and saw, over her shoulder, the fleeting sight of him turning slowly onto his back.

She ran down the hall and jerked open the front door. Dying sunlight flooded the sky with its blood.

With a choking gasp, she jumped down the porch steps and ran in desperate, erratic strides around the house, not even feeling the pebbles her feet ran over. She kept looking at the silent row of cages she was running toward. It's not true, it's not true—the words kept running through her brain—he lied to me. A sob pulled back her lips. He *lied!*

Darkness was falling like a rapid curtain as she dashed up to the first cage on trembling legs.

Empty.

Another sob pulsed in her throat. She ran to the next cage. He was lying!

Empty.

"*No.*"

"*Les!*"

"Marian!" He leaped across the cage floor, a sudden wild hope flashing across his face.

"Oh *darling.*" Her voice was a shaking, strengthless murmur, "He told me—"

"Marian, open the cage. Hurry! It's *coming.*"

Dread fell over her again, a wave of numbing cold. Her head jerked to the side instinctively, her shocked gaze fled out across the darkening desert.

"Marian!"

Her hands shook uncontrollably as she tried one of the keys in the lock. It didn't fit. She bit her lip until pain flared up. She tried another key. It didn't fit.

"*Hurry.*"

"Oh God." She whimpered as her palsied hands inserted another key. That didn't fit.

"I can't find the—"

Suddenly, her voice choked off, her breath congealed. In a second, she felt her limbs petrify.

In the silence, faintly, a sound of something huge grating, and hissing over the earth.

"Oh, *no*." She looked aside hurriedly, then back at Les again.

"It's all right, baby," he said. "All right, don't get excited. There's plenty of time." He drew in a heavy breath. "Try the next key. That's right. No, no, the other one. It's *all* right now. There. No, that doesn't work. Try the next one." His stomach kept contracting into a tighter, harder knot.

The skin of Marian's lower lip broke beneath her teeth. She winced and dropped the key ring. With a gagging whimper, she bent over and snatched it up. Across the desert, the wheezing, squashing sound grew louder.

"Oh, Les, I can't, I *can't!*"

"All right, baby," he heard himself say suddenly, "never mind. Run for the highway."

She looked up at him, suddenly expressionless. "*What?*"

"Honey, don't stand there for God's sake!" he cried. "*Run!*"

She caught the breath that shook in her and dug her teeth again into the jagged break on her lip. Her hands stopped shaking and, almost numbed, she tried the next key, the next, while Les stood watching her with terrified eyes, looking over her shoulder toward the desert.

"Honey, don't—"

The lock sprang open. With a breathless grunt, Les shoved open the door and grabbed Marian's hand as the lathing sibilance shook in the twilight air.

"Run!" he gasped. "Don't look back!"

They ran on wildly pumping legs away from the cages, away from the six-foot high mass of quivering life that flopped into the clearing like gelatine dumped from a gargantuan bowl. They tried not to listen, they kept their eyes straight ahead, they ran without breaking their long, panic-driven strides.

The car was back in front of the house again, its front bashed in. They jerked open the doors and slid in frantically. His shaking hand felt the key still in the ignition. He turned it and jabbed in the starter button.

"Les, it's coming this way!"

The gears ground together with a loud rasp and the car jerked forward. He didn't look behind, he just changed gears and kept pushing down on the accelerator until the car lurched into the lane again.

Les turned the car right and headed for the town he remembered passing through—it seemed like years before. He pushed the gas pedal to the floor and the car picked up speed. He couldn't see the road clearly without the headlights but he couldn't keep his foot up, it seemed to jam itself down on the accelerator. The car roared down the darkening road and Les drew in his first easy breath in four days as . . .

the being foamed and rocked across the ground, fury boiling in its tissues. The animal had failed, there was no food waiting, the food had gone. The

being slithered in angry circles, searching, its visual
cells picking at the ground, its sheathed and lumi-
nous formlessness scouring away the flaky dirt.
Nothing. The being gurgled like a viscid tide for the
house, for the clicking sound in . . .

Merv Ketter's arm jerked spasmodically and he sat up,
eyes wide and staring. Pain drove jagged lines of
consciousness into his brain—pain in his head, pain
in his arm. The cone was like a burrowing spider
there, clawing with razor legs, trying to cut its way
out of his flesh. Merv struggled up to his knees, teeth
gritted together, eyes clouding with the pain.

He had barely gained his feet when the crashing,
splintering sound shook the house. He twitched violently, his lower jaw dropping. The digging, gouging
fire in his arm increased and, suddenly he knew. With
a whining gasp, he leaped into the hall and looked
down the dark stairway pit as

the being undulated up the stairs, its seventy ingot
eyes glowering, its shimmering deformity lurching
up toward the animal. Maddened fury hissed and
bubbled through its amorphous shape, it flopped
and flung itself up the angular steps. The animal
turned and fled toward

the back steps!—it was his only chance. He couldn't
breathe, air seemed liquid in his lungs. His boot heels
hammered down the hall and through the darkness
of his bedroom. Behind, he heard the railings buckle
and snap as the being reached the second floor, bent

itself around into a U-shaped bladder, then threw its sodden form forward again.

Merv flung himself down the steep stairway, his palsied hand gripping at the railing, his heartbeat pounding at his chest like mallet blows. He cried out hoarsely as the pain in his arm flared again, almost making him lose consciousness.

As he reached the bottom step, he heard the doorway of his bedroom shattered violently and heard the gushing fury of the being as it

heaved and bucked into the backstair doorway and smashed it out to its own size. Below, it heard the pounding of the fleeing animal. Then adhesiveness lost hold and the being went grinding and rolling down the stairway, its seven hundred feelers pricking the casing and scraping at the splintering wood.

It hit the bottom step, crushed its huge misshapen bulk through the doorway and boiled across the kitchen floor while

in the living room Merv dashed for the mantel. Reaching up, he jerked down the Mauser rifle and whirled as the distended being cascaded its luminescent body through the doorway.

The room echoed and rang with sharp explosions as Merv emptied the rifle into the onrushing hulk. The bullets sprayed off its casing impotently and Merv jumped back with a scream of terror, the gun flung from his hands. His outflung arm knocked off the picture of his wife and he heard it shatter on the floor and, in his twisted mind, had the fleeting vision of it lying on the floor, Elsie's face smiling behind jagged glass.

Then his hand closed over something hard. And, suddenly, he knew exactly what to do.

As the glittering mass reared up and threw its liquidity toward him, Merv jumped to the side. The mantel splintered, the wall cracked open.

Then, as the being pulled itself up again and heaved over him, Merv jerked out the pin of the grenade and held it tightly to his chest.

Stupid beast! I'll kill you now for—
PAIN!!

Tissues exploded, the casing split, the being ran across the floor like slag, a molten torrent of protoplasms.

Then silence in the room. The being's minds snuffed out one by one as tenuous atmosphere starved each tissue of its life. The remains trembled slightly, agony flooded through the being's cells and glutinous joints. Thoughts trickled.

Vital fluids trickling. Lamp beams giving warmth and life to pulsing matter. Organisms joining, cells dividing, the undulant contents of the food vat swelling, swelling, overpowering. Where are they! Where are the masters who gave me life that I might feed them and never lose my bulk or energy?

And then the being, which was born of tumorous hydroponics, died, having forgotten that it, itself, had eaten the masters as they slept, ingesting, with their bodies, all the knowledge of their minds.

On Saturday of the week of August 22nd, that year, there was a violent explosion in the desert and people twenty miles away picked up strange metals in their yards.

"A meteor," they said, but that was because they had to say *something*.

THE TEST

THE NIGHT BEFORE THE TEST, LES HELPED HIS FATHER study in the dining room. Jim and Tommy were asleep upstairs and, in the living room, Terry was sewing, her face expressionless as the needle moved with a swiftly rhythmic piercing and drawing.

Tom Parker sat very straight, his lean, vein-ribbed hands clasped together on the table top, his pale blue eyes looking intently at his son's lips as though it might help him to understand better.

He was 80 and this was his fourth test.

"All right," Les said, reading from the sample test Doctor Trask had gotten them. "Repeat the following sequences of numbers."

"Sequence of numbers," Tom murmured, trying to assimilate the words as they came. But words were not quickly assimilated any more; they seemed to lie upon the tissues of his brain like insects on a sluggish carnivore. He said the words in his mind again—*sequence of . . . sequence of numbers*—there he had it. He looked at his son and waited.

"Well?" he said, impatiently, after a moment's silence.

"Dad, I've already given you the first one," Les told him.

"Well . . ." His father grasped for the proper words. "Kindly give me the—the . . . do me the kindness of . . ."

Les exhaled wearily. "Eight-five-eleven-six," he said.

The old lips stirred, the old machinery of Tom's mind began turning slowly.

"Eight . . . f—ive . . ." The pale eyes blinked slowly. "Elevensix," Tom finished in a breath, then straightened himself proudly.

Yes, good, he thought—very good. They wouldn't fool him tomorrow; he'd beat their murderous law. His lips pressed together and his hands clasped tightly on the white table cloth.

"What?" he said then, refocusing his eyes as Les said something. "Speak up," he said, irritably. "Speak *up*."

"I gave you another sequence," Les said quietly. "Here, I'll read it again."

Tom leaned forward a little, ears straining.

"Nine-two-sixteen-seven-three," Les said.

Tom cleared his throat with effort. "Speak slower," he told his son. He hadn't quite gotten that. How did they expect anyone to retain such a ridiculously long string of numbers?

"What, *what?*" he asked angrily as Les read the numbers again.

"Dad, the examiner will be reading the questions faster than *I'm* reading them. You—"

"I'm quite aware of that," Tom interrupted stiffly.

"Quite aware. Let me remind you . . . however, this is . . . not a test. It's study, it's for *study*. Foolish to go rushing through everything. *Foolish*. I have to learn this—this . . . this *test*," he finished, angry at his son and angry at the way desired words hid themselves from his mind.

Les shrugged and looked down at the test again. "Nine-two-sixteen-seven-three," he read slowly.

"Nine-two-six-seven—"

"*Sixteen*-seven, Dad."

"I said that."

"You said six, Dad."

"Don't you suppose I know what I said!"

Les closed his eyes a moment. "All right, Dad," he said.

"Well, are you going to read it again or not?" Tom asked him sharply.

Les read the numbers off again and, as he listened to his father stumble through the sequence, he glanced into the living room at Terry.

She was sitting there, features motionless, sewing. She'd turned off the radio and he knew she could hear the old man faltering with the numbers.

All right, Les heard himself saying in his mind as if he spoke to her. All right, I know he's old and useless. Do you want me to tell him that to his face and drive a knife into his back? You know and I know that he won't pass the test. Allow me, at least, this brief hypocrisy. Tomorrow the sentence will be passed. Don't make me pass it tonight and break the old man's heart.

"That's correct, I believe," Les heard the dignified voice of his father say and he refocused his eyes on the gaunt, seamed face.

"Yes, that's right," he said, hastily.

He felt like a traitor when a slight smile trembled at the corners of his father's mouth. I'm cheating him, he thought.

"Let's go on to something else," he heard his father say and he looked down quickly at the sheet. What would be easy for him? he thought, despising himself for thinking it.

"Well, come on, Leslie," his father said in a restrained voice. "We have no time to waste."

Tom looked at his son thumbing through the pages and his hands closed into fists. Tomorrow, his life was in the balance and his son just browsed through the test paper as if nothing important were going to happen tomorrow.

"Come on, come on," he said peevishly.

Les picked up a pencil that had string attached to it and drew a half-inch circle on a piece of blank paper. He held out the pencil to his father.

"Suspend the pencil point over the circle for three minutes," he said, suddenly afraid he'd picked the wrong question. He'd seen his father's hands trembling at meal times or fumbling with the buttons and zippers of his clothes.

Swallowing nervously, Les picked up the stop watch, started it, and nodded to his father.

Tom took a quivering breath as he leaned over the paper and tried to hold the slightly swaying pencil above the circle. Les saw him lean on his elbow, something he wouldn't be allowed to do on the test; but he said nothing.

He sat there looking at his father. Whatever color there had been was leaving the old man's face and Les could see clearly the tiny red lines of broken vessels under the skin of his cheeks. He looked at the dry skin, creased and brownish, dappled with liver spots. Eighty years old, he thought—how does a man feel when he's eighty years old?

He looked in at Terry again. For a moment, her gaze shifted and they were looking at each other, neither of them smiling or making any sign. Then Terry looked back to her sewing.

"I believe that's three minutes," Tom said in a taut voice.

Les looked down at the stop watch. "A minute and a half, Dad," he said, wondering if he should have lied again.

"Well, keep your eyes on the watch then," his father said, perturbedly, the pencil penduluming completely out of the circle. "This is supposed to be a test, not a—a—a *party.*"

Les kept his eyes on the wavering pencil point, feeling a sense of utter futility at the realization that this was only pretense, that nothing they did could save his father's life.

At least, he thought, the examinations weren't given by the sons and daughters who had voted the law into being. At least he wouldn't have to stamp the black INADEQUATE on his father's test and thus pronounce the sentence.

The pencil wavered over the circle edge again and was returned as Tom moved his arm slightly on the table, a motion that would automatically disqualify him on that question.

"That watch is slow!" Tom said in a sudden fury.

Les caught his breath and looked down at the

watch. Two and a half minutes. "Three minutes," he said, pushing in the plunger.

Tom slapped down the pencil irritably. *"There,"* he said. "Fool test anyway." His voice grew morose. "Doesn't prove a thing. Not a thing."

"You want to do some money questions, Dad?"

"Are they the next questions in the test?" Tom asked, looking over suspiciously to check for himself.

"Yes," Les lied, knowing that his father's eyes were too weak to see even though Tom always refused to admit he needed glasses. "Oh, wait a second, there's one before that," he added, thinking it would be easier for his father. "They ask you to tell time."

"That's a foolish question," Tom muttered. "What do they—"

He reached across the table irritably and picked up the watch and glanced down at its face. "Ten-fifteen," he said, scornfully.

Before Les could think to stop himself, he said, "But it's eleven-fifteen, Dad."

His father looked, for a moment, as though his face had been slapped. Then he picked up the watch again and stared down at it, lips twitching, and Les had the horrible premonition that Tom was going to insist it really was 10:15.

"Well, that's what I meant," Tom said abruptly. "Slipped out wrong. Course it's eleven-fifteen, any fool can see that. Eleven-fifteen. Watch is no good. Numbers too close. Ought to throw it away. Now—"

Tom reached into his vest pocket and pulled out his own gold watch. "Here's a *watch*," he said, proudly. "Been telling perfect time for . . . sixty years! That's a watch. Not like this."

He tossed Les's watch down contemptuously and it flipped over on its face and the crystal broke.

"Look at that," Tom said quickly, to cover the jolting of embarrassment. "Watch can't take anything."

He avoided Les's eyes by looking down at his own watch. His mouth tightened as he opened the back and looked at Mary's picture; Mary when she was in her thirties, golden-haired and lovely.

Thank God, she didn't have to take these tests, he thought—at least she was spared that. Tom had never thought he could believe that Mary's accidental death at fifty-seven was fortunate, but that was before the tests.

He closed the watch and put it away.

"You just leave that watch with me, tonight," he said grumpily. "I'll see you get a decent . . . uh, *crystal* tomorrow."

"That's all right, Dad. It's just an old watch."

"That's *all* right," Tom said. "That's all right. You just leave it with me. I'll get you a decent . . . crystal. Get you one that won't break, one that won't break. You just leave it with me."

Tom did the money questions then, questions like *How many quarters in a five dollar bill?* and *If I took 36 cents from your dollar, how much change would you have left?*

They were written questions and Les sat there timing his father. It was quiet in the house, warm. Everything seemed very normal and ordinary with the two of them sitting there and Terry sewing in the living room.

That was the horror.

Life went on as usual. No one spoke of dying. The

government sent out letters and the tests were given and those who failed were requested to appear at the government center for their injections. The law operated, the death rate was steady, the population problem was contained—all officially, impersonally, without a cry or a sensation.

But it was still loved people who were being killed.

"Never mind hanging over that watch," his father said. "I can do these questions without you . . . hanging over that watch."

"Dad, the examiners will be looking at their watches."

"The examiners are the examiners," Tom snapped. "You're not an examiner."

"Dad, I'm trying to help y—"

"Well, help me then, *help* me. Don't sit there hanging over that watch."

"This is your test, Dad, not mine," Les started, a flush of anger creeping up his cheeks. "If—"

"My test, yes, my test!" his father suddenly raged. "You all saw to that, didn't you? All saw to it that—that—"

Words failed again, angry thoughts piling up in his brain.

"You don't have to yell, Dad."

"I'm not yelling!"

"Dad, the boys are sleeping!" Terry suddenly broke in.

"I don't care if—!" Tom broke off suddenly and leaned back in the chair, the pencil falling unnoticed from his fingers and rolling across the table cloth. He sat shivering, his thin chest rising and falling in jerks, his hands twitching uncontrollably on his lap.

"Do you want to go on, Dad?" Les asked, restraining his nervous anger.

"I don't ask much," Tom mumbled to himself. "Don't ask much in life."

"Dad, shall we go *on?*"

His father stiffened. *"If you can spare the time,"* he said with slow, indignant pride. *"If you can spare the time."*

Les looked at the test paper, his fingers gripping the stapled sheets rigidly. Psychological questions? No, he couldn't ask them. How did you ask your eighty-year-old father his views on sex?—your flint-surfaced father to whom the most innocuous remark was "obscene."

"Well?" his father asked in a rising voice.

"There doesn't seem to be anymore," Les said. "We've been at it almost four hours now."

"What about all those pages you just skipped?"

"Most of those are for the . . . the physical, Dad."

He saw his father's lips press together and was afraid Tom was going to say something about that again. But all his father said was, "A fine friend. Fine friend."

"Dad, you—"

Les's voice broke off. There was no point in talking about it anymore. Tom knew perfectly well that Doctor Trask couldn't make out a bill of health for this test the way he'd done for the three tests previous.

Les knew how frightened and insulted the old man was because he'd have to take off his clothes and be exposed to doctors who would probe and tap and ask offensive questions. He knew how afraid Tom was of the fact that when he re-dressed, he'd be watched from a peephole and someone would mark on a chart how well he dressed himself. He knew how it frightened his father to know that, when he ate in the government cafeteria at the midpoint of the day-long examination, eyes would be watching him again to see if he dropped a fork or a spoon or knocked over a glass of water or dribbled gravy on his shirt.

"They'll ask you to sign your name and address," Les said, wanting his father to forget about the physical and knowing how proud Tom was of his handwriting.

Pretending that he grudged it, the old man picked up the pencil and wrote. I'll fool them, he thought as the pencil moved across the page with strong, sure motions.

Mr. Thomas Parker, he wrote, *2719 Brighton Street, Blairtown, New York*.

"And the date," Les said.

The old man wrote, *January 17, 2003*, and something cold moved in the old man's vitals.

Tomorrow was the test.

They lay beside each other, neither of them sleeping. They had barely spoken while undressing and when Les had leaned over to kiss her goodnight she'd murmured something he didn't hear.

Now he turned over on his side with a heavy sigh and faced her. In the darkness, she opened her eyes and looked over at him.

"Asleep?" she asked softly.

"No."

He said no more. He waited for her to start.

But she didn't start and, after a few moments, he

said, "Well, I guess this is . . . it." He finished weakly
because he didn't like the words; they sounded ridiculously melodramatic.

Terry didn't say anything right away. Then, as if
thinking aloud, she said, "Do you think there's any
chance that—"

Les tightened at the words because he knew what
she was going to say.

"No," he said. "He'll never pass."

He heard Terry swallowing. Don't say it, he thought,
pleadingly. Don't tell me I've been saying the same
thing for fifteen years. I know it. I said it because I
thought it was true.

Suddenly, he wished he'd signed the *Request For
Removal* years before. They needed desperately to be
free of Tom; for the good of their children and themselves. But how did you put that need into words without feeling like a murderer? You couldn't say: I hope
the old man fails, I hope they kill him. Yet anything
else you said was only a hypocritical substitute for
those words because that was exactly how you felt.

Medical terms, he thought—charts about declining crops and lowered standard of living and hunger
ratio and degrading health level—they'd used all
those as arguments to support passage of the law.
Well, they were lies—obvious, groundless lies. The
law had been passed because people wanted to be left
alone, because they wanted to live their own lives.

"Les, what if he passes?" Terry said.

He felt his hands tightening on the mattress.

"Les?"

"I don't know, honey," he said.

Her voice was firm in the darkness. It was a voice at the end of patience. "You have to know," it said.

He moved his head restlessly on the pillow. "Honey, don't push it," he begged. "Please."

"Les, if he passes that test it means five more years. *Five more years,* Les. Have you thought what that means?"

"Honey, he can't pass that test."

"But, what if he does?"

"Terry, he missed three-quarters of the questions I asked him tonight. His hearing is almost gone, his eyes are bad, his heart is weak, he has arthritis." His fist beat down hopelessly on the bed. "He won't even pass the *physical,*" he said, feeling himself tighten in self-hatred for assuring her that Tom was doomed.

If only he could forget the past and take his father for what he was now—a helpless, mind-jading old man who was ruining their lives. But it was hard to forget how he'd loved and respected his father, hard to forget the hikes in the country, the fishing trips, the long talks at night and all the many things his father and he had shared together.

That was why he'd never had the strength to sign the request. It was a simple form to fill out, much simpler than waiting for the five-year tests. But it had meant signing away the life of his father, requesting the government to dispose of him like some unwanted garbage. He could never do that.

And yet, now his father was 80 and, in spite of moral upbringing, in spite of life-taught Christian principles, he and Terry were horribly afraid that old Tom might pass the test and live another five years with them—another five years of fumbling around the house, undoing instructions they gave to the boys, breaking things, wanting to help but only getting in the way and making life an agony of held-in nerves.

"You'd better sleep," Terry said to him.

He tried to but he couldn't. He lay staring at the dark ceiling and trying to find an answer but finding no answer.

The alarm went off at six. Les didn't have to get up until eight but he wanted to see his father off. He got out of bed and dressed quietly so he wouldn't wake up Terry.

She woke up anyway and looked up at him from her pillow. After a moment, she pushed up on one elbow and looked sleepily at him.

"I'll get up and make you some breakfast," she said.

"That's all right," Les said. "You stay in bed."

"Don't you want me to get up?"

"Don't bother, honey," he said. "I want you to rest."

She lay down again and turned away so Les wouldn't see her face. She didn't know why she began to cry soundlessly; whether it was because he didn't want her to see his father or because of the test. But she couldn't stop. All she could do was hold herself rigid until the bedroom door had closed.

Then her shoulders trembled and a sob broke the barrier she had built in herself.

The door to his father's room was open as Les passed. He looked in and saw Tom sitting on the bed, leaning down and fastening his dark shoes. He saw the gnarled fingers shaking as they moved over the straps.

"Everything all right, Dad?" Les asked.

His father looked up in surprise. "What are you doing up this hour?" he asked.

"Thought I'd have breakfast with you," Les told him.

For a moment they looked at each other in silence. Then his father leaned over the shoes again. "That's not necessary," he heard the old man's voice telling him.

"Well, I think I'll have some breakfast anyway," he said and turned away so his father wouldn't argue.

"Oh . . . *Leslie.*"

Les turned.

"I trust you didn't forget to leave that watch out," his father said. "I intend to take it to the jeweler's today and have a decent . . . decent crystal put on it, one that won't break."

"Dad, it's just an old watch," Les said. "It's not worth a nickel."

His father nodded slowly, one palm wavering before him as if to ward off argument. "Never-the-less," he stated slowly, "I intend to—"

"All right, Dad, all right. I'll put it on the kitchen table."

His father broke off and looked at him blankly a moment. Then, as if it were impulse and not delayed will, he bent over his shoes again.

Les stood for a moment looking down at his father's gray hair, his gaunt, trembling fingers. Then he turned away.

The watch was still on the dining room table. Les picked it up and took it in to the kitchen table. The old man must have been reminding himself about the watch all night, he thought. Otherwise he wouldn't have managed to remember it.

He put fresh water in the coffee globe and pushed the buttons for two servings of bacon and eggs. Then he poured two glasses of orange juice and sat down at the table.

About fifteen minutes later, his father came down wearing his dark blue suit, his shoes carefully polished, his nails manicured, his hair slicked down and combed and brushed. He looked very neat and very old as he walked over to the coffee globe and looked in.

"Sit down, Dad," Les said. "I'll get it for you."

"I'm not helpless," his father said. "Stay where you are."

Les managed to smile. "I put some bacon and eggs on for us," he said.

"Not hungry," his father replied.

"You'll need a good breakfast in you, Dad."

"Never did eat a big breakfast," his father said, stiffly, still facing the stove. "Don't believe in it. Not good for the stomach."

Les closed his eyes a moment and across his face moved an expression of hopeless despair. Why did I bother getting up? he asked himself defeatedly. All we do is argue.

No. He felt himself stiffening. No, he'd be cheerful if it killed him.

"Sleep all right, Dad?" he asked.

"Course I slept all right," his father answered.

"Always sleep fine. Fine. Did you think I wouldn't because of a—"

He broke off suddenly and turned accusingly at Les. "Where's that watch?" he demanded.

Les exhaled wearily and held up the watch. His father moved jerkily across the linoleum, took it from him and looked at it a moment, his old lips pursed.

"Shoddy workmanship," he said. "Shoddy." He put it carefully in his side coat pocket. "Get you a decent crystal," he muttered. "One that won't break."

Les nodded. "That'll be swell, Dad."

The coffee was ready then and Tom poured them each a cup. Les got up and turned off the automatic griller. He didn't feel like having bacon and eggs either now.

He sat across the table from his stern-faced father and felt hot coffee trickling down his throat. It tasted terrible but he knew that nothing in the world would have tasted good to him that morning.

"What time do you have to be there, Dad?" he asked to break the silence.

"Nine o'clock," Tom said.

"You're sure you don't want me to drive you there?"

"Not at all, not at all," his father said as though he were talking patiently to an irritably insistent child. "The tube is good enough. Get me there in plenty of time."

"All right, Dad," Les said and sat there staring into his coffee. There must be something he could say, he thought, but he couldn't think of anything. Silence hung over them for long minutes while Tom drank his black coffee in slow, methodical sips.

Les licked his lips nervously, then hid the trembling

of them behind his cup. Talking, he thought, talking and talking—of cars and tube conveyers and examination schedules—when all the time both of them knew that Tom might be sentenced to death that day.

He was sorry he'd gotten up. It would have been better to wake up and just find his father gone. He wished it could happen that way—*permanently*. He wished he could wake up some morning and find his father's room empty—the two suits gone, the dark shoes gone, the work clothes gone, the handkerchiefs, the socks, the garters, the braces, the shaving equipment—all those mute evidences of a life gone.

But it wouldn't be like that. After Tom failed the test, it would be several weeks before the letter of final appointment came and then another week or so before the appointment itself. It would be a hideously slow process of packing and disposing of and giving away of possessions, a process of meals and meals and meals together, of talking to each other, of a last dinner, of a long drive to the government center, of a ride up in a silent, humming elevator, of—

Dear God!

He found himself shivering helplessly and was afraid for a moment that he was going to cry.

Then he looked up with a shocked expression as his father stood.

"I'll be going now," Tom said.

Les's eyes fled to the wall clock. "But it's only a quarter to seven," he said tensely. "It doesn't take that long to—"

"Like to be in plenty of time," his father said firmly. "Never like to be late."

"But my God, Dad, it only takes an hour at the

most to get to the city," he said, feeling a terrible sinking in his stomach.

His father shook his head and Les knew he hadn't heard. "It's early, Dad," he said, loudly, his voice shaking a little.

"Never-the-less," his father said.

"But you haven't *eaten* anything."

"Never did eat a big breakfast," Tom started. "Not good for the—"

Les didn't hear the rest of it—the words about lifetime habit and not good for the digestion and everything else his father said. He felt waves of merciless horror breaking over him and he wanted to jump and throw his arms around the old man and tell him not to worry about the test because it didn't matter, because they loved him and would take care of him.

But he couldn't. He sat rigid with sick fright, looking up at his father. He couldn't even speak when his father turned at the kitchen door and said in a voice that was calmly dispassionate because it took every bit of strength the old man had to make it so, "I'll see you tonight, Leslie."

The door swung shut and the breeze that ruffled across Les's cheeks chilled him to the heart.

Suddenly, he jumped up with a startled grunt and rushed across the linoleum. As he pushed through the doorway he saw his father almost to the front door.

"Dad!"

Tom stopped and looked back in surprise as Les walked across the dining room, hearing the steps counted in his mind—*one, two, three, four, five.*

He stopped before his father and forced a faltering smile to his lips.

"Good luck, Dad," he said. "I'll . . . see you tonight." He had been about to say, "I'll be rooting for you"; but he couldn't.

His father nodded once, just once, a curt nod as of one gentleman acknowledging another.

"Thank you," his father said and turned away.

When the door shut, it seemed as if, suddenly, it had become an impenetrable wall through which his father could never pass again.

Les moved to the window and watched the old man walk slowly down the path and turn left onto the sidewalk. He watched his father start up the street, then straighten himself, throw back his lean shoulders and walk erect and briskly into the gray of morning.

At first Les thought it was raining. But then he saw that the shimmering moistness wasn't on the window at all.

He couldn't go to work. He phoned in sick and stayed home. Terry got the boys off to school and, after they'd eaten breakfast, Les helped her clear away the morning dishes and put them in the washer. Terry didn't say anything about his staying home. She acted as if it were normal for him to be home on a weekday.

He spent the morning and afternoon puttering in the garage shop, starting seven different projects and losing interest in them.

Around five, he went into the kitchen and had a can of beer while Terry made supper. He didn't say anything to her. He kept pacing around the living room, staring out the window at the overcast sky, then pacing again.

"I wonder where he is," he finally said, back in the kitchen again.

"He'll be back," she said and he stiffened a moment, thinking he heard disgust in her voice. Then he relaxed, knowing it was only his imagination.

When he dressed after taking a shower, it was five-forty. The boys were home from playing and they all sat down to supper. Les noticed a place set for his father and wondered if Terry had set it there for his benefit.

He couldn't eat anything. He kept cutting the meat into smaller and smaller pieces and mashing butter into his baked potato without tasting any of it.

"What is it?" he asked as Jim spoke to him.

"Dad, if Grandpa don't pass the test, he gets a month, don't he?"

Les felt his stomach muscles tightening as he stared at his older son. *Gets a month, don't he?*—the last of Jim's question muttered on in his brain.

"What are you talking about?" he asked.

"My Civics book says old people get a month to live after they don't pass their test. That's right, isn't it?"

"No, it *isn't*," Tommy broke in. "Harry Senker's grandma got her letter after only two weeks."

"How do *you* know?" Jim asked his nine-year-old brother, "Did you see it?"

"That's enough," Les said.

"Don't *have* t'see it!" Tommy argued. "Harry told me that—"

"That's *enough!*"

The two boys looked suddenly at their white-faced father.

"We won't talk about it," he said.

"But what—"

"*Jimmy,*" Terry said, warningly.

Jimmy looked at his mother, then, after a moment, went back to his food and they all ate in silence.

The death of their grandfather means nothing to them, Les thought bitterly—nothing at all. He swallowed and tried to relax the tightness in his body. Well, why *should* it mean anything to them? he told himself; it's not their time to worry yet. Why force it on them now? They'll have it soon enough.

When the front door opened and shut at 6:10, Les stood up so quickly, he knocked over an empty glass.

"Les, *don't,*" Terry said suddenly and he knew, immediately, that she was right. His father wouldn't like him to come rushing from the kitchen with questions.

He slumped down on the chair again and stared at his barely touched food, his heart throbbing. As he picked up his fork with tight fingers, he heard the old man cross the dining room rug and start up the stairs. He glanced at Terry and her throat moved.

He couldn't eat. He sat there breathing heavily, and picking at the food. Upstairs, he heard the door to his father's room close.

It was when Terry was putting the pie on the table that Les excused himself quickly and got up.

He was at the foot of the stairs when the kitchen door was pushed open. "Les," he heard her say, urgently.

He stood there silently as she came up to him.

"Isn't it better we leave him alone?" she asked.

"But, honey, I—"

"Les, if he'd passed the test, he would have come into the kitchen and told us."

"Honey, he wouldn't know if—"

"He'd know if he passed, you know that. He told us about it the last two times. If he'd passed, he'd have—"

Her voice broke off and she shuddered at the way he was looking at her. In the heavy silence, she heard a sudden splattering of rain on the windows.

They looked at each other a long moment. Then Les said, "I'm going up."

"Les," she murmured.

"I won't say anything to upset him," he said. "I'll . . ."

A moment longer they stared at each other. Then he turned away and trudged up the steps. Terry watched him go with a bleak, hopeless look on her face.

Les stood before the closed door a minute, bracing himself. I won't upset him, he told himself; I *won't*.

He knocked softly, wondering, in that second, if he were making a mistake. Maybe he should have left the old man alone, he thought unhappily.

In the bedroom, he heard a rustling movement on the bed, then the sound of his father's feet touching the floor.

"Who is it?" he heard Tom ask.

Les caught his breath. "It's me, Dad," he said.

"What do you want?"

"May I see you?"

Silence inside. "Well . . ." he heard his father say then and his voice stopped. Les heard him get up and heard the sound of his footsteps on the floor. Then there was the sound of paper rattling and a bureau drawer being carefully shut.

Finally the door opened.

Tom was wearing his old red bathrobe over his clothes and he'd taken off his shoes and put his slippers on.

"May I come in, Dad?" Les asked quietly.

His father hesitated a moment. Then he said, "Come in," but it wasn't an invitation. It was more as if he'd said, This is your house, I can't keep you from this room.

Les was going to tell his father that he didn't want to disturb him but he couldn't. He went in and stood in the middle of the throw rug, waiting.

"Sit down," his father said and Les sat down on the upright chair that Tom hung his clothes on at night. His father waited until Les was seated and then sank down on the bed with a grunt.

For a long time they looked at each other without speaking, like total strangers, each waiting for the other one to speak. How did the test go? Les heard the words repeated in his mind. How did the test go, how did the test go? He couldn't speak the words. How did the—

"I suppose you want to know what . . . happened," his father said then, controlling himself visibly.

"Yes," Les said. "I . . ." He caught himself. "Yes," he repeated and waited.

Old Tom looked down at the floor for a moment. Then, suddenly, he raised his head and looked defiantly at his son.

"*I didn't go,*" he said.

Les felt as if all his strength had suddenly been sucked into the floor. He sat there, motionless, staring at his father.

"Had no intention of going," his father hurried on. "No intention of going through all that foolishness. Physical tests, m-mental tests, putting b-b-*blocks* in a board and . . . Lord knows what all! Had no intention of going."

He stopped and stared at his son with angry eyes as if he were daring Les to say he had done wrong.

But Les couldn't say anything.

A long time passed. Les swallowed and managed to summon the words. "What are you . . . going to do?"

"Never mind that, never mind," his father said, almost as if he were grateful for the question. "Don't you worry about your Dad. Your Dad knows how to take care of himself."

And suddenly Les heard the bureau drawer shutting again, the rustling of a paper bag. He almost looked around at the bureau to see if the bag were still there. His head twitched as he fought down the impulse.

"W-ell," he faltered, not realizing how stricken and lost his expression was.

"Just never mind now," his father said again, quietly, almost gently. "It's not your problem to worry about. Not your problem at all."

But it is! Les heard the words cried out in his mind. But he didn't speak them. Something in the old man stopped him; a sort of fierce strength, a taut dignity he knew he mustn't touch.

"I'd like to rest now," he heard Tom say then and he felt as if he'd been struck violently in the stomach. I'd like to rest now, to rest now—the words echoed down long tunnels of the mind as he stood. Rest now, rest now . . .

He found himself being ushered to the door where he turned and looked at his father. *Good-bye.* The word stuck in him.

Then his father smiled and said, "Good night, Leslie."

"*Dad.*"

He felt the old man's hand in his own, stronger than his, more steady; calming him, reassuring him. He felt his father's left hand grip his shoulder.

"Good night, son," his father said and, in the moment they stood close together Les saw, over the old man's shoulder, the crumpled drugstore bag lying in the corner of the room as though it had been thrown there so as not to be seen.

Then he was standing in wordless terror in the hall, listening to the latch clicking shut and knowing that, although his father wasn't locking the door, he couldn't go into his father's room.

For a long time he stood staring at the closed door, shivering without control. Then he turned away.

Terry was waiting for him at the foot of the stairs, her face drained of color. She asked the question with her eyes as he came down to her.

"He . . . didn't go," was all he said.

She made a tiny, startled sound in her throat. "But—"

"He's been to the drugstore," Les said. "I . . . saw the bag in the corner of the room. He threw it away so I wouldn't see it but I . . . saw it."

For a moment, it seemed as if she were starting for the stairs but it was only a momentary straining of her body.

"He must have shown the druggist the letter about

the test," Les said. "The . . . druggist must have given him . . . pills. Like they all do."

They stood silently in the dining room while rain drummed against the windows.

"What shall we do?" she asked, almost inaudibly.

"Nothing," he murmured. His throat moved convulsively and breath shuddered through him. "*Nothing.*"

Then he was walking numbly back to the kitchen and he could feel her arm tight around him as if she were trying to press her love to him because she could not speak of love.

All evening, they sat there in the kitchen. After she put the boys to bed, she came back and they sat in the kitchen drinking coffee and talking in quiet, lonely voices.

Near midnight, they left the kitchen and just before they went upstairs, Les stopped by the dining room table and found the watch with a shiny new crystal on it. He couldn't even touch it.

They went upstairs and walked past the door of Tom's bedroom. There was no sound inside. They got undressed and got in bed together and Terry set the clock the way she set it every night. In a few hours they both managed to fall asleep.

And all night there was silence in the old man's room. And the next day, silence.

ONE FOR THE BOOKS

WHEN HE WOKE UP THAT MORNING, HE COULD TALK French.

There was no warning. At six-fifteen, the alarm went off as usual and he and his wife stirred. Fred reached out a sleep-deadened hand and shut off the bell. The room was still for a moment.

Then Eva pushed back the covers on her side and he pushed back the covers on his side. His vein-gnarled legs dropped over the side of the bed. He said, "*Bon matin*, Eva."

There was a slight pause.

"Wha'?" she asked.

"*Je dis bon matin*," he said.

There was a rustle of nightgown as she twisted around to squint at him. "*What'd* you say?"

"All I said was good—"

Fred Elderman stared back at his wife.

"What *did* I say?" he asked in a whisper.

"You said '*bone mattin*' or—"

"Je dis bon matin. C'est un bon matin, n'est-ce pas?"

The sound of his hand being clapped across his mouth was like that of a fast ball thumping in a catcher's mitt. Above the knuckle-ridged gag, his eyes were shocked.

"Fred, what *is* it?"

Slowly, the hand drew down from his lips.

"I dunno, Eva," he said, awed. Unconsciously, the hand reached up, one finger of it rubbing at his hair-ringed bald spot. "It sounds like some—some kind of foreign talk."

"But you don't know no foreign talk, Fred," she told him.

"That's just it."

They sat there looking at each other blankly. Fred glanced over at the clock.

"We better get dressed," he said.

While he was in the bathroom, she heard him singing, *"Elle fit un fromage, du lait de ses moutons, ron, ron, du lait de ses moutons,"* but she didn't dare call it to his attention while he was shaving.

Over breakfast coffee, he muttered something.

"What?" she asked before she could stop herself.

"Je dis que veut dire ceci?"

He heard the coffee go down her gulping throat.

"I mean," he said, looking dazed, "what does this mean?"

"Yes, what *does* it? You never talked no foreign language before."

"I *know* it," he said, toast suspended halfway to his open mouth. "What—what kind of language is it?"

"S-sounds t'me like French."

"*French?* I don't know no French."

She swallowed more coffee. "You do now," she said weakly.

He stared at the tablecloth.

"*Le diable s'en mêle,*" he muttered.

Her voice rose. "Fred, *what?*"

His eyes were confused. "I said the devil has something to do with it."

"Fred, you're—"

She straightened up in the chair and took a deep breath. "Now," she said, "let's not profane, Fred. There has to be a good reason for this." No reply. "Well, *doesn't* there, Fred?"

"Sure, Eva. *Sure.* But—"

"No buts about it," she declared, plunging ahead as if she were afraid to stop. "Now is there any reason in this world why you should know how to talk French"—she snapped her thin fingers—"just like that?"

He shook his head vaguely.

"Well," she went on, wondering what to say next, "let's see then." They looked at each other in silence. "Say something," she decided. "Let's—" She groped for words. "Let's see what we . . . have here." Her voice died off.

"Say somethin'?"

"Yes," she said. "Go on."

"*Un gémissement se fit entendre. Les dogues se mettent à aboyer. Ces gants me vont bien. Il va sur les quinze ans—*"

"Fred?"

"*Il fit fabriquer une exacte représentation du monstre.*"

"Fred, hold on!" she cried, looking scared.

His voice broke off and he looked at her, blinking.

"What . . . what did you say this time, Fred?" she asked.

"I said—a moan was heard. His mastiffs began to bark. These gloves fit me. He will soon be fifteen years old and—"

"What?"

"And he had an exact copy of the monster made. *Sans même l'entamer.*"

"*Fred?*"

He looked ill. "Without even scratchin'," he said.

At that hour of the morning, the campus was quiet. The only classes that early were the two seven-thirty Economics lectures and they were held on the White Campus. Here on the Red there was no sound. In an hour the walks would be filled with chatting, laughing, loafer-clicking student hordes, but for now there was peace.

In far less than peace, Fred Elderman shuffled along the east side of the campus, headed for the administration building. Having left a confused Eva at home, he'd been trying to figure it out as he went to work.

What was it? When had it begun? *C'est une heure,* said his mind.

He shook his head angrily. This was terrible. He tried desperately to think of what could have happened, but he couldn't. It just didn't make sense. He was fifty-nine, a janitor at the university with no education to speak of, living a quiet, ordinary life. Then he woke up one morning speaking articulate French.

French.

He stopped a moment and stood in the frosty October wind, staring at the cupola of Jeramy Hall. He'd cleaned out the French office the night before. Could that have anything to do with—

No, that was ridiculous. He started off again, muttering under his breath—unconsciously. "*Je suis, tu es, il est, elle est, nous sommes, vous êtes—*"

At eight-ten, he entered the History Department office to repair a sink in the washroom. He worked on it for an hour and seven minutes, then put the tools back in the bag and walked out into the office.

"Mornin'," he said to the professor sitting at a desk.

"Good morning, Fred," said the professor.

Fred Elderman walked out into the hall thinking how remarkable it was that the income of Louis XVI, from the same type of taxes, exceeded that of Louis XV by 130 million livres and that the exports which had been 106 million in 1720 were 192 million in 1746 and—

He stopped in the hall, a stunned look on his lean face.

That morning, he had occasion to be in the offices of the Physics, the Chemistry, the English and the Art Departments.

The Windmill was a little tavern near Main Street. Fred went there Monday, Wednesday, and Friday evenings to nurse a couple of draught beers and chat with his two friends—Harry Bullard, manager of Hogan's Bowling Alley, and Lou Peacock, postal worker and amateur gardener.

Stepping into the doorway of the dim-lit saloon

that evening, Fred was heard—by an exiting patron—to murmur, *"Je connais tous ces braves gens,"* then look around with a guilty twitch of cheek. "I mean . . ." he muttered, but didn't finish.

Harry Bullard saw him first in the mirror. Twisting his head around on its fat column of neck, he said, "C'mon in, Fred, the whiskey's fine," then, to the bartender, "Draw one for the elder man," and chuckled.

Fred walked to the bar with the first smile he'd managed to summon that day. Peacock and Bullard greeted him and the bartender set down a brimming stein.

"What's new, Fred?" Harry asked.

Fred pressed his mustache between two foam-removing fingers.

"Not much," he said, still too uncertain to discuss it. Dinner with Eva had been a painful meal during which he'd eaten not only food but an endless and detailed running commentary on the Thirty Years War, the Magna Charta and boudoir information about Catherine the Great. He had been glad to retire from the house at seven-thirty, murmuring an unmanageable, *"Bon nuit, ma chère."*

"What's new with you?" he asked Harry Bullard now.

"Well," Harry answered, "we been paintin' down at the alleys. You know, redecoratin'."

"That right?" Fred said. "When painting with colored beeswax was inconvenient, Greek and Roman easel painters used *tempera*—that is, colors fixed upon a wood or stucco base by means of such a medium as—

He stopped. There was a bulging silence.

"Hanh?" Harry Bullard asked.

Fred swallowed nervously. "Nothing," he said hastily. "I was just—" He stared down into the tan depths of his beer. "Nothing," he repeated.

Bullard glanced at Peacock, who shrugged back.

"How are your hothouse flowers coming, Lou?" Fred inquired, to change the subject.

The small man nodded. "Fine. They're just fine."

"Good," said Fred, nodding, too. "*Vi sono pui di cinquante bastimenti in porto.*" He gritted his teeth and closed his eyes.

"What's that?" Lou asked, cupping one ear.

Fred coughed on his hastily swallowed beer. "Nothing," he said.

"No, what did ya say?" Harry persisted, the half-smile on his broad face indicating that he was ready to hear a good joke.

"I—I said there are more than fifty ships in the harbor," explained Fred morosely.

The smile faded. Harry looked blank.

"What harbor?" he asked.

Fred tried to sound casual. "I—it's just a joke I heard today. But I forgot the last line."

"Oh." Harry stared at Fred, then returned to his drink. "Yeah."

They were quiet a moment. Then Lou asked Fred, "Through for the day?"

"No. I have to clean up the Math office later."

Lou nodded. "That's too bad."

Fred squeezed more foam from his mustache. "Tell me something," he said, taking the plunge impulsively. "What would you think if you woke up one morning talking French?"

"Who did that?" asked Harry, squinting.

"Nobody," Fred said hurriedly. "Just . . . *supposing*, I mean. Supposing a man was to—well, to *know* things he never learned. You know what I mean? Just *know* them. As if they were always in his mind and he was seeing them for the first time."

"What kind o' things, Fred?" asked Lou.

"Oh . . . history. Different . . . languages. Things about . . . books and painting and . . . and atoms and—chemicals." His shrug was jerky and obvious. "Things like that."

"Don't get ya, buddy," Harry said, having given up any hopes that a joke was forthcoming.

"You mean he knows things he never learned?" Lou asked. "That it?"

There was something in both their voices—a doubting incredulity, a holding back, as if they feared to commit themselves, a suspicious reticence.

Fred sloughed it off. "I was just supposing. Forget it. It's not worth talking about."

He had only one beer that night, leaving early with the excuse that he had to clean the Mathematics office. And, all through the silent minutes that he swept and mopped and dusted, he kept trying to figure out what was happening to him.

He walked home in the chill of night to find Eva waiting for him in the kitchen.

"Coffee, Fred?" she offered.

"I'd like that," he said, nodding. She started to get up. "No, *s'accomadi, la prego*," he blurted.

She looked at him, grim-faced.

"I mean," he translated, "sit down, Eva. I can get it."

They sat there drinking coffee while he told her about his experiences.

"It's more than I can figure, Eva," he said. "It's . . . scary, in a way. I know so many things I never knew. I have no idea where they come from. Not the least idea." His lips pressed together. "But I *know* them," he said, "I certainly know them."

"More than just . . . French now?" she asked.

He nodded his head worriedly. "Lots more," he said. "Like—" He looked up from his cup. "Listen to this. Main progress in producing fast particles has been made by using relatively small voltages and repeated acceleration. In most of the instruments used, charged particles are driven round in circular or spiral orbits with the help of a—you listenin', Eva?"

He saw her Adam's apple move. "I'm listenin'," she said.

"—help of a magnetic field. The acceleration can be applied in different ways. In the so-called betatron of Kerst and Serber—"

"What does it *mean*, Fred?" she interrupted.

"I don't know," he said helplessly. "It's . . . just words in my head. I know what it means when I say something in a foreign tongue, but . . . this?"

She shivered, clasping at her forearms abruptly.

"It's not right," she said.

He frowned at her in silence for a long moment.

"What do you mean, Eva?" he asked then.

"I don't know, Fred," she said quietly and shook her head once, slowly. "I just don't know."

She woke up about midnight and heard him mumbling in his sleep.

"The natural logarithms of whole numbers from ten to two hundred. Number one—*zero*—two point three oh two six. *One*—two point three nine seven nine. *Two*—two point—"

"Fred, go t'sleep," she said, frowning nervously.

"—four eight four nine."

She prodded him with an elbow. "Go t'*sleep*, Fred."

"*Three*—two point—"

"Fred!"

"Huh?" He moaned and swallowed dryly, turned on his side.

In the darkness, she heard him shape the pillow with sleep-heavy hands.

"Fred?" she called softly.

He coughed. "What?"

"I think you better go t'Doctor Boone t'morra mornin'."

She heard him draw in a long breath, then let it filter out evenly until it was all gone.

"I think so, too," he said in a blurry voice.

On Friday morning, when he opened the door to the waiting room of Doctor William Boone, a draft of wind scattered papers from the nurse's desk.

"Oh," he said apologetically. *"Le chieggo scuse. Non ne val la pena."*

Miss Agnes McCarthy had been Doctor Boone's receptionist-nurse for seven years and in that time she'd never heard Fred Elderman speak a single foreign word.

Thus she goggled at him, amazed. "What's that you said?" she asked.

Fred's smile was a nervous twitch of lips.

"Nothing," he said, "Miss."

Her returned smile was formal. "Oh." She cleared her throat. "I'm sorry the doctor couldn't see you yesterday."

"That's all right," he told her.

"He'll be ready in about ten minutes."

Twenty minutes later, Fred sat down beside Boone's desk and the heavy-set doctor leaned back in his chair with an, "Ailing, Fred?"

Fred explained the situation.

The doctor's cordial smile became, in order, amused, fixed, strained and finally nonexistent.

"This is really so?" he demanded.

Fred nodded with grim deliberation. *"Je me laisse conseiller."*

Doctor Boone's heavy eyebrows lifted a noticeable jot. "French," he said. "What'd you say?"

Fred swallowed. "I said I'm willing to be advised."

"Son of a gun," intoned Doctor Boone, plucking at his lower lip. "*Son* of a gun." He got up and ran exploring hands over Fred's skull. "You haven't received a head blow lately, have you?"

"No," said Fred. "Nothing."

"Hmmm." Doctor Boone drew away his hands and let them drop to his sides. "Well, no apparent bumps or cracks." He buzzed for Miss McCarthy. Then he said, "Well, let's take a try at the x-rays."

The x-rays revealed no break or blot.

The two men sat in the office, discussing it.

"Hard to believe," said the doctor, shaking his head. Fred sighed despondently. "Well, don't take on so," Boone said. "It's nothing to be disturbed about. So you're a quiz kid, so what?"

Fred ran nervous fingers over his mustache. "But there's no sense to it. Why is it happening? What is it? The fact is, I'm a little scared."

"Nonsense, Fred. *Nonsense*. You're in good physical condition. That I guarantee."

"But what about my—" Fred hesitated "—my brain?"

Doctor Boone stuck out his lower lip in consoling derision, shaking his head. "I wouldn't worry about that, either." He slapped one palm on the desk top. "Let me think about it, Fred. Consult a few associates. You know—*analyze* it. Then I'll let you know. Fair enough?"

He walked Fred to the door.

"In the meantime," he prescribed, "no worrying about it. There isn't a thing to worry about."

His face as he dialed the phone a few minutes later was not unworried, however.

"Fetlock?" he said, getting his party. "Got a poser for you."

Habit more than thirst brought Fred to the Windmill that evening. Eva had wanted him to stay home and rest, assuming that his state was due to overwork; but Fred had insisted that it wasn't his health and left the house, just managing to muffle his *"Au revoir."*

He joined Harry Bullard and Lou Peacock at the bar and finished his first beer in a glum silence while Harry revealed why they shouldn't vote for Legislator Milford Carpenter.

"Tell ya the man's got a private line t'Moscow," he said. "A few men like that in office and we're in for it, take my word." He looked over at Fred staring into his beer. "What's with it, elder man?" he asked, clapping Fred on the shoulder.

Fred told them—as if he were telling about a disease he'd caught.

Lou Peacock looked incredulous. "So that's what you were talking about the other night!"

Fred nodded.

"You're not kiddin' us now?" Harry asked. "Y'know *everything*?"

"Just about," Fred admitted sadly.

A shrewd look overcame Harry's face.

"What if I ask ya somethin' ya *don't* know?"

"I'd be happy," Fred said in a despairing voice.

Harry beamed. "Okay. I won't ask ya about atoms nor chemicals nor anythin' like that. I'll just ask ya t'tell me about the country between my home town Au Sable and Tarva." He hit the bar with a contented slap.

Fred looked hopeful briefly, but then his face blanked and he said in an unhappy voice, "Betweeen Au Sable and Tarva, the route is through typical cut-over land that once was covered with virgin pine (*danger: deer on the highway*) and now has only second-growth oak, pine and poplar. For years after the decline of the lumber industry, picking huckleberries was one of the chief local occupations."

Harry gaped.

"Because the berries were known to grow in the wake of fires," Fred concluded, "residents deliberately set many fires that roared through the country."

"That's a damn dirty lie!" Harry said, chin trembling belligerently.

Fred looked at him in surprise.

"You shouldn't ought t'go around tellin' lies like that," Harry said. "You call that knowin' the countryside—telling *lies* about it?"

"Take it easy, Harry," Lou cautioned.

"Well," Harry said angrily, "he shouldn't ought to tell lies like that."

"I didn't say it," Fred answered hopelessly. "It's more as though I—I read it *off*."

"Yeah? Well . . ." Harry fingered his glass restlessly.

"You really know *everything*?" Lou asked, partly to ease the tension, partly because he was awed.

"I'm afraid so," Fred replied.

"You ain't just . . . playin' a trick?"

Fred shook his head. "No trick."

Lou Peacock looked small and intense. "What can you tell me," he asked in a back-alley voice, "about orange roses?"

The blank look crossed Fred's face again. Then he recited, "Orange is not a fundamental color but a blend of red and pink of varied intensity and yellow. There were very few orange roses prior to the Pernatia strain. All orange, apricot, chamois and coral roses finish with pink more or less accentuated. Some attain that lovely shade—*Cuisse de Nymphe émue*."

Lou Peacock was open-mouthed. "Ain't that something?"

Harry Bullard blew out heavy breath. "What d'ya know about Carpenter?" he asked pugnaciously.

"Carpenter, Milford, born 1898 in Chicago, Illi—"

"Never mind," Harry cut in. "I ain't interested. He's a Commie; that's all I gotta know about him."

"The elements that go into a political campaign," Fred quoted helplessly, "are many—the personality of the candidates, the issues—if any—the attitude of the press, economic groups, traditions, the opinion polls, the—"

"I tell ya he's a Commie!" Harry declared, voice rising.

"You voted for him last election," Lou said. "As I re—"

"I did *not!*" snarled Harry, getting redder in the face.

The blank look appeared on Fred Elderman's face. "Remembering things that are not so is a kind of memory distortion that goes by several names such as *pathological lying* or *mythomania*."

"You callin' me a liar, Fred?"

"It differs from ordinary lying in that the speaker comes to believe his own lies and—"

"Where did you get that black eye?" a shocked Eva asked Fred when he came into the kitchen later. "Have you been fighting at *your age*?"

Then she saw the look on his face and ran for the refrigerator. She sat him on a chair and held a piece of beefsteak against his swelling eye while he related what had happened.

"He's a bully," she said. "A bully!"

"No, I don't blame him," Fred disagreed. "I insulted him. I don't even know what I'm saying any more. I'm—I'm all mixed up."

She looked down at his slumped form, an alarmed expression on her face. "When is Doctor Boone going to do something for you?"

"I don't know."

A half hour later, against Eva's wishes, he went to clean up the library with a fellow janitor; but the moment he entered the huge room, he gasped, put his hands to his temples and fell down on one knee, gasping, "My head! My *head!*"

It took a long while of sitting quietly in the downstairs hallway before the pain in his skull stopped. He sat there staring fixedly at the glossy tile floor, his head feeling as if it had just gone twenty-nine rounds with the heavyweight champion of the world.

Fetlock came in the morning. Arthur B., forty-two, short and stocky, head of the Department of Psychological Sciences, he came bustling along the path in porkpie hat and checkered overcoat, jumped up on the porch, stepped across its worn boards and stabbed at the bell button. While he waited, he clapped leather-gloved hands together energetically and blew out breath clouds.

"Yes?" Eva asked when she opened the door.

Professor Fetlock explained his mission, not noticing how her face tightened with fright when he announced his field. Reassured that Doctor Boone had sent him, she led Fetlock up the carpeted steps, explaining, "He's still in bed. He had an attack last night."

"Oh?" said Arthur Fetlock.

When introductions had been made and he was alone with the janitor, Professor Fetlock fired a rapid series of questions. Fred Elderman, propped up with pillows, answered them as well as he could.

"This attack," said Fetlock, "what happened?"

"Don't know, Professor. Walked in the library and—well, it was as if a ton of cement hit me on the head. No—*in* my head."

"Amazing. And this knowledge you say you've acquired—are you conscious of an *increase* in it since your ill-fated visit to the library?"

Fred nodded. "I know more than ever."

The professor bounced the fingertips of both hands against each other. "A book on language by Pei. Section 9-B in the library, book number 429.2, if memory serves. Can you quote from it?"

Fred looked blank, but words followed almost immediately. "Leibnitz first advanced the theory that all language came not from a historically recorded source but from proto-speech. In some respects he was a precursor of—"

"Good, good," said Arthur Fetlock. "Apparently a case of spontaneous telepathic manifestations coupled with clairvoyance."

"Meaning?"

"Telepathy, Elderman. Telepathy! Seems every book or educated mind you come across, you pick clean of content. You worked in the French office, you spoke French. You worked in the Mathematics office, you quoted numbers, tables, axioms. Similarly with all other offices, subjects and individuals." He scowled, purse-lipped. "Ah, but why?"

"*Causa qua re,*" muttered Fred.

A brief wry sound in Professor Fetlock's throat. "Yes, I wish I knew, too. However . . ." He leaned forward. "What's that?"

"How come I can learn so much?" Fred asked worriedly. "I mean—"

"No difficulty there," stated the stocky psychologist. "You see, no man ever utilized the full learning capacity of the brain. It still has an immense potential. Perhaps that's what's happening to you—you're realizing this potential."

"But how?"

"Spontaneously realized telepathy and clairvoyance plus infinite retention and unlimited potential." He whistled softly. "Amazing. Positively amazing. Well, I must be going."

"But what'll I do?" Fred begged.

"Why, enjoy it," said the professor expansively. "It's a perfectly fantastic gift. Now look—if I were to gather together a group of faculty members, would you be willing to speak to them? Informally, of course.

"But—"

"They should be entranced, positively entranced. I must do a paper for the *Journal*."

"But what does it mean, Professor?" Fred Elderman asked, his voice shaking.

"Oh, we'll look into it, never fear. Really, this is revolutionary. An unparalleled phenomenon." He made a sound of delighted disbelief. "In-credible."

When Professor Fetlock had gone, Fred sat defeatedly in his bed. So there was nothing to be done—nothing but spout endless, inexplicable words and wonder into the nights what terrible thing was happening to him. Maybe the professor was excited; maybe it was exciting intellectual fare for outsiders. For him, it was only grim and increasingly frightening business.

Why? Why? It was the question he could neither answer nor escape.

He was thinking that when Eva came in. He lifted his gaze as she crossed the room and sat down on the bed.

"What did he say?" she asked anxiously.

When he told her, her reaction was the same as his.

"That's all? Enjoy it?" She pressed her lips together in anger. "What's the matter with him? Why did Doctor Boone send him?"

He shook his head, without an answer.

There was such a look of confused fear on his face that she reached out her hand suddenly and touched his cheek. "Does your head hurt, dear?"

"It hurts inside," he said. "In my . . ." There was a clicking in his throat. "If one considers the brain as a tissue which is only moderately compressible, surrounded by two variable factors—the blood it contains and the spinal fluid which surrounds it and fills the ventricles inside the brain we have—"

He broke off spasmodically and sat there, quivering.

"God help us," she whispered.

"As Sextus Empiricus says in his *Arguments Against Belief in a God,* those who affirm, positively, that God exists cannot avoid falling into an impiety. For—"

"Fred, stop it!"

He sat looking at her dazedly.

"Fred, you don't . . . know what you're saying. Do you?"

"No. I never do. I just—Eva, what's going on!"

She held his hand tightly and stroked it. "It's all right, Fred. Please don't worry so."

But he did worry. For behind the complex knowledge that filled his mind, he was still the same man, simple, uncomprehending—and afraid.

Why was it happening?

It was as if, in some hideous way, he were a sponge

filling more and more with knowledge and there would come a time when there was no room left and the sponge would explode.

Professor Fetlock stopped him in the hallway Monday morning. "Elderman, I've spoken to the members of the faculty and they're all as excited as I. Would this afternoon be too soon? I can get you excused from any work you may be required to do."

Fred looked bleakly at the professor's enthusiastic face. "It's all right."

"Splendid! Shall we say four-thirty then? My offices?"

"All right."

"And may I make a suggestion?" asked the professor. "I'd like you to tour the university—all of it."

When they separated, Fred went back down to the basement to put away his tools.

At four twenty-five, he pushed open the heavy door to the Department of Psychological Sciences. He stood there, waiting patiently, one hand on the knob, until someone in the large group of faculty members saw him. Professor Fetlock disengaged himself from the group and hurried over.

"Elderman," he said, "come in, come in."

"Professor, has Doctor Boone said anything more?" Fred insisted. "I mean about—"

"No, nothing. Never fear, we'll get to it. But come along. I want you to—Ladies and gentlemen, your attention, please!"

Fred was introduced to them, standing in their midst, trying to look at ease when his heart and nerves were pulsing with a nervous dread.

"And did you follow my suggestion," Fetlock asked loudly, "and tour all the departments in the university?"

"Yes . . . sir."

"Good, good." Professor Fetlock nodded emphatically. "That should complete the picture then. Imagine it, ladies and gentlemen—the sum total of knowledge in our entire university—all in the head of this one man!"

There were sounds of doubt from the faculty.

"No, no, I'm serious!" claimed Fetlock. "The proof of the pudding is quite ample. Ask away."

Fred Elderman stood there in the momentary silence, thinking of what Professor Fetlock had said. The knowledge of an entire university in his head. That meant there was no more to be gotten here then.

What now?

Then the questions came—and the answers, dead-voiced and monotonous.

"What will happen to the sun in fifteen million years?"

"If the sun goes on radiating at its present rate for fifteen million years, its whole weight will be transformed into radiation."

"What is a root tone?"

"In harmonic units, the constituent tones seem to have unequal harmonic values. Some seem to be more important and dominate the sounding unity. These roots are—"

All the knowledge of an entire university in his head.

"The five orders of Roman architecture."

"Tuscan, Doric, Corinthian, Ionic, Composite. Tuscan being a simplified Doric, Doric retaining the triglyphs, Corinthian characterized by—"

No more knowledge there he didn't possess. His brain crammed with it. Why?

"Buffer capacity?"

"The buffer capacity of a solution may be defined as dx/dpH where dx is the small amount of strong acid or—"

Why?

"A moment ago. French."

"*Il n'y a qu'un instant.*"

Endless questions, increasingly excited until they were almost being shouted.

"What is literature involved with?"

"Literature is, of nature, involved with ideas because it deals with Man in society, which is to say that it deals with formulations, valuations and—"

Why?

"Rule for masthead lights on steam vessels?" A laugh.

"A steam vessel when under way shall carry (a) on or in front of the foremast or, if a vessel without a foremast, then in the forepart of the vessel, a bright, white light so constructed as to—"

No laughter. Questions.

"How would a three-stage rocket take off?"

"The three-stage rocket would take off vertically and be given a slight tilt in an easterly direction, Brennschluss taking place about—"

"Who was Count Bernadotte?"

"What are the by-products of oil?"

"Which city is—?"

"How can—?"

"What is—?"

"When did—?"

And when it was over and he had answered every question they asked, there was a great, heavy silence. He stood trembling and yet numb, beginning to get a final knowledge.

The phone rang then and made everyone start.

Professor Fetlock answered it. "For you, Elderman."

Fred walked over to the phone and picked up the receiver.

"Fred?" he heard Eva say.

"*Oui.*"

"What?"

He twitched. "I'm sorry, Eva. I mean yes, it's me."

He heard her swallowing on the other end of the line. "Fred, I . . . just wondered why you didn't come home, so I called your office and Charlie said—"

He told her about the meeting.

"Oh," she said. "Well, will you be—home for supper?"

The last knowledge was seeping, rising slowly.

"I'll try, Eva. I think so, yes."

"I been worried, Fred."

He smiled sadly. "Nothing to worry about, Eva."

Then the message sliced abruptly across his mind and he said, "Goodbye, Eva," and dropped the receiver. "I have to go," he told Fetlock and the others.

He didn't exactly hear what they said in return. The words, the transition from room to hall were blurred over by his sudden, concentrated need to get out on the campus.

The questioning faces were gone and he was hurrying down the hall on driven feet, his action as his speech had been—unmotivated, beyond understanding. Something drew him on. He had spoken without knowing why; now he rushed down the long hallway without knowing why.

He rushed across the lobby, gasping for breath. The message said, *Come. It's time.*

These things, these many things—who would want to know them? These endless facts about all earthly knowledge.

Earthly knowledge . . .

As he came half tripping, half running down the building steps into the early darkness, he saw the flickering bluish-white light in the sky. It was aiming over the trees, the buildings, straight at him.

He stood petrified, staring at it, and knew exactly why he had acquired all the knowledge he had.

The blue-white light bore directly at him with a piercing, whinning hum. Across the dark campus, a young girl screamed.

Life on the other planets, the last words crossed his mind, *is not only possibility but high probability.*

Then the light hit him and bounced straight back up to its source, like lightning streaking in reverse from lightning rod to storm cloud, leaving him in awful blackness.

They found the old man wandering across the campus grass like a somnambulant mute. They spoke to him, but his tongue was still. Finally, they were obliged to look in his wallet, where they found his name and address and took him home.

A year later, after learning to talk all over again, he said his first stumbling words. He said them one

night to his wife when she found him in the bathroom
holding a sponge in his hand.

"Fred, what are you doing?"

"*I been squeezed,*" he said.

STEEL

THE TWO MEN CAME OUT OF THE STATION ROLLING A covered object. They rolled it along the platform until they reached the middle of the train, then grunted as they lifted it up the steps, the sweat running down their bodies. One of its wheels fell off and bounced down the metal steps and a man coming up behind them picked it up and handed it to the man who was wearing a rumpled brown suit.

"Thanks," said the man in the brown suit and he put the wheel in his side coat pocket.

Inside the car, the men pushed the covered object down the aisle. With one of its wheels off, it was lopsided and the man in the brown suit—his name was Kelly—had to keep his shoulder braced against it to keep it from toppling over. He breathed heavily and licked away tiny balls of sweat that kept forming over his upper lip.

When they reached the middle of the car, the man in the wrinkled blue suit pushed forward one of the seat backs so there were four seats, two facing two. Then the two men pushed the covered object between the seats and Kelly reached through a slit in the covering and felt around until he found the right button.

The covered object sat down heavily on a seat by the window.

"Oh, God, listen to'm squeak," said Kelly.

The other man, Pole, shrugged and sat down with a sigh.

"What d'ya expect?" he asked.

Kelly was pulling off his suitcoat. He dropped it down on the opposite seat and sat down beside the covered object.

"Well, we'll get 'im some o' that stuff soon's we're paid off," he said, worriedly.

"If we can find some," said Pole who was almost as thin as one. He sat slumped back against the hot seat watching Kelly mop at his sweaty cheeks.

"Why shouldn't we?" asked Kelly, pushing the damp handkerchief down under his shirt collar.

"Because they don't make it no more," Pole said with the false patience of a man who has had to say the same thing too many times.

"Well, that's crazy," said Kelly. He pulled off his hat and patted at the bald spot in the center of his rust-colored hair. "There's still plenty B-twos in the business."

"Not many," said Pole, bracing one foot upon the covered object.

"*Don't,*" said Kelly.

Pole let his foot drop heavily and a curse fell slowly from his lips, Kelly ran the handkerchief around the lining of his hat. He started to put the hat on again, then changed his mind and dropped it on top of his coat.

"Christ, it's hot," he said.

"It'll get hotter," said Pole.

Across the aisle a man put his suitcase up on the rack, took off his suit coat and sat down, puffing. Kelly looked at him, then turned back.

"Ya think it'll be hotter in Maynard, huh?" he asked.

Pole nodded. Kelly swallowed dryly.

"Wish we could have another o' them beers," he said.

Pole stared out the window at the heat waves rising from the concrete platform.

"I had three beers," said Kelly, "and I'm just as thirsty as I was when I started."

"Yeah," said Pole.

"Might as well've not had a beer since Philly," said Kelly.

Pole said, "Yeah."

Kelly sat there staring at Pole a moment. Pole had dark hair and white skin and his hands were the hands of a man who should be bigger than Pole was. But the hands were as clever as they were big. Pole's one o' the best, Kelly thought, one o' the best.

"Ya think he'll be all right?" he asked.

Pole grunted and smiled for an instant without being amused.

"If he don't get hit," he said.

"No, no, I mean it," said Kelly.

Pole's dark, lifeless eyes left the station and shifted over to Kelly.

"So do I," he said.

"Come *on*," Kelly said.

"Steel," said Pole, "ya know just as well as me. He's shot t'hell."

"That ain't true," said Kelly, shifting uncomfortably. "All he needs is a little work. A little overhaul 'n' he'll be good as new."

"Yeah, a little three-four grand overhaul," Pole said, "with parts they don't make no more." He looked out the window again.

"Oh . . . it ain't as bad as that," said Kelly. "Jesus, the way you talk you'd think he was ready for scrap."

"Ain't he?" Pole asked.

"No," said Kelly angrily, "he *ain't*."

Pole shrugged and his long white fingers rose and fell in his lap.

"Just cause he's a little old," said Kelly.

"Old." Pole grunted. "*Ancient*."

"Oh . . ." Kelly took a deep breath of the hot air in the car and blew it out through his broad nose. He looked at the covered object like a father who was angry with his son's faults but angrier with those who mentioned the faults of his son.

"Plenty o' fight left in him," he said.

Pole watched the people walking on the platform. He watched a porter pushing a wagon full of piled suitcases.

"Well . . . is he okay?" Kelly asked finally as if he hated to ask.

Pole looked over at him.

"I dunno, Steel," he said. "He needs work. Ya know that. The trigger spring in his left arm's been rewired so many damn times it's almost shot. He's got no protection on that side. The left side of his face's all beat in, the eye lens is cracked. The leg cables is worn, they're pulled slack, the tension's gone to hell. Christ, even his gyro's off."

Pole looked out at the platform again with a disgusted hiss.

"Not to mention the oil paste he ain't got in 'im," he said.

"We'll get 'im some," Kelly said.

"Yeah, *after* the fight, *after* the fight!" Pole snapped. "What about *before* the fight? He'll be creakin' around that ring like a goddamn—*steam shovel*. It'll be a miracle if he goes two rounds. They'll prob'ly ride us outta town on a rail."

Kelly swallowed. "I don't think it's that bad," he said.

"The *hell* it ain't, said Pole. "It's worse. Wait'll that crowd gets a load of 'Battling' Maxo from Philadelphia. Oh—*Christ,* they'll blow a nut. We'll be lucky if we get our five hundred bucks."

"Well, the contract's signed," said Kelly firmly. "They can't back out now. I got a copy right in the old pocket." He leaned over and patted at his coat.

"That contract's for Battling Maxo," said Pole. "Not for this—steam shovel here."

"Maxo's gonna do all right," said Kelly as if he was trying hard to believe it. "He's not as bad off as you say."

"Against a B-*seven*?" Pole asked.

"It's just a *starter* B-seven," said Kelly. "It ain't got the kinks out yet."

Pole turned away.

"Battling Maxo," he said. "One-round Maxo. The battling steam shovel."

"Aw, shut the hell up!" Kelly snapped suddenly, getting redder. "You're always knockin' 'im down. Well, he's been doin' okay for twelve years now and he'll keep on doin' okay. So he needs some oil paste. And he needs a little work. So *what*? With five hundred bucks we can get him all the paste he needs. And a new trigger spring for his arm and—and new leg cables! And everything. Chris-*sake*."

He fell back against the seat, chest shuddering with breath and rubbed at his checks with his wet handkerchief. He looked aside at Maxo. Abruptly, he reached over a hand and patted Maxo's covered knee clumsily and the steel clanked hollowly under his touch.

"You're doin' all right," said Kelly to his fighter.

The train was moving across a sun-baked prairie. All the windows were open but the wind that blew in was like blasts from an oven.

Kelly sat reading his paper, his shirt sticking wetly to his broad chest. Pole had taken his coat off too and was staring morosely out the window at the grass-tufted prairie that went as far as he could see. Maxo sat under his covering, his heavy steel frame rocking a little with the motion of the train.

Kelly put down his paper.

"Not even a word," he said.

"What d'ya expect?" Pole asked. "They don't cover Maynard."

"Maxo ain't just some clunk from Maynard," said Kelly. "He was big time. Ya'd think they'd"—he shrugged—"remember him."

"Why? For a coupla prelims in the Garden three years ago?" Pole asked.

"It wasn't no three years, buddy," said Kelly.

"It was in 1994," said Pole, "and now it's 1997. That's three years where I come from."

"It was late '94," said Kelly. "Right before Christmas. Don't ya remember? Just before—Marge and me . . ."

Kelly didn't finish. He stared down at the paper as if Marge's picture were on it—the way she looked the day she left him.

"What's the difference?" Pole asked. "They don't remember *them* for Chrissake. With a coupla thousand o' the damn things floatin' around? How could they remember 'em? About the only ones who get space are the champeens and the new models."

Pole looked at Maxo. "I hear Mawling's puttin' out a B-nine this year," he said.

Kelly refocused his eyes. "Yeah?" he said uninterestedly.

"Hyper-triggers in both arms—*and* legs. All steeled aluminum. Triple gyro. Triple-twisted wiring. God, they'll be beautiful."

Kelly put down the paper.

"Think they'd remember him," he muttered. "It wasn't so long ago."

His face relaxed in a smile of recollection.

"Boy, will I ever forget that night?" he said. "No one gives us a tumble. It was all Dimsy the Rock, Dimsy the Rock. *Three* t'one for Dimsy the Rock. Dimsy the Rock—fourth rankin' light heavy. On his way t'the top."

He chuckled deep in his chest. "And did we ever put him away," he said. "*Oooh*." He grunted with savage pleasure. "I can see that left cross now. *Bang!* Right in the chops. And old Dimsy the Rock hittin' the canvas like a—like a *rock*, yeah, *just* like a rock!"

He laughed happily. "Boy, what a night, what a night," he said. "Will I ever forget that night?"

Pole looked at Kelly with a somber face. Then he turned away and stared at the dusty sun-baked plain again.

"I wonder," he muttered.

Kelly saw the man across the aisle looking again at the covered Maxo. He caught the man's eye and smiled, then gestured with his head toward Maxo.

"That's my fighter," he said, loudly.

The man smiled politely, cupping a hand behind one ear.

"My fighter," said Kelly. "Battling Maxo. Ever hear of 'im?"

The man stared at Kelly a moment before shaking his head.

Kelly smiled. "Yeah, he was almost light heavyweight champ once," he told the man. The man nodded politely.

On an impulse, Kelly got up and stepped across the aisle. He reversed the seatback in front of the man and sat down facing him.

"Pretty damn hot," he said.

The man smiled. "Yes. Yes it is," he said.

"No new trains out here yet, huh?"

"No," said the man. "Not yet."

"Got all the new ones back in Philly," said Kelly.

"That's where"—he gestured with his head—"my friend 'n I come from. And Maxo."

Kelly stuck out his hand.

"The name's Kelly," he said. "Tim Kelly."

The man looked surprised. His grip was loose.

"Maxwell," he said.

When he drew back his hand he rubbed it unobtrusively on his pants leg.

"I used t'be called 'Steel' Kelly," said Kelly. "Used t'be in the business m'self. Before the war o' course. I was a light heavy."

"Oh?"

"Yeah. That's right. Called me 'Steel' cause I never got knocked down once. Not *once*. I was even number nine in the ranks once. Yeah."

"I see." The man waited patiently.

"My fighter," said Kelly, gesturing toward Maxo with his head again. "He's a light heavy too. We're fightin' in Maynard t'night. You goin' that far?"

"Uh—no," said the man. "No, I'm—getting off at Hayes."

"Oh." Kelly nodded. "Too bad. Gonna be a good scrap." He let out a heavy breath. "Yeah, he was—fourth in the ranks once. He'll be back too. He—uh—knocked down Dimsy the Rock in late '94. Maybe ya read about that."

"I don't believe . . ."

"Oh. Uh-huh." Kelly nodded. "Well . . . it was in all the East Coast papers. You know. New York, Boston, Philly. Yeah it—got a hell of a spread. Biggest upset o' the year."

He scratched at his bald spot.

"He's a B-two y'know but—that means he's the second model Mawling put out," he explained, seeing the look on the man's face. "That was back in—let's see—'90, I think it was. Yeah, '90."

He made a smacking sound with his lips. "Yeah, that was a good model," he said. "The best. Maxo's still goin' strong." He shrugged depreciatingly. "I don't go for these new ones," he said. "You know. The ones made o' steeled aluminum with all the doo-dads."

The man stared at Kelly blankly.

"Too— . . . flashy—flimsy. Nothin' . . ." Kelly bunched his big fist in front of his chest and made a face. "Nothin' *solid*," he said. "No. Mawling don't make 'em like Maxo no more."

"I see," said the man.

Kelly smiled.

"Yeah," he said. "Used t'be in the game m'self. When there was enough men, o' course. Before the bans." He shook his head, then smiled quickly. "Well," he said, "we'll take this B-seven. Don't even know what his name is," he said, laughing.

His face sobered for an instant and he swallowed.

"We'll take 'im," he said.

Later on, when the man had gotten off the train, Kelly went back to his seat. He put his feet up on the opposite seat and, laying back his head, he covered his face with the newspaper.

"Get a little shut-eye," he said.

Pole grunted.

Kelly sat slouched back, staring at the newspaper next to his eyes. He felt Maxo bumping against his side a little. He listened to the squeaking of Maxo's joints. "Be all right," he muttered to himself.

"What?" Pole asked.

Kelly swallowed. "I didn't say anything," he said.

When they got off the train at six o'clock that evening they pushed Maxo around the station and onto the sidewalk. Across the street from them a man sitting in his taxi called them.

"We got no taxi money," said Pole.

"We can't just push 'im through the streets," Kelly said. "Besides, we don't even know where Kruger Stadium is."

"What are we supposed to eat with then?"

"We'll be loaded after the fight," said Kelly. "I'll buy you a steak three inches thick."

Sighing, Pole helped Kelly push the heavy Maxo across the street that was still so hot they could feel it through their shoes. Kelly started sweating right away and licking at his upper lip.

"God, how d'they live out here?" he asked.

When they were putting Maxo inside the cab the base wheel came out again and Pole, with a snarl, kicked it away.

"What're ya *doin'*?" Kelly asked.

"Oh . . . sh—" Pole got into the taxi and slumped back against the warm leather of the seat while Kelly hurried over the soft tar pavement and picked up the wheel.

"Chris-*sake*," Kelly muttered as he got in the cab. "What's the—?"

"Where to, chief?" the driver asked.

"Kruger Stadium," Kelly said.

"You're there." The cab driver pushed in the rotor button and the car glided away from the curb.

"What the hell's wrong with you?" Kelly asked Pole in a low voice. "We wait more'n half a damn year t'get us a bout and you been nothin' but bellyaches from the start."

"Some bout," said Pole. "Maynard, Kansas—the prizefightin' center o' the nation."

"It's a start, ain't it?" Kelly said. "It'll keep us in coffee 'n' cakes a while, won't it? It'll put Maxo back in shape. And if we take it, it could lead to—"

Pole glanced over disgustedly.

"I don't *get* you," Kelly said quietly. "He's our fighter. What're ya writin' 'im off for? Don't ya want 'im t'win?"

"I'm a class-A mechanic, Steel," Pole said in his falsely patient voice. "I'm not a day-dreamin' kid. We got a piece o' dead iron here, not a B-seven. It's simple mechanics, Steel, that's all. Maxo'll be lucky if he comes out o' that ring with his head still on."

Kelly turned away angrily.

"It's a *starter* B-seven," he muttered. "Full o' kinks. *Full* of 'em."

"Sure, sure," said Pole.

They sat silently a while looking out the window, Maxo between them, the broad steel shoulders bumping against theirs. Kelly stared at the building, his hands clenching and unclenching in his lap as if he was getting ready to go fifteen rounds.

"That a B-fighter ya got there?" the driver asked over his shoulder.

Kelly started and looked forward. He managed a smile.

"That's right," he said.

"Fightin' t'night?"

"Yeah. Battling Maxo. Maybe ya heard of 'im."

"Nope."

"He was almost light heavyweight champ once," said Kelly.

"That right?"

"Yes, sir. Ya heard o' Dimsy the Rock, ain't ya?"

"Don't think so."

"Well, Dimsy the—"

Kelly stopped and glanced over at Pole who was shifting irritably on the seat.

"Dimsy the Rock was number *three* in the light heavy ranks. Right on his way t'the top they all said. Well, my boy put 'im away in the fourth round. Left-crossed 'im—*bang!* Almost put Dimsy through the ropes. It was beautiful."

"That right?" asked the driver.

"Yes sir. You get a chance, stop by t'night at the stadium. You'll see a good fight."

"Have you seen this Maynard Flash?" Pole asked the driver suddenly.

"The Flash? You bet. Man, there's a fighter on his way. Won seven straight. He'll be up there soon, ya can bet ya life. Matter o' fact he's fightin' t'night too. With some B-two heap from back East I hear."

The driver snickered. "Flash'll slaughter 'im," he said.

Kelly stared at the back of the driver's head, the skin tight across his cheek bones.

"Yeah?" he said, flatly.

"Man, he'll—"

The driver broke off suddenly and looked back. "Hey, you ain't—" he started, then turned front again. "Hey, I didn't know, mister," he said. "I was only ribbin'."

"Skip it," Pole said. "You're right."

Kelly's head snapped around and he glared at the sallow-face Pole.

"*Shut up*," he said in a low voice.

He fell back against the seat and stared out the window, his face hard.

"I'm gonna get 'im some oil paste," he said after they'd ridden a block.

"Swell," said Pole. "We'll eat the tools."

"Go to hell," said Kelly.

The cab pulled up in front of the brick-fronted stadium and they lifted Maxo out onto the sidewalk. While Pole tilted him, Kelly squatted down and slid the base wheel back into its slot. Then Kelly paid the driver the exact fare and they started pushing Maxo toward the alley.

"Look," said Kelly, nodding toward the poster board in front of the stadium. The third fight listed was

MAYNARD FLASH
(B-7, L.H.)
VS.
BATTLING MAXO
(B-2, L.H.)

"Big deal," said Pole.

Kelly's smile disappeared. He started to say something, then pressed his lips together. He shook his head irritably and big drops of his sweat fell to the sidewalk.

Maxo creaked as they pushed him down the alley

and carried him up the steps to the door. The base wheel fell out again and bounced down the cement steps. Neither one of them said anything.

It was hotter inside. The air didn't move.

"Refreshing like a closet," Pole said.

"Get the wheel," Kelly said and started down the narrow hallway leaving Pole with Maxo. Pole leaned Maxo against the wall and turned for the door.

Kelly came to a half-glassed office door and knocked.

"Yeah," said a voice inside. Kelly went in, taking off his hat.

The fat bald man looked up from his desk. His skull glistened with sweat.

"I'm Battling Maxo's owner," said Kelly, smiling. He extended his big hand but the man ignored it.

"Was wonderin' if you'd make it," said the man whose name was Mr. Waddow. "Your fighter in decent shape?"

"The best," said Kelly cheerfully. "The best. My mechanic—he's class-A—just took 'im apart and put 'im together again before we left Philly."

The man looked unconvinced.

"He's in good shape," said Kelly.

"You're lucky t'get a bout with a B-two," said Mr. Waddow. "We ain't used nothin' less than B-fours for more than two years now. The fighter we was after got stuck in a car wreck though and got ruined."

Kelly nodded. "Well, ya got nothin' t'worry about," he said. "My fighter's in top shape. He's the one knocked down Dimsy the Rock in Madison Square year or so ago."

"I want a good fight," said the fat man.

"You'll get a good fight," Kelly said, feeling a tight pain in his stomach muscles. "Maxo's in good shape. You'll see. He's in top shape."

"I just want a good fight."

Kelly stared at the fat man a moment. Then he said, "You got a ready room we can use? The mechanic 'n' me'd like t'get something t'eat."

"Third door down the hall on the right side," said Mr. Waddow. "Your bout's at eight thirty."

Kelly nodded. "Okay."

"Be there," said Mr. Waddow turning back to his work.

"Uh . . . what about—?" Kelly started.

"You get ya money after ya deliver a fight," Mr. Waddow cut him off.

Kelly's smile faltered.

"Okay," he said. "See ya then."

When Mr. Waddow didn't answer, he turned for the door.

"Don't slam the door," Mr. Waddow said. Kelly didn't.

"Come on," he said to Pole when he was in the hall again. They pushed Maxo down to the ready room and put him inside it.

"What about checkin' 'im over?" Kelly said.

"What about my *gut?*" snapped Pole. "I ain't eaten in six hours."

Kelly blew out a heavy breath. "All right, let's go then," he said.

They put Maxo in a corner of the room.

"We should be able t'lock him in," Kelly said.

"Why? Ya think somebody's gonna *steal* 'im?"

"He's valuable," said Kelly.

"Sure, he's a priceless antique," said Pole.

Kelly closed the door three times before the latch caught. He turned away from it, shaking his head worriedly. As they started down the hall he looked at his wrist and saw for the fiftieth time the white band where his pawned watch had been.

"What time is it?" he asked.

"Six twenty-five," said Pole.

"We'll have t'make it fast," Kelly said. "I want ya t'check 'im over good before the fight."

"What for?" asked Pole.

"Did ya *hear* me?" Kelly said angrily.

"Sure, sure," Pole said.

"He's gonna take that son-of-a-bitch B-seven," Kelly said, barely opening his lips.

"Sure he is," said Pole. "With his teeth."

"Hurry up," Kelly said, ignoring him. "We ain't got all night. Did ya get the wheel?"

Pole handed it to him.

"Some town," Kelly said disgustedly as they came back in the side door of the stadium.

"I told ya they wouldn't have any oil paste here," Pole said. "Why should they? B-twos are dead. Maxo's probably the only one in a thousand miles."

Kelly walked quickly down the hall, opened the door of the ready room and went in. He crossed over to Maxo and pulled off the covering.

"Get to it," he said. "There ain't much time."

Blowing out a slow, tired breath, Pole took off his wrinkled blue coat and tossed it over the bench standing against the wall. He dragged a small table over to where Maxo was, then rolled up his sleeves. Kelly took off his hat and coat and watched while Pole worked loose the nut that held the tool cavity door shut. He stood with his big hands on his hips while Pole drew out the tools one by one and laid them down on the table.

"Rust," Pole muttered. He rubbed a finger around the inside of the cavity and held it up, copper colored rust flaking off the tip.

"Come on," Kelly said, irritably. He sat down on the bench and watched as Pole pried off the sectional plates on Maxo's chest. His eyes ran up over Maxo's leonine head. *If I didn't see them coils,* he thought once more, *I'd swear he was real.* Only the mechanics in a B-fight could tell it wasn't real men in there. Sometimes people were actually fooled and sent in letters complaining that real men were being used. Even from ringside the flesh tones looked human. Mawling had a special patent on that.

Kelly's face relaxed as he smiled fondly at Maxo.

"Good boy," he murmured. Pole didn't hear. Kelly watched the sure-handed mechanic probe with his electric pick, examining connections and potency centers.

"Is he all right?" he asked, without thinking.

"Sure, he's great," Pole said. He plucked out a tiny steel-caged tube. "If this doesn't blow out," he said.

"Why should it?"

"It's sub-par," Pole said jadedly. "I told ya that after the last fight *eight months* ago."

Kelly swallowed. "We'll get 'im a new one after this bout," he said.

"Seventy-five bucks," muttered Pole as if he were watching the money fly away on green wings.

"It'll hold," Kelly said, more to himself than to Pole.

Pole shrugged. He put back the tube and pressed in the row of buttons on the main autonomic board. Maxo stirred.

"Take it easy on the left arm," said Kelly. "Save it."

"If it don't work here, it won't work out there," said Pole.

He jabbed at a button and Maxo's left arm began moving with little, circling motions. Pole pushed over the safety-block switch that would keep Maxo from counterpunching and stepped back. He threw a right at Maxo's chin and the robot's arm jumped up with a hitching motion to cover his face. Maxo's left eye flickered like a ruby catching the sun.

"If that eye cell goes . . ." Pole said.

"It *won't*," said Kelly tensely. He watched Pole throw another punch at the left side of Maxo's head. He saw the tiny ripple of the flexo-covered cheek, then the arm jerked up again. It squeaked.

"That's enough," he said. "It works. Try the rest of 'im."

"He's gonna get more than two punches throwed at his head," Pole said.

"*His arm's all right*," Kelly said. "Try something else I said."

Pole reached inside Maxo and activated the leg cable centers. Maxo began shifting around. He lifted his left leg and shook off the base wheel automatically. Then he was standing lightly on his black-shoed feet, feeling at the floor like a cured cripple testing for stance.

Pole reached forward and jabbed in the FULL button, then jumped back as Maxo's eye beams centered on him and the robot moved forward, broad shoulders rocking slowly, arms up defensively.

"Christ," Pole muttered, "they'll hear 'im squeakin' in the back row."

Kelly grimaced, teeth set. He watched Pole throw another right and Maxo's arm lurch raggedly. His throat moved with a convulsive swallow and he seemed to have trouble breathing the close air in the little room.

Pole shifted around the floor quickly, side to side. Maxo followed lumberingly, changing direction with visibly jerking motions.

"Oh, he's *beautiful*," Pole said, stopping. "Just beautiful." Maxo came up, arms still raised, and Pole jabbed in under them, pushing the OFF button. Maxo stopped.

"Look, we'll have t'put 'im on defense, Steel," Pole said. "That's all there is to it. He'll get chopped t'pieces if we have 'im movin' in."

Kelly cleared his throat. "No," he said.

"Oh for—will ya use ya *head*?" snapped Pole. "He's a B-two f'Chrissake. He's gonna get slaughtered anyway. Let's save the pieces."

"They want 'im on the *off*ense," said Kelly. "It's in the contract."

Pole turned away with a hiss.

"What's the use?" he muttered.

"Test 'im some more."

"What for? He's as good as he'll ever be."

"Will ya do what I say!" Kelly shouted, all the tension exploding out of him.

Pole turned back and jabbed in a button. Maxo's left arm shot out. There was a snapping noise inside it and it fell against Maxo's side with a dead clank.

Kelly started up, his face stricken. "Jesus, what did ya *do!*" he cried. He ran over to where Pole was pushing the button again. Maxo's arm didn't move.

"I *told* ya not t'fool with that arm!" Kelly yelled. "What the hell's the *matter* with ya!" His voice cracked in the middle of the sentence.

Pole didn't answer. He picked up his pry and began working off the left shoulder plate.

"So help me God, if you broke that arm . . ." Kelly warned in a low, shaking voice.

"If *I* broke it!" Pole snapped. "Listen, you dumb mick! This heap has been runnin' on borrowed time for three years now! Don't talk t'me about breakages!"

Kelly clenched his teeth, his eyes small and deadly.

"Open it up," he said.

"Son-of-a—" Pole muttered as he got the plate off. "You find another goddamn mechanic that coulda kep' this steam shovel together any better these last years. You just *find* one."

Kelly didn't answer. He stood rigidly, watching while Pole put down the curved plate and looked inside.

When Pole touched it, the trigger spring broke in half and part of it jumped across the room.

Kelly stared at the shoulder pit with horrified eyes.

"Oh, Christ," he said in a shaking voice. "Oh, *Christ.*"

Pole started to say something, then stopped. He looked at the ashen-faced Kelly without moving.

Kelly's eyes moved to Pole.

"Fix it," he said, hoarsely.

Pole swallowed. "Steel, I—"

"*Fix* it!"

"I can't! That spring's been fixin' t'break for—"

"You broke it! Now fix it!" Kelly clamped rigid fingers on Pole's arm. Pole jerked back.

"Let go of me!" he said.

"What's the matter with you!" Kelly cried. "Are you crazy? He's got t'be fixed. He's got t'be!"

"Steel, he needs a new spring."

"Well, get it!"

"They don't *have* 'em here, Steel," Pole said. "I *told* ya. And if they *did* have 'em, we ain't got the sixteen-fifty t'get one."

"Oh—Oh, *Jesus*," said Kelly. His hand fell away and he stumbled to the other side of the room. He sank down on the bench and stared without blinking at the tall motionless Maxo.

He sat there a long time, just staring, while Pole stood watching him, the pry still in his hand. He saw Kelly's broad chest rise and fall with spasmodic movements. Kelly's face was a blank.

"If he don't watch 'em," muttered Kelly, finally.

"What?"

Kelly looked up, his mouth set in a straight, hard line. "If he don't watch, it'll work," he said.

"What're ya talkin' about?"

Kelly stood up and started unbuttoning his shirt.

"What're ya—"

Pole stopped dead, his mouth falling open. "Are you *crazy?*" he asked.

Kelly kept unbuttoning his shirt. He pulled it off and tossed it on the bench.

"Steel, you're out o' your mind!" Pole said. "You can't do that!"

Kelly didn't say anything.

"But you'll—Steel, you're *crazy!*"

"We deliver a fight or we don't get paid," Kelly said.

"But—Jesus, you'll get *killed!*"

Kelly pulled off his undershirt. His chest was beefy, there was red hair swirled around it. "Have to shave this off," he said.

"Steel, *come on,*" Pole said. "You—"

His eyes widened as Kelly sat down on the bench and started unlacing his shoes.

"They'll never let ya," Pole said. "You can't make 'em think you're a—" He stopped and took a jerky step forward. "Steel, fuh Chrissake!"

Kelly looked up at Pole with dead eyes.

"You'll help me," he said.

"But they—"

"Nobody knows what Maxo looks like," Kelly said. "And only Waddow saw me. If he don't watch the bouts we'll be all right."

"But—"

"They won't know," Kelly said. "The B's bleed and bruise too."

"Steel, *come on,*" Pole said shakily. He took a deep breath and calmed himself. He sat down hurriedly beside the broad-shouldered Irishman.

"Look," he said. "I got a sister back East—in Maryland. If I wire 'er, she'll send us the dough t'get back."

Kelly got up and unbuckled his belt.

"Steel, I know a guy in Philly with a B-five, wants t'sell cheap," Pole said desperately. "We could scurry up the cash and—Steel, fuh Chrissake, you'll get *killed!* It's a B-seven! Don't ya understand? A B-*seven!* You'll be mangled!"

Kelly was working the dark trunks over Maxo's hips.

"I won't let ya do it, Steel," Pole said. "I'll go to—"

He broke off with a sucked-in gasp as Kelly whirled and moved over quickly to haul him to his feet. Kelly's grip was like the jaws of a trap and there was nothing left of him in his eyes.

"You'll help me," Kelly said in a low, trembling voice. "You'll help me or I'll beat ya brains out on the wall."

"You'll get killed," Pole murmured.

"Then I will," said Kelly.

Mr. Waddow came out of his office as Pole was walking the covered Kelly toward the ring.

"Come on, come on," Mr. Waddow said. "They're waitin' on ya."

Pole nodded jerkily and guided Kelly down the hall.

"Where's the owner?" Mr. Waddow called after them.

Pole swallowed quickly. "In the audience," he said.

Mr. Waddow grunted and, as they walked on, Pole heard the door to the office close. Breath emptied from him.

"I should've told 'im," he muttered.

"I'd o' killed ya," Kelly said, his voice muffled under the covering.

Crowd sounds leaked back into the hall now as they turned a corner. Under the canvas covering, Kelly felt a drop of sweat trickle down his temple.

"Listen," he said, "you'll have t'towel me off between rounds."

"Between what rounds?" Pole asked tensely. "You won't even last one."

"Shut up."

"You think you're just up against some tough fighter?" Pole asked. "You're up against a machine! Don't ya—"

"I said shut up."

"Oh . . . you dumb—" Pole swallowed. "If I towel ya off, they'll know," he said.

"They ain't seen a B-two in years," Kelly broke in. "If anyone asks, tell 'em it's an oil leak."

"Sure," said Pole disgustedly. He bit his lips. "Steel, ya'll never get away with it."

The last part of his sentence was drowned out as, suddenly, they were among the crowd, walking down the sloping aisle toward the ring. Kelly held his knees locked and walked a little stiffly. He drew in a long, deep breath and let it out slowly. He'd have to breathe in small gasps and exhalations through his nose while he was in the ring. The people couldn't see his chest moving or they'd know.

The heat burdened in around him like a hanging weight. It was like walking along the sloping floor of an ocean of heat and sound. He heard voices drifting past him as he moved.

"Ya'll take 'im home in a box!"

"Well, if it ain't *Rattlin'* Maxo!"

And the inevitable, *"Scrap iron!"*

Kelly swallowed dryly, feeling a tight drawing sensation in his loins. Thirsty, he thought. The momentary vision of the bar across from the Kansas City train station crossed his mind. The dim-lit booth, the cool fan breeze on the back of his neck, the icy, sweat-beaded bottle chilling his palm. He swallowed again. He hadn't allowed himself one drink in the last hour. The less he drank the less he'd sweat, he knew.

"Watch it."

He felt Pole's hand slide in through the opening in the back of the covering, felt the mechanic's hand grab his arm and check him.

"Ring steps," Pole said out of a corner of his mouth.

Kelly edged his right foot forward until the shoe tip touched the riser of the bottom step. Then he lifted his foot to the step and started up.

At the top, Pole's fingers tightened around his arm again.

"Ropes," Pole said, guardedly.

It was hard getting through the ropes with the covering on. Kelly almost fell and hoots and catcalls came at him like spears out of the din. Kelly felt the canvas give slightly under his feet and then Pole pushed the stool against the back of his legs and he sat down a little too jerkily.

"Hey, get that derrick out o' here!" shouted a man in the second row. Laughter and hoots. "Scrap iron!" yelled some people.

Then Pole drew off the covering and put it down on the ring apron.

Kelly sat there staring at the Maynard Flash.

The B-seven was motionless, its gloved hands hanging across its legs. There was imitation blond hair, crew cut, growing out of its skull pores. Its face was that of an impassive Adonis. The simulation of muscle curve on its body and limbs was almost perfect. For a moment Kelly almost thought that years had been peeled away and he was in the business again, facing a young contender. He swallowed carefully. Pole crouched beside him, pretending to fiddle with an arm plate.

"Steel, *don't*," he muttered again.

Kelly didn't answer. He felt a desperate desire to suck in a lungful of air and bellow his chest. He drew in small patches of air through his nose and let them trickle out. He kept staring at the Maynard Flash, thinking of the array of instant-reaction centers inside that smooth arch of chest. The drawing sensation reached his stomach. It was like a cold hand pulling in at strands of muscle and ligament.

A red-faced man in a white suit climbed into the ring and reached up for the microphone which was swinging down to him.

"Ladies and gentlemen," he announced, "the opening bout of the evening. A ten-round light heavyweight bout. From Philadelphia, the B-two, *Battling Maxo*."

The crowd booed and hissed. They threw up paper airplanes and shouted "*Scrap iron!*"

"His opponent, our own B-seven, the *Maynard Flash!*"

Cheers and wild clapping. The Flash's mechanic touched a button under the left armpit and the B-seven jumped up and held his arms over his head in the victory gesture. The crowd laughed happily.

"Jesus," Pole muttered, "I never saw that. Must be a new gimmick."

Kelly blinked to relieve his eyes.

"Three more bouts to follow," said the red-faced man and then the microphone drew up and he left the

ring. There was no referee. B-fighters never clinched—
their machinery rejected it—and there was no knock-
down count. A felled B-fighter stayed down. The new
B-nine, it was claimed by the Mawling publicity staff,
would be able to get up, which would make for live-
lier and longer bouts.

Pole pretended to check over Kelly.

"Steel, it's your last chance," he begged.

"*Get out,*" said Kelly without moving his lips.

Pole looked at Kelly's immobile eyes a moment,
then sucked in a ragged breath and straightened up.

"Stay away from him," he warned as he started
through the ropes.

Across the ring, the Flash was standing in its corner,
hitting its gloves together as if it were a real young
fighter anxious to get the fight started. Kelly stood up
and Pole drew the stool away. Kelly stood watching
the B-seven, seeing how its eye centers were zeroing
in on him. There was a cold sinking in his stomach.

The bell rang.

The B-seven moved out smoothly from its corner
with a mechanical glide, its arms raised in the tradi-
tional way, gloved hands wavering in tiny circles in
front of it. It moved quickly toward Kelly who edged
out of his corner automatically, his mind feeling,
abruptly, frozen. He felt his own hands rise as if
someone else had lifted them and his legs were like
dead wood under him. He kept his gaze on the bright
unmoving eyes of the Maynard Flash.

They came together. The B-seven's left flicked out
and Kelly blocked it, feeling the rock-hard fist of the
Flash even through his glove. The fist moved out again.
Kelly drew back his head and felt a warm breeze across

his mouth. His own left shot out and banged against the Flash's nose. It was like hitting a door knob. Pain flared in Kelly's arm and his jaw muscles went hard as he struggled to keep his face blank.

The B-seven feinted with a left and Kelly knocked it aside. He couldn't stop the right that blurred in after it and grazed his left temple. He jerked his head away and the B-seven threw a left that hit him over the ear. Kelly lurched back, throwing out a left that the B-seven brushed aside. Kelly caught his footing and hit the Flash's jaw solidly with a right uppercut. He felt a jolt of pain run up his arm. The Flash's head didn't budge. He shot out a left that hit Kelly on the right shoulder.

Kelly back-pedaled instinctively. Then he heard someone yell, "Get 'im a bicycle!" and he remembered what Mr. Waddow had said. He moved in again, his lips aching they were pressed together so tightly.

A left caught him under the heart and he felt the impact shudder through his frame. Pain stabbed at his heart. He threw a spasmodic left which banged against the B-seven's nose again. There was only pain. Kelly stepped back and staggered as a hard right caught him high on the chest. He started to move back. The B-seven hit him on the chest again. Kelly lost his balance and stepped back quickly to catch equilibrium. The crowd booed. The B-seven moved in without making a single mechanical sound.

Kelly regained his balance and stopped. He threw a hard right that missed. The momentum of his blow threw him off center and the Flash's left drove hard against his upper right arm. The arm went numb. Even as Kelly was sucking in a teeth-clenched gasp the B-seven shot in a hard right under his guard that slammed into Kelly's spongy stomach. Kelly felt the breath go out of him. His right slapped ineffectively across the Flash's right cheek. The Flash's eyes glinted.

As the B-seven moved in again, Kelly side-stepped and, for a moment, the radial eye centers lost him. Kelly moved out of range dizzily, pulling air in through his nostrils.

"Get that heap out o' there!" some man screamed. "Scrap iron, scrap iron!"

Breath shook in Kelly's throat. He swallowed quickly and started forward just as the Flash picked him up again. Taking a chance, he sucked in breath through his mouth hoping that his movements would keep the people from seeing. Then he was up to the B-seven. He stepped in close, hoping to out-time electrical impulse, and threw a hard right at the Flash's body.

The B-seven's left shot up and Kelly's blow was deflected by the iron wrist. Kelly's left was thrown off too and then the Flash's left shot in and drove the breath out of Kelly again. Kelly's left barely hit the Flash's rock-hard chest. He staggered back, the B-seven following. He kept jabbing but the B-seven kept deflecting the blows and counterjabbing with almost the same piston-like motion. Kelly's head kept snapping back. He fell back more and saw the right coming straight at him. He couldn't stop it.

The blow drove in like a steel battering-ram. Spears of pain shot behind Kelly's eyes and through his head. A black cloud seemed to flood across the ring. His muffled cry was drowned out by the screaming crowd as he toppled back, his nose and mouth